EARTHDOM

Book Three of the
ETHER COLLAPSE Series
Written by RYAN DEBRUYN

MOUNTAINDALE
PRESS

TABLE OF CONTENTS

Acknowledgments

Being a part of the LitRPG community now for three years has been a life changing experience. The first book was something I had always needed to write, something that I had dreamed of doing since childhood. The second was to prove I could make it into a career.

Now with the third in your hands, I have realized that I write these books for you, the fans. Wherever you currently are, wherever you curl up to read or listen to this installment, I thank you. I write for you, and I hope we have a long future of great stories together.

Thank you again, and I hope you are safe and healthy during this troubled time in history.

RECAP

Oh, welcome back! I've been waiting on you. Let me catch you up on what's been happening—I might need your help getting through this.

My name is Rockland Barkclay. Yeah, I know—the short form, Rocky, reminds you of the boxer. Or the flying squirrel. Look, we can talk about that, or we can talk about my Territory. Your choice.

Yeah, I thought so.

After the planet came to life, I was desperate to find my family. Nadine, Lacy and Benoit weren't with me when this started, and I was doing everything I could to find them. My team and I crisscrossed most of Ontario, surviving all of the chaos that the Planetary God threw at us. We even collected and transported nearly five thousand people back home from Ottawa. I'm going to gloss over the hundreds of thousands that died. Trying to stay upbeat and positive because I didn't find my family. And they *are* still out there!

Once we arrived in Algonquin Valley, Selaphelia Ardensai—my Ancestral Guide and a billion year old hottie—brought the thousands of people to the Grotto, which is a valley surrounded by three cliffs and a river. On first glance, the Grotto was woefully unprepared for the influx. Of course, at the time, I thought the biggest difficulty would be finding housing, food, and growing the Grotto's infrastructure. You know, economic basics.

I quickly discovered I was looking through horse blinders, because that part turned out to be easy. With some help from the system.

That's when the fan got painted brown. We learned that a Void God had taken over a Dungeon at the site of the nuclear meltdown in Chalk River. Ether Storms were ravaging our Territory border and the surrounding lands. And a particularly ugly Necromonger—I'm talking papery skin, greasy hair, and a penchant to keep undead as pets—named Apothis wanted us all dead as part of his master's quest for world domination. In other words, the dungeon adventurer life I planned was on hold.

If you're a little squeamish, you might have blanked about the whole undead, necromancer, and dreadful abomination portion of our escapades. Trust me, even recalling it causes *me* to shudder. You ever try going sword-to-spell against a Master Class Necromonger? Probably avoid that experience—I don't recommend it. At all.

With a lot of luck—not the system stat, but honest to goodness situational luck—some help from powerful allies, and a rescued dragon, we survived Apothis' first assault. The undead lover had somehow found a place of power below our Grotto that we didn't know about. We had a six-hour window to wrest control from Apothis—and rushed headlong into the tunnels below the Grotto. I learned a hard lesson that day when my fast friend, Joe, was slain while saving my life.

In the end, I sacrificed some Dragonscale and a Heartstring to the Altar of Michabo and ported that pontificating Necromonger back to his Dungeon. Yeah, it turns out he was the final boss in the Dungeon, and that in a week, his cooldowns would reset. I pictured him at full power and besieging the Grotto! We couldn't let Apothis remain—I mean, would you be able to sleep with a horde of undead controlled by a megalomaniac for neighbors?

I couldn't.

Smith the Medicine Man, Amber the Fencer, Zippo the Fire Mage, Sela the Druid, and I ventured into the depths of the Apep Dungeon and destroyed it. I'll spare you the specifics of the grueling fight and horrific scenes we saw below. We essentially sacrificed our lives in the final chamber.

So, yeah, we're dead. I'm speaking to you from the great beyond. Okay, I'm being dramatic, but I *am* speaking to you from the Spirit Realm. The Territories' place of power was far more powerful than any of us could have guessed. Michabo—a weird bunny hybrid Native American dude—was able to pull our Spirits here and save our living bodies.

I made a deal with Michabo to transfer all of my stored Etherience. In return, Michabo promised the Rebirth of as many members as he could manage. Fingers crossed that the other members of my group felt just as philanthropic—then we will all be able to return.

I think that covers everything.

Rottweiler, I spoke too soon.

The Apocalypse is at it again. Gaia is just throwing one curveball after another. I'm not asking for much—maybe just a fastball, something straightforward so I can have a second to breathe. I've already broken almost every bone in my body. Twice.

Do you think I am being unreasonable?

Probably. Look, I've gotta go deal with this before people start dying. You coming or what?

PROLOGUE

Etherless Void—Guild Collective Armada

Dahrix sat in his captain's seat. He was jacked into most of the Battleship's system and led the entirety of the Guild Collective assault fleet. Far too busy to listen to Hectar blathering on and on. He ran a hand over his metal face, blinked and then slowly tuned back in. Would this maggot ever shut up? He would task whichever Mechanoid had let him onto the ship with degreasing the tune up bay.

"Dahrix, this is only the ninth planet. We must send another team to run diagnostics! Just because the others were desiccated wastelands doesn't mean this one will be. We don't have enough data to ensure they are all dead!" Hectar screamed.

Silence fell as Dahrix regarded Hectar coolly; the ungrateful biologist was only on this mission because of his lucky discovery of the powerful Essence. Normally, Dahrix wouldn't have to put up with a biologist on his mission into the Etherless Void, but the Guild Prime had deemed it necessary.

Dahrix let some of his displeasure show and watched the researcher swallow in response. It was hard for Hectar to meet his red-eyed visage, framed by his robotic face, and he knew it. Add this to the militaristic and sterile environment of his control room, and most individuals squirmed.

Dahrix let the relative silence linger, coolly regarding Hectar as he began to sweat. Normally, the Control Room hummed with conversation. But not on Dahrix's deck. Each Mechano-Lord on deck worked seamlessly together, communicating silently and only when necessary. Dahrix smiled as Hectar began to crumble under the unnerving clacking of keys. Hectar had come on deck so confident, too.

Dahrix finally spoke, emphasizing each word. "These excursions cost our expedition speed."

"*Sir*, it's just...It's just a small delay. We, uh, don't have a bearing yet. Can we just throttle back and wait for the return of the Alchemy and Biology Guild's research ships?" Hectar stuttered.

Dahrix's jaw servos whined as he clenched his teeth. Dahrix wasn't upset about the loss of speed. He was furious about the lack of directional bearing. The Flow Ridians were supposed to have had the beacon up days ago. What was the holdup?

"Hectar, you will take a guard from the Mechano-Lords with you. This is not the time to lose any piece of the armada. You have exactly one hour to set up your equipment, and then you shall return to formation. Understood?"

Hectar lurched from the room, barely in control of his body functions. Dahrix's anger surged and he debated firing his eye ports at the imbecile. He blinked instead, and waited for the second soft hiss of the metal doors. Hectar had finally left his deck. Good riddance.

Dahrix's body relaxed. He turned and faced the central navigational projection globe. Its blinking blue lights and sectional grids highlighted every ship in the two hundred and twenty-five strong fleet. This was ninety percent of the power that the Guild Collective could muster, and he was its glorious leader.

Geb and Tirahnya, the heads of other guilds, had joined this foray into the abyss. Each commanded a battleship of their own and led a portion of the fleet during combat situations.

As Mission Commander, by order of Dario, the Guild Prime, he alone would shoulder any failures.

He wasn't naive. Other commanders sent daily reports to Dario about his actions. Dahrix posted regular updates to the Guild Prime himself, after all. His pertained to the information that the Flow Ridians revealed. His coolant circulation increased as he thought about the creatures described by the humans—the

Etherience that they would give—the loot! Imagine constructs made of asphalt, concrete, and other building materials. Creatures so large they were literal moving mountains. And best of all, each of these mountainous 'Golems' apparently held an Epic Class rank. That was the same as his own!

How fast would his guild level on a planet with Masterclass wildlife? How rich would they become? So many untapped Dungeons, Territories, and quests. All they needed was a heading.

Dahrix scratched his cheek, an unnecessary habit he hadn't been able to break in his hundreds of years of life. He continued to study the globe as he spoke aloud to his Lieutenant, "You are absolutely sure you made the beacon's higher functions undetectable?"

"As I explained, it is impossible to completely hide those functions. However, we used our best—"

The smell of burning metal cut off his Lieutenant's report. Dahrix shut his eyes and took a deep breath. He had been wanting to vent his laser ports all day and finally had. That imbecile Hectar always brought it out in him.

The weapons had only damaged the globe, luckily. Dahrix sighed. "Get maintenance up here to replace the Radar globe—please." No point venting more anger on a fellow Mechano-Lord. It wasn't their fault that all these illogical sapient beings existed.

A notification light blinked to life, and Dahrix strode to the station where another crew member sat. Dahrix's subordinate reported, "Guild Leader, the beacon has gone live!"

Dahrix's coolant circulated even faster as the crew member zoomed out of the two-dimensional representational map. The cycling fluid slowed back down as the map finished resolving at an appropriate distance. The beacon was exceptionally far away; probably more than a year of travel at full speed.

"That explains the timing delay of the signal," Dahrix surmised to the room. He turned to his Lieutenant. "How many days ago would the beacon need to be set up to travel this distance?"

With a few key clicks, his Lieutenant responded, "Sir, at least one day, twenty-one hours, thirty-five minutes, and twelve seconds. Assuming no planets or debris lies between us and it."

"Order all ships back to formation. Send in the 'Back-Up Plan,'" said Dahrix. He returned to his captain's chair. His facial muscles creaked, forming something he had been told resembled a 'wolf smile.' With the signal streaming, he now had an Ether connection to his converted minions. Perhaps it was best to hold off on taking too much control. For now. He needed more information and a better feel for the situation.

His mood began to sour again, and he slammed his gauntlet down on a glowing red mushroom-button set within a pedestal beside his chair.

Outside the ship's window, eight balls of fluorescent green light bloomed in the darkness of space. He thought about the eight planets that Hectar had painstakingly established monitoring equipment on. Hectar's reports held hope that life might one day return to their barren surfaces. Unfortunately, that just wouldn't do.

While the bombs that had been placed on the planets by his Mechano-Lord Guards wouldn't destroy them, they would make them uninhabitable for many years to come. He knew he would receive an earful from Hectar for dispersing toxic gas, but his directive was clear. If they couldn't occupy the planets, ensure that no one else could.

As the Back-Up Plan passed Hectar's ship, the imbecile's squeaky voice came over the emergency channel. "What are you doing? Dahrix, please recall those torpedos. Wait—why are all the sensors on the other planets going haywire? Dahrix, are you insane? They're Planetary Gods—you can't just bomb them."

Dahrix let the speed of 'The Back-Up Plan' speak for him. The torpedoes detonated and showered the darkness with bright yellow light directly to the fleet's port side, spilling a potent nerve block onto the surface of the planet. It would be hundreds of years before the toxins would fully dissipate. The sound of twisting metal filled the room as a maniacal grin stretched over the dark black metal of Dahrix's face.

Dahrix wouldn't allow people easy access to power. Not this time. Never again. No one would ever look down on him or his people again. He would find the means to grow stronger still.

CHAPTER ONE

"Wake up! Do you want your living body to actually die?" Michabo shouted as he popped back into the Spiritual Grotto where Rocky currently resided.

Rockland Barkclay rolled over on the meticulously groomed grass and groaned. He wasn't sure he wanted to wake up today. He had been in this idyllic landscape for what felt like weeks, and could remember the scenery without opening his eyes. At first, he had marveled at the perfectly cultivated Grotto, which was an exact copy of his Territorial Grotto. A three-story, black residential building surrounded the massive yellow Guild Tent that once dominated the center of the space. Approximately twelve Dragonscale Longhouses provided shelter for about five hundred people in their dorm-style rooms. There were a further three that had been designated as small apartment complexes, while a short distance from the Longhouses was the Mess Hall. He wished he could eat in this place.

What kind of supposed paradise doesn't have any food?

"Didn't you hear me? I said, wake up."

"Oh, I heard you." Rocky slowly opened his eyes. His exaggerated yawn matched his arms, stretching widely and melodramatically. "I'll stand up if you answer some questions about all of this. Let's start with something easy. What is this place?"

Michabo was some sort of mix between Native American and a cute furry creature. He was either wearing a living bunny skin robe, complete with floppy-eared hood, or he was part rabbit himself.

"I already told you. It's the Spirit Realm. Now get up." Michabo thumped his rabbit foot.

"How is that a helpful answer? "Rocky yawned again and pressed his body further into the soft earth.

Michabo's foot thumped faster and faster.

"Hold on now. Don't get your ears in a knot." He had been with Michabo in this place for far too long already, and the stupid, limp-eared bunny-man refused to answer any questions.

Like every other day since his arrival, Rocky stood up and began his Seraphim Sword forms. He yawned once more— there was really no way of telling if it was morning, afternoon, or night in the Spirit Realm. His usual routine was sleep, annoy the rabbit-man, practice sword forms, and top it off with Meditation.

"Just because time flows more quickly here than the Gaian Plane doesn't mean you should stay longer." Michabo grumped at Rocky's slow-paced forms.

Rocky sensed the man glaring as he completed the first thrust and parry of the 'Kata.' He geeked out a bit at being able to use the word for the training Sela had drilled him on, relentlessly. Before the apocalypse, a kata was something an anime character performed—not him.

"Listen, you are here while your body is still alive, and holding that connection taxes this place greatly. All of your crushed and dying bodies have been fully restored, and they are awaiting the spirit's return." Michabo glanced at his hand and fidgeted with his drooping rabbit ear, then looked up at Rocky and said, "Some of the others have already left, which has helped. Still, we used all of our stored Etherience rescuing you and your party from that Dungeon collapse."

Perhaps the silent treatment was the correct response— Michabo had *shared* more information than Rocky had managed to tease out of the infuriating floppy-eared man to date. Rocky continued to flow into the high horizontal parry forms of the Kata.

Michabo sighed heavily and sucked on his pipe.

Well, at least Michabo was committed to attempting to convince him to leave. He was on his second Kata when Michabo spoke again. "Rockland, the longer you stay here, the more you put your citizens at risk. What is holding you here? Is it the loss of the Revenant class?"

Rocky's teeth clicked, and his sword wavered for a moment before he locked it down. Yes, that was a huge problem. If only it was that easy to select a new class. Problem number one—only four options were open to him. Since Michabo had pulled him into the Spirit Realm, Rocky had lost access to classes that didn't require Rebirth. From the information he had extracted from Michabo, Rebirth was somehow different from Resurrection. The only distinction that made sense was that Resurrection required you to die, and Rebirth somehow took your living self and recreated it.

Problem number two—of the four classes available, only one was selectable, and Rocky wanted none of it.

He finished his Kata and sat cross-legged on the ground to Meditate as he perused the four classes again. Maybe this time he would see something he had missed. He closed his eyes, entered his meditative state, and flipped through the classes available.

Chimera Knight (Assassin)
- **A free and intelligent chimera is nearly impossible to tame. Now that you have bonded a chimera of the manticore subspecies, you can discover how to tame others for the creation of the order of Chimera Knights. As an owner of a manticore, your class will appear as Chimera Knight, but you will be a variant—assassin class.**

1) One must find a chimera kit before they're a year old.

2) One must either obtain permission from the parent or the parent must have died from a cause other than at the owner's hands.

3) One must not use any item to subjugate or tame the creature through magical or physical means.

> A Chimera Knight is strongly linked to his pet. Together, they grow and become a powerful force.
>
> This class keeps all stats from the previous rank.

Chimera Knight

- o All skills from the previous rank remain.
- o All Etherience requirements for Levels are 60% higher.
- o +1 Strength per Level
- o +1 Stamina per Level
- o +1 Dexterity per Level
- o +1 Agility per Level

--

Seraphim

- A Seraphim must be reborn to ascend. During Rebirth, all automatically assigned stats during the previous rank are consumed, and the worthy shall have the free stat points to redistribute upon Rebirth.
  - o A Seraphim is a class that is locked to individuals who are descendants of the Cathodiem guild leadership lines.

Seraphim

- o All skills from the previous rank remain.
- o All Etherience requirements for Levels are 90% lower.
- o +1 Strength per Level
- o +1 Stamina per Level
- o +1 Dexterity per Level
- o +1 Agility per Level

--

Dark-Hunter

- A Dark-Hunter is a powerful force of darkness. Death is but another side of the life coin, and a Dark-Hunter metes out death to those who deserve it. To become a Dark-Hunter, one must be reborn, and all stat points, including free stat points, will be consumed in the process.

Dark-Hunter

- o All skills from the previous rank are refreshed and can be reassigned in the Dark-Hunter tree.
- o All Etherience requirements for Levels are 50% lower.
- o +2 Agility per Level
- o +2 Dexterity per Level

--

Demon

- Demons are mighty beings that care only for themselves. To become a Demon, one must be reborn, and all stat points become free stat points. A Demon may choose to place them as they wish upon Rebirth.

Demon

- o All skills from the previous rank remain.
- o All Etherience requirements for Levels are 90% higher.
- o +2 Intelligence per Level
- o +1 Strength per Level
- o +1 Stamina per Level

Mentally, Rocky clicked on Seraphim again and received the same error message he'd seen a dozen times.

Error!

To select the Seraphim class, one must be in control of each individual emotion. Would you like to see a representation of your emotional state?
<Yes> | No

For the hundredth time, he selected yes, and a blob of colors took shape in front of him. A swirling kaleidoscope seemed intangible one moment, and concrete the next. The way they intertwined, then moved was eerie. Almost like machine gears and cogs that kept jamming and lighting on fire. Anytime Rocky tried to untangle the myriad of red and gold knots, the whole network would flash and squirm out of his grasp. The next second, he would be apoplectic, hopelessly sorrowful, ecstatic, and deranged. Today, he forewent trying to mess with this disaster. Last time, he ended up pacing for over an hour as his body came down from its adrenaline high.

Michabo choked. "Every time I look at your Chidi, I am disgusted. That creature you have created looks back at me with such coldness." Michabo shook his head as if he could dislodge the image. "Did you tie your anger to your competitive spirit on purpose?"

As Rocky studied it, each throbbing vein of color snaked around a colossal aorta of red. Based on its pulsing pattern and his current mood, he guessed that was his anger. Michabo was partially right in his analysis, but Rocky corrected him and muttered, "More like I tied *everything* to my anger."

The only emotion that was nearly free of the entanglement was a dark, cloudy color. A sharp pang of pain hit his chest and he knew—this was sadness. Was he really so depressed? This new world had a strange way of bringing it out in him. Magnifying it.

He shook his head. He'd been sitting here for too long, trying to untangle his emotions, with no success. He considered another class. One that he had tried to select out of desperation.

But it also wanted him to fiddle with his emotional state. The Demon class wanted him to literally cram all of them into a single ball, each emotion indiscernible from the other.

I refuse to do that. I can't imagine not being able to tell where anger ends, and something else begins.

Dark-Hunter, on the other hand, required him to basically reset his entire class, and he had just gotten used to being a Revenant. Rocky dismissed those issues and swirled his Ether along his inner channels. Soon, he had figure eights looping idly and creating a beautiful pattern that looked like a lopsided flower.

Chimera Knight, he admitted, seemed like an excellent choice, but he needed to have completed a defense of the Grotto before he could access it. Defeating Apothis hadn't counted. Even though the bag of bones had assaulted his Territory, he didn't count. No, when the timer ran out for Ether Assisted Protection, something would attack his people.

Michabo interrupted the perfect quiet of the Spirit Realm. "It doesn't matter how hard you work, Rockland. I can tell you, from my own experience, that hard work doesn't always beat talent. Sela, for example, is a natural leader, a fighter, and she has been chosen by a higher being. You, sadly, were just a means for her return."

This was new information. Rocky didn't understand this new knowledge. He cracked one eye open and stared at the infuriating little rabbit-man. Michabo puffed on his pipe, the smoke forming a replica of the pattern Rocky had fashioned with his Ether flow. Was confusing information better than none?

Michabo smiled. "How many days have you been working to increase your strength in this new world? A few cycles of the moon? I worked for centuries, and still, the talented of this world practically chewed my family up before they spit out the fat."

An image of a woman in chains popped into Rocky's mind. The line of women who tried to save the chained one. And the subsequent slaughter of a bunny woman and girl. Could they be Michabo's wife and daughter? He took a deep breath and asked, "What happened, Michabo? Why are you in this place?"

Michabo tapped the stem of his pipe against his chin, and Rocky closed his eyes and returned to his peaceful Meditation. He had just created a thin layer of flowing Ether below his skin when Michabo spoke again.

"This place is simple in some ways, and infinitely complex in many others. I can perhaps enlighten you to a part of it." Michabo took a deep drag and then exhaled a smoky cloud. "You have seen some powerful creatures upon the surface world already, correct?"

Rocky nodded. The hovering smoke formed into an army of golems. Michabo frowned at it and then brought his hands together, forcing the smoke to join and create one giant golem that could be considered Everest, when compared to the foothills that the other golems represented.

Michabo pointed to the monstrous smoky golem. "Right now, the surface has even more impressive creatures upon it. Creatures so large and deadly that seeing one would result in catatonia for most humans. These creatures can neither be reasoned with nor beaten without resorting to extreme measures."

After a moment, he clicked his tongue and raised a hand. "There is good news, though. These creatures, while immensely strong, aren't inherently evil. They have no wicked agenda. If they do have a goal, they aren't actively trying to hurt people to achieve it."

Michabo took another deep puff of his pipe and blew more smoke, wiping away his gauzy Ether art. An army of undead, led by massive Abominations and Apothis—complete with his staff and riding atop his massive champions—slowly replaced the mountainous golem.

Rocky shivered.

"Creatures with ambition destroy everyone and everything in their way. They will stop at nothing to get what they want. Then you have inconsolable Evil. You have faced this evil, and beaten it back, but failed to defeat it. Apep lingers out there, on Gaia. His agents are still attempting to subvert all living creatures to their will." Michabo held up his hand, with his index extended, "Apep is but a finger of the greater Evil my people faced."

Rocky met Michabo's eyes as a tear rolled down the rabbit-man's cheek.

Michabo paused and collected himself. "Now picture a world where Evil has combined with a power that can't be reasoned with."

Rocky's eyes widened. What Michabo described was horrific. He pictured the world overrun with undead and shivered.

I can't allow that to happen, but if this evil is stronger than Apep—where would I even start?

"That is not even the whole of the problem, Rockland!" shouted Michabo. "Envision a world where that all-powerful Evil is so hidden that, on the surface, everything looks serene. The lake where Evil resides is deep—so deep that when it moves, all that can be seen is a small ripple on the surface."

Rocky held Michabo's gaze and eventually nodded. "Is the Spirit Realm an escape from that unseen Evil?" Rocky held his breath, hoping he wasn't right. He didn't relish the possibility of the rabbit-man telling him that this powerful place was an escape. But what else could it be?

Michabo laughed bitterly. "Absolutely not. The Spirit Realm is just a tiny part of the massive undertaking to stop that Evil. It was created to preserve the memory of the past. To hold the Evil at bay long enough to free Gaia, so she could one day fight and win against that creature. To teach the future not to ever create such unspeakable Evil again."

"Do you mean Apep?"

Michabo laughed harder, almost choking on the smoke of his pipe. "Apep is powerful, but like Odin or Gaia, his power has limits. No, the Evil I speak of was created by sapient beings. The Evil I speak of spawned Apep and brought that chaos here. The Evil I speak of uses lesser evils like Apep to mask their slowly sprawling desiccation."

"Did you succeed in removing this Evil from Gaia with the creation of the Spirit Realm?"

Michabo shrugged. "It is too soon to tell. At first, I had thought so. However, recent events have led me to believe that it still has some influence here."

Rocky waited for Michabo to elaborate, but he didn't. Instead, the rabbit-man dumped out the ashen contents of his pipe and looked off into the distance.

Rocky shook his head and seized the opportunity of his host's talkative mood. "I can't pick a class, Michabo. Don't pretend you aren't aware of my dilemma. I want to leave, but unless you want me to reset my class or become a Demon, I'm going to need your help."

Michabo turned to Rocky.

A surge of hope flooded his body. "You seem to have some power in this place—can't you do something?"

Michabo lifted his pipe and refilled it with tobacco—slowly. Rocky struggled not to punch the Native American rabbit-man. This was one of Michabo's favorite time-wasting displays, and next, rabbit-wonder would say something completely unhelpful!

Michabo lit up and breathed out the smoke. "I can do nothing to help someone unwilling to help themselves. You must look deep within yourself and find the answer you seek—"

Rocky's jaw and hands clenched and he glared at the man. Michabo stared blankly at the space in front of him. Rocky recognized that look. He probably looked the same way when he was receiving a notification. Michabo blinked rapidly at whatever he was reading and then looked between Rocky and the notice.

"Well, isn't this interesting…" Michabo drawled.

"What is it?" Rocky was getting really tired of having to pull every piece of information out of Floppy. Maybe if he stole Michabo's pipe and began stomping on it?

Michabo tapped his chin with the stem. "Your territorial protection has run out, and something is coming to invade in the next twenty-four hours. You are being granted temporary access to the Chimera Knight class. If you can defeat it and pass the assigned quest, you can keep the class—"

Rocky was already nodding his head. He was ready to accept the quest, but Michabo held up his hand.

"Do not accept so quickly, Rockland. If you fail to defeat this threat in twenty-four hours, not only will you lose the Apprentice Revenant skill tree and the Leadership Class, but you will be randomly assigned a class and start at Apprentice rank again. That's if you survive."

Rocky didn't have to think too long. If a monster was invading his Territory, then its residents needed him. This wasn't really an option for him. He had vowed to never let someone invade and kill his citizens again. And he meant to keep that promise.

"I will defend them," he whispered as a wicked smile spread across his face. "Or I will die trying."

Protection Quest
> **Leader of Territory Chimera Roost– Chimera Knight**
>> **Safeguard the Sanctum**

The time of your Ether-Assisted Territorial Protection elapsed. A creature has taken notice and wishes to claim your Territory. Within twenty-four hours, it will enter Algonquin Valley and attempt to kill everyone located within.

You will be given temporary access to the Chimera Knight Class during this quest. Failure will remove this temporary class, all Etherience gains beyond Apprentice Rank, and revoke access to your Ancestral Class skill tree.

Stop this threat in the time limit given, or die trying. A knight is only as good as their oath.

Rewards:
Etherience
Chimera Knight Journeyman Class

Good luck, Leader!

CHAPTER TWO

Rocky woke for the second time in what felt like hours. Michabo's last words rang in his head. *Do not panic, Rockland. You are being Reborn. Ask Sela about the strong women in her life.*

An object rolled off his chest, and the sound of something soft hitting the floor nearby followed it. He shot up to a sitting position and froze. He felt his body, but his eyes couldn't distinguish between open and closed.

What's wrong with my eyes?

His heart rate increased in tempo, and sweat prickled his skin as the weight of desperation pressed on his chest. How would he do this in twenty-four hours with no sight?

His trembling hands clutched the flat surface under him. His hands explored the cold but well-defined—almost sharp— edges of some sort of table. The time between the feeling of something falling from his chest and the soft percussive sound told him that he was elevated.

Echoing voices—sometimes distant, sometimes next to him—bounced against the walls of this unfamiliar place.

He summoned his Soul Blade, preparing for a fight. His eyes watered as the Ether-blue light from his skill pushed back the darkness and blinded him.

They work!

As he blinked away the tears, he could make out some of his surroundings. The space almost looked like a large, open hospital room. But that couldn't be right, could it? The blue light from his skill reflected off shiny surfaces and hopped over metallic-looking screens and desks.

Is this a morgue?

The blade dropped into his hands and the weight of it made him feel slightly better as he eased off of the cold slab table. He held the blade, admiring its honed edges and intricate hilt in the fading light. A link to his lost class and ancestor.

He jerked his head back. The blade was humming in his hands. It felt different than the last time he'd wielded it. Almost like it was more alive. The room was nearly black again. He Analyzed it quickly as the voices continued to echo in the background.

Congratulations! Your Soul Blade "Dark Tidings" has consumed enough souls to gain a level!

Dark Tidings – Soul Blade

Level 9

0 / 210 Ether Pool

The Strength of Arms IX
+18 Strength as long as the Blade has Ether from its pool to draw on. Unlock higher levels of your Soul Blade for more.

The Strength of Body IX
+9 Stamina as long as the Blade has Ether from its pool to draw on. Unlock higher levels of your Soul Blade for more.

* Dark Tidings refuses to absorb any more golem Essence. Find a new source of sustenance. *

* Dark Tidings has found its favorite sustenance. Sapient Essence will count double. *

He left the blue screen open. At least his eyes could see something. It relaxed him slightly.

The echoing voices became clearer as sounds drifted toward him. He strained his ears, listening closely for something, anything, that hinted whether danger was approaching. He felt his way around the table and crouched beside it, muscles tensed, ready to surprise his attackers.

"Jeff really needs to get better at telling time. He left his post hours before his duty finished," said a female voice. The voice was conversational. Not at all hostile. Were they just lulling him into a false sense of security? He shifted his weight, shaking the tingling sensation in his feet. Who was Jeff?

"You know how disturbing and oppressive it is down here. Isn't that why you always make me come with you and keep you company? That, or you're afraid of the dark," said a second, deeper female voice.

A musical laugh resonated from the hallway leading to the room. "Keep that attitude up, and you'll be covering your next shift down here alone."

The voices continued advancing. It wouldn't be long before they'd walk through the door. His breathing quickened and he tightened his grip on the sword's hilt.

"The Ether Protection has been down for a day now, and the hunters are seeing more dangerous creatures at the edges of the Territory. If more of the saviors don't show up soon…"

These must be allies if they're worrying about protecting my Territory.

He relaxed his shoulders and lowered his sword.

"You worry too much. Zippo and Sela are back already. They don't have any equipment or gear, but they are still Journeyman rank."

Relief flooded Rocky's body—Zippo and Sela were safe. *Alive.* He patted his chest and legs. Bare skin. Nothing but bare skin.

A torchlight flickered from the doorway. It wasn't enough to illuminate the inky darkness of the room, but it did tell him that his 'rescue party' was about to save him. And his stark-naked body.

His eyes darted left and then right, searching for something to cover himself with. He paused and shook his head. How could he miss the obvious? He activated his Dark Cloak skill. The deepest shadows of the room revealed the edges of their secrets. The sliver of light from the doorway wasn't enough for his Dark Cloak's dark vision to penetrate the farthest corners. Yet, with his new sight, he recognized his surroundings.

He had managed a small victory in this very chamber—by a hair-thin margin.

He had been reborn on the Altar of Michabo.

I was with that rabbit-eared jerk for an entire week, and he didn't tell me. I am going to choke him with his own ears next time I see him.

He wiped at his behind, trying to clear it of a billion years of dust. He didn't feel anything on his smooth posterior. Right, this place was magically renovated—with the shimmering black Dragon scale. Still, his skin crawled. Waking up naked in cold, ancient ruins wasn't exactly the most sanitary experience.

Two women rounded the corner, their torches lighting up the circular room. Their mouths dropped open. Rocky looked around for the danger and saw the torch lights failure to dispel the fog of his Dark Cloak. He smiled and turned to see the women level their beam rifles in his direction. His smile fled, and he crossed his arms in front of himself, double-cupping his prized jewels.

"Don't shoot!" His voice cracked, betraying his fear. While he was pretty sure his Dark Cloak would protect him, he didn't want to test that theory out. Especially in his state of undress. "It's me. Rocky." He removed one hand from his junk and took a pause. They couldn't see his nakedness through the cloak. Right?

They hadn't reacted to the removal of his hand. He unrounded his shoulders and cleared his throat, "I kind of woke up naked…"

Both women flushed beet red as he Analyzed them.

--

Victoria Faris
Apprentice-Partisan
Level 18
Health Points: 230 / 230

--

Letoya Deckman
Apprentice-Competitor
Level 19
Health Points: 160 / 160

--

Victoria pulled off her backpack. She dug inside and pulled out some sort of fluffy pink robe. She walked up to his black cloud and held it out. "I—umm—didn't recognize you…"

He swallowed hard and snatched the plush pink apparel from her hand. Victoria jumped.

"Sorry, sorry," he muttered as he put on the pink robe and cinched the waist. The hem reached his mid-thigh but it didn't hurt to have a little help protecting his *virtue* under his Skill.

Letoya pointed to something near his feet. "Is that yours?"

He looked down and spotted a leather satchel on the floor beside the Altar of Michabo. He analyzed it and his mouth twitched.

Dungeon Bag of Holding
Soul-Bound: Rockland Barkclay

- **This bag contains a link through clever Enchanting to a pocket dimension of Ethereal Space. It has Enchantments to prevent time from working inside the storage space. It has a gravity Enchantment and subdivides into compartments automatically.**
  Size: Vast
  Weight Reduction: 90%

"Yes, that is mine." He scooped up his most precious item. He tied it on to the cinch of the pink robe. The weight of the items inside dragged the sash down slightly. But the knot tied across his upper stomach was strong enough to hold the reduced weight of the bag.

"Ladies, I am in a bit of a rush to get back to the surface. Any chance we can get out of here?"

Stupid ticking timers, elapsed Ether protections, and Michabo—you know what, it's mostly Michabo!

They exited the room and Letoya pointed down a hallway he wasn't familiar with. "Shortcut," she explained as she led. "This is the way—the way that Apothis sent his minions into the Grotto."

Rocky swallowed. His people, protected by Tao and Gamma, had fought off a massive undead horde, while he, Sela, Smith, Zippo, and Joe fought their way to the place of power. His fist clenched. Never again.

Victoria interrupted his maudlin. "We do have some good news. You have only been gone for five days…"

Really, she was struggling to find anything else that would be considered good news? She clearly had more to say, too.

Letoya chimed in. "The planting grove is producing food."

Rocky rolled his eyes. "Just tell me the bad news already!"

Victoria and Letoya's shoulders slumped. Victoria frowned as she whispered, "Well...with the Ether Protection gone, larger monsters are slowly edging into the Valley. This has greatly impacted our hunting parties' production. The cooks are managing the shortage from the Territorial Inventory reserve, but they will have to start rationing soon, if something doesn't change."

Letoya revisited her earlier assessment. "While the grove is bearing fruit..." she smiled broadly and Rocky groaned. A pun *and* bad news. Perfect.

Her smile faded as she continued. "The farmers had to keep more than half of it to replant and expand. While this will help in the future, it's contributing to the immediate food shortages."

Gotta enjoy the little things that make you happy in the Apocalypse, I guess. However, fleeting.

Rocky stopped them with a question. "Just Zippo and Sela have returned—no one else?"

"From the group that went into Apep's Dungeon? Just those two and you. Azoth has been flying over Chalk River every day since you disappeared, and he didn't return until Sela did," said Victoria, regaining some volume. "Bathilda left the area. She said she would stop in from time to time, but she has further sites to cleanse."

"Tao and Gamma are still around, helping us build and training everyone in the mornings," added Letoya, grinning once again. "They have tried to help with some of the larger monsters on the Territory edge, but there are only the two of them. They are the only new group to beat the Arena Dungeon, Maximus, but they are too large to enter the Long-Forgotten Dungeon." She tapped her chin and continued, "The other three Knights haven't returned, but Tao keeps hinting that they are coming this way. Not sure how he knows that, though…"

He put up his hand, nodding solemnly to the two women, indicating that was enough information on the groups for now.

The new topic dislodged some more good news. Letoya looked at his fog-shrouded hand and switched topics. "People have been able to use the Citizen Accessible Shop for all manner of items. The council used the Crystals that your group left behind to supply all of the Longhouses, Mess Hall, and City Hall with power."

Victoria jumped in, "One hunting group has even managed to rent an apartment complex with their earnings."

That was excellent news. Rocky set up those three Longhouses as apartments, as a way for the economy of the Grotto to grow. He nodded. "Has the council considered buying foodstuffs from the shop if the food shortages continue to grow?"

The women looked at each other and shrugged. "Above our paygrade," Letoya said. "People are pretty upset up there, and the council has its hands full."

Victoria squeaked, and her face grew red. Letoya's face fell a moment later. It appeared they hadn't wanted to tell him about something. Rocky shook his head. "Tell me. Might as well rip off the bandaid."

"People were really upset with you for just adding them to the guild. It became a pretty major issue after you left. Luckily, the benefits of membership have become so apparent that most people have forgiven you. Then people heard about the jobs available through the Territory, and their anger flared back up. Everyone wants the increased skill growth. Why do only one hundred people get it?" Victoria almost slurred her barrage of words.

Note to self, find a way to add more jobs or positions to current jobs.

"Victoria! Tell him everything." Letoya said.

Victoria glared at her *friend*, then sighed. "Many groups of delvers that attempted the Long-Forgotten Dungeon are being held captive within." She licked her lips and her face paled. "Family members and citizens are concerned that those missing are dead. If Sela hadn't returned and talked to LFD and the mob, there would have been a riot."

Letoya huffed, "Honestly, people still might. LFD is holding them hostage, and it's increasing our food shortages. Why is that nutcase holding them, anyway?"

Rocky groaned. He had twenty-four hours to beat back an invasion, and some of his people were trapped in a Dungeon!

He really didn't need another problem to deal with.

Always curveballs...

CHAPTER THREE

The sun blinded Rocky, scorching his face and forcing his eyes to blink as they adjusted to the late summer day. He stepped out and took a satisfying breath of fresh, non-stagnant air. Nothing would ruin this moment. Not even the timer hovering over his new class and possible class reset.

Victoria led the way toward the guild tent, and Rocky followed, considering his new class skill options.

40,000 Etherience remaining until level 2.

The system must be imposing a multiplier of some sort. He did some quick calculations—the multiplier change in level requirements from Apprentice to Journeyman was a thousand, plus his Chimera Knight's sixty percent increase. If he had thought the end of Apprentice ranks had been a grind, he was going to be ground down to a fine pulp in the Journeyman Ranks.

He browsed his skills and saw his Revenant skills displayed, but he could no longer see the rest of the tree they had come from. He sucked his teeth to prevent clenching them. Revenant had definitely been a rare class. Now he only had those five skills to remind him of it. Perhaps the Chimera Knight Class would be just as rare.

Soul Blade
Dark Mend
Dark Blade
Dark Cloak
Shadow Clone
Chimera Knight Skill Tree
Tier 1
Poison Pool

- **For each venom/poison the Chimera Knight suffers and survives, he gains immunity. The toxic makeup of that poison will be added to his Venom Pool. In time, the Chimera Knight can add his unique venom to strikes or weapons. Do be careful as a Chimera Knight; not all poisons can be survived.**

0 / 5

Skill gained at 1/5 'Envenom.'

Envenom

- **Create an applicable venom from your Chimera Venom. This venom increases in strength with each additional poison and venom added to its base.**

--

Knight's Resolve

- **Increases the knight's resistances to all elements, poisons, and venoms.**

0 / 5

Passive buff received at 1/5 "Stalwart."

Stalwart

- **At 1/5, Stalwart increases elemental, poison, and venom resistances by 10%.**

He pulled his head out of his screens and realized he was drawing strange looks from any citizens they passed. The bright light of day highlighted the low hovering black cloud of his Dark Cloak skill.

Considering that I am wearing an extra-small, pink-fluffy bathrobe under it… I think I will leave the skill up!

It would appear that his first level of Skills were mostly something that gamers referred to as Passive Skills. While Passive Skills were powerful, they didn't really grant great variety for combat. If he was to choose right now, he would pick Poison

Pool, as it was a talent that could gain immeasurable strength one day. He considered having a poison as powerful as Azoth's, and goosebumps rose on his arms.

Knight's Resolve was also desirable. Resistance to fire would have been extremely handy during those final moments in the fight against Apothis. Not to mention that if he had a safeguard against venoms and poisons, he could strengthen his Poison Pool easily.

Choosing to assign his single skill point later, he continued toward the Town Hall to find Sela.

A massive group of people milled near the structure. A buzz of angry voices disturbed the tranquil summer day. Sela's voice cut through the din, and his heart soared.

"I told you yesterday, and I'll tell you again today. Calm down."

The crowd lobbed their outrage at Sela. Rocky could no longer pinpoint her voice as the throng of voices drowned her out. Other voices of contention bled through the knot of people. "That's my husband … Why are you allowing … Tell the stupid Dungeon…"

As Rocky circumvented the outside edge of the crowd, people took notice of the floating, black cloud that weaved around them. The intense hum of the mob diminished as one by one, people turned and stared at him. Or rather, at the dark cloud that surrounded him.

Rocky had been given a lot of time to think and stare at his emotional turmoil while he was stuck in the Spirit Realm. He had pledged to be a better leader. He had sworn to get a better handle on his emotions. He just wasn't sure how he would do this.

As the crowd quieted and he rounded its edge, Sela came into view, standing a few meters away from the front of the semi-circle of closely pressed bodies, eyebrows drawn together as she squinted at the mob. At their unexpected silence, her head whipped around to the cluster of foggy darkness.

Sela's eyebrows flew up, nearly to her hairline, and she cried, "Rockland!" She raced toward him and reached to hug him through the fog. Dark Cloak was a defensive skill, and as she touched it, the automated response of the cloak adjusted her course, away from him. He reached out his arms and helped guide her trajectory back to him.

She hit him hard enough to drive the air from his lungs. The tight grasp of her embrace prevented him from fully drawing breath, but the hug felt terrific.

A few people in the crowd turned to their neighbors, "Who is Rockland? Does she mean the other leader? Is he a black cloud?"

Rocky's heart sank. These people didn't even know what he looked like? His earlier commitment to bettering himself grew. How do you gain the trust of people who don't even know your face? But he couldn't think about that now. All he wanted was to bask in the moment, in his reunion with Sela. He didn't want it to end, but he placed his hands on her shoulders and moved her away from him. An invasion was coming, and it could start at any moment. All these people gave him an opportunity to introduce himself.

Rocky released Dark Cloak and strode to the front of the mob to address them. He wanted the people he was responsible for to see him. Right—that would put a face to the name.

Sela facepalmed and muttered, "What in Atlantis is he wearing?"

He blushed, adjusting the robe to cover more of his skin. But it was no use. The robe just wasn't big enough. At least the crowd had settled.

I guess that's a blessing.

The people gawked at him as he positioned himself where Sela had stood and addressed them.

"What does he think he is, a bathrobe knight?" said a voice in the crowd.

He relaxed at the connection that comment made. He had once read a story about a strong leader who wore a bathrobe, and perhaps he could channel some of that man today.

To be that leader, I am just missing the Demon class—I even had the opportunity.

He needed a bit more information. So, face flushed, he turned to Sela, "Have you figured out how long the Dungeons have been open?"

She didn't bother to remove her palm from her face as she held up her other hand, splaying all five fingers. Five days. Alright. He could work with that. According to the contract with LFD, people were due to return in two days.

He faced the crowd once more and said, "The captured members of our guild will return in two days. Guaranteed. However, there is a more pressing issue that requires our immediate attention."

Someone in the crowd prodded a neighbor and said, "Who is this clown?"

The man's comment garnered more attention than his announcement had. Hadn't these people seen him at the welcoming ceremony a few months ago?

"Listen up." His voice sliced through the rising din. "There is going to be an attack from a mighty creature against our Territory sometime in the next twenty-four hours. If we want our loved ones to have a place to return to, we need to prepare a defense."

As one, like a bunch of lemmings, the mob lost focus. Had something just happened? He turned to Sela. She was focusing on a screen as her eyes flicked from side to side. She had granted him access to view her screens on the first day of the apocalypse. Rocky smiled at the memory as he returned his attention to the crowd.

Well, that's handy!

"Gather everyone and meet me at the training grounds. Now."

As the crowd scattered, he walked to Sela. She pointed at his robe and gripped her stomach with her other hand as convulsive laughter wracked her body.

"I hope you realize that you look like a fool." She motioned to his Bag of Holding and took on a pointed stare. "I am pretty sure you have some clothing or gear in that thing."

Now it was his turn to facepalm. He had forgotten entirely about the suits of Nanoweave Under Armor, not to mention all the unidentified pieces of gear. He bowed his head and rubbed the back of his neck. Digging into his bag, he pulled the black ball of Nanoweave out and pushed it to his chest.

Well, this is much better.

The form-fitting suit of black fabric that cleaned and repaired itself felt good against his skin. Sela was never going to let him forget this. Beside him, Victoria cleared her throat, averted her eyes and extended her hand. "Think I could...umm...have my robe back? Please?" Her face was almost as pink as the bathrobe.

He shrugged it off and handed it to her. Sela and Letoya held on to each other for support as they dissolved into laughter.

"It's just so *pink*—" Sela wheezed and held her stomach.

"—and *fluffy*," said Letoya as she gasped for air.

"Alright, alright. Can we move on now?"

Letoya stifled her laughter and asked, "How long do we have until the creatures attack?"

Rocky shrugged. He wasn't sure of the exact timing but answered as best as he could, "It will attack sometime in the next twenty-four hours. Probably sooner, rather than later."

Letoya saluted and said, "I will go get the military, sir." Rocky saluted back and she jogged off.

Victoria, no longer red in the face, stepped forward. "I would like to offer my services as what I am told is termed a tank, sir."

Rocky's mouth curled up in delight at her words. He turned to Sela, who nodded eagerly, and asked, "Victoria, do you know a good healer?"

Victoria tugged on her shirt and bit her lip. "Do we absolutely need him? He is a bit—eccentric."

Rocky narrowed his eyes. "Eccentric enough for you to risk your life?"

Victoria's face paled. "I just assumed—how did you all survive without a healer?"

Rocky glanced at Sela, drew his mouth into a line and said, "I am not sure we did…"

"You don't know if…Letoya may bring him along. Hopefully. He might need some persuading, though. He hangs around the military a lot. He isn't really one of us."

"Let's head to the training grounds," said Rocky. He didn't want to be late to his own meeting. Not a good start for a leader.

"What did Michabo say to you in the Spirit Realm?" Sela asked.

"My new class is dependent on beating this invasion in twenty-four hours." He didn't want to say too much when so much was unknown. She would have to be satisfied with that answer for now. Michabo's words filled his thoughts.

Ask Sela about the strong women in her life.

She gazed at a screen that popped up in front of her. "I don't understand. Why didn't you just take the Revenant class for your Journeyman ranks?"

Victoria trailed behind them, pretending she wasn't listening, but her footsteps edged closer, and her head tilted forward to catch every word. Rocky cracked his neck and rolled his shoulders, unsure of how much to say in front of Victoria. He had just met her, after all. "I couldn't pick any of the classes. To be honest, I was lucky to get out of there without becoming a Demon."

Victoria's mouth fell open. Sela glanced at the woman before frowning at Rocky with knitted brows. "You had the option to pick Demon as a class? What about Seraphim?"

Rocky raised both arms out beside him. "Both, yes—" he lowered his voice "—but I don't want to talk about it." He flicked his gaze to Victoria, who was following closer than ever. "Not here. I wasn't able to select them. Let's leave it at that for now."

"Those classes should be locked to the Cathodiem leadership bloodline. Azrael was never considered a guild leader. What is going on?"

Rocky raised his voice for Victoria's benefit. If she got any closer, she would be tripping over his feet. "Where are Azoth and Zippo?"

"I think Zippo is at the cooking fires. As for Azoth," Sela looked northeast, toward Chalk River, and Rocky felt his heart stop.

No. No. No. No. No. No.

"He won't stop flying over Chalk River." Her voice was light, and warm, as she spoke of their good friend. "Maybe try calling him back, I bet he will be here instantly."

His shoulders drooped and he kicked a loosened stone on the path. He had already tried mentally contacting Azoth. He sent a quick, <Azoth, buddy?>, and received no answer. He weaved slightly as waves of worry washed over him. He ran his hands through his hair. Where was Azoth? Why wasn't he answering him?

"Can you call him?"

"No, he is out of my range, but your ring—" she stared at his finger and her voice fell—"has a further range."

He wasn't sure how long he could hide his worry for Azoth. Yes, he was enormous, and his ferocity was impressive, but he was just a kit. Barely a few months old.

Sela rested her hand on his arm. "It's okay, Rocky. I'm worried about him too. But we will get the ring back. I'm sure we can dig—"

He tugged his arm loose from her grasp. "It's fine." He shook his head as if he could shake the pain off himself. Shrugging it off and hoping the wind could take it away. "I am sure my class will have something. Or, yeah, we will dig it up." He steadied his voice. "Nothing I can do about it right now. Let's go prepare for the—"

Sela crossed her arms, elbows pressed to her sides. "Right. Well, Amelia wants to meet us in the shop right away. Garnell left a message saying that there is something urgent to discuss."

I don't have time for this. Doesn't anyone care that an invasion is going to start at any moment?

He clenched his jaw and muttered, "As long as it's quick." His tone was sharper than he meant it to be. He closed his eyes for a moment and took a few deep breaths. "Victoria, please ensure the healer joins us and start getting people organized."

***

The shop was situated in a vacant quadrant of the Grotto. Rainbows, refracted off of the metal surface, that stood out more because of the long unkempt grass behind it. Considering all of the add-ons they might one day need for the shop, Rocky planned to build this quadrant up last, if possible. He and Sela sprinted to the round dome of the Seed Shop and touched the Arbuckle to open the door. They changed into their kimonos and fox masks, which Rocky pulled from his Bag of Holding.

Oh, right, another piece of clothing I could have worn in front of that crowd. I'm not sure the reception would have been any warmer.

They stepped through the dark doorway and into the strange alien metal dome. The early morning sun blinded them as it shone from the mountaintop Bazaar. Rocky always enjoyed the atmosphere of the Aretrean Bazaar. The familiar buzz of people negotiating for wares, sellers hocking, and muted conversations floated through the air.

Sela nudged him. He looked up as two patrons walked directly through him.

What the—? How could he interact with Sela but not others? It must be because we're right beside each other in the Seed Shop.

They rushed toward the stall of the Karacy, Garnell. The merchant was speaking with a tall, black nightmare of a creature. It reminded Rocky of a stretched out black stick figure. Its appendages were sharpened to fine points, and its perfectly round head had no mouth or eyes. Then it spoke. Its abdomen, layered with chitin, opened in multiple places to reveal several mouths filled with rows of shark-like teeth.

Sela pushed him forward and he dug his heels into the ground. He didn't want to be anywhere near that thing. He was a solid dozen feet away and that still wasn't far enough.

"We. Are. In. A. Shop. You. Big. Chocobo." Sela shoved him, drawing Gernell's attention.

"Ow. Geez, I'm just, you know, taking it all in," Rocky said.

A screen offering the cheaper and far less opulent private sales room appeared in front of him. He accepted and found himself and Sela inside the concrete room. The room was barren, only containing a metal desk and four simple chairs.

Rocky paced, waiting for Garnell to finish his negotiations. It was probably five minutes, but it felt like half an hour with the imminent threat of invasion.

Garnell ported into the room. Amelia wasn't with him, and Rocky's stress increased. They didn't have time to wait for her. His territory could be breached at any moment.

"Rocky, it is very impolite to stare openly at any creature in the bazaar. Lad, have ye never seen a Rictus before?" asked Garnell.

Rocky dropped his gaze to the floor and shook his head. Garnell chuckled, "Not to worry. I had ye out of there before the Rictus took offense. Unfortunately, Amelia is rather busy trying to capitalize on the departure of a large portion of the Guild Collective. She won't be joining us." He coughed and added, "The words are still hers. So, I apologize for any rudeness."

The affable merchant pulled out a scroll, "First, what took ye so long?"

"We have been a little swamped defending ourselves from the threats on our world." Rocky snarked under his breath.

Garnell heard him. Luckily, he took no offense and even shrugged his shoulders. "Two hundred and twenty-five ships left Helion Prime three days ago. That is over ninety percent of the strength of the Guild Collective. If you don't start preparing for their invasion, you will be but a page in the history of your world."

Rocky exchanged looks with Sela, who had removed her fox mask. She tilted her head and asked, "Garnell, this can't be the issue. Unless the time before the invasion has decreased?"

Garnell scanned the paper. "It doesn't appear to be the case, lass. However, she goes on. The Flow Ridians have set up the beacon, and Dahrix now has a bearing for the armada. This beacon needs to be destroyed immediately if your world has any chance of repelling the invasion."

Rocky took a deep breath, closed his eyes, and removed his own mask. They didn't have time for this. The problems of the Grotto, building a space fleet, and saving his fam—more survivors.

"We cannot attack other humans without cause. I don't even think we have time to make the trip. Our Territory needs to be defended. Our borders need to be reestablished. People need to be rescued. Killing humans when we could be saving others isn't my first choice, Garnell," said Rocky.

Garnell held up a hand. "I understand, lad. I am just passing on her message. I will make sure she is here next time to explain herself."

Warning! A powerful creature has crossed your Territory's Boundary!
Algonquin Valley has numerous invaders crossing the border! Push back these invaders or risk losing your Territory.

- **10 Semi-Sapient and 2 Boss creatures have crossed the threshold.**

Follow the gold string to find the invaders!

"We are all out of time for today. Sorry, Garnell, but we have some things to take care of on our front. Tell Amelia we will meet with her as soon as we can, but we aren't going to go gallivanting to destroy the beacon. They would have found us eventually, anyway. Either way, killing humans over a beacon is not our top priority right now."

He ported out of the shop, underscoring his point.

CHAPTER FOUR

They exited the shop and Rocky spotted two large, pulsing golden threads surrounded by ten smaller silver ones that led to the northwest. Second by second, the threads grew thicker. This could only mean one thing—the threat was approaching the Grotto.

He sprinted toward the entrance, urging his legs to pump faster. Ahead, two figures loomed. As he neared them, the forms took shape—Tao and Gamma waited with the military and a few other citizens.

The two massive golems looked around and loosened their weapons from where they rested on their backs. Rocky moved toward them, spying the green samurai-style armor. The crowds of humans gave the creatures a large berth before filling the space and edging closer to Rocky and Sela.

He glanced around and hesitated, searching for the right words to appease the worried crowd. "Tao, Gamma, can you stay here and watch over the NPC's? There are ten attackers and two bosses. I need you and the military to make sure none of them make it further than this entrance." They had been attacked in the Grotto once before, and he wasn't interested in a repeat performance. He was counting on the golems to act as the final line of defense. Again.

The crowd murmured, some worried about their safety while others were concerned about his return.

Rocky raised his voice, overpowering the clamor. "Anyone who doesn't wish to fight, go to the guild tent. If you wish to defend the Grotto, go to the military barracks for your orders. Tao and Gamma, please go collect the people at the training grounds. Relay my orders."

Tao and Gamma moved through the parting crowd as the people erupted, fear spreading through them like spilled water. With confidence he didn't feel, he shouted, "If you wish to attack the creatures, follow me!"

In the past, before the Spirit Realm, he would have taken Tao and Gamma with him. Now Rocky knew better. It was too risky to take all of their strength out in a single group. He tightened his jaw and walked as confidently as he could manage in his tight-fitting under armor.

"You shouldn't go out there without any gear," said Sela.

He stopped and smiled. She was right, but there was no time to visit more merchants in the shop.

Her mouth set into a line as she raised a hand. "I will meet you outside the entrance—wait for me." She grabbed his Bag of Holding and ran off.

Hoping she would return quickly, Rocky walked toward a massive crack in the protective rockface. The crack led to a corridor through the grey stone. That narrow passage was the only entrance through the thick, natural Grotto walls. The only other option was to cross the river, but the fast-moving water had only one bridge and wouldn't be easy to ford.

He strode through the parting groups of people. At first, they averted their eyes, his bravery overwhelming their fear. He smiled at those who met his eyes. They didn't need to join him— it was okay. He would protect them.

The crowd kept parting to make a path for him, and he continued his walk alone, meeting each person's eyes as he passed them. If one of those people gained a bit of confidence from his show, that would be enough. Rocky blinked, each set of eyes he met started to become fervent. The people behind those gazes—dressed in smithing aprons, torn rags, or low-level gear— nodded and conveyed something to Rocky.

At first, he didn't feel their support. Still, the more that nodded, the more his shoulders relaxed. The easier his walk became. These were the people he had sworn to defend, and they believed in him.

Victoria joined him, matching her stride to his, but her stiff footfalls betrayed her inner struggle. Rocky patted her on the shoulder, hoping to pass some of the citizens' energy to her. This reminded him of walking the tunnel before a basketball game. He swore to himself that this would be a career high.

She was risking her life by joining him, and he acknowledged it, but—

No one will die before I do. If it is within my power, I will protect those who follow me beyond these walls.

Mr. Pips and Bart fell in step with them, adding their strength to his. They walked through the press of bodies and finally strode unimpeded.

Zippo came into view in front of the group and turned to stand, watching their approach, and Rocky's heart stuttered. He couldn't help the broad smile, and he increased his pace to outdistance the others. The last few meters were closed quickly as the young man rushed to him, arms wide.

The air rushed out of his lungs as Zippo collided with him and closed his arms in a powerful embrace, "You're back!" Zippo crowed into his ear. Rocky was surprised that the young man's feet were still on the ground.

It was hard not to see him as the crying little boy he had met.

Rocky lifted his young friend off the ground and swung him around. He placed Zippo back on the ground and gripped his shoulders.

"It's good to see you. I can't wait to hear about your time in the Spirit Realm. Learn any new recipes?"

The other members of his party stood beside him, having caught up to them. Zippo noticed their presence and said, "There will be time for all that later."

Rocky watched Zippo turn and lead the group. He took a deep satisfying breath. His chest swelled with more than just the air. Zippo definitely wasn't that scared little kid anymore.

They reached the break in the sheer rock walls surrounding the Grotto—the most common entrance. Rocky inspected the group. Mr. Pips stood tall and lanky as always—like an emaciated teenager, despite his middle age. Bart crossed his arms, looking unapproachable in his Harley leathers and greaser vibe. Victoria, laden with a shield, mace, and armor, chatted with Zippo. She seemed shy and hesitant next to the red-haired, exuberant young man.

Rocky scanned the area. "Victoria, where is the healer?"

She looked from side to side. "Letoya said he would be here. He likes to brag about his valor to anyone who will listen. But he is basically a coward. Has anyone seen Gaston?"

"Yes, actually!" Sela half led, half dragged a man along behind her. He either had deplorable hygiene or had just woken up. Sela pointed at him. "This is Gaston, and he has graciously volunteered—" Gaston made a noise as if to protest, and Sela cuffed his head before continuing, "—to heal for us. I have told him that Bart and Mr. Pips will stay at his side at all times. For his *protection*."

Gaston gulped as he eyed his new bodyguards..

Rocky wasn't keen on forcing an unwilling participant to tag along, but there was no stopping Sela once she got started.

"Gaston, here, has been charging the citizens to heal injuries that would heal on their own. If they refused to pay, he browbeat them into it, using foreign laws that don't exist in the Grotto." She smiled. All teeth. "Now he is going to earn those Crystals."

Mr. Pips and Bart stood beside him, looking very grim, and Rocky almost felt sorry for Gaston. *Almost.* A rustle and some buckles clanking brought his attention back to Sela. She balanced a pile of mismatched armor in front of her.

"I didn't have time to grab anything from the shop, but some crafter lent me some of their stock," Sela said as she lowered the items to the ground.

She put on a set, and Zippo and Rocky did the same.

Rocky analyzed the gear. None of the pieces were Enchanted. They were probably the pieces the Territory produced while waiting for someone to learn Enchanting. He committed to examining Enchanted gear and discovering how it was created when he returned.

The armor wouldn't do much but add another layer for monsters to rip through. But it was still better than nothing. "There are twelve invaders who want some attention. Let's go give it to them."

The group exited and circled the Grotto's exterior walls. They took off, heading along the golden threads.

Sela ran beside him in her human form and exclaimed, "Azoth just came into range. I told him to scout."

His heart thudded hollowly, and he tried to reach his pet again.

<Azoth?>

Nothing. He gritted his teeth, determined to find a way to talk to Azoth again.

"Sela, ask him to scout the attackers and figure out what they are."

Sela laughed. "He says 'big and ugly.'"

That sounded exactly like Azoth.

Having Azoth join the party was a boon. They were fighting from a numerical disadvantage, and Rocky wasn't sure of the strength of their opponents yet.

He summoned his shadow clone and mentally sent it ahead to scout. Using a new trick, he entered a half-Meditative state in order to see what his clone was seeing.

The clone outpaced the group, which was easy to do as a shadow clone. There was no need to conserve energy or be stealthy. Or be held back by Victoria's slow running speed.

Rocky was excited to see a tanking class that had survived this long in action. He was willing to trade speed for someone who could divert attention away from him. He had met a few people who had chosen front-line classes early on, but not a single one had made it this far.

If we are going to win this fight, we will need better tactics.

His mind's vision through his clone sprinted on, but he slowed down, eventually coming to a stop. The rest of the adventurers followed his lead and came to a halt. They chattered, questioning the action.

"Rocky?" Zippo asked.

He scrutinized his troops, considering the group's composition.

"Bart, Mr. Pips, you two are the most experienced hunters. Do you have any traps or skills that lend themselves to ambushes?" Both men nodded, scratching their heads. Rocky continued, "Sela, you can set up pitfalls. Anything else?"

His clone ran on in his mind, following the strings.

"Are we going to try to set up an ambush here, then? That does seem like a better plan than a headlong attack," Sela mused.

Rocky motioned his sword tip to himself and said, "I want to see the enemy and figure out what we are up against, as well as how long we have to prepare." He turned to Bart and Mr. Pips. "Have you hunted this area? Where is the best spot for an ambush?" He motioned with his arm along the golden strings.

"I had a group of noobies out here the other day. We found a large clearing and shot some low-level boars from the treetops." Bart indicated the direction with this chin. "This way."

In his mind's eye, he searched for signs of monsters. He almost gave up when the massive pink leg of a humanoid swung out from behind a tree. His clone Analyzed the limb.

Northern Ogre
Master-Goliath
Level 11
Health points 3200/3290

While the ogre wasn't as big as Tao or Gamma, it was easily twenty-five feet tall and thick limbed. The Northern Ogre carried a carved tree club that dragged on the ground, leaving deep trenches in its wake. He willed his clone to go into stealth and find the boss creatures.

Everything went blank. The feed cut off as something flattened his clone.

Rocky flinched momentarily, but at the concerned looks, he explained, "My clone just ran into an ogre and got flattened from behind. They are definitely big and ugly!" The party entered a long grass clearing surrounded by massive trees on all sides. The canopy parted and opened to the cloudless blue sky as they entered the meadow.

Bart turned and spread his arms in an open gesture. "Here we are. The tree heights are tiered, which allowed the new hunters to fire from a safe spot while I trapped the area and drew the quarry back to them. Will this do?"

Rocky nodded. "Victoria, we're going to need you to act as the bait. We want to draw in the whole lot of them. You good with that?"

Victoria crossed her arms, hugging her small shield. She opened her mouth, then closed it. Sela put both of her hands on the woman's shoulders, and Victoria nodded stiffly.

"They are coming from that direction—" he pointed to the gold strings, "—so let's start setting it up. No need to tell you your business, right?"

Bart and Mr. Pips looked at each other and then at Gaston. Gaston stared at Sela, his face quite pale. Rocky pulled mines out of his Bag of Holding and tossed them to Bart. "Don't worry. Zippo will ensure Gaston is *safe*."

"Sela, tell Azoth to harry them from above, group them up, and force them this way," said Rocky.

"You know he won't understand that, right?"

His head fell. Azoth would definitely not understand that. He mimicked the birdbrain's response. *"Hairy. Rocky want Ogre's hair?"*

Sela laughed and gave him a thumbs up. She would take care of it. She knelt and placed a hand on the earth, still chuckling softly, setting up her Pitfalls. Zippo climbed a tree, also preparing for the fight.

Rocky summoned his Shadow Clone again. It popped into sight with a duplicate of his own bare backside mooning him. Rocky shook his head.

I'm not the one who crushed you. Go attack an ogre with your behind.

He checked his Ether pool. One hundred and fifty points. But it was slowly creeping up. There was nothing left to do but wait. He jumped into a tree opposite Zippo, closer to the border where the ogres would enter.

A cursory glance down made Rocky's stomach roil. He jumped a few trees away. His body's reaction to his Perception skill wasn't a comfortable experience. Most akin to the intense desire to find a toilet, however, he couldn't deny its effectiveness. Mid-jump, his eyes alighted on a few large Fusion mines half-hidden in the forest foliage. He kept jumping from tree to tree until his stomach settled. He landed on his final tree and placed his skill point into Knight's Resolve. He had no use for Envenom in this upcoming fight, but a mine going off could deal some serious fire damage.

His tree vibrated under his palm just as his ears picked up on distant crashing noises. A massive crack jolted him, and he winced as the noise assaulted his highly attentive ears. A huge roar accompanied the death of that unseen tree. Wind whipped the leaves around Rocky as a tree flew through the air. A fraction of a second later, Azoth winged by. His pet was definitely getting to the ogres.

Azoth banked and easily avoided a boulder that whistled by. Thunderous thumps accompanied an animalistic human-like roar. Rocky studied his pet and his cheeks began to hurt from smiling. He wanted nothing more than to hug the beastie.

Azoth faltered in the air for a moment before shooting straight up, almost performing a wingover. Rocky lost sight of Azoth.

A Louisville Slugger cracked a homerun beside Rocky. Every muscle in his body clenched tight. What had happened?

Underneath him, the branch twanged. He registered a second crack. Then he was freefalling along with something huge and very dark.

He converted his sword to liquid, narrowly avoiding impaling himself. His wild eyes searched for the enemy. Two black orbs met his gaze.

Azoth. We need to talk about timing. Oh—right—dammit.

Azoth landed first, grunting as his four mismatched legs absorbed the fall. Rocky landed atop the semi-truck-sized Chimera. His short-lived relief vanished and his lungs compressed due to the impact. His body ejected the air in his lungs causing his diaphragm to spasm.

Azoth rolled and leaped excitedly, bucking Rocky off his back. The loud breaking branches and crashing leaps of his pet were not subtle. Rocky tried to catch his breath and calm Azoth.

The ogres would hear his pet's rambunctious dance. At least he didn't step on a mine.

His heart beat loudly in his chest. Despite the counter-productiveness of what was happening, his breath caught. Azoth hopped around with happy feet. His pet jumped up onto his back feet, spread his wings to lift briefly into the air, and landed before bouncing again. Rocky wiped away a happy tear with the back of his hand.

His stomach tried to exit through his mouth. Rocky opened his hands and tried to place them on Azoth's bouncing chest, hoping to calm the enormous puppy. "Whoa, buddy. Calm down—" A gargantuan tongue assaulted him, followed rapidly by a horned head prodding him and knocking him over. Rocky laid on his back, pinned by the Chimera's enthusiasm. "Azoth, I can't hear you. I have lost my ring."

Sela popped out of stealth in her cat form and head-bumped Azoth, which freed Rocky. Sela and Azoth locked eyes, connecting in a way that Rocky couldn't. Not without his ring. He missed his pet more than ever. He didn't like being separated, but he didn't expect the stabbing pain when he finally saw Azoth.

Azoth looked back and forth between Sela and Rocky. His eyes were dimmed and his ears fell. Azoth took off while wistfully peeking at Rocky. Sela nodded briefly to Rocky before vanishing back into stealth.

What just happened?

His feet on the ground picked up tremors through his leather boots, and the sound of large footfalls was unmistakable. He quickly jumped back up the broken tree. Rocky's brow furrowed. Would the ogres avoid the loud noises Azoth had caused?

His eye caught movement as a massive tree-club whipped toward him. He pistoned his legs out of the crouch and shot backwards toward another tree. The echoing boom of the club's impact put Azoth's recent attempt to shame. Buckshot splinters peppered him, and he crossed his arms to protect his face. He flinched as small paper cuts bloomed on his exposed skin.

His heart pounded against his rib cage and his hands pulsed as adrenaline pumped through his system, intensifying his focus. He turned on Stealth and Dark Cloak. His emotions warred within him, tangled and messy. He was going to fix that problem, but for now, he wanted the anger. Maybe even needed it.

His eyes were glued to the pudgy face of his assailant when the tree that he landed on vibrated. His eyes scanned the area and landed on a second ogre. The ogre who must have just rung the proverbial bell that he was crouched in. The first Ogre charged at his new perch and the second struck again. The healthy tree wasn't meant for this kind of abuse and split down the center, its dying whine assaulting Rocky along with the stench of ogre breath.

The second ogre's eyes locked onto the patch of blackness and roared. His Dark Cloak managed to steer the spittle away from him, at least.

You just let two ogres sneak up on you. You have to be better Rockland. Or there won't be a next time—next time.

He leaped out of the tree toward the clearing and released both his Skills. He needed the ogre to pursue him.

Most of the guiding strings were gone. The four that remained included the two golden ones, and he faltered. A stuttering step corrected the slip and he sprinted, tempting the ogre to chase after him. These two needed to die first.

He scanned the clearing in front of him and found that the others were fighting ogres of their own. He wanted to help, but he had his own problems.

The ground shook as a mine exploded, launching a distant ogre into the air. The violent shockwave rippled the terrain, and Rocky half-hopped when the subsequent wind buffeted him.

His gut clenched—his Perception warning him of a pitfall—and he leaped over it, clearing the twenty feet he needed to avoid disaster.

A furtive look over his shoulder made him gasp. The two ogres had followed and hit the pitfall like a train derailed by a broken track. A thud echoed as their chests struck the far edge of the hole. Fat-fingered hands scrabbled on the ground, gripping and tearing out long grass. But to no avail. Rocky skidded to a stop and charged back to the pit. He was going to finish these blockheads.

He darted toward his quarry. His sword hummed, almost whispering, about the taste of blood and their defeated souls.

An ogre emerged from his hiding spot just beyond the hole and advanced toward him. Its calves flexed, and it shot over the pit effortlessly. The creature's leap made his look like a child playing kindergarten hopscotch. He Analyzed his airborne foe.

Bam-Bam
Master-Yabba-Dabba
Level 23
Health Points 2322/ 2450
Boss

His assailant sailed toward him, and Rocky desperately charged his Dark Blade skill.

C'mon, then. Step up to the plate.

The ground groaned as Bam-Bam landed in a two-foot stomp that vibrated up Rocky's feet. He released his Skill with three charges and entered Dark Cloak. Bam-Bam braced a two-story metal I-beam in front of his chest and face, successfully blocking Rocky's attack.

Rocky's black phantasmal blades struck the steel, and a cacophony filled the air. The momentum of the blades pushed past the right side of the I-Beam and cut into Bam-Bam's right arm. The boss' roar joined the screech.

Rocky resumed his charge, crouching and pumping his legs. He dropped two more Dark Blade's worth of Ether into his sword, 'Dark Tidings.' He held the Skill in the blade and slashed at Bam-Bam's Achilles tendon—and the blade stuck. Panicking, he added his torquing core to the blow. With the ease of a butter knife in teflon, his edge breached Bam-Bam's tough skin. The resistance turned his blow and his slash cut into the ogre's calf. The boss howled louder as the blade's darkness spread up and down the spasming calf.

He liquified his blade, releasing it from the clenching muscles of the ogre's calf. Without a moment to spare, he reformed his blade and turned.

Bam-Bam shifted his foot and sidekicked at the dark cloud that had attacked his calf. All the air whooshed out of Rocky's lungs as the ogre's massive foot connected with his chest. He bit his lip as pain blossomed along his front. Only the disgusting pinky toe had fully connected, luckily. Bam-Bam swayed further onto the heel of his injured leg.

Rocky rolled back to his feet, spitting the iron taste out of his mouth. Bam-Bam attempted to balance on his single injured leg and fight against Rocky's phantasmal blades simultaneously. Even with ogre strength, he failed. Just as the two trapped ogres reached hands and heads out of the pit, Bam-Bam fell right on top of them. They all crumpled back down into the hole, and Rocky surveyed the battle during the respite.

Three cooling ogre corpses laid around the clearing while three others battled on.

An ogre and Victoria stood toe-to toe. Her opponent grunted as it teed off, and she caught the tree-club on her small shield. He expected this diminutive woman to fly away or be reduced to a cloud of misty blood. Her shield glowed, and the tree rebounded viciously. The ogre managed an, "Oooyyy" before the club smashed its teeth and nose in a sickly wet crunch.

Sela dodged the feet of another ogre as Zippo threw fireballs at its face. Meanwhile, Mr. Pips stood beside Gaston and held up two hands. Rocky's gaze followed the direction the man's reach indicated. The final ogre struggled to free its leg from an enormous fluorescent glowing bear trap.

Bart got into position on the other side of Gaston. He extended one arm and braced it with the other, squinting down the length of his arm and over his extended finger. He raised his thumb forming a finger gun, then dropped the thumb. A bolt of glowing blue pumped out, racing at Mr. Pip's trapped foe. The skill cut through the creature's tough hide and dug a deep furrow into the muscle beneath. The ogre rocked back.

Rocky turned around in time to see Bam-Bam leap out of the pit. The enraged boss vented a roar that bounced off the trees, and his bleeding calf pulsed out a misty red aura that quickly surrounded Bam-Bam. Amidst the chaos, another ogre exited the trees behind the pit.

Rocky Analyzed his foe again.

Bam-Bam
Master-Yabba-Dabba
Level 23
Health Points 1843/ 2450
Boss
Bloodlust-Aura

He saw the same aura climbing up the ogre behind Bam-Bam and Analyzed … her?

Pebbles
Master-Doo

Level 29
Health Points 1250/ 1250
Boss
Bloodlust-Aura

The two minions, now covered in a red aura, leaped out of the pit.

Rocky tried to curse, "Frakkin Cylons!"

CHAPTER FIVE

The sound of tribal drums resounded in the clearing, vibrating every air molecule and sending a chill down Rocky's spine. There was only one thing that could make that sound—Bloodlust-Aura. There was no time to see how his fellow warriors fared as four ogres stared at him, ready to attack. The ogres didn't need the makeshift tree-club weapons they left in the pit—their smart car-sized fists were deadly enough.

Pebbles raised her gnarled tree staff and smashed the bottom of it into the ground. She backed up into the trees, joining two other shadowy outlines. Rocky didn't see or feel anything change, and yet he couldn't shake off the thought of her retreat. The only reason that made sense was if those were the final three invaders. Rocky sent his clone to track them. He didn't want to send the clone away—it would weaken his position. Being down one attack option was never good, but he had no choice. He needed to know where Pebbles and her guards were heading.

He might not have his clone, but at least he still had Azoth. He hadn't seen the chimera attacking ogres during his last scan of the clearing, but he hoped his pet was around and ready to help. He dreaded facing the three remaining ogres and took a step backward, unleashing the coiled-hell in front of him. As if a gunshot for the hundred-meter dash went off, the three ogres flashed forward, each hairy foot boring furrows into the soft earth beneath them.

Hundreds of options raced through his mind. He needed a plan. Fast. And then it hit him. He wasn't sure he liked the idea, but he couldn't overthink it. Sports had taught him that. He shuffled, then sprinted, and sped toward the opposite edge of the clearing. His days in track and field had trained him not to check how close his opponents were. But that didn't mean it was easy, and he fought the urge to glance back. The tribal drums still pumped out their haunting cadence, but now heavy feet and guttural growls joined it. The ogres were pursuing him. He hoped his agility and spacing would be enough.

His eyes surveyed the ground in front of him, searching for what he needed. They hit on something about forty meters in front of him, and his stomach lurched, warning him of danger. He adjusted his course. His stomach heaved harder in warning and he leaped into the air, trying to avoid the fusion mine under him.

He soared over the grass, over the mine, and chanced a look back. His heart stuttered—grasping fingers less than a meter behind him.

Bam-Bam ran, hand outstretched and slowed by his calf injury, which were probably the only reasons Rocky wasn't already dead. The two other lesser ogres closely flanked Bam-Bam, their arms pumping beside them.

Rocky barely made it to this spot before the other three. But he hadn't been quick enough to buy himself the space he needed. A miniature sun bloomed under a minion's ugly, bulbous foot. The air pressure bombarded his Dark Cloak, compressing it before connecting with his back. He shot up diagonally, and a scream ripped from his throat. The heat from the wave of air scorched him, and for a moment, he thought he saw the icon for his passive skill, Stalwart, flare in his interface.

Debris pierced his skin where his compressed Dark Cloak failed to adjust course, and his health dropped precariously. He had no air left in his lungs but managed a squeak as the razor-sharp shrapnel cut him. Still airborne, he cast Dark Mend and downed a Health Potion. There was a hard landing in his immediate future.

He bumped into something soft in the air, and talons dug painfully into his left shoulder. The joint burned from being forced to bear Rocky's full weight. And the puncture wounds from the claws caused his muscles to convulse uncontrollably.

Unable to handle the sudden added weight and projectile force, Azoth retracted his claw, releasing Rocky. The momentum dump allowed his lungs to suck in a stuttering breath of air. His pet now with all of Rocky's transferred force overcorrected and pinwheeled, hissing as he attempted to correct his flight. Azoth began to attempt a few acrobatic movements just as Rocky lost sight of his pet. He fell.

The ground rushed to meet him. He absorbed as much of the impact as he could in the spring of his knees, then slackened the joints and rolled. Thankfully he came out uninjured and immediately whipped his head, searching the sky for his pet. He winced as Azoth's wing snapped and the Chimera crash landed with a roar. Rocky scoured the landscape, attempting to locate impending threats.

A cloud of debris and dirt hung in the air where the mine had detonated. He'd never seen anything like it. The debris was encompassed by a strange purple dome that refracted light like a bubble of soap. He wrenched his gaze away, and his eyes flitted over the other battle in the distance. Three blood-lusting ogres were still engaged in combat with the smaller figures of his group. Bam-Bam's ability must have a powerful effect. How else would the ogres still be alive?

His eyes alighted on Azoth, who was extricating himself from the churned soil.

Rocky didn't waste a second, and bolted toward the Chimera, casting a Dark Mend. Once he reached his pet's side, Azoth was shaking his massive lion's head, and his wing lay broken on the grass. Rocky's Dark Mend coalesced thickly upon the wing, and the bones snapped back into place. He cast another one, just in case, and pulled out his last Health Potion. He unstoppered it and showed it to his pet, but Azoth's head wouldn't stop shaking.

He recorked it—he couldn't afford to spill his last health restoring bottle—and kept a comforting hand on his Chimera's neck as he studied the frozen debris field. Within the debris, two shapes slowly moved away from a small, blinding sun. Outside the field, smoke rose from a third legless shape. He analyzed the creature, confirmed it was dead, and shifted his gaze to study the retreating ogres, suspended in the debris.

Bam-Bam got a foot clear of the backside of the field, and the rest of his body crept out. His second minion followed closely, and as soon as they were out of harm's way, the bubble sped up, and debris washed over the two ogres. The bubble allowed them to clear the deadly detonation—the ground and air—dissipating the detonation damage.

Rocky tilted his head back and groaned. He'd bet ten crystals that was a time spell Pebbles had used. As the dirt settled, two eyes like hot coals glared at him. Bam-Bam. The ogre moseyed toward a tree to rearm, Rocky took advantage of the further reprieve to examine Azoth.

His pet had stopped thrashing and he uncorked the bottle, tipping the liquid into Azoth's mouth. The liquid sped up the healing, and Rocky sighed in relief.

Bam-Bam had touched his first tree. Rocky expected him to wrench it out of the ground, but instead, the tree started changing. Bam-Bam walked to a second and third tree, repeating the same motions. Just like the first one, these trees altered their shape.

The tree branches realigned themselves into unique patterns. An empty feeling settled in the pit of his stomach. Had Bam-Bam made treants or something similar?

The trees cracked and Rocky protected his ears from the sound. No feet or limbs formed and he sighed in relief. He relaxed too soon. The trees finished rearranging themselves, and Rocky Analyzed them.

Totem of Healing
Master-Totem

Level 23
Health Points 500/ 500

--

Totem of Barkskin
Master-Totem
Level 23
Health Points 500/ 500

--

Totem of Haste
Master-Totem
Level 23
250/ 250

He should have seen that Skill coming. Years of gaming taught him that Shaman classes often had Bloodlust—and the twisted totems were a clear confirmation of a Shaman-like class.

Rocky whispered to Azoth, "We need to take those totems out. If I distract them, do you think you can knock them down?"

The orbs of his pet's eyes dimmed for a moment and then shone fiercely. Azoth head-butted Rocky and nodded.

"Let's do this, buddy."

Rocky began charging his sword with a single Dark Blade and turned toward Bam-Bam and the ogre minion. Azoth sprinted in the opposite direction of the fight.

Bam-Bam pointed and barked out a laugh at the retreating Chimera. Rocky sneered and spit. That ugly jerk was going to regret laughing at his pet.

Rocky blinked. The ogre strode forward. Each step was invisible, almost like Bam-Bam was walking with a picture shutter capture.

He checked his Ether pool. It was critically low, sitting at a measly twenty-five points of his total two hundred and thirty. With his free hand, he retrieved and chugged one of his last few bottles of Ether Draught. The tingling taste of electrified berries shot over his tongue and down his throat. He dropped the flask into his Bag of Holding before returning his second hand to the hilt of his longsword.

He lunged forward and released a vertical slash with all of his might. The phantasmal shadow blade careened forward, and he charged his sword again.

His first blade sped toward Bam-Bam and he immediately released another phantasmal blade, . stepping forward with his other foot to return his sword on a diagonal path up to above his right shoulder. His second Skill flew at the totems.

The deep grooves, caused by his Skills, ate up ground like a drag car race and seemed to be on a crash course with their targets, when Bam-Bam blurred. One moment, he was standing behind the first slash, and the next, he was in front of it. Rocky stepped back and a second blur shot in front of the totems before the minion clapped its hands onto each side of the second slash.

Alright, note to self Totem of Haste goes down first.

The minion's hands held his Dark Blade, shedding skin and instantly healing it back. He didn't know what to do. How was he supposed to take them down?

Think, Rocky, think.

Wait. Bam-Bam wasn't coming to attack him. He was fast enough to obliterate Rocky in a half second, but he didn't. Why?

There must be a range on the totems. That's got to be it, and Azoth is headed right for them. Shoot.

Rocky pushed off the ground and began charging his blade. He didn't release this Skill but held it in the edge, hoping to hit Bam-Bam. The minimal damage to Bam-Bam's calf was still visible, despite the healing Totem. A melee version of his skill was his chance to hurt the grotesque creature—if he got lucky.

Bam-Bam smiled, his rotten, yellow teeth on display, as Rocky began to sprint toward him.

The other minion is still battling with my second Dark Blade. I've got their attention. Alright, Chuckles—time for you to pay.

Bam-bam countercharged.

Something niggled at him. Another oddity. Bam-Bam should be reacting faster than before, but he waited a few seconds to start a charge. If Rocky stopped his rush… Bam-Bam would probably do the same, not wanting to exit the ward's range.

Rocky adjusted his sprint by the smallest margin, slowing down. He hoped he was right.

The boss ogre devoured the space between them, unaware of Rocky's change in speed.

The ogre tried to slow down as realization dawned, it was too late. Still, all that built-up speed and momentum didn't just vanish. Bam-Bam stumbled and jammed his heel into the earth, skidding and sliding. Rocky bared his teeth. Bam-Bam wasn't going to stop in time.

As the creature exited the Totem of Haste's field of effect, his arms pinwheeled. His unsteady movements toppled him into a faceplant.

Rocky, a few feet away from his final landing spot, slashed mid-step at Bam-Bam's bald head. A forearm shot up, blocking his blade from reaching the ogre's cranium. His sword sliced cleanly into Bam-Bam's meaty forearm, leaving behind spreading darkness. Rocky narrowly missed the pudgy head behind the arm. The ogre opened its mouth and roared its putrid breath right in Rocky's face.

His Ether was critically low again.

Ogre spittle overwhelmed his Dark Cloak, soaking him and making his bile rise. He closed his eyes in disgust and shook his head and arms, dislodging the ogre sludge the way a dog shakes off water. Stepping forward, he positioned his blade to slash the beast again and slipped on a slimy, ogre-sized snot-wad. His calculated lunge turned into awkward splits. Rocky squeaked as a stretch he had never performed, never intended—and never wanted to experience—overwhelmed his pain tolerance.

Adrenaline surged through his body, and he drove his sword toward the roaring Boss.

Bam-Bam's eyes glinted, and his neck shot out like a snake. His gaping mouth opened wider, and horror gripped Rocky as the cavernous mouth lunged at him.

This is not the way I planned to go.

He had no way of retreating as he continued to slide in ogre mucus toward his toothy-demise.

His front foot connected with Bam-Bam's chin, halting his latest gymnastic move before he did something really painful, like tearing his groin. His front leg was fully extended and he still couldn't use it to retreat.

His back foot had the tiniest bit of power left in his ankle and calf. He made the only decision left to him. Go toward the mouth, and jump in deep enough to get passed the front rotting wall of teeth.

He used his back leg to shove himself, toward the snapping teeth. His front leg gained a bend and coiled as his back foot closed the split posture. He pushed again with his now bent front leg toward the closing mouth. The clack of teeth echoed through the clearing as Bam-Bam's mouth shut, trapping Rocky inside.

He had made it.

In the dark, a kneeling Rocky teetered and staggered as Bam-Bam swung his head side to side. A warm liquid oozed from the mouth's walls, coating him in head-to-toe ogre juice. The tongue under his knees bucked violently and tossed him around like a kid in a bouncy castle.

The writhing organ gave him a moment's reprieve and he grabbed onto its fleshy sides. He refused to be a snack. The ogre abruptly opened his mouth, flinging his tongue and Rocky forward.

Rocky was ejected from the orifice as quickly as he had been trapped within. He saw the blessed sun.

Hurtling through the air, he thudded onto the grass. The rest of the contents of Bam-Bam's mouth sloshed over him—thick and chunky. He doubled over, clutched his stomach, and retched.

He wiped his mouth as he stood up and looked around. Blood soaked into the grass. Was it his? He patted his arms and legs, probing for a wound.

The sound of a stream of water from a hose startled him. It was a few feet from him, and he jerked his head, searching for the ogre.

Bam-Bam shook uncontrollably and held his head with both hands—blood was streaming from its mouth. Rocky clenched his hand. Wait. Where was his sword? He didn't remember losing the weapon.

The boss creature slumped to the ground, twitching, which gave Rocky the chance to Analyze him.

Bam-Bam
Master-Yabba-Dabba
Level 23
Health Points 0/ 2450
Boss
Dead

Rocky peeked inside Bam-Bam's mouth, disgusted at the rot and decay.

I was inside that? Come on! Ever heard of a dentist?

It was further nauseating to acknowledge he had just been in there. And was still covered in blood and mucus. His stomach attempted to revolt again, and he fought it back down.

Rocky peeked further into the ogre's maw—lodged in the roof of Bam-Bam's mouth was the familiar hilt of a sword. Rocky would resummon it. There was no way he was going back in there and retrieving it. One ogre mucus shower was enough to last a lifetime.

He scanned the area behind the boss—there should be one final minion guarding the totems. Spotting movement among the trees, he couldn't help barking out a short laugh as he found Azoth and the final minion played chase. Azoth had the clear advantage, since the minion's red bloodlust aura had faded. Behind them stood two splintered symbols, and Azoth positioned his little game to score a final blow.

The ogre overextended, and his pet's quick reflexes juked back, overbalancing the clumsy oaf. A few fast gallops, and Azoth collided, horn nubs first, with the third and final Totem of Healing. A boom followed by long creaks confirmed the Totem's structural damage. The Totem cracked and fractured, surrendering as it fell to the ground.

Azoth had more or less one-shotted that Totem. No longer concerned for his pet, he scanned the battlegrounds. Everyone looked at him. Frozen. He held up both mucus-soaked hands and mimed a 'Don't ask, I don't want to talk about it' gesture and pointed to Azoth's opponent— the final remaining enemy in the clearing.

If they could down it quickly, they could pursue Pebbles. The group combined their attacks and killed it instantly.

Rocky did his best to clean himself off, even going as far as to put on a new set of under armor. Zippo jumped onto Azoth's back, and he followed, slightly cleaner. Sela shifted into a raven, while the rest of the group looted the corpses and would catch up later.

The three strings in his interface led directly toward the Grotto. Leaving Gamma and Tao had been a good decision. A true leader's decision.

The flight cut the distance they needed to travel in half. Rocky looked through the eyes of his clone on multiple occasions, trying to discern what he was seeing. His clone was hiding up in a tree as they approached, watching Pebbles and her two guards.

The three ogres stood at the Grotto's entrance. Pebbles kneeled with her staff planted, and it slowly sank into the ground. The two guards flanked her and surveyed the horizon for enemies.

He couldn't decide if they should fly into the Grotto to regroup or to immediately attack the ogres outside of it.

A few minutes of flight brought them over the three ogres. Rocky switched his perception to his own eyes and studied the scene from above. It was still just as strange to see from above as it was from the clone's perspective.

Tao and Gamma waited on the far side of the pathway into the Grotto, and two military personnel watched the strange ogre's group from the top of the cliffs.

The head of Pebbles' staff touched the ground, and purple light radiated from it, blinding the onlookers. He cursed and turned away, blinking away the spots that clouded his vision. Azoth faltered, and Rocky patted his shoulder. "It's okay, buddy, just blink away the spots and hover here. Don't panic; they didn't attack us."

Azoth calmed down and Rocky continued to blink away the spell's purple afterglow. When his vision returned, he couldn't believe what he was seeing.

He closed his eyes and opened them. Nothing had changed. The Pathway into the Grotto was crowded with ogres. Tao and Gamma were encased in a familiar glowing purple field-bubble—nearly identical to the one that had saved Bam-Bam. His vision cleared and he Analyzed a familiar figure leading the charge into the Grotto.

Bam-Bam
Master-Yabba-Dabba
Level 23
Health Points 1225/ 2450
Boss

He tilted his head and counted the ogres moving toward Tao and Gamma. There were nine of them, and he was absolutely sure that they were the same minions they had just killed.

Pebbles collapsed and her two guards caught her. They swung her onto their shoulders like she was a log and ran from the Grotto.

Follow her! he thought to his clone.

He ordered Azoth to the ground outside of the purple dome that encased Tao and Gamma. They hadn't moved yet.

"Tao, Gamma, are you two alright?" asked Rocky. No response.

He peered closer. It was barely visible, but Tao moved, just enough for Rocky to notice. They were moving as if they were paddling through the thickest molasses ever created. He cursed and looked at the army behind the two golems.

"Form up around the golems. I am not sure if the enemy can move normally in there, either, so let's not give them the chance."

The tanks clacked forward.

A roar came from the Grotto's entrance.

The first ogre to emerge was a glowing, red Bam-Bam. Tribal drums gave cadence to the haunting sight. It threw three round objects, and trees grew from the spots where the objects landed.

"Fire!" he shouted. He wasn't going to let the Totems have a chance to form. Minions streamed out of the tunnel and formed up in front of the Totems, shielding them.

The second volley flew forward in a kaleidoscope of ionized light, and Rocky waited for the ogres to fall under the barrage.

They didn't, and he Analyzed Bam-Bam again.

Bam-Bam
Master-Yabba-Dabba
Level 23
Health Points 1500/ 2450
Boss
Blood Lust

Bam-Bam was healing under the onslaught, not dying.

"Zippo, get up in the air and take out those Totems! Sela, get some vines ready!"

Zippo hopped onto the Chimera's back, and the wind from Azoth's wings stirred the dirt and leaves, forcing Rocky to turn his face away.

When it was safe to look back, something had changed. Bam-Bam flexed his muscles against the onslaught. The ogres took tiny steps forward, like linebackers in football slowly collapsing the pocket of protection. This time, though, the protected quarterback was all of Rocky's military, Tao, Gamma, Sela, and himself.

He checked his Ether. Not great. He charged up two stacks of Dark Blade and let them fly horizontally. They collided first with Bam-Bam, stopping him in his tracks.

Rocky smiled for a split second, until eight ogres stepped up and extended their hands to his double-stacked Skill. They began moving again, chewing up the ground.

Rocky searched the sky anxiously. What was taking Zippo so long?

Fireballs rained down on the Totems, splashing against an invisible umbrella that dissipated the fire twenty feet above the ogres.

He Analyzed the new totems and found one change. The Totem of Haste was missing.

Totem of Single-Direction Shielding
Master-Totem
Level 23
250/ 250

The Totem must have blocked some of the earlier attacks. How did he let the other ogres distract him to the point that he'd miss that? The advancing ogres protected the front while the Totem guarded the skies.

Rocky cursed. The gap was quickly closing—no more than ten feet left.

Sela's vines sprang from the earth and wrapped around the bodies of the ogres.

"The aura is eating them faster than I can repair them," Sela grunted.

The vines snapped, and the ogres took another huge step, cutting the distance to eight feet.

Rocky prepared his melee version of Dark Blade with the last of his Ether, readying himself for a fight.

An object whizzed by Rocky's head. His eyes followed a black frying pan as it sailed through the air, clanged off the thick-skinned arms of an ogre minion, and fell in the dirt.

His eyebrows joined his hairline. He traced the pan's flight path to a man heaving a black metal wok. The man tossed the wok through the air and ran straight ahead, followed by thousands of other people.

Rocky scanned the horizon. The army's numbers increased as more and more people bolstered it. What started as roughly seven hundred military men swelled to two thousand, and kept growing.

A man in a chef's apron waved his hands in multiple directions, dancing in place.

A flock of short blades flew around an ogre minion, crisscrossing tough skin. The ogre roared and fell to one knee. Its mouth opened to roar, and thousands of projectiles joined the onslaught. Glowing skills rocketed forward, growing brighter.

Tank operators shouted over the tumult, "Empty!" and "Switching to rifle fire!"

One soldier yelled, "Cease fire!" and the onslaught tempered but didn't stop. The four thousand untrained citizens kept going until they exhausted their Ether pools. Several minutes elapsed before the firing ceased. Smoke swirled where weapons once rained.

Azoth landed beside him with Zippo on his back. "We didn't hit the totems at all. That shield kept diverting my attacks." He gestured between the four thousand citizens and the smoke. "This was them."

Rocky's heart swelled with pride as he looked over the citizens who braved the fight. When the Grotto was under threat, everyone stood together.

But there was still Pebbles to contend with. First, he needed to ensure that the ogres were dead. But, if Pebbles escaped, this could all start again.

"Azoth, can you give that smoke some help with dispersing?" Rocky asked. There was no response, of course. He still wasn't used to it—he missed Azoth's broken, childish speech pattern.

Azoth flapped his wings, as if he was playing a new game, and the smoke cleared to reveal nine ogre corpses.

Tao and Gamma were slowly extricating themselves from the time bubble. This battle hadn't lasted long.

Rocky pointed to the hulking bodies and addressed the man who had ordered the cease-fire. "Loot the corpses, and then stack them in front of the Dungeons. Make sure the boss gets placed with Maximus."

The man saluted and ordered his tank squadrons to hook the corpses up to the chassis.

Rocky checked in with his clone. He couldn't believe what he was seeing—the ogre minions were being attacked by someone. He recognized it as the exiles immediately, since there was a particular Skill involved in the fight. Derik had hurled that same attack at Rocky a few weeks before.

"Zippo, oversee the cleanup."

He searched the crowd for Sela and spotted her a few feet away, talking with a group of citizens. What was she doing? Pebbles was top priority. Whatever they were gossiping about could wait.

"Sela, let's get on Azoth and find Pebbles."

She excused herself and joined him on Azoth's back. The group she chatted with shot them worried looks. Maybe he was mistaken. He patted his friend and asked, "Can you see the gold string? Good. Follow it!"

CHAPTER SIX

Rocky and Sela flew over the tops of the enlarged Territory trees. Even the thickened canopy couldn't contain the sounds of battle below them. Rocky scanned for a safe spot to land, but Azoth, being Azoth, chose his own.

Rocky and Sela leaped from the saddle as Azoth entered the fray. As she dropped, Sela shifted into her cat form to help with her landing. He didn't have that option. He mentally turned on Dark Cloak, praying it would help with his.

As he hurtled to the ground, branches whipped him, tearing at his arms and back. He shouted his pain and lost count of how many hit him. Abruptly, he slammed into a tree trunk, and his compressed lungs cut his shout short. Dark Cloak had some severe limitations. Like stopping a thousand branches of the ugly tree from beating him. Oh, and one trunk.

He landed on the forest floor with a crack. He wasn't sure if he'd broken a bone ,but it sure felt like it. He struggled to catch his breath. He wheezed and gasped for air, wincing with each cough. Gritting his teeth against the pain, he cast Dark Mend and silently berated Azoth. And himself—he needed to take at least partial blame.

He cast a second Dark Mend, and the pain receded enough for him to roll onto his back.

He groaned at a new notification.

Congratulations! You have learned a new skill.
Falling
- **You have fallen numerous times in your life, and have always gotten back up. Let the system help you with that. Reduces damage from falling by 0.5% per level in weak ranks.**
Current level Weak level 1

Thanks a lot. Did the system have to rub it in?

Rocky gingerly rose to his feet and surveyed the corpses of the three ogres. Azoth was atop one with his claws dug in, and Rocky covered his ears as his pet roared.

He shook his head and walked over. "Azoth, before you eat that disgusting thing, let us loot it first."

Azoth had pumped his wings to gain altitude, still towing the minion corpse, then reluctantly dropped the corpse at his command.

Rocky knelt beside the body and thought, *Loot.* Five Crystallized Ether appeared in one of his hands.

That's a significant amount. I wonder if it's because they are humanoid?

He glanced at his other hand. Some sort of leather? He Analyzed it.

Ogre Loincloth

- **This loincloth is made from the fiercest creature the ogre has slain. Often, it carries immense strength, due to the inherent Ether of the original occupant.**

He dropped the Loincloth like it had burned him.

He grimaced at the thing on the ground, and bile rose in his throat. He caught an eyeful of what it had been covering and turned away.

"Azoth, you can take it away now." He coughed, nearly misspeaking.

The gusts of wind that built up and then dissipated told of his pet leaving with the corpse in tow. He sure was getting stronger if he could carry something so substantial now. Maybe Azoth could even carry a third person.

He headed toward the boss's corpse, already imagining the loot he'd get, when a voice stopped him in his tracks.

"You wait right there! We stopped these creatures and would have killed them without your pet's interference. I'm pretty sure you did some damage to that tree trunk, though."

He didn't miss that voice one bit.

Derik pushed and shoved through his fellow exiles, wrenching his arms free from those who tried to hold him back.

If he had felt any goodwill toward the man, it vanished with Derik's tone. And the man pointing out his fall.

He had a decision to make. Should he allow them to loot the corpses? The rules of their exile were clear. The loot of their kills was to be given to the Territory. He scrolled through his screens and noticed his waiting notifications. Shaking his head, and recalling his vow to be a good leader, he made the fair decision.

They had killed these bosses and helped the Territory. Rocky shouldn't let his dislike of Derik cloud that. He ignored a few notifications and navigated to a screen that allowed Derik and the exiles to loot the corpses in front of them.

Rocky motioned that the loot was Derik's. He didn't trust his voice to stay neutral.

"Very humble of you, *Mister Leader*. Thanks for offering us the loot of our own kill," Derik spat out.

"Consider yourself lucky that this meeting doesn't end with my fist in your face. *Again.*"

Sela interposed herself and Rocky blinked.

Oops. I really need to work on that anger management.

He turned his back, signaling that he was done with Derik, and checked the notification he had closed to loot the corpses.

Congratulations! You have completed a quest.
Protection Quest
Leader of Territory Algonquin Valley – Chimera Knight

- **You have successfully safeguarded the sanctum and even renewed a new timer for your Ether-Assisted Protection. You have upheld your oath and successfully defeated the invading monsters in the time limit.**

    A knight is only as good as their oath.

Rewards:

    0 Personal Etherience (250,000 Etherience diverted to Spirit Realm as per Michabo agreement)

    You have successfully claimed the Chimera Knight Journeyman Class

Great job, Leader!

The Etherience of the quest diverting to the Spirit Realm reminded him of his earliest conversation with Michabo. He quickly pulled up his other completed quest and searched through the Greater Territorial Perks. Michabo had stressed the importance of obtaining one of the perks listed, and he needed to find it before the timer lapsed. According to Michabo, he had exactly a week from the completion of a quest to select a reward, if offered; otherwise, it would randomize your selection.

He opened the quest, which was awaiting completion.

Congratulations! You have completed a quest.

Chain Quest

    Red Quest

        Party Quest - Druid

Cleanse the Land

- **The land around your Territory has been infected by the Irradiated Ether and needs to be cleansed by fire. To ensure that this infection does not linger, remove its source, Apep's Dungeon, and its Leader. Failure to eradicate**

this plague will result in future attacks on your Territory and erosion of borders.

Rewards:

1 Greater Territorial Perk (Awaiting selection 4 hours, 13 minutes, 3 seconds remaining)
0 Etherience (250,000 Etherience diverted to Territorial Etherience)
1000 Crystallized Ether to party Leader.
Choose your reward to finalize.

He clicked the Greater Territorial Perk and scrolled through the list of twenty-five items, skipping over those he wasn't looking for. With four hours remaining, he couldn't afford to look at the others, especially due to knowing himself well enough to admit he would probably end up believing the Territory needed one of the other twenty-four options more.

Not that he fully trusted Michabo, but the weird bunny-man had told him the Atlantean Guild Tower would be required to keep the Spirit Realm functioning. The fact that the space had recently saved his entire party's life made a good argument for keeping it.

He clicked on the Atlantean Guild Tower and was shocked when it gave him an additional option within the building tab.

Atlantean Guild Tower

- **An Atlantean Guild Tower creates a conduit for a Territory, increasing the Territorial Etherience conversion from 1 for every 100 citizens to 1 for every 10 citizens. It also provides a Guild or Palace living area within the dome, which is attached to its base. This building can be continuously upgraded to better serve your Territory. It even comes with an**

additional option upon creation, if Orbital Satellites exist.

  ○ **For an additional 500,000 Territorial Etherience, this Tower creates a Satellite Uplink, which will allow remote access to the Atlantean Net. The single Satellite Uplink will also enable the owner to view areas below its orbit.**

Would you like to Uplink to a Satellite?
<Yes> | No

Would you like to accept this as your Greater Territorial Perk?
<Yes> | No

A Satellite uplink would be invaluable, but he wasn't sure if the price would be worth it. He searched around for Sela and found her chatting with the other exiles while Derik looted Pebbles. She laughed at something, and his heart clenched. He rolled his shoulders, forcing out the physical tightness, and called, "Sela, can I borrow you for a moment?"

She turned, smiled, and excused herself from the group. Once she had joined him, he motioned toward the hovering Guild Perk option.

"Michabo, told me that we needed this Tower. What do you think?"

Sela's smile vanished like the sun at night. She finished reading the screen and asked "How much Territorial Etherience do we have?"

He heard something in her voice. He would have called it excitement, but it wasn't bubbly. It was too intense and made his heart stutter. Was it because the tone made him worried, or was it his own desire?

He opened Algonquin's Territorial page and scanned it to find the current total. He hadn't yet had the time to delve into most of the options—only really recalling that for every one hundred people in residence, the Territory created 1 Ether per day for the pool.

He scanned the lists of options for spells, buildings, and conversions. But there was a new tab that he'd never seen before.

Territorial Management Page
Click a tab to open the options within.
<Spells> | Buildings | Conversions | Resources | Rebirths
Total Population: 3,693 Individuals within Borders
Total Etherience per day: 37 Territorial Etherience
Current Etherience Total: 1,265,213 (2,265,213 – 1,000,000 for current Rebirth)

One million points per Rebirth? Michabo had said they needed the entire group's Etherience for resurrections. If his Etherience transferred point for point, he had more than enough for the Satellite. Rocky alone had transferred two hundred million at least! Had Michabo needed the group's collective Etherience? Maybe there was a conversion rate. Etherience wasn't exactly Territorial Etherience—right?

Rocky had no reason not to trust Michabo, and figured he would try to get the rabbit man to explain later. He clicked the Rebirth tab.

Territorial Management Page
Rebirths
- **Thanks to your place of power, the Altar of Michabo, you have access to Rebirths. You can**

only use this option on Spirits that reside in the spirit realm to place them in a physical body. Spirits need to have a constant stream of Territorial Etherience to be sustained in the Spirit Realm. If it runs out, they may either die a true death or be demoted to the 7th Layer.

Joaquim Smith
- **Journeyman Level 1**
  - **<Cancel>**
    - ○ **Cancel refunds 1,000,000 Territorial Etherience. 12 hours, 13 minutes, 35 seconds of 48 hours remaining until Rebirth.**

Amber Dell (In Queue)
- **Journeyman Level 1**
  - **<Rebirth>**
    - ○ **Costs 1,000,000 Territorial Etherience**
    - ○ **48 hours total time required for Rebirth**

Sela's eyes welled and she pressed her lips together. She met his eyes, a tear tracking through the dirt on her face, and his stomach fell.

She looked away and whispered, "I know we all donated our Etherience to be Reborn. But after seeing this? I think we *have* to take the Uplink."

Every knotted emotion flared. His heart pumped fire through his veins, and his eyes welled with tears. His face wrinkled and his breath caught. It was impossible to discern which of his emotions had triggered the web. He felt around the edges of his anger, sadness, disgust, and surprise. Was that his shame? Did he feel the same way as Sela?

He placed a hand on her shoulder. "Sela, I—"

"All done looting this thing. We left anything we can't use for the Territory. Goodbye."

He forgot they weren't alone and he held on to Sela's shoulder, squeezing accidentally. She wriggled away and his teeth clacked together. Was there anything Derik couldn't ruin?

He snatched his hand back like he had touched fire, taking a deep, controlled breath as he watched the man walk away. He could send his clone in stealth after him. He would have the perfect alibi. No one would suspect him of—he shook his head. Derik wasn't worth it.

His cheeks suffused with heat, and he turned to apologize to Sela.

Sela wasn't there. She was back with the group of exiles, talking with the exiles, worry painted on their faces. She made calming gestures, and after a few more exchanges, the refugees followed Derik.

His apology settled at the back of his mouth and he blurted, "What was that about?"

Sela shrugged. "They were worried that we thought they felt the same way as Derik. They saw your face and feared that it meant they would never be allowed back into the Grotto." She paused and smiled, "I assured them that you wouldn't hold the actions of one man against the whole. I pointed out that you let them loot their kill. Relationships are mending." Her smile slipped for a moment, and she rubbed her shoulder.

Rocky opened his mouth to speak, but Sela cut in.

"No worries, I was surprised too. What are we going to do with these two ogre corpses?"

"I think I can just place them in my Bag of Holding. Remember we did it with Ragnar?" He crossed his arms, hugging himself, as goosebumps popped onto his arms. "I wish I had thought of this with Joe."

He bent down and put Pebbles in his Bag of Holding. The bag yanked him to the ground. He dumped Pebbles back out of the bag and stood up, brushing off the dirt from his butt.

He looked at the ground, avoiding Sela's eyes, his cheeks heating up.

Sela giggled. It was infectious, and he soon joined in. It felt good to laugh after the last few hours.

"I want to give them to the Dungeons. We will have to either get some tanks or Tao and Gamma to drag them back, though. Tell Azoth to bring what's left of his corpse back, too."

Giving the corpses to the dungeons sparked something. His eyes flew open.

"Sela, do you think Ragnar might be released from Apep if another Dungeon absorbed him?"

Sela touched her lips and shrugged. "I doubt anyone else has ever tried it. I vote to be the first. Let's grab the loot and get back to the Grotto. We should call the council as well. We will want everyone's input on the decision with the Tower. Have you looked through the other options?"

Rocky shook his head. "No, I didn't want to get bogged down. Michabo was pretty annoying and specific about choosing this one…"

"He wasn't very friendly with me." She scowled and crossed her arms. "I am not sure I trust anything he says." She sighed and added, "Let's at least look through the other ones. I will admit a connection to the Atlantean Net is crucial."

Rocky nodded and gingerly placed the three loincloths into his Bag of Holding. He shivered with disgust. He definitely needed to burn his fingertips after this to get *that* off his skin. Then he remembered he was also still covered in dried ogre slobber.

Maybe the system can heal me if I rip my own skin off?

He assumed the Exiles had taken anything else of value for themselves and wondered what Bam-Bam and the other eight minions had dropped. He and Sela made their way back to the Grotto as he studied his notifications and levels.

Congratulations, you have reached Level 4! You have been awarded 3 Stat Points and 3 Skill Points!
Stasis Entered! 0 Etherience Remaining till next Level!
--
Rockland Barkclay Level 4

Class: Journeyman-Dark Chimera Knight, Level 3 Strategist

Class Skills: Dark Blade, Dark Mend, Soul Blade, Dark Cloak, Shadow Clone, Knight's Resolve

Health Points = 340/340

Dark Ether Pool = 230/230

You have 8 stat points and 4 skill points to distribute.

Stamina – 34 (Strength of Body +9)

Strength – 36 (Strength of Arms +18)

Agility – 40

Dexterity – 37

Intelligence – 23

Wisdom – 35

Charisma – 37

Luck – 10

Weak Skills

Non-Class Combat Skills: Ether Cleanse - 10

Common Skills: Barter – 8, Camouflage – 7, Endurance – 27 (+2), Falling - 1, Tracker – 19 (+3), Trance Meditation – 24 (+5)

Profession Skills: Actor – 5, Butcher – 23, Cook – 2, Herbalist – 19, Miner – 1, Skinner – 22, Teacher – 18, Trader – 5

Moderate Skills

Non-Class Combat Skills: Combatant – 2 (+1), Ether Channels – 3 (+2),

Ether Manipulation 4 (+3), Stealth
– 13, Swordsmanship – 9
Common Skills: Analyze – 16 (+2),
Perception – 7 (+3), Sneak – 18
Profession Skills

Stasis

He noticed a change he hadn't accounted for. His Level in his Leader Class had risen. He checked through his notifications and found the one he was looking for.

Congratulations, you have successfully defended your Territory from the first Territorial Invasion. The timer for Ether-Assisted Protection has been reset to one moon cycle. You have been awarded 2 Leadership Levels for defeating 2 bosses.

Rockland smiled, realizing that he had found at least one way to increase his Leadership Class Level. It would take a long time to gain more of the levels if he had to wait approximately 29 days for each one, but at least he had finally discovered a way to do it.

He placed his new Skill points into Knight's Resolve. He wanted to view the second tier of skills and held off putting anything into Poison Pool just yet. As Rocky placed his skill points, more became available until he reached level six. He fully filled the first tier of skills and accessed the new unlocked skills.

Soul Blade
Dark Mend
Dark Blade
Dark Cloak
Shadow Clone

Chimera Knight Skill Tree

Tier 1

Poison Pool

- For each venom/poison the Chimera Knight suffers and survives, he gains immunity. The toxic makeup of that poison will be added to his Venom Pool. In time, the Chimeran Knight can add his unique venom to strikes or weapons. Do be careful; as Chimera Knight, not all poisons can be survived.

0 / 5

Skill gained at 1/5 "<u>Envenom.</u>"

Envenom

- Create an applicable venom from your Chimera Venom. This venom increases in strength with each additional poison and venom added to its base.

--

Knight's Resolve

- Increases the knight's resistances against all elements, poisons, and venoms.

5 / 5

Passive buff gained, "<u>Stalwart.</u>"

Stalwart

- Stalwart increases elemental, poison, and venom resistances by 50%.

--

Tier 2

Knight's Quest

- Increases the Etherience received from completed quests.

Passive buff received at 1/5 "<u>Questing.</u>"

0/5

Questing

- **At 1/5 Questing, buff increases Etherience received from completed Quests by 5%.**

--

Knight's Action
- **Allows the user to increase an attack or perform a dodge at double their usual Strength or Speed. Skill gained at 5/5 "<u>Knight's Action.</u>"**
  0/5

He was disappointed that he didn't get a new powerful offensive Skill. Although tempted by Knight's Action, Knight's Quest was a no-brainer. Having increased experience was a bonus in every game he had ever played. He hoped this world would treat it the same way.

Not to mention that the vast majority of his Etherience had been awarded from Quests in the Apprentice ranks.

CHAPTER SEVEN

The walk back to the Grotto was pleasant, and Rocky enjoyed the noises of the lush forest as the warm summer sun shone through the leaves.

Sela finally spoke again. "Michabo essentially insulted my entire family and my guild." She crossed her arms in front of her and dropped her gaze to the forest floor.

Rocky had asked her why she didn't like Michabo nearly five minutes ago. She had changed the subject to the weather. Had the silence finally allowed her to work out her feelings?

He glanced at her. Clenched jaw. Lowered brows. Eyes down. He was going to have to let her speak when she was ready.

Do I trust Michabo? I mean, his claims that no woman ever made it past Master Class seem a bit far-fetched.

Five more minutes passed in tense silence. Rocky couldn't go back to enjoying the walk. Not when Sela was stomping angrily by his side.

"He said horrible things. He even took away all of my senses. Torturing me by sending me back to a replica of that place." Sela shuddered.

Rocky hugged her. He recalled her intense fear of the place she had resided before her return to be his guide. He didn't have any other response to give. Michabo had been an annoying host—but torture?

Sela's shuddering eased, and she pushed him away, still refusing to meet his eyes.

They walked on. Rocky kept opening his mouth to tell her what had happened to him in the Spirit Realm. But the time wasn't right.

Maybe I should investigate some of his claims first.

Her body language and those few sentences accomplished one thing. By the time they passed through the Grotto entrance, his opinion was muddled. Her experience was so different from his that he wasn't sure which Michabo was the real one. The disregard for Sela convinced him that they should look through the other options for the Greater Territorial Perk—if nothing else.

Sela and Rocky didn't expect the clamoring scene that greeted them. Tao, Gamma, and the military surrounded what remained of the unmoved ogre corpses. A ring of citizens encircled the golems and military.

Rocky and Sela froze in the entrance. The citizens didn't seem aggressive. On the other side, the military and golems glanced around, searching for answers. What was going on?

Sela arched an eyebrow.

"Let's go see what this is about, then," he said.

The crowd noticed their approach and returned to their bickering.

"That leather is a rare ingredient."

"I got given a quest to make something with the ogre earrings."

"My quest is more important."

Rocky and Sela pushed their way through the closely packed bodies, eventually reaching the center of the mob. Gamma had collected all the visible loot into a pile.

"People all say that they have a right to the loot because they have a quest. There are too many people for the number of components here, though," said Gamma.

Rocky nodded and wondered why he hadn't received a quest to create something.

He looked at the crowd again and Analyzed a few people. The group of about five hundred citizens consisted of all crafting classes. All Non Power Classes.

"Think you two—" he turned to Gamma and Tao, "—can go collect the corpses of the two others we fought outside the Grotto? Maybe check them for earrings and the like? I kind of...forgot."

Tao nodded and placed a hand on Gamma's shoulder, preventing him from responding. Gamma clearly wasn't happy about his request. Rocky had only intended to give them an escape from the situation. Tao whispered something to Gamma. Why couldn't the angry ax-golem see that?

Hi, pot. I'm a kettle.

The crowd parted around the golems as they made their way to the Grotto entrance.

"Seen anything like this before?" asked Rocky, turning to Sela.

"It's prevalent when a rare material comes into a Territory. Usually, we auctioned the items to the highest bidder. Rare materials are a great way to increase class levels and professional skills," she responded.

Rocky considered the pile of loot. None of the gear was exceptional, except for a single locked ring.

Ring of Pebbles' Champion
- **This ring is part of a set. Both rings must be worn together to harness the power of its Enchantments.**
  Quality: Excellent
  Stats: Unknown

Rocky picked up the ring, then pulled a bundle of robes, a sword, an ax, and a few other pieces of locked gear, from his Bag of Holding. He handed everything to a few men in military fatigues.

"Give all of this to Zippo, please, and ask him to unlock it before bringing it back."

The men saluted and shoved their way through the crowd, heading toward the cafeteria. Rocky wasn't sure if Zippo could identify in the Citizen Acceptable Shop, but figured it was worth a try.

He puffed out his chest. He could get used to this whole delegating thing.

The rest of the pile was mostly ogre leather, bone weapons, plain metal adornments, and herb sacks.

"The quests you have should *all* be completed. Seek out those who have the same quest prompt as you and form a group. The military will dole out the materials you need." Rocky dumped the loot from Pebbles' group into a pile and marched off to the Dungeons, ready to negotiate.

Due to the Grotto's unrest with one of them—he started with LFD. Rocky and Sela found a stack of ogre corpses waiting just outside the entrance. As they crossed the bridge over the river, they heard LFD practically begging for the military to drag the bodies to him. "Why are you stacking the corpses outside of my Dungeon! Obviously, you misinterpreted the order—"

"They didn't misinterpret anything, LFD."

"But—"

"LFD, we must negotiate before you get all of these Master level corpses. I believe the contract said that for each 'kill' you managed, we would provide equivalent goods. Right?"

LFD groaned, vibrating the soil under Rocky. "You would just let the corpses rot away, then?"

"No, I am sure Maximus would be more than willing to receive these corpses," said Sela with a smirk.

"Ready to deal?" asked Rocky.

"Yes—"

"Good. Release all of your captives!" Rocky initiated.

"But Rocky, I still get to hold them for two more days. It's in the contract."

"We aren't negotiating until you let them go, LFD."

"Fine. It will take a moment for them to get outside. They're on my second level."

They waited patiently, and before long, their people came out of the entrance, blinking as they transitioned to the sun. "Is everyone okay? No one is hurt?" Rocky asked the group.

Sela checked with each person individually. He left that to her, and oversaw everyone who came out.

A young woman approached him, "He treated us pretty good, all things considered. But he totally ruined our leveling plans."

Rocky focused on the speaker. It was Bailey. Rocky remembered her; she even had the same five guys with her from their last run-in.

"Still getting into trouble, I see," Rocky grinned, including the entire group.

"She gave you trouble, too? This one and her friends kept escaping and killing my mobs for Etherience. Eventually, I had to give them their own room and lock them in!" LFD tattled.

Rocky's eyebrows rose and Bailey shrugged. "We needed to level somehow. I told you the morning after the party, we *are* going to be hunters for the Grotto. The food in there, though," she finished by mimicking a gag.

All of the groups that emerged began to make their way toward the Mess Hall. "LFD, how many did you have? And what did you feed them?"

"Sustenance. I assure you it had all of the necessary vitamins and nutrients required by humans. Exact count was four hundred and eighteen 'dead.'"

Rocky didn't want to imagine what all of the nutrients and required vitamins would taste like.

He pictured LFD lumping it into a slimy ball. Gross. "For the kills, we will give you half of one of these corpses for all of them."

"No way, Rocky! The two more days of captivity and eating them would amount to way more than that!"

Rocky stored away that tidbit of information. Dungeons got something from holding people. "Okay, well, for another corpse and the other half of this one, all you need to do is go loot the Dungeon at Chalk River. The one we killed and collapsed."

Sela peeked inside and walked over. "That was the last of them. No one was hurt. LFD, you have to recover all of our gear from that dungeon. I wonder why Michabo left it there." She grumpily added the last side comment to Rocky under her breath.

"Oh, really? I can go take back my body that's outside the Territory, then. I mean, that seems like a fair price." The eccentric dungeon always gave away too much. Rocky did like its straightforwardness. He crossed his fingers—his ring that connected him to Azoth was down there.

Sela looked at him, and he shrugged. He couldn't think of anything else to negotiate for. "The final four corpses, you can have, but we get a large favor to be named later, and two thousand 'deaths' paid for."

"A thousand deaths, and a minor favor."

"Guess we will go talk to Maximus—"

"Deal. Two thousand 'deaths' and your large favor sound totally reasonable."

This is a stopgap measure, for sure. I need to go through LFD in the future to figure out why his Dungeon is so hard. Or maybe we need to stop groups from entering altogether, in order to teach him a lesson. That, or use the large favor to get him to reorganize.

Zippo joined them on their trek to Maximus.

"The council is ready to meet as soon as you arrive," Zippo informed them. "Genius plan with the ogre crafting materials, Rock." He passed the gear he had been asked to identify back to Rocky. "What would you do without me? Now, do you need my help with Maximus, or should I go get started on cooking something for the meeting?"

Rocky turned to Sela. She stood stock still with her mouth hanging open. She hadn't told Zippo to do this?

He blinked and turned back to the young man, "Thank you, Zippo. Get to cooking! I could eat a dragon, I think."

"Fresh out of dragon, unfortunately, but I think I can manage something." Zippo laughed as he jogged off toward the Mess Hall.

Rocky swallowed his drool. He was starving after all that ogre killing. He picked up his pace and hurried to reach Grotto's northern wall.

I can't wait. Zippo loves to cook meat, too.

"Men and their food," mumbled Sela from behind him.

Outside the entrance of the Arena Dungeon stood two enormous advertisements. One displayed a list of dead arena combatants, with a countdown timer. The other was titled 'Current Champions' and had six names listed—Sela, Zippo, Rocky, Azoth, Tao, and Gamma.

"Hello, Maximus. I am sure you have noticed this pile of ogre corpses outside your entrance," Rocky greeted the dungeon cheerfully.

"Hmm, I did notice their stench, yes. I think you are covered in one of them."

Rocky looked down at himself. He really needed a dunk in the river. He waited for the Dungeon to say more, but it was apparent that Maximus wasn't planning on speaking again. He cleared his throat and continued, "I would like to negotiate with you for their value. How many names are on the list here?"

"Eight-hundred and forty-five." A hint of pride tinted his bodiless voice. "Since I don't hold the people captive for the week, it seems they prefer my sands over the depths of that Delving Dungeon."

"Ahh, so you believe that you are the superior choice to our Delving Dungeon, do you?" asked Sela.

"Of course, I am. I bring the monsters to you and create scaling challenges that bring out the best in your combatants.

LFD's second floor is filled with mobs that are copies of his first-floor boss. That Dungeon has no creativity, no passion."

Rocky facepalmed.

Of course, it is!

Their quick fix wasn't going to last long, if that was the case. They would have to go back and have another discussion with LFD. If his floors escalated that sharply, it was no wonder that most of the populace failed his challenges.

"Well, Sela, I am sure those six ogre corpses we gave LFD will allow him to increase his Dungeon size. Once we mention to him a possible way to increase attendance—"

"You already gave him six of these corpses? You wouldn't give him more, then," Maximus sputtered.

Rocky let the silence linger. He was prepared to wait the dungeon out to keep the upper hand in the negotiation.

"What do you want for them?"

They exchanged four of the corpses, including Azoth's meal, for similar concessions as those they had earned from LFD. They scored a monthly tournament held by the Dungeon, twelve hundred deaths to be named at a later date, and had paid for this week's kills.

Rocky fought hard for one last prize—a final advertisement wall. If he was honest, he would have given the corpses to the Dungeon for this one treasure alone. It would be a wall of remembrance. On this board, people could request names to be added. Names of family, friends, and loved ones lost since the start of the Apocalypse. Joe would be the first name. It was only fitting.

Benoit, Nadine, and Lacy. Is it time for me to give up? Should I put my family's names on the list?

He clutched what was left of the hope that he would find them alive. He thumbed at a tear running down his cheek. He would find his mother, sister, and brother-in-law.

"I wonder what we should do with these Champion and boss corpses?" He tried to make his voice carefree and sounded like a prepubescent boy instead.

Sela patted him on the shoulder and he turned to her. She placed her other hand on her chin. Rocky got caught in her eyes but attempted the same thinking pose, distractedly.

They held their breath. The sounds of the Grotto echoed over the grass.

"Arena Dungeons collect boss mobs. I could use them to help advance your population. Perhaps if they are intelligent enough, they can even help train your people. Please don't give them to LFD. Delving Dungeons can create new mobs in time. I can only collect creatures that venture into my traps or sands."

Rocky and Sela breathed out in unison, the moment broken.

Rocky summoned Ragnar's corpse out of his Bag of Holding and placed it at the entrance. "Can you do anything with this boss from Apep's Dungeon?"

Something stirred in the air, giving Rocky goosebumps. He looked around, feeling something but unable to see anything. The feeling increased in intensity—his skin broke out in cold sweats. He closed his eyes and used his Ether Manipulation to find the cause. Thick tentacles of navy blue extended from Maximus' entrance to Ragnar's corpse. It poked and prodded the body.

"Use your Ether Manipulation skill, Sela." Fascinated, he couldn't tear his eyes away as Maximus examined every inch of Ragnar.

"It will take quite a bit of strength, but I may be able to break his bond. It is already stretched thin," Maximus declared.

"How much power do you need?" asked Rocky.

"For this? At least the equivalent of a thousand apprentice-level creatures, perhaps more. It depends on their potency."

Sela pointed to the two Ogre-Boss corpses. "And how much are these worth in that assessment?"

A shiver ran down Rocky's back. Twice as cold as the first shudder. He closed his eyes and found two tentacles examining the ogre corpses.

"Their value for Ether and Essence is only moderately above the other corpses you brought me."

"You honestly expected us to believe that? Their true value for Ether and Essence would bring you halfway to the required amount," Sela said.

"Perhaps." The silence stretched out, like Maximus' tentacles.

"You know these are worth more. You can respawn them. That should double their worth," Rocky added.

"Alright, I will take them as a trade for this deed, but it will take me weeks to recover and begin utilizing the new mob."

"Only if Ragnar is allowed to exit your Dungeon and train the villagers of the Grotto," said Rocky.

"As long as he returns if I need him for defense, and your people vow not to kill him outside of my depths."

***

Negotiations finished, Rocky and Sela walked away. Maximus had their permission to take the corpses. Ragnar would be allowed to live in the Grotto six days of seven. However, he would need to return to Maximus for a full week before each month's Tournament.

His quest was updated as Maximus finished absorbing Ragnar's body.

Request
> **Party Quest – Request**
>> **Release Ragnar**

You have found a way to release Apep's hold on Ragnar. If successful, Ragnar will return as a Champion in your Arena Dungeon. Ensure your Dungeon resurrects him for your reward.

> **Rewards:**
>> **Etherience**
>> **Weapons trainer**
>> **Arena organizer**
>> **Speak with Ragnar for other possible options**

The very thought of the formidable Vanir training his citizens instilled hope equal to his trepidation. This also reminded him of the sword they had taken from Ragnar; the same sword Zippo had delivered with the rest of unlocked loot.

Ring of Pebbles' Champion

- **This ring is part of a set. Both rings must be worn together to harness the power of its Enchantments.**
  Set item (1 of 2)

Enchantments: Bloodlust, Time Bubble

Bloodlust (Locked)

- **If both rings are worn at the same time, the wearer can cast Bloodlust. Skill information hidden until rings are worn together.**

Time Bubble (Locked)

- **If both rings are worn at the same time, the wearer can cast Time Bubble. Skill information hidden until rings are worn together.**

His mouth twisted when he realized who had the ring that accompanied this one. He passed the ring to Sela. Her face bore the same expression as his.

He would have to talk with Derik. That idiot really did ruin everything.

He checked the other items, hoping to cheer himself up.

Great Ax of the Vanir
- This Ax is extremely heavy and unwieldy but has an edge that never dulls.

> Ether Pool Size: Large
>
> Current Ether Pool: 42 / 100

Enchantments: Sharp V (+50%), Savage Blow (+50 / -50 Strength)

Sharp V
- This blade projects a thin layer of Ether across the length of the blade. This Ether layer increases its cutting power while also protecting its edge. This ensures the Ax never dulls.

Savage Blow V
- This Enchantment adds 50 Strength to the wielder during a swing. Once the swing has completed, the Strength will vanish.

—

Ragnar's Longsword
- This sword is far too big to be used as a longsword by most living beings. Its craftsmanship and history are ancient.

> Ether Pool: Huge
>
> Current Ether Level: 100 / 410

Enchantments: Vanir's Might (One-Handed), Monster's Bane (Wildlife)

Vanir's Might
- This Enchantment reduces the weight of this weapon to a wieldable level by a single hand. The magic activates only if the Strength and Stamina of the individual are above 50.

Monster's Bane

- **When fighting wildlife, this blade ignores the inherent Ether of its opponent.**

—

Rattleshirt's Breastplate of Protection

- **This breastplate is made from a bone so dark, it is nearly black, and appears to be unbreakable.**
    - **Ether Pool: Large**
    - **Current Ether: 42 / 140**

Enchantments: Protection V (50%), Stamina V (+10)

—

Apep's Void Shroud

- **This armor was created from a Dungeon under the control of a Void God.**
    - **Ether Pool: Small**
    - **Current Ether Pool: 10 / 25**

Enchantment: Intellect II (+3), Wisdom I (+1)

—

Apep's Void Stick

- **These staffs are rumored to be all that is left of an entire planet's vegetation. Ether Pool: Small**
    - **Current Ether Pool: 11 / 25**

Enchantments: Intellect I (+1), Wisdom II (+3)

There was nothing that he could really use, other than the breastplate. But even that would be better off for a class like Victoria's. The robes would offer him some stats, but he'd probably trip over long flowing material in combat.

With nothing more of immediate concern, Rocky and Sela headed to the fire they traditionally used for town meetings and took seats on one of the logs ringing the fire pit.

"How are we the first ones to arrive?" Rocky wondered.

"Perhaps the new council members are involved in the quests from ogre drops?"

He ran his hand through his drool-crusted hair. The old council had consisted entirely of combat classes. Considering that the A-Team had been halved in numbers, and Joe was no longer with them, the council must have been nearly depleted. Who would show up today?

He glanced at Sela, who seemed to be rooted in thought. He cleared his throat to ensure his voice didn't startle her and asked, "Did anyone tell you who was added to the Council when we were in the Spirit Realm?"

The sun was sinking in the distance, its light painting a mural of colors behind her as she turned to face him. Her hair became a halo as her face entered the shadow of light disparity. Rocky squinted. Her features were shrouded in darkness, surrounded by her nearly glowing hair, which the sun intensified.

"I have heard the names, but I am unsure if I have met the individuals personally. Mr. Pips asked me to approve the additions during our first meeting." She paused and added, "I guess that falls to us now."

He bristled at the mention of Mr. Pips seeking Sela's approval. He should be involved in these decisions. He was the leader, after all. According to the system, he owned Algonquin Valley. He should be the person his people counted on. But everyone seemed to go to her first for everything.

Rocky shook his head, dispelling his negativity. Until recently, he had wanted nothing to do with being a leader. But things were different now. He was ready to be the leader. As people saw his new determination, his willingness, they would come to him. They would follow him.

"I don't think I know more than a handful of people who reside here," he said, stifling any trace of jealousy in his words.

The sun setting behind Sela's head still shadowed her face, and he couldn't read her reaction to his admission. He shifted his gaze to the river. Maybe he had time for a dunk? He was still covered in ogre goobers.

"What are you two doing here? The town hall is where meetings are held now. Did no one tell you?" Zippo called from fifty feet away as he strode toward them. He stopped and motioned them in his direction." Everyone is there already. We are just waiting on you."

Late for his first official council meeting. People seemed to understand, though; at least, no one showed open anger or disappointment when they arrived.

The meeting began with introductions all around. Rocky missed the first few opening statements by Mr. Pips that prompted the ensuing presentations. He was too busy, staring at the two empty chairs. One of those would be filled shortly, but the other—

You don't need the Satellite connection. You haven't had one 'til now.

A woman Rocky didn't recognize stood up. She had brown curly hair and seemed to be in her mid-forties. The woman's eyes gleamed, and her smile accentuated her crow's feet." My name is Astrid, and I was a seamstress in the village of Dorset, mostly tailoring new suits and patching old ones. I have chosen the class of Tailoress and was voted onto the council." She paused and smiled sheepishly. "Because I played video games, I kind of fell into being the leader of the group from Dorset."

Another person stood up and told a similar story, and Rocky wondered what had led them to Algonquin Park. The man was in his twenties, and his heavily scarred face added a dangerous vibe. His hair covered his forehead in a comb-over style made famous by a Canadian celebrity. His voice was surprisingly gravelly. "Thank you for having me. My name is Gerard, and my group is from Brent. We were a small group of gamers who played together at a local gaming shop, and we were mid-session when the Ether Wave hit. I had always played games as a warrior tank, and chose that class again—in what I believed to be a bizarre dream."

Another tank in the Grotto. There might be hope for us, after all. I didn't think so many humans were this sadistic.

Gerard continued, "The group believed that the most dangerous mobs were the converted buildings. So, we entered Algonquin Park, hoping to find some low-level mobs to level from. Instead, we found the Territory—" he nodded to Sela, and then Rocky, "—and we have become hunters and adventurers. I was also voted into my position."

As he sat down, another individual stood. His face was completely shadowed by the hood of his cloak, and his loose-fitting black Karate Gi made the outline of his body impossible to discern. "I am Jorge, Shadow class." He sat down. How did this *charismatic* fellow get onto the council?

The final new member stood up and said, "My name is Yuri, and I am a Smith. The people recognized that we have worked hard. They voted one of us into a council seat. My compatriots chose me to represent." The balding, silver-bearded man stood there awkwardly, still wearing his smithing apron. Rocky, who wasn't an expert on accents, would have guessed he was Slavik of some sort. Yuri nodded to indicate he was finished before sitting down.

The group turned their eyes on Zippo, Sela, and Rocky, attentively listening to their brief introductions. Zippo went first, and after he was done, he moved to a side table. As Rocky spoke, Zippo distributed rough clay plates heaped with food. The delicious smell filled Rocky's nose and he stuttered in his introduction.

As everyone ate, small issues were discussed. Items like electricity for a few final buildings that had yet to acquire their own Ether converters. Rocky placed most of the new equipment on the side table and asked people to find appropriate homes for it, reserving the chestpiece for Victoria. While it might be beneficial to sell the gear, he preferred to strengthen his people.

As he sat back down, he noticed the distance everyone had left around him. His skin itched, and he wrinkled his nose. He definitely needed a dunk in that river. At least he was nose blind to whatever odor he was giving off.

With the *housekeeping* topics out of the way, the discussion moved to more serious issues.

"One of our Dungeons held my group captive for four days. This is extremely counterproductive to a growing population," Gerard remarked, referring to LFD and its captive policy.

Rocky nodded. Gerard wasn't wrong—four hundred people had missed leveling for a maximum of five days. It wasn't time they could afford to squander.

"The food he gave us tasted of playdoh, and nearly everyone but my group had 'died' on the first floor," Gerard continued. "My group made it to the second floor where everyone was held, but the basic patrol mobs were all boss-level creatures. What can we do about this?"

Rocky held up his hand to get the council's mutterings under control. "LFD is often difficult to deal with. However, if we post guards in front of his entrance to warn people regarding how difficult it is and his hostage policy, we will see a dramatic decline in delvers."

A few people shrugged. It wasn't exactly enthusiastic, but Rocky took it as a good sign. "I would suggest we start there. LFD will slowly learn what gets him more attendance and what gets him less. Earlier, he let slip that keeping people inside his depths gives him something. So, I am pretty sure this will work. On another topic, I am interested in this food he created." The Grotto was facing food shortages. While the new Ether Assisted Protection was in place again, the fact that the Dungeon could provide food seemed a boon he hadn't expected.

The group agreed with his suggestion and a military runner was sent out to stand guard at LFD's entrance to provide warning to all who would enter of the dangers involved. Rocky assumed that most people would wait until later in the week to attempt the Dungeon. The problem, of course, was that if everyone attempted to run the Dungeon on the same few days, the Etherience penalties would likely mount.

At least they had a plan of action, and while LFD was erratic, if people didn't want to enter his depth, he would likely want to change it. The council discussed taxes and the sale of their non-Enchanted goods to the shop.

"I wish to hold off on selling the created gear, as I believe we can discover how to Enchant it. Once Enchanted, the value should increase exponentially," Rocky explained.

Astrid's chair squeaked as she stood. "Crafters don't have a reliable source of income! We can't just go out and hunt creatures, hoping for Crystals to drop. Leatherworkers and tailors were trading unenchanted crafted gear for the supplies, and some money on top. That market has run dry, as hunters in the Grotto now have serviceable armor. We need another source of income so we can buy new materials and continue to improve."

Gerard's chair flew out from under him. "The adventurers and hunters risk their lives everyday. We pay taxes on all of our loot. The crafters are just sitting here, safe in the Grotto."

Okay, I sense this is a topic of some friction.

Rocky slowly stood before anyone else could wade into the issue. "Everyone has important jobs, Gerard. Astrid is just asking for a way for crafters to recoup some of their costs. This way, they can continue to create stronger gear to provide the adventurers with more safety when they are out hunting. Right, Astrid?" Astrid nodded emphatically while she wrung her hands. "Gerard?"

Gerard nodded once with his arms crossed.

"What if Rocky placed five hundred Crystallized Ether into the Guild Bank? The crafters could sell their gear to the Meliora Guild," Sela chimed in while seated.

Everyone around the table nodded at this, and Rocky's jaw clenched. He had been building to something similar. He sat down and tried to relax. He hadn't known that there was a Guild Bank that could function as a merchant, so he had been planning to buy the gear himself.

These and other small problems brought them to the most crucial decision. The Greater Territorial Perk.

Sela shared the options on the Atlantean System meeting functions, and each member took some time to read through the possibilities. While there was a bit of interest in farms, research, or production buildings, everyone agreed that knowing the state of the world was paramount.

Rocky waited for Sela to tell them about the price for the satellite, but she didn't. He tilted his head, and upon catching his expression, she shook her head so that only he would notice.

"The connection to the Atlantean Net and a satellite needs to be decided on, as well. It is costly and will require a huge portion of our Territorial Ether," Sela divulged, skirting around the exact figures. And problem.

Most people nodded, as if accepting the cost—for the benefit. Still, Sela held up a finger and continued, "This is not as easy of a decision as it seems. It may take us months to regain what we spend and could delay certain options immediately."

She walked back to her seat, allowing everyone to discuss the question with neighbors. As soon as she sat down, she whispered, "We cannot ask a group to make a decision on what they may see as murder. We can stress the severity of the decision and gather their collective opinion, but this is why all final decisions need to be left to us."

Was she really suggesting they keep Amber's Rebirth a secret? His stomach flipped, and he observed the group while they were discussing the problem. Most were smiling and considering the question, unaware that someone's life was directly tied to it. White-hot rage bubbled in his chest, and Sela put a soothing hand on his knee as Gerard stood to speak. She shook her head at him and motioned with her free hand at the adventurer.

Gerard addressed the group. "If this tower increases our Territorial Ether gains, then it will not take as long to gather the amount we would need to use for the Satellite link."

As Gerard continued, Rocky felt his raging heart decrease its pace—that was a good point. Probably not the first line of thinking that would have been addressed if the council was aware of the life riding on the decision. Rocky's mouth was still twisted as Gerard continued to discuss the benefits of the tower and why spending the life-giving resource was a good option.

As Gerard sat down, Rocky had to admit they were all excellent points. "Let's hear the negatives of making this decision next," he said.

Mr. Pips stood up, his biking leathers hanging loosely on his thinning form. "We would not have the ability to speed up building construction or research for the next few months. Something we have yet to discuss tonight is the pending invasion from the Guild Collective. Could these points be used to increase defenses against them?" Rocky and Sela nodded, and Mr. Pips continued, "Sela has told us we have a while before they arrive. However, she has also insisted that we cannot hope to win without greater defenses in place."

"Wouldn't having a connection to the Satellite help us locate more survivors? Could we not use them to help us build defenses faster?" Zippo countered.

Watching Zippo, Rocky's pride swelled. Zippo was no longer the scared child he met so long ago. He was becoming a man. He hoped that someone was looking out for the boy's extended family the way he looked out for Zippo.

"Sela, will the uplink let us know if people are still alive, and where they are?" asked Rocky.

Sela moved her hand back and forth. "It will let us know if someone is still alive, but the system never tracked where on the planet someone was."

Maybe it was selfish, but that made Rocky's decision easy. He needed it to find his family.

The group ended their discussions, many swayed by the system's ability to confirm if someone was alive or dead, and the group unanimously voted for the uplink.

CHAPTER EIGHT

The council left shortly after the vote, leaving the action of pushing the button to Rocky. They hadn't known what pressing the button meant for him. For his friend, Amber, who had no idea what this would do to her. Rocky had tried to imagine his family back in his arms. It hadn't worked—his hand still hovered over the button. He pictured an unseen monster chasing his family, and this time, he had the courage to press the button. They needed him. Or he needed them.

The decision still rankled. He traded someone's life for this. What if it didn't work? Or if Michabo had tricked him? How would he live with himself? He would bet that his clone wouldn't be able to look at him. Or want to.

It was too late now. He had pushed the button. He grimaced at the ghostly tentacles in the dark that had suddenly shot from the ground beneath the guild tent. Luckily, the people inside had escaped unharmed.

He knew from experience that they would construct the tower, but was surprised that they hadn't needed to provide materials. He and Sela had even been given a countdown timer of twelve hours. He shook his head as the guild tent flapped like a flag in the wind from the top of the eighteen-hundred-foot-tall writhing structure.

Why can't we have nice things?

Rocky recalled Azoth cutting a hole in the same tent as soon as it had unfurled and had to admit that this was the worse of the two to befall the cloth structure. His only hope was that they could find a way to get it down, once the structure finished construction. Otherwise, it was a colossal waste of a thousand Crystals.

It had taken him the better part of an hour to finally accept the inevitable decision. Sela had stayed with him in the meeting room, talking to him and answering most of his baseless questions.

He was happy to have a moment alone, now that he was in his private suite within the City Hall. He moved away from the window—he couldn't watch the construction so soon after pressing that button—and turned to the comfort of his new opulent room. His four-poster bed was more extravagant than a traditional king size from before the crash. Bedding and far too many pillows for one man were laid out for his use. He touched the mattress and his hand sank into its softness, and he couldn't wait to rest his muscles on it. He wondered if everyone received a bed like this during the week he was away—or if it had just been Sela and himself.

He removed his sword, frog, and belt, placing them on a rack at the foot of the bed. Other stands held his current armor. Wearing only his Nano-weave under-armor, he poked his head into the room that led off of his bedchamber. He stood frozen, mid-step. It was the holy grail. Something he'd often dreamed of, now more than ever.

A shower.

A bathroom. Equipped with a tub, toilet, washbasin, and that gorgeous shower as its crowning jewel.

He stood in the shower. He was so focused on this luxury that he didn't recall crossing the floor to the tiled, heavenly space.

He stared at the black knob that looked like every heat adjustment shower knob he had seen in the past. He turned the contraption and a hiss of air left the black nozzle. His excitement dried up, much like the nozzle—as air continued to stream without a drop of water.

Of course.

He was about to give up and take his ogre boogers to the river when a burst of cold water struck. He shivered as the glacial liquid pelleted his skin and chilled his bones.

He reached for the knob with shaking hands, and the water began to warm.

Comforting, pleasant—and scalding.

He jumped out of the stream of water and adjusted the nozzle to find the perfect mix. He removed his soaking Under Armor and pranced into the running water like a child through a sprinkler.

He hadn't purchased soap or any sort of cleaning product, but that didn't matter. All his worries washed away under the constant flow of hot water over his head and tight muscles. He roughly rubbed his hair and beard, feeling the accumulation of dirt and oil slough away. Could he feel the ogre mucus falling off?

His fingers caught in his beard and he desperately wanted a razor. But perhaps there was another way...

He summoned his Soul Blade, for one hundred Ether, in the form of a very sharp, flat dagger.

That was probably the most frivolous use of Ether I could have come up with. But it is going to be worth it.

Without shaving cream, he cut himself several times removing the beard. Still, the increased healing factor of the system made those cuts close up almost instantly.

He received a new skill and he laughed sharply before nearly crying.

Congratulations! You have learned a new skill. Grooming

- **Even primates take better care of themselves than a human without a shower. 1% greater cleanliness per level at the Apprentice ranks.**

Current level Apprentice-Groomer Level 1.

He was tempted to chop at his hair, which was probably an absolute disaster, but ultimately decided he would simply purchase some shampoo and soap from the shop later.

He doubted the cue ball look would suit him. A friend had once told him, "Bald is beautiful," and he agreed that the style had suited the man. He just doubted his misshapen noggin could pull it off.

He got out of the shower and looked at the vanity that, based on his typical life experience, would have contained a mirror. That mirror would have been fogged up after the scalding shower he had just taken, but alas this vanity only contained a washbasin. For a fleeting moment, he missed the days of swiping his hand across a foggy mirror to see his reflection.

He sighed and stood on the tiled floor, letting the air dry his body, and made another note to find some towels and a bathrobe—that weren't pink. Maybe some clothes that would be more comfortable, and ogre gunk-free.

The ball of Nanoweave armor cleaned itself, but he didn't want to touch it. Somehow, the thought of putting on his old clothes was an affront to his freshly cleaned skin. He pulled a brand-new ball out of his bag and moved it to his chest. It unfurled to provide skintight protection ending below his eyes. Surprisingly, it displaced the water, drying him, and he touched his ear to lower the face shield. Time for bed.

A hesitant knock sounded at the door.

He wondered who would be out there at this hour. He cracked the door open, then allowed it to swing further when he saw the visitor. He stood there, gaping like an idiot. Sela, wearing only her Nanoweave armor—which did absolutely nothing to hide her figure—asked him a question.

His face grew red and he realized Sela was talking

"… hot water. Would it be okay if I used your shower?"

He nodded and stepped aside.

I swear I felt tired a moment ago. Now would be a good time to close your mouth, Rocky. Smooth, real smooth.

"Thanks." Sela smiled and made her way to the washroom. "You shaved—" her eyes traveled from his smooth skin up to his unmanageable hair, "—but you should have someone take a look at that mane of yours. At least you got the grass and ogre blood out of it."

He turned a deeper shade of red at her—compliments?

She watched him and must have decided that he wasn't going to respond as she shrugged and entered the bathroom.

Rocky didn't move, his desire warring with his previous civilization and all its unspoken rules. His bathroom didn't have a door on it, and it was everything he could do to remain at the entrance to his suite.

His front door was still wide open, and he began closing it when he heard the shower turn on. Then a ball of black substance rolled out of the bathroom, accompanied by a squeal of delight. Sela must have made the noise when the hot water hit her naked—

He exited his room and shut the door behind him. He had some Enchanting to investigate and a few odds and ends to pick up at the store. It was time to go shopping. Yep.

He practically fled from the room, as if it contained an unbeatable monster. Outside, the chilly night air hit him, but he didn't dare turn back for his gear upstairs.

He headed to the Citizen Accessible Shop.

As he walked, he selected some blank leather armor pieces from the Territorial Inventory. He really wished he could talk to Azoth right then. As he felt his heart sink, he decided that he would go sit with the beastie as he worked. He needed the company, and he missed the goofy Chimera.

Once in the shop, he picked up the cheapest Enchanted gear he could find and grabbed three, hoping that they were Enchanted by a Skill. If he was going to learn to Enchant, he needed to study how the other races did it, not the Dungeons. Before leaving, he asked, "Attendant, can you search for anything the shop sells related to Enchanting?"

The attendant took a moment before replying in her ambiguous voice, which emitted from a distinctive feminine human hologram, "Complete. There is one item that is related to Enchanting. Enchanter's Kit. Would you like to see it?"

He briefly studied the hologram as he nodded. Somehow the shop had pulled the likeness of a very charismatic and attractive Hollywood actress. Who exactly it was, Rocky couldn't recall, but he definitely had seen that face in movies.

A blue screen popped up, and he scanned the information.

Enchanter's Kit
- **This Enchanter's Pen, Mortar, and Pestle set is a necessity for any serious Enchanter.**
   Cost: 1000 Crystals

He nearly choked at the price that followed the lackluster description. "Can you negotiate that down?"

"Negative. The seller is also artificial intelligence, and at your request, provided proof that this price is non-negotiable. Would you like to see the purchase transcripts of every Enchanter's Kit bought at the market for the last ten years?"

He wanted to throw up, but all of his gaming experience dictated that this profession was crucial to success and exorbitant. He glanced at his Bag of Holding and read the figure it claimed it held, for Crystals—1,780 and change. They had already placed the five hundred into the Guild bank to purchase the blanks and continue to pay wages.

He bought the expensive kit and studied it. In retrospect, he probably should have waited and discussed the purchase with Sela, Zippo, and the soon-to-be-resurrected Smith. Still, they would need the item if they were going to gain strength and survive the invasions.

The purchase came with three items: one was the pen, the others, a mortar, and pestle. The pen appeared to be crafted of diamond and looked like an oversized writing instrument. His entire hand could wrap around it, but just barely. Upon first inspection, he assumed it was a solid diamond, but the weight in his palm felt off. Turning the stylus over in multiple directions under the blinding interior light of the shop, he noticed a seam at the top. He jiggled the cap off and found an empty hollow tube running down the center of the diamond.

He glanced at the diamond mortar and pestle and realized he was supposed to create the ink to fill it. Was he supposed to grind up herbs that could create an ink...or he might not even need the pen, mortar or pestle for low level enchantments? Who was to say?

He turned to the attendant. "What do I put in here?" he asked, indicating the hollow Pen.

The attendant paused, chirped a few times, and said, "We personally do not have access to the answer. Instead, we asked the seller. Their response was, 'Only the strongest and most fragile of mediums can hold Enchanted Ether.' Did we answer your question?"

"No, that doesn't answer the question at all."

"Would you like us to search the shop for a book or item that may contain the answer?"

He nodded.

"Complete. There is one item that is related to Enchanting. Enchanter's Pen. Would you like to see it?"

He was ready to scream. He placed his purchases in his Bag of Holding and stalked out of the shop. Like everything else in this place, he would figure it out on his own. He knew better than to count on people sharing knowledge in this new world.

He paused, letting his eyes adjust from the darkness of the night to the brightness of the interior shop. Where was Azoth? Usually, he would contact the birdbrain, but that wasn't possible now. He closed his eyes and tried to feel out the location of his friend.

Their connection existed, though whether it was system-generated or something else, he didn't know. Still, he knew it had to be there. He was about to give up when he felt something—it wasn't Ether, though. Whatever the thin strand was, it acted like an Ether channel but was invisible to his Ether Manipulation. He followed it, not sure what it was, but his gut told him it would lead him to his pet.

The strand guided him to a cleared space beside stacks of 2x4s, nails, shingles, and other building materials. Azoth was curled up with his back to a pile of cut timber.

Rocky approached him and sat in front of the tight bundle of fur and feathers. He laid out his purchases on the ground in front of him and prepared for some work. Before Rocky could begin, a pulse shot along the new external connection. It alarmed him for a split second and then Azoth purred. Rocky reached back, patting the gigantic lion paw. The thread hummed with energy, and Rocky enjoyed the connection.

He settled into the silent companionship and turned his attention back to the task at hand. He entered his Meditation and began some of the exercises that Tao had taught the citizens of the Grotto. After fifteen minutes, he had cleaned up and reinvigorated his internal channels. Feeling refreshed, he reached forward to pick up his first Enchanted purchase. His hands closed around the Jerkin of Protection, and he brought it close to his chest.

Gortuk Jerkin of Protection
- **This item is made from Gortuk skin.**
   Ether Pool level: Tiny

Current Ether Pool Level: 20/20
Enchantments: Protection I (15%)
Protection I

- **Ether Pool will be used to directly reduce melee damage to any area covered by this armor. Magical damage requires three times the amount of Ether from Ether Pool to reduce damage. Damage reduced up to 15%, depending on the strength of the blow. This effect can be increased by having an Enchanter increase the rank of the Enchantment.**

He took a deep breath, steadied himself, and forced out a tendril of his internal Ether. It was surprisingly more straightforward this time than it had been in the past, By no means easy, but definitely easier. Sweat broke out on his forehead as he examined the item.

He had been right. He could replicate this effect.

There was a pool of Ether, and off that pool ran intricate channels of viridian blues. It was almost identical to his internal channels—but this one almost formed what he guessed were letters. He studied the pattern and memorized them before placing the item down and pulling a blank leather chest piece out of the Territorial inventory.

He didn't need the pen to replicate this enchantment, either. Maybe he was right and only needed it for high level enchantments? Wouldn't that be a waste of Crystals.

He studied the leather and immediately found an empty place where a pool could reside. He filled the void with his own Ether and sensed when it reached its limit. He pulled a thread of Ether and wove it into the intricate patterns he had memorized. It took some time, and when he had finished, his body was hot, and his face was drenched in a thick layer of sweat.

Excited, he pulled his awareness back and mentally let go of the Ether. His head pounded as his Ether pool dropped by one hundred and fifty points. He pushed the headache out of his Meditative state and watched. The Ether was flowing in the same patterns as the Enchanted Jerkin. Pain registered dimly on his awareness, and he ignored it. He had just figured out how to Enchant gear! Not only that, but his entire populace possessed the ability to Enchant.

His hands screamed in agony, breaking his Meditation. His eyes flew open and he cried out, throwing the flaming piece of leather away from himself. His hands were blackened and bubbling with blisters. He nearly vomited at the smell of burnt leather and human skin.

Azoth shot up behind him and trampled the burning chest piece, but the fire wouldn't go out. His pet's actions broke his shock, and he cast Dark Mend on his hands and Azoth.

"Azoth, stand back. That fire is fueled by Ether." Rocky forced out between clenched teeth.

Azoth retreated from the blue-flaming leather. He stepped gingerly, avoiding too much pressure on his burnt front paws.

Shit, I should have bought Health Potions.

Without Health or Elixir potions, they watched as the leather burned until it was nothing but a wisp of smoke. Every time his Ether pool ticked up enough, he added a stack of Dark Mend to himself or Azoth.

Well, that hadn't worked out the way he had planned.

Azoth curled back up on the ground behind Rocky. He leaned into his pet, the exhaustion of the day overwhelming him. He would just rest his head and wait for his pool to fully regenerate before his next attempt at Enchanting. His eyelids grew heavy as Azoth's warmth enveloped him. As he fell into a deep sleep, the last thing he saw was Sela, jogging toward him and shaking her head.

CHAPTER NINE

Azoth moved beneath Rocky, jostling him awake. A sizable wet cat tongue scraped its way up to his scalp.

"Gah, Azoth, are you planning to eat me?"

Sela chuckled from where she lay wrapped in his arm.

When did she end up cuddled in my arms? Stop thinking about how nice it feels. Damnit!

"He says you taste cleaner than normal. Maybe you would be tastier, too."

Azoth stared at him with dog-like eyes. His pet licked its snout, and a laugh escaped from Rocky. He disentangled himself from Sela.

"Just try me. I'm nothing but bone and sinew." He shoved the behemoth and only succeeded in moving himself a few steps back. He mimicked a battle roar and jumped on Azoth, performing a graceless scratch attack.

Sela's laughter cut through the quiet morning air. Azoth's feathers and fur smelled of wet dew, and Rocky reveled in what they had built in the Grotto. What they had achieved.

Sela stopped laughing and stared at the sky. Rocky disentangled himself and followed the beautiful Ancestral guide's gaze. How in the hell had he missed the colossal tower that dominated the clearing? The flapping guild tent mocked him as it fluttered from the tip.

"What do you think that massive dome at the bottom is?" asked Rocky.

The dome at the bottom of the tower easily doubled the height of every building in the Grotto and formed a wide, black semi-circle around the base. From its center rose a pillar that supported a small sphere at the top of the tower. After the sphere there was clearly some sort of lightning rod structure but it was hard to tell from the bottom as the center skewered the guild tent. Most of the hanging fabric kept flapping over the top of the dome obscuring it from view. His neck spasmed, reminding him that he had craned his neck for too long. He looked away and rubbed his complaining muscles.

"I have no idea, but we should probably go find out."

Azoth flew off above them and inspected the tower from the air.

"Sela, can you remind him not to break anything? Offer him a treat if he figures out how to get the Guild tent down—without damaging it."

Rocky continued after Sela's chuckle, "How far away from here do you think people can see this Tower?"

Sela shrugged, lost in thought.

They turned down a grass-filled path between two Longhouses. Early risers wiped sleep from their eyes and congregated, gaping at the newest pitch-black building. Threading through the crowd, they approached a set of double doors that even Bathilda the dragon could fit through.

"You going to stand here staring or find out what's inside?" said a familiar voice Rocky hadn't heard in a while.

All the gawkers whipped their heads around to find Smith in a fluffy pink robe, escorted by Victoria and Letoya.

Sela hugged him, welcoming the Native American man.

Someone in the crowd wolf whistled, and another man crowed, "Smith is back, and he is wearing that fluffy pink robe. Pay up, I told you all that's the outfit you are reborn in."

A kaleidoscope of red spread over Victoria's face, and Rocky laughed along with the crowd.

He pulled a spoon out of his Bag of Holding, and handed it to Smith. The fluffy robed man frowned and squinted at the spoon, then slowly looked up at Rocky. A few others in the crowd looked between the pink-accented Smith, holding a spoon, and Rocky. He didn't explain, he just laughed harder. This was picture perfect!

Smith's return lifted a weight off Rocky's shoulders that he hadn't known he was carrying. But something else would take its place. He couldn't shake what would happen to Amber—or his role in it. The burr that was Amber wormed its way into his subconscious, but he wasn't going to let it overshadow this happy reunion.

It took about five minutes before the crowd calmed enough to allow for any sort of conversation.

"Why are you three sweating and out of breath?" asked Sela.

Victoria stepped forward, planting her feet at parade rest, with her hands behind her back. The stance highlighted her new black bone-chestpiece. "Smith appeared last night, right after many quakes assaulted the tunnels. Letoya and I were just about to retreat when we found him on top of the altar. Shortly after, the quakes intensified, and tunnels began to collapse. We were forced to use the cave your group first entered through as an alternate exit. We were forced to sprint to stay ahead of the tunnel collapse."

The onlookers murmured worriedly.

Those tunnels had always been a backup plan. They added a layer of safety the Territory could fall back on. He opened his mouth to ask a follow-up, but Sela beat him to it.

"Is the altar gone, then?"

"I would have said yes, but since we got to the surface and saw this—" Smith indicated the dome and tower, "—I have been thinking. The collapse was strange. It wasn't due to weight or instability. All the networks of tunnels and that central room seemed to be moving upwards."

"Oh—Oh!—we didn't know, guys. Holy hells, we just chose to build this thing last night too," Rocky confessed.

Smith waved away the apology. "No way you could have known. If my theory is correct, I bet we could have just stayed put in the altar room. My guess is that it's somewhere there." He pointed up the tower, indicating where he thought the room had relocated itself. "Want to go find out?"

"First, can we get you out of that wardrobe slip waiting to happen?" Rocky reached into his bag and pulled out a set of Nanoweave under armor and handed it to Smith.

Smith pulled Rocky in close, and growled, "You gave me a spoon instead of this?" Then he took the orb and pulled away. Rocky tilted his head as his resurrected friend held the metal ball to his chest before trading the pink bathrobe back to Victoria. The man wasn't exactly angry, but...

Maybe I shouldn't tell him that was my set of Nanoweave that was inside an ogre.

Rocky offered Smith a plain tunic and breeches from the Guild's inventory. His friend lowered the facemask and put on proper clothes over the skin tight garment.

The crowd followed Rocky to the dome. He tried the doors but they wouldn't open, and onlookers released a collective sigh of disappointment.

Sela sorted through notifications and whispered, "It needs three Ether converters to gain functionality. We need to go pick those up or force the doors open with brute strength."

Rocky looked around, searching for Tao or Gamma, who were nowhere to be found.

"It just needs power, folks. We will be right back!"

***

Rocky and Sela entered the shop.

"A message from Garnell awaits you, Lady Sela," said the attendant.

Rocky raised an eyebrow.

Why is it a message for Sela?

His Ancestral guide accepted the envelope and read it quickly.

"Amelia wants to meet with us at our earliest convenience."

Rocky narrowed his eyes. If the invitation was for both of them, why was the note addressed to Sela?

She handed him the letter as she approached the counter to find the Ether converters.

He read over the missive, wanting to make sure Sela hadn't left anything out. There were only a few sentences, and he didn't find any information that differed from what Sela had said. He shook his head, freeing it of his suspicious feelings, and breathed deeply to center himself. He needed to relax. The letter was probably addressed to Sela because she did most of the talking in the meetings. She was co-leader of the Grotto, after all.

His Bag of Holding got heavier. He looked up to find the last Ether Converter vanishing inside and Sela sternly frowning at him.

"What happened to the majority of our Crystals, Rocky?"

He ran his hand through his hair and looked down. Collecting his nerves, he forced himself to meet her gaze. "Umm...I purchased an Enchanter's Kit." He braced himself for an explosive reaction.

"Actually, we really do need that. Was that what you were doing last night?"

On the way back to the tower, Rocky and Sela discussed his failed Enchantment attempt, and she pointed out the obvious. He hadn't used the pen at all. He had gotten ahead of himself last night. Maybe he had been overtired. He should have thought harder about that. Why would there be a pen if he wasn't supposed to use it?

Dad used to love to say that Rocky was a 'leap before you look' kind of idiot.

The unexpected memory of his dad saddened him. But the Tower, once powered, may be able to finally give him an answer about the rest of his family.

The domed base of the tower came back into view, an even larger crowd amassed beneath it.

He turned to Sela and whispered, "Where do we even put these Ether converters?"

"No idea."

As they approached, Gamma and Tao were present, having taken up positions on the opposite side of the dome. There was another set of doors ninety degrees offset from the ones he had attempted to open that morning. Tao and Gamma's position, and the people clustered around them, highlighted a pattern of gatherings. Each large gathering would likely be in front of doors. They veered in that direction.

As they reached the two, Gamma said, "Well, can we go inside now? *Tao*."

Rocky was used to the rudeness of the ax-wielding Knight. "Good morning to you as well, Gamma. Good morning, Tao."

Tao bared his teeth in an attempted smile and managed to only look partially constipated—which was an improvement. "The weather is fair today, and the excitement of a new toy tints the air. Perhaps we shall explore what Gaia has granted us?"

Sela clapped, having always shared a kindred bond with the wise Knight. She bounced excitedly on her heels and said, "Yes, please, Sir Tao."

Gamma and Tao stepped up to the double doors, each taking a side.

The Knights, now dwarfed by the entrance, would understand how the humans felt around them. And now more than ever, Rocky felt small.

This new world was vast.

The two strained under the weight of the doors, and their feet sunk into the grass. Nothing like seeing Newton's third law in action. The door moved an inch, cracking loudly, and a whoosh of air escaped. The two continued pushing, and the door began to swing faster on its fresh new hinges until they were able to hold the doors fully open.

Gamma strained to keep his side open. Through clenched teeth, he said, "Rocky, Sela, these doors are going to swing shut as soon as we let go. Hurry up."

"Everyone stays here. Tao, Gamma, Sela, and I will get the power converters in place." A sleepy-eyed young man pushed his way through the crowd, his red hair in disarray. "And Zippo."

They jogged through the doorway, and Zippo conjured a fireball.

Clear of the colossal slabs as thick across as Tao and Gamma, Rocky said, "You two can let go now. We're going to need your strength." Both Knights released the doors and sidestepped the swinging motion created by the release of pressure. The doors boomed shut, echoing the crash in all directions.

The sound ricocheted off the hard Dragonscale surfaces further and further away from the group.

Zippo's fireball highlighted an arched ceiling that towered above the Knights' heads, revealing a passage on each side of the chamber that led to closed doors. His vision couldn't penetrate past the illumination of the fireball, and he suspected that they would find doors at regularly spaced intervals.

"Probably time to figure out where we should place these Ether converters," Rocky said. His voice echoed off the surrounding walls.

The group continued down the unadorned hallway. He had been right—enormous doors barred their entry to regularly-spaced side rooms. Or maybe other hallways.

Should we examine every doorway? I mean, we've already walked by eight.

He glanced back but kept following the current hallway, hoping that some sort of electrical room would be in the center of the dome. The hall was straight and could only be leading them to the base of the tower. Two sets of doors later, they entered a circular room. The roof of the corridor sloped up and created a cathedral ceiling.

In the center of the room, a large, square column rose from the floor straight up to the ceiling and probably continued up into the tower above. "Is this a counter, or a half-wall?" Rocky wondered. He patted the circular chest-high slab that ringed the base of the column.

Sela took a few steps up to stand on a platform that ran inside the circular counter. "This looks like a guild headquarters; from everything I have seen so far. This would be the receptionist area, where adventurers can come collect their promised rewards or find parties for questing." She pointed to the walls.

Rocky followed the path of her finger to several stone pillars of varying sizes, each displaying a flat-screen-like face and a small circular indentation.

"Those look like Guild kiosks for finding active quests or creating quests. The little indentation is for your hand. It almost feels like I am standing in the Cathodiem guild offices, in the Silver Spires," Sela said. She shivered and struggled to contain her tears.

He climbed the few stairs up to her and placed a hand on her shoulder. He hated to see her in pain but never knew what to say or do.

She looked up at him, tears welling in her eyes, and flung herself at him, wrapping her arms around him and burying her face in his chest. Zippo made a disgusted sound, which earned him a warning glare, and Rocky patted Sela on the back as she trembled.

He couldn't be sure, but he thought he heard her mutter, "Don't you miss those bastards." She stopped crying but held Rocky a heartbeat longer before pushing herself away. The tears were gone, and a fierce look took their place.

He knew what that meant. He'd had the same look when he thought about his family.

"Anyone see something that looks like a place to connect the power converters?" asked Rocky.

Zippo nodded, and his elongated shadow bobbed on the wall along with his head. "Yeah, if you two would stop being all gross, maybe we could get some work done." He stuck out his chin. "I think it's right there."

Rocky ruffled Zippo's hair as he walked by him. The young man protested and tried to flatten his beautiful bed head, 'that Rocky had just ruined.'

Tao and Gamma stood sentry as the three humans approached the recessed portion on the side of the central pillar. Rocky pulled out an Ether converter from his bag. Unfortunately, the dimensions of the recess could only contain one of the contraptions.

He placed the converter inside and felt something at the back of the recess, akin to a magnet, wrench the converter from his hands. He must have done something right as it clicked into place. Lights on the central pillar flickered to life, accompanied by mechanical noises.

A ding sounded from the opposite side of the pillar, and the group jogged toward it.

Rocky stared into a hollow shaft through double doors that had receded into the walls beside them. Beside the doors was a button with a lit, red arrow pointing up. An electronic plaque that read, 'Reception' hung above the opening.

Scratching his head, he asked, "An elevator?"

"It's a lift," said Sela.

Zippo chuckled softly at her unneeded correction. Clearly, the term elevator wasn't widely used back in her day. Rocky just nodded—he was used to her doing this.

Gamma and Tao waved their hands in front of themselves, excluding themselves from the ride. "Why don't you all try it out first? If you don't die, we will test its capabilities in the future," Gamma said.

"More loot for us then, you big concrete chocobos," said Sela.

Zippo, now fireball-less, Rocky, and Sela walked through the doors onto the platform. Once inside, Sela approached a wall that displayed three buttons.

Observatory and Crew Quarters
Control Room
Utilities & Medical Facilities

She reached for 'Control Room,' and Rocky stopped her.

"Utilities might be where we place the other Ether converters?"

She nodded and pressed 'Control Room' anyway. "Let's take a quick peek while we still have privacy."

The doors closed, and his knees jerked in response to the increased pressure of the accelerating *lift*.

He caught his breath as the group exited the roof of the dome. The elevator was glass, and the tower was transparent from the inside. They were now well above the trees. Below them stretched their Territory, and beyond that, the recovering, blackened Earth. It had only been a week, but the green tendrils crawling across the scorched landscape indicated that plant life was regrowing quickly.

Guess I should have known Bathilda's cleansing would heal absurdly fast, thanks to the system.

The view opened up further, out past the cleansing. The world was alive and vibrant. Leafy green contrasted the crystalline blue skies, and fluffy white clouds. From his vantage point, he spotted small shapes of terrifying creatures scouring the terrain outside of the sooty-cleansed Earth. A shadow thumped into the tower wall as they sped past, and everyone jumped.

"Azoth thinks that the moving box is his new toy," laughed Sela.

During the ascent, Azoth managed one further 'assault' before they reached the second sphere atop the tower. The whole ride had lasted no more than thirty seconds.

The doors dinged open to a pitch-black room. Zippo stepped forward and conjured another red ball. Rocky hadn't noticed earlier, but Zippo no longer had to hold a hand under his creation.

The illuminated room held a familiar, if slightly rearranged, sight. Smith had been right—it was the same room that had previously been located deep underground. The altar stood straight out from the elevator, and the starshipesque captain-chairs still occupied the space behind it. The place had always felt like a cockpit from the distant past. The workstations all around him only added to that ambiance.

After a quick look around, the group didn't find anything that looked like an area for a power converter.

"Alright, I think that is what we expected. Let's head down a floor and see if we can find a way to 'pay our hydro bill,'" said Sela.

Zippo groaned, but Rocky was impressed by her relatively proper use of the saying. She was acclimatizing to this world far faster than he thought she would.

They made their way down to the utility floor and discovered a considerable number of contraptions that Rocky couldn't identify. At least Sela knew what they were.

"Those are water tanks—" she pointed to a pile, "—those would be batteries, oxygen scrubbers, plasma generators, missile ports, forcefield generators, supplement converters, and back there is all the infirmary and medical equipment. Don't ask me what the things are, because I have only been on the receiving end of their use."

Rocky hated any reminders of how Sela had died slowly at the hands of a potent poison in her first life. He pointed to two open, hollow rigs near the batteries. "Those look like the places for these converters. Is this thing a ship?"

"I was wondering the same thing," said Zippo.

"I don't think so. I think it just has some defenses and some large reserves in case of sieges." Sela scanned the room. "I don't see any engines, just some alternative power sources." She patted what she had deemed the Plasma Generators. "Probably only to be used in an emergency."

Like when the entire planet lost Ether?

He pulled the converters out and handed one to Zippo. They put the devices in place, with the same magnetic assistance and click.

Everything around them came to life. Mechanical clicks and electric beeps resounded through the room, and a progress bar notification appeared in front of Rocky and Sela.

Satellite found.
Connection to Goggle Satellite XZ143 established.
Uplink successful.
Downloading Atlantean Net Updates
0%

An explosion of announcements followed the first notification. They scrolled through the corner of his interface so fast that he knew it would take a while to get through them.

CHAPTER TEN

"So, all of those notifications were available quests in the region?" Rocky asked as they rode the elevator back up a floor.

After supplying power, Sela had been preparing to enter the elevator, only to find Rocky and Zippo trying to sort through hundreds of notices.

"Yes, they are something akin to the billboard advertisements you explained to the Ottawa Knights. You can go to the quest kiosk and see what exactly each one entails before accepting them," Sela said.

The elevator doors opened, and they entered a scene from a Sci-fi movie. Each surface was lit up, with a screen dominating its controls. Some of the stations had scrolling text on screen, others had three dimensional representations of—the Territory?

Those caught his attention, but one—one screen glued his feet to the floor.

"Quests are broken down into categories. For example, system generated quests, survival quests and the like. People can create quests down below as well. Since those aren't system generated and only one reward is available, those quests need to be handled differently. Only one group, no sharing—" Sela hadn't noticed she was walking by herself and turned. "Is this the first time you have seen interactive screens? No, you both told me about computers, I think. These are mostly the same thing."

Rocky hadn't been staring because of the computers, at least not entirely. There were so many computers in the room, but one specific screen caught his attention. The screen displayed a real-time satellite image of the earth. Zoom buttons dotted the sides of the screen.

Rocky ran over to the screen. "No, Sela, we have seen computers. This is a world map in real-time. Right now, we can see North America, Greenland, and even some of Europe!"

Sela turned and studied the map, head tilted back and eyes wide. The landmasses on display were far different than the Pangaea continent she would have grown up on.

Before he zoomed in on anything, he pointed out the more significant land masses they could see. He tried to name some countries, tracing borders where he recalled their existence.

Once finished, he zoomed in on the Greater Toronto Area. To call it a mess was an understatement. He couldn't get close enough to make out much more than the overall state of the 'city.' The school campuses and hospitals in the city had, like Ottawa, become the only buildings left. Grey gravel still marked where roads once were, but the vegetation was slowly growing in.

Something strange stood out to him. He squinted at the map, focusing on the few patches of remaining buildings. A few of them seemed to be encircled by golems.

Some time ago, the Ottawa Knights had accepted a quest to protect humans. Was that what these golems were doing?

Out of the hundred billboard notices he received; he recalled a specific one. 'Save the Survivors of North Bay.'

He zoomed out and in again and found the remains of the city just north of them. Like Toronto and Ottawa, it contained patches of remaining buildings where schools, hospitals, and other spared buildings still stood. Unlike Toronto, every parcel of buildings was surrounded by golems. Save them from what?

Oh no.

"Can you see the system quests from up here?" asked Rocky.

"I am sure you should be able to. Why, what is it?" Sela replied.

Rocky wasn't sure if he should voice his suspicions and instead, ran from screen to screen.

"Over here, Rocky," Zippo said.

He sprinted over and searched the quest list, using an on-screen keyboard to type 'North Bay.'

The quest came up, and his gut clenched as his heart attempted to stop beating.

Preservation of Champion Life Quest
    Chain Party Quest – Atlantean Net Generated Save the North Bay Survivors I
- **Champions in North Bay are starving. While they are being protected by the golems, they haven't been able to hunt for food. Bring them food and find a way to handle the situation.**
    Rewards:
           Etherience
    Possible Increased Reputation with Survivors
    Atlantean Statutes, Preservation of Life, Section XII

Sela and Zippo read over his shoulders and growled. He went to the filter function, cleared the search tab, and chose the option to sort by distance. A few townships in and around Algonquin Valley popped to the front of the queue. The closest were Brent, Madawaska, and Barry's Bay.

An overwhelming weight settled onto his shoulders. People were starving to death. Too weak to free themselves from guarded isolation. Unable to find a way to collect food and water. His family might—he sharply inhaled through his nose and banished that line of thinking. They had to do something.

Rocky tapped the screen. "How do we accept these quests? Will they give us directional arrows to help?" The majority of small townships could be in a great many directions.

"The list keeps growing," Zippo noted, scrolling through the quests.

The total continued to climb. He checked the progress bar for the uplink to the Ethernet—one percent.

Is this only one percent of the quests?

"There is a lot of other information the Ethernet will pass onto the Control Room. It has probably packaged the quests in the first few percentages." Sela rested a hand on Rocky's shoulder. "Yes, we can definitely go help as many of these survivors as possible. I think our group should try to target groups slightly farther away first and organize some of our hunting parties for the groups closer in. What do you think?"

Rocky was already walking toward the elevators. "Sure, that's fine. The kiosks let you accept quests, right?"

Sela put herself between him and the doors. She extended her hands toward him, and they collided with his chest. "We need to collect some food and organize some groups first. Rushing off on our own will save only a few, Rockland. Taking thirty minutes now will save countless."

Rocky restarted his walk, pushing her along in front of him. "We will save others as we go. My family might be out there!"

Sela's jaw clenched and she slapped him across the face.

He stopped and raised a hand to his cheek. Realization of what just happened struck him like a freight train, and his face darkened. "Get out of my way, Sela."

Sela pointed her finger in his face. "No. You are acting like a child with power. Right now, those people out there need a leader. Someone who will *create* a chance for thousands instead of hundreds. What are you going to give the people you rush to rescue? Raw meat to eat? Your small water bottle to drink? Think like the leader you are, not the man scared for his family."

He felt the blood drain from his face as quickly as it had flooded it. She had hit his trigger word—twice. She was right. He had the bare minimum of travel rations and water in his Bag of Holding. To perform multiple quests, they would need far larger quantities.

He closed his eyes and took a deep breath. Then nodded.

The group rode the elevator down to the ground floor, and the air was charged with tension.

Rocky's skin tingled as his blood pumped heat through his limbs. "How come we didn't get these quests earlier?"

"Without a connection to the Ethernet, these quests are only available if you can see the people in need. Then the Atlantean system pushes out the quest to you. Now, we are able to see all the quests currently generated by the system." She hesitated before adding, "It's going to be impossible to get to everyone, Rockland."

There was truth in her words, but he wasn't ready to accept them.

The rest of the descent was blanketed by the return of heavy silence. Zippo was the only one unaffected as he bounced from foot to foot, eager for what came next.

The doors dinged and opened to the Atrium. To his surprise, the room was still empty. "Why didn't the doors open to admit people?" Rocky asked.

"Permissions," Sela murmured as she navigated through her status screens.

Now with the interior lights on, it was clear that the atrium had four large hallways leading off it. Each corridor was identical and led to two double doors, similar to the others they encountered.

Tao and Gamma turned to face a hallway as one of the double doors they had struggled so hard to open coasted inwards with an electric hum. The doors held themselves ajar, and then the three others followed suit with similar buzzing.

"There are a lot of permissions to sort through. For now, I gave everyone access to the building. Only Smith and the three of us have access to the elevator, though," said Sela.

People streamed through the doors into the new Guild Hall and Control Tower.

Sela yelled, "If you can hear me, go collect everyone else. Grotto meeting right here, right now!"

Rocky clenched his fists. There she went again, taking on the leadership role. He breathed out a sigh and shook his head. He knew he wouldn't have come to that realization as quickly as she did. He couldn't become a perfect leader with one pep talk.

Some people turned around, jostling back through the crowd and conveying her orders to others.

Rocky approached a kiosk and chose a quest for a town he didn't recognize—Burk's Fall. He had never been to Burk's Fall and had no idea where it was geographically. He wanted to see if the system would guide parties to their destinations. Sure enough, a gold thread appeared in his interface, and he sighed with relief.

***

The meeting took the place of the usual morning training, causing a stir among the citizens. Rocky and Sela explained the predicament of the surrounding towns and many of the hunters committed to help.

Smith volunteered to organize the teams and coordinate. Mr. Pips tried to sneak away, and Smith grabbed his riding leathers, pulling him back.

"Pips, I need you to get up to the Control Room and figure out what everything does."

"But, Smith, I can help out there. I am one of the strongest hunters in the village."

"You also know the groups of hunters better than anyone else. You are hands down the best choice for deciding which groups can handle this and which can't. I also know that you loved rebuilding electronics and working with computers.

Well, we have a room filled with them up there, and we need that expertise."

Smith's words caused Mr. Pips' head to fall. When he looked back up, he had a fire in his eyes. "You can count on me, Smith."

Rocky immediately flushed. That was a very similar confrontation to the one Sela and he just had.

Rocky ensured that Smith had the ability to grant tower permissions to other people. A runner approached, and Rocky listened distractedly. "Smith there are living quarters down all of these hallways. Thousands of them."

Smith looked at Rocky, and he nodded, confirming he had heard the news. Now wasn't the time.

Not that we need more right now, but we will if we start bringing more people back!

Smith was now in charge of this operation. Rocky and Sela were given the task of heading into the shop and purchasing plenty of rations for the groups. Smith had also split up the military to accompany the hunters, ensuring a tank traveled with each group. The foodstuffs would then be packed onto the machines for ease of travel.

***

Rocky's disguise barely masked his impatience as he and Sela entered the seed shop and were teleported into the Aretrean Bazaar. Once inside, they caught sight of Mechano-Lords—one in each cardinal direction. Cloaked in their kimonos and fox masks, Rocky hoped that they wouldn't draw attention to themselves.

He followed Sela as she made her way toward Lingren's Choo-Sentani.

Be cool. These are not the humans you are looking for, droids.

As they walked by, he made a small motion with his hand deep inside the sleeves of his kimono. He missed his 'May the Force be With You' sweater that had become rags after his first days in this new world.

The Mechano-Lords ignored them, and after a short walk and wait, they met with Lingren to gear themselves up.

Sela made her voice deeper and growled, "Need gear for younglings. What you have? Cheap but serviceable!"

Lingren didn't offer them tea as was his usual custom. The masks must have thrown him off—quite the feat for a man native to the planet. Rocky was glad for the reprieve from the elves' sewer water he had sipped last time.

"How many younglings are you looking to supply? How much do you have to spend?" asked the tanned and wrinkled elven-featured man.

His palms instantly slicked with sweat, and he fidgeted in his robe. What if Lingren was only willing to sell this gear in bulk? The Territory could always use more equipment, but he wasn't sure his meager funds could afford it.

"Tribe has few taking trials this season. Traditional gear only for combatants," said Sela.

"Dumb animal probably can't even count," muttered Lingren. He held up his fingers, adding one at a time to the displayed number. "How. Many. Sets. Do. You—"

Rocky reached out to grab the man's hand and his enrobed arm swept through Lingren's up ticking fingers.

The man stopped and looked at his own hand. "Four sets, then." He pulled roped bundles out of thin air. "At least these moonfolk could count my fingers. I swear elven dogs are more intelligent than the moonfolk. Imagine someone of my rank serving the likes of them. Disgusting."

Rocky opened and clenched his fists. He wanted to scream at the racist prick. Sela lightly touched his fist and shook her head.

He tamped his anger down, and it simmered, ready to boil over at any moment. His previous esteem for Lingren plummeted with the casual racism on display. He was no better than Jessebihr, that sleazy Skills trader. In his previous life, he had been raised to stand up to acts like this. He bit down hard, his teeth grinding together, as he fought against his instincts. He'd like nothing more than to dropkick the big jerk, but he couldn't afford to cause a scene. Not while the Mechano-Lords roamed the Bazaar on high alert.

Lingren placed the four bundles between them. "Fifteen Crystals!"

Sela held out one long sleeve of her robe. Crystals shone in the fabric covering her palm.

"I said fifteen. This is six and change."

Sela offered him the money again and growled, "Take?"

The sleazy elf threw his hands up and attempted multiple times to explain the problem to Sela. She tilted her mask, feigning confusion, and gestured entreatingly with her gem-filled hand.

The merchant snatched the proffered Crystals.

Sela swept the gear into Rocky's bag, and they walked past the small line that had formed outside the merchant's stall. Behind them, Lingren growled, "Have a great day, moon-moon's!"

For once, they had fleeced the fleecer. It looked like Lingren was the one dumber than a pack of elven dogs. Rocky sloughed the derogatory statement off his shoulders. As long as Lingren continued this behavior, Rocky intended to keep cutting into his profit margin. Maybe Lingren would finally learn a lesson.

Rocky and Sela headed to Garnell's booth next. For once, there wasn't a line. Rocky perused the stacks of building materials and tools on display as they approached. He knew that Garnell also sold building and territorial blueprints, as well as a few items that were on a reserve list. The dwarf didn't share that list with all of his customers, though.

Garnell recognized them through their disguises. It wasn't an exceptional feat of perception—he had been the one to sell them the Beastkin garb. They had also been here the day before in the same disguises'

As they approached the merchant's stall, an offer to enter a low-scale meeting room appeared, and they both accepted.

They were transported to the same cold concrete room as their last visit. The decor hadn't changed—four metal chairs and a single table. It was one two-way mirror short of being a lousy interrogation room.

"I'll contact Amelia—" said Garnell.

"No," interrupted Rocky. "Sorry, Garnell, we don't have time to meet with her today. We have some very pressing problems to deal with right now."

Garnell tilted his head, and his bushy eyebrows drew together. "Then why are ye here?"

Sela took her mask off and shook out her long hair. "We need plenty of rations. Figured you would be the best person to talk to."

Garnell smiled, transforming into the jovial man Rocky remembered. The merchant nodded and scratched his dwarven beard. "Alright, how much is plenty?"

Rocky was loath to trust any merchant after the sickening display Lingren had just put on. Garnell was different—he hoped. "One hundred Crystals' worth to start?"

Garnell's eyes went wide and he tugged on his beard. "Is ye Settlement that bad?"

Sela shook her head. "No, Garnell, we need to save others. Also, I think one hundred Crystals will be more than we can carry out of here." She glared at Rocky, who shrugged. They could use as much food as they could get their hands on.

"By the great Crom—for one hundred Crystals, I can provide ye with ten pallets of travel rations today. Another ninety pallets can be brought tomorrow. Each pallet is stacked with approximately two hundred- and fifty-days' worth of rations for one Karacy."

Tallying some mental math, Rocky determined that meant that today they could feed up to twenty-five hundred saved humans. Too bad the quests didn't give numbers.

"Done," said Rocky. Sela would probably want less, but having too many rations was better than too few.

Garnell produced the pallets which were swept into the Bag of Holding—nearly dragging Rocky to the floor.

"Ye really do need to make time for Amelia."

Rocky nodded a bit chagrined and looked to Sela. "Later tonight? Maybe we can take an Elixir of Shortened Sleep and spare an hour?"

"I agree, Rockland, but obviously, it is you who seems more hesitant in losing an hour for this task," Sela said.

She was right, of course. Even asking if they could spare the time was a cop-out. His heart felt like it was being ripped in two. They needed to save the humans, but would taking an hour to meet Amelia cost people their lives? He had delegated tasks to others. An hour now could save his entire Territory later.

"We will send you a message tonight, Garnell. I apologize for any lack of sleep that may cause you."

He ported out and staggered from the shop building, immediately transferring nine ration pallets into the Territorial Inventory. He sighed as his legs shook with relief from the removal of the strain they had been under.

CHAPTER ELEVEN

Zippo, Sela, and Rocky rode atop Azoth, scanning the landscape below. The Chimera had grown so much—and not just in size—Azoth could now carry three humans.

The group followed one of five golden threads that were displayed in their interfaces. Each thread would lead to a pocket of starving apocalypse survivors. There had been nine other rescue parties created from the group of volunteers. Each group was given a single pallet's worth of rations to distribute across the tanks that accompanied them.

He studied the new gear that he and Sela had equipped. Zippo also wore part of the set, but he had opted to add a robe and staff from the cultists of Apep.

Tunic of Initiation
- **This tunic is a regulated item and must meet the criteria laid out by the Beastfolk council to be sold as part of the Initiation set.**
     Ether Pool: Small
     Current Ether Pool: 50 / 50
Enchantments: Stats V (+1), Protection I (10%)
     Stats V
- **All stats except luck are increased by one.**

The pants, boots, and gloves carried the exact same Enchantments. Leaving them and Smith with a plus four to all stats except luck. That was better than nothing, and the added protection Enchantments would hopefully give them some minor help in upcoming fights.

Rocky shouted to Sela over the wind, "What initiation is this gear talking about?"

Her arms gripped his waist tighter, sending shivers through his body. Using her strength, she brought her chin up to his shoulder. "The Beastfolk are particularly strong melee fighters. All their children have to undergo a trial by their 'god' to become an adult. The cubs and kits used to enter the trial the way they were born—with nothing but their fur, nails, and teeth. Many millennia passed like this, and due to the Beastfolk's number one export—their mercenaries—the clans couldn't keep up with the death rates."

"How do you know all of this?" Rocky was impressed. Sela had told him she disliked school. But for someone who admitted they hated school and classes, this seemed like a lot of knowledge to him.

Sela dug her chin into his shoulder. "I went to the Atlantean Academy with a Beastfolk. He was from the Bear Tribe. Back to your first question, though. This gear was commissioned to increase the success rate in the trial. Each set must be identical to create an equal chance, and because of the constant demand, the supply increased. Thus, the lowered costs. This was all during my time, of course, but it seems that the market for it still exists."

"Look," Sela changed the subject as their course adjusted. She must have directed Azoth mentally, because he banked left.

Rocky tightened his grip on the saddle as the wind buffeted him. Once Azoth leveled back out, Rocky saw a cluster of buildings growing larger.

His tension eased now that action was finally going to be taken. Azoth began his descent and touched down a kilometer away from the school grounds. Rocky counted the golems he could see. Fifteen.

He Analyzed the closest golem, from just under five hundred meters away. That was a large increase for his Skill.

Bio Enhanced Golem
Journeyman-Crusher

Level 10
Health Points: 2500 / 2500

The levels were an entire rank higher than the golem mobs they had faced early on in the Apocalypse. He didn't spot any leader golems in the blockade, which was a blessing. He previously fought a particularly scary Basalt golem shortly after the first wave of Ether had struck.

Facing Golem Leaders after the second wave isn't appealing at all.

Sela slid from the saddle. "Alright, it is fifteen golems. Want to isolate and pick them off one by one, or group them up for some area of effect spells?"

They were the strongest fighters individually, and the strongest party. They could probably wipe out the creatures with large spells, save the survivors, and move on. Still, he knew from his sports career that the 'easy wins' often became the upsets you suffered.

"I am hesitant to take any fight lightly," said Rocky. "Zippo, I know you have your Fire Tornado; anything new from Journeyman level? What about you, Sela?"

"No new spells, but I did learn how to dual cast! Drains my Ether like crazy. Still, I can use Fire Wall and Tornado simultaneously, if they are grouped up enough," said Zippo.

"I have a Blight skill that will do extra damage because of the golems' Bio Enhancement. It should also hold them in an area so Zippo can cast freely," said Sela.

Rocky looked at his own frustrating skill tree. Why was he the only one not getting new powerful skills? No, the real question was why he was the only one forced out of his original class tree? Was Michabo—

He felt like someone had tossed pebbles into his stomach.

"Azoth claims he can use a roar that has a chance to disorient enemies—I am paraphrasing—a lot," Sela said.

Thanks, Sela. Now my stomach feels like it is digesting those stones. I'm stagnating in my growth.

He inspected his Soul Blade and the red rubies of the raven eyes stared back. The silence stretched until Sela punched him in the chest, startling him.

"We are waiting on you to answer the same question, and you are just standing there—thinking?" she stated.

"Sorry, I still have Dark Blade. I was just weighing the options."

"We can try an area of effect, and if it doesn't work, Azoth can probably carry three now," Sela recapped.

The three humans got into position and sent Azoth to lure the golems. The Chimera was dwarfed by the gargantuan constructs he ran toward. The first one to notice him swung its enormous fist down at the ground. Azoth nimbly jumped aside, and the golem dug a crater into the soft, grassy soil. The earth shuddered from the strength of the blow, sending small tremors through the soles of Rocky's boots and into his legs.

His stomach and heart trembled with the quake, as if he was on a roller coaster. His friend was in real danger. Azoth bounced around, gathering more and more of the golem's attention. Rocky's heart pounded harder as increasing numbers of titans struck at his friend.

Sela laughed, and he stared at her. How could she laugh at a time like this?

"He is playing with them, I told him the school is a safe zone. He is using it to his advantage. His running commentary is something like, 'You'll never catch Azoth—missed Azoth—Gamma and Tao would be disappoint."

He stared at the battle and saw what he had missed the first time. Azoth was modulating his speed to keep the golems close. Even though Rocky laughed, he couldn't help but feel distanced from his pet, unable to hear Azoth's commentary firsthand.

"He has them all, and is going to swing them this way," Sela said.

The fifteen golems attacking Azoth were bunched up in a tightly tangled mess of concrete limbs. The creatures circled the school grounds, as if an invisible forcefield prevented the golems from entering.

Azoth used his freedom to dart in and out of that zone to his full advantage. His tactics forced the golems to walk the circumference in a tight group, all vying to attack the 'enemy.'

Azoth led the golems to the area directly in front of Zippo, Sela, and Rocky before darting toward them. As the golems stepped forward, the grass under their feet blackened and curled in on itself like a dying snake.

A fetid odor washed over Rocky, and he coughed and spluttered. The golems' feet sank into the ground as if they had stepped into a thick bowl of swampy soup. Suddenly, the soil and grass that was protecting their bodies quickly began to brown and slough off their frames.

Zippo cast a spell, and a pillar of fire formed in the center of the group, catching four of the golems. He raised his other hand, and a dark swirling cloud of ash formed, obscuring the rest from view. The darkness flashed like ember lightning as the ash spun in slow, concentric circles.

Rocky added his Dark Blade Skill, charged five times, and Azoth roared. The wind buffeted the group as Zippo's Tornado disturbed the equilibrium of the area. Rocky's Skill disappeared into the swirling blackness and screeched as it contacted the first golems.

Zippo held the spells for approximately ten seconds before he crumpled to the ground, sweat drenching his skin. A few seconds later, the ash blew away in the gale force.

What remained of the fifteen golems was laughable. Half-sunken into the bog of Sela's Blight skill were square chunks of blackened stone and flaming wood.

Sela released her skill, and the ground solidified. The grass returned a moment later, seeming to grow from nothing. A few blades of the new grass withered and died from the fire, and Zippo held out a shaking hand and extinguished the puttering flames.

"Nice work. Now let's loot and get those survivors some food and water," Rocky said, dusting himself off.

The group looted the corpses and crushed the golem cores under their feet. Sela insisted on it, going so far as to pull the ones Rocky looted out of his Bag of Holding and doing it herself.

"My connection to Gaia says this is the right thing to do," Sela said as she stomped on a core.

As they approached the school, Rocky expected people to rush out of the building to greet them. They must have heard the noise and felt the vibrations of the combat.

He opened the doors to the building and almost vomited. The smell of stale urine and drying excrement assaulted his nose, a stench worse than even the Blighted Bog. Azoth sneezed and moved away.

"This isn't good at all. Even animals don't defecate where they live. Either the people inside are too weak to venture out onto the grounds, or something else is very wrong," Sela said. "Azoth, go back to the Territory and bring three people here to take care of the people inside."

"If it is as bad as I fear, these people will not be able to leave for at least a day, even with the system's help," she continued.

The three entered the school and searched through classroom after classroom. They found unused makeshift bedrooms in most. They didn't find the cause of the smell until they reached the cafeteria. A quick headcount told him that fifty-two people lay on the floor. Each body smelled like a sewage treatment plant, had sallow, sunken skin, oily hair, cracked lips and bed sores. They looked like corpses all laid out in neat rows. Three people knelt beside some of the immobile bodies and dripped water from dirty cups into their mouths.

He couldn't bring himself to Analyze the bodies just yet. Instead, Rocky pulled out the pallet of rations and a large water tank. He moved to one of the still cognizant and mobile humans and said, "We are here to help. We have food and water."

The person looked at him with weary eyes and then continued to drip water into the person's mouth.

Rocky didn't understand why the person was ignoring him. He tried again, pulling out his water bottle and pressing it into the hands of the dirty...man?

Finally, his touch elicited a response. The nearly desiccated individual croaked, "You aren't hallucinations?"

The other two mobile survivors glanced in his group's direction. He could have shouted for joy at this sign of life. "We are here to help you all."

Thirty minutes later, Azoth returned with three very dizzy and pale citizens of the Grotto. Their reaction to Azoth's full speed was bad, and their stomachs couldn't handle the school and its smells. In those thirty minutes, Rocky, Sela, Zippo, and the three mobile survivors had given water and a small piece of rations to each prone body.

In some cases, the person was so weak that Rocky had to chew the food and spit it into his hand before feeding the mash to the downed body. The act wasn't pleasant, but if it saved a life, he would chew for each of the forty-nine survivors.

The three helpers from the Grotto began tending to the survivors, once their stomachs had settled.

Rocky brought the water jug over to the sinks. The group only had a thin layer of water left at the bottom of two industrial-sized kitchen sinks. He hefted the jug and poured the contents into the two containers until they were full.

"I have topped up your water, and am leaving a great deal of the rations. Three of us need to go help other groups. Wait here, and we will ensure that an escort comes to bring you to safety very soon. Right now, just focus on getting better, okay?"

Rocky, Sela, and Zippo walked back down the hallway they had entered through. The smell that had originally shaken the three combatants no longer bothered Rocky. Either his nose had gotten used to it, or finding people alive had helped.

They passed a room with a closed door on their way out. For a heartbeat, the smell of death intensified. He didn't open the door—he didn't need to. He knew what would greet him if he did.

Congratulations, you have completed a Chain Quest! Preservation of Champion Life Quest
Chain Party Quest – Atlantean Net Generated Save the McDougall Survivors I
- **You have managed to save 52 survivors from starvation. By this act, you have unlocked the second part of the chain quest.**
  Rewards:
260,000 (+13,000 Knight's Quest) Etherience to each party member.
Talk to the survivors to offer them the choice to become permanent members of your Territory.
Atlantean Statutes, Preservation of Life, Section XII
--

You have been offered a 2nd part in a Chain Quest! Preservation of Champion Life Quest
Chain Party Quest – Atlantean Net Generated Save the McDougall Survivors II
- **Escort 50% of the survivors successfully back to your Territory. This quest difficulty has been**

**adjusted due to distance to Territory.
Approximately 100 miles (160 km)
Rewards:**

**Etherience
New members of your Territory.**
Atlantean Statutes, Preservation of Life, Section XII

The quest Etherience, combined with the kills of the twelve golems outside, barely pushed him to level seven. It was already costing him more than two million per level, and he wasn't excited at the prospect of how slow levels would be coming now. The only good news was that the escort quest seemed to share Etherience across anyone he doled the quest out to. When he got back, he would have to make sure everyone in the Territory got every escort quest. Perhaps it would be a good way to level everyone together.

Rocky assigned his skill points and chose to increase Knight's Quest. The extra 13,000 Etherience was an obvious reason to do so. Putting another point in the Skill increased the gain from five to ten percent. Rocky felt his blood heat up as he directly countered his earlier thoughts on high Etherience.

The last decision to make was where to put his free stat points. He was extremely close in a few stats to what Sela had termed a 'breakthrough'. He placed two points into Luck, keeping with his previous decisions when awarded a five-block of free points. Then he deliberated; he only needed three points in Agility to pass that breakthrough point.

**Rockland Barkclay Level 7
    Class: Journeyman-Dark Chimera Knight
    Level 3 Strategist
Class Skills: Dark Blade, Dark Mend, Soul Blade, Dark
Cloak, Shadow Clone, Knight's Resolve, Knight's
Quest**

Health Points = 410/410

Dark Ether Pool = 280/280

You have 6 stat points and 0 skill points to distribute.

Stamina – 41 (Strength of Body +9) (+4 Stat V)

Strength – 43 (Strength of Arms +18) (+4 Stat V)

Agility – 50 (+3) (+4 Stat V)

Dexterity – 44 (+4 Stat V)

Intelligence – 28 (+4 Stat V)

Wisdom – 42 (+4 Stat V)

Charisma – 44 (+4 Stat V)

Luck – 12 (+2)

Weak Skills

Non-Class Combat Skills: Ether Cleanse - 10

Common Skills: Barter – 8, Camouflage – 7, Endurance – 30 (+3 *Rank Up?*), Fall - 1, Tracker – 19 , Trance Meditation – 26 (*Rank Up?*)

Profession Skills: Actor – 5, Butcher – 24 (+2 *Rank Up?*), Cook – 2, Grooming - 3(+2), Herbalist – 19, Miner – 1, Skinner – 25 (+3 *Rank Up*), Teacher – 20 (+2), Trader – 5

Moderate Skills

Non-Class Combat Skills: Combatant – 11 (+9), Ether Channels – 4 (+1), Ether Manipulation 5 (+1) , Stealth – 15 (+2), Swordsmanship – 14 (+5)

Common Skills: Analyze – 18 (+2), Perception – 11 (+4), Sneak – 19 (+1)

Profession Skills:

He quickly ranked up the non-class skills available to him, then placed three Stat points into agility. His skin tingled with the anticipation of reaching the next level of growth. Fifty points. He selected yes on the prompt as they made it back outside the school.

"Wait, Rockland," Sela cried.

He fell to the ground, and his body twitched violently. Pain shot through his muscles as if they were burning him to ash from the inside out. He screamed as his body convulsed.

"Shoot. He has just hit a breakthrough. Zippo, go fill up this jug with water. He is going to need to be cleaned off after this." Sela removed his equipment as best she could. At times, he thought she was holding him down; at others, it seemed like she was fighting with him.

Five minutes of hell later, Rocky was embarrassed to admit he had soiled himself. He laid there, naked and covered in his own piss and shit. He was grateful that Sela had removed his clothes, but it didn't make up for the humiliation.

Rocky took the jug of water Zippo had brought and sheltered himself around the corner of the building. As he scrubbed his skin, black grit fell away. He scraped off heaps of the dried substance.

He reapplied his Nano-Armor and called out, "What was that black stuff all over me, Sela?"

"Your breakthroughs are going to be very similar to this in the future. I should have told you sooner. I hadn't realized how close you were. As you break through the limitations of your body, it is forced to change. It removed imperfections and counterproductive materials inside your body. That black stuff is that accumulated material."

Rocky opened his mouth to yell at her, and she cut him off. "I wouldn't get dressed just yet. From my brief glance, you broke through in Agility, correct?"

He nodded stiffly.

"Take everything back off and hit your breakthrough in Dexterity as well. Right now, you are likely to fall over when you use your speed. It is always wise to break through linked stats together."

"I have to go through that again?"

He began to sweat.

Sela nodded.

CHAPTER TWELVE

Rocky and his team used the same tactics on the four other towns—Key River, Britt, Pointe au Baril, and Parry Sound—and saved three hundred and two people in total.

After his breakthroughs, Rocky sensed a subtle difference in the fights. His movements were a bit faster, and he could adjust the course of his blade within centimeters. Still, they attacked with Area of Effect spells, and he wasn't entirely sure of the new extent of his speed after the breakthrough.

Not every saved group was in as bad of shape as the first, but each one had suffered. The story from the starving groups seemed to be the same. They just didn't think they had the firepower to down one of the Bio Enhanced golems. No one wanted to risk attacking the behemoths either, in case it broke the protection of the school. When they realized they would starve, it was already too late. They only grew weaker.

Azoth touched down next to the guild building. The group slid off his back and jogged inside to gather more quests and get an update to verify the escorts were en route to the recovering survivors.

Azoth headed toward the butcher's yard in search of an effortless meal, rather than hunting for one. According to Sela, that hadn't been a fun conversation. Understandably, the massive predator enjoyed the hunt.

Military personnel swarmed around the building, rushing out of corridors to deliver messages. Some carried clothing that Rocky hadn't considered to bring on the first trip. Most of the survivors they had seen wore rags, often soiled. He'd have to pack some into his Bag of Holding before setting back out.

He approached Smith, who was conveying orders from atop the raised circular countertop. The Native American man sent three runners on their way, then hopped down as Rocky neared. He smiled wearily and followed Rocky's eyes to the retreating runners. "I wish I were out there with you. Trust me. At any rate, we have sent a group with five tanks and thirty soldiers to complete the escort quests your group relayed. The last group is just prepping to leave," he said.

Taking out his Knowledge Tablet, he swiped the screen a few times. "Currently, the other ten volunteer groups have managed to locate the towns. Three of them are inside the school grounds, and two are dispatching golems individually. The other four parties ran into large groups of monsters that they had to retreat from for the time being. We have been able to track them using the satellite to some degree as well. I have ordered those groups who made it inside to stay the night and escort their charges back in the morning. At current, you are the only active group I have left. Please tell me you can take on more?"

Rocky looked over his shoulder to spot Sela and Zippo standing at a kiosk. "I think that's what they are searching for right now. I asked them to get Huntsville and Bancroft in this grouping, since I am hoping to cover the closer towns to our South. While there are many small towns near us, we need to start planning for longer trips. Got any ideas?"

Smith shook his head. "I will start coming up with some options while you are out. One other option to consider is to approach the exiles. They would be willing to help, I am sure. We also know they are powerful."

Rocky's anger flared, but he pushed it down. Frank had controlled the exiles during their attack on Rocky. He took a deep breath and let it out. His emotions were such a roiling mess that he couldn't be sure if his reaction to the exiled group had been fair in the first place. "What about Tao and Gamma?" he asked instead.

"They are not allowed to leave the Territory, despite a clear wish to do so. I believe they are awaiting their final three members." Smith called Sela over. Once she was close enough,

Smith asked, "Are you sure there is nothing in the shop we can buy to help speed up the escort of the groups you save?"

Unbelievable. He was standing right there. Why wouldn't Smith ask him? Why summon his Ancestral guide? He may not have known the answer, but that wasn't the point. Tempting as it was, he wasn't going to tear into his friend. This time.

Sela bit her lip."Rocky, I think we should talk to Garnell and Amelia about this later today. Perhaps they can sell us something that is not completely worthless. It will be expensive, of course, and may require more Crystals."

"You let me worry about that. I think people will be willing to chip in some of their Crystals for that cause. I will keep thinking of other options while you're out this afternoon. Good luck." Smith's last words seemed to be his exit from the conversation. Rocky hadn't noticed them at first, but a large group of runners were waiting for his return to the raised counter.

Zippo jogged over. "I did my best, like Sela showed me. I think I grabbed the final two quests that match up well. We have Huntsville, Dorset, Haliburton, Bancroft, and Minden. That sound, right?"

Rocky tried to open up a mental map, recalling what he knew of the cities mentioned. "Sounds reasonable."

They walked down the corridor and Sela puffed air out between clenched teeth.

"What is it?" asked Rocky.

"The birdbrain is ignoring me."

They made their way to the butcher's yard and found Azoth devouring what the hunters assured them was his fifth deer corpse.

"Azoth, you've had enough. The Territory needs the rest of that food," Rocky said.

Azoth didn't even look up from his meal.

One of the hunters said, "Actually, with the border back up, the larger monsters have exited Algonquin Valley. The hunting groups are back to catching more. Unfortunately, some of our strongest groups are out right now. So, maybe..."

The group allowed Azoth to finish his meal.

When Azoth finished and went for a sixth, Sela and Rocky stepped in his path. "I think that's enough, buddy. There will be plenty of time to gorge later." Rocky turned to the hunters and apologized for his pet's gluttony.

Azoth growled and his stinger rose over his head. "Azoth, no! Bad Azoth!" Rocky shouted.

Azoth's eyes widened and he shook his head, as if trying to fight against an unseen foe. His scorpion tail sank between his legs and his head fell.

"I'm sorry, buddy. I didn't mean it. You are a good boy. I will just remember not to come between you and your food in the future." Rocky shuddered. Azoth's poison was no joke, and if his pet attacked someone over food, they would die. It wasn't like a dog who bit a hand.

They mounted back up, and Sela directed Azoth to fly south, toward the Minden area. Her chiding voice fell on Rocky's ears alone. "The 'bad Azoth' might have been a bit harsh, Rocky. He's really hurt."

He felt his chest tighten, and his breathing grew shallow. Rocky hadn't meant to hurt his pet. Not being able to mentally communicate was so strange. Was Azoth's aggressive display part of that?

Note to self: 'bad boy' and all of its variations are off limits.

***

They had been in the air for fifteen minutes when he saw a group of aerial creatures performing diving attacks against something on the ground. Their wings and bodies glistened with a dark, leathery sheen. Azoth veered toward the fight.

As they neared the combat, Rocky's body tightened at the sight of the bird-bats' prey. Three familiar green-armored golems attempted to repel the attackers, while more nearby golems defended a large column of survivors from hairless wolf-like creatures.

His first thought was to rush past the aerial assault, but they would pass by it no matter what. "Try to knock the birds from the sky, Zippo." Rocky pulled a Plasma Grenade from his bag. "Azoth, fly above the creatures, buddy, then continue south to the survivors."

Azoth pumped his wings, causing moments of intense pressure followed by weightlessness. Rocky had yet to get used to the jumpy flight his pet provided during intense combat, but it bothered him less than it had originally.

As they closed in on three of the airborne creatures, his heart pounded in his ears. The bird-like beasts were as big as Bathilda. He used Analyze as soon as he hit the range for the spell.

Batwing Bird
Master-Amalgamated Dive Bomber
Level 21
Health Points: 4213 / 4515

In the air, five hundred meters wasn't a large distance. Zippo's fireball spells whooshed toward the wings of two of the creatures, Rocky depressed the pin of his grenade and heaved it, intentionally aiming at a point that would miss the animals. A second grenade, tossed by Sela, flew toward a parallel point on the opposite side of the flying birds.

Just as one of the bat-birds folded its wings to dive, Zippo's spell exploded on the creature's back. The other fireball burned a smallish hole through the wing of another. The remaining creature banked away instinctively, directly into the path of Rocky's grenade. Two miniature suns bloomed and one disabled the creature's wing as the group flew past the pandemonium they just caused. They should protect the survivors first. The master class Knights below were fully capable of handling the cleanup.

He glanced over his shoulder and surveyed the damage. Two creatures fell to the earth, while the third poised to dive, changed course, and flapped its wings to follow the new threat.

"Christmas Carols," Rocky swore. One of the bat-birds was now hot on Azoth's tail.

"Azoth, think you can drop us off without that thing catching up?"

Sela grabbed him tightly and shouted, "You. Idiot. Hold on!"

Azoth folded his wings, and Rocky instantly regretted his request. His cheeks flapped as the wind and G-force threatened to rip him from the saddle. He fought the buffeting blast with his core, pulling his upper body closer to Azoth's back and maintaining his white-knuckled death grip on the rope lashing.

Sela, whose chest was pressed to his back, placed a drag on Rocky's action. Perhaps even Zippo was added to the Herculean pull. It certainly felt like a tug of war with a concrete pillar.

He inched forward, and once the equilibrium broke, their speed increased, until he and Sela were as tight as they could be. He hoped Zippo was gripping Sela like she was him.

I can't hear him screaming, which I think is a good sign—my stupid big mouth.

Azoth unfurled his wings and the forces reversed, pushing Rocky painfully into the Chimera's back. He didn't feel the touchdown—thankfully—and he righted himself to a spinning world. Azoth landed near the front of the combat, just behind the backs of the golems that were grappling with the wolves.

He untied himself and dropped from the saddle, bruising his hip and shoulder in the process. The impact knocked the breath from his lungs, but he held back his vomit. A silver lining. The wolves towered over the golems, trying to withstand the assault. Two of the golems were barely restraining one single, ugly creature. Projectiles volleyed over and over at each leather-skinned wolf. But the monsters barely registered the strikes.

Rocky rolled over and groaned. The bat-bird approached from behind, coming into striking range of the unarmed human survivors.

He levered himself to his knees as the now-familiar chafe storm followed Azoth's takeoff. His pet would handle the bat-bird. That left the wolves to him.

Rocky shoved his palms into the dirt and managed to get to all fours. The world spun for a moment, and he had to pause. On his debuff bar, a stick figure with a circle of stars caught his attention, and he focused on it.

Vertigo
- **The equilibrium of your inner ear has been significantly upset. Usually caused by a severe blow to the head, a sudden change in pressure, or just wax buildup.**
  Extreme dizziness, reducing Agility and Dexterity to 10% of the current value
  Inhibited thought processes, reducing Intelligence and Wisdom to 50% of the current value.
Time remaining: 43 seconds.

He clenched his jaw and surveyed the battlefield as best he could. As he had hoped, Azoth was distracting the final visible Batwing Bird. The Chimera was either leading him high into the sky—or straight into the ground? Tough to say, with the world revolving so quickly.

One of the more ferocious-looking wolves clamped its jaw and two layers of teeth around a golem's arm. The teeth screeched and grated over the concrete, and Rocky covered hunkered his ears toward his shoulders.

He stared in horror as the wolf's lower jaw shifted backwards and forwards, like a... reciprocating saw? The golem's limb fell to the ground with a reverberating boom.

Another golem was—floating? Somersaulting? Cartwheeling?—away from a second wolf.

Rocky dug his fingers further into the damp earth pushing under his fingernails. The world continued to spin, and he couldn't tell if he was hanging from the soil or not, but he wasn't going to risk letting go. The ground shook as the debuff timer ticked down to zero, simultaneously the sound of a boulder cascading down a mountainside assaulted his ears. He slumped back to the ground as the sky became the ground. Or was it the ground becoming the sky? The acidic taste of bile rose in his throat, and he swallowed it back down. He finally got to his feet, and Sela and Zippo followed suit.

Blue above, and green below. That feels better.

"Pick a target; those golems are getting torn apart—literally," Rocky said, sprinting in the direction of the fight. He targeted the wolf who had launched one of its containment golems into the air. It was half fighting, half dragging its other golem restraint toward the line of ranged human attackers. Checking his line of attack, Rocky found no human between himself and the beast—just the golem. He charged Dark Blade as he used Analyze.

Rat-Wolf
Master-Shredder
Level 22

Health Points: 4300 / 7000

The ranged attackers had done more damage than he had initially thought. Blood ran from numerous small wounds on the creature's rat-like hide.

He loaded three charges of his skill during his approach, and released it with a vertical slash. A quick thought triggered Dark Cloak, and he raced to the edge of his released Dark Blade. The triple-charged ability tore through the dirt and sped toward the back of the golem holding the Shredder, leaving three straight ditches in its wake.

Rocky flew over the ground, moving faster than any car he had ever driven. He hadn't realized how fast he was going—this would take some getting used to. He adjusted his speed, attempting not to overshoot his next target, just as the Dark Blades collided with the golem. The dismemberment of the golem that he had forgotten to Analyze took mere seconds.

His ability, which the enemy hadn't seen coming, inched the Rat-Wolf back along its previous path. Rocky expected the slow retreat, and he continued his sprint, triggering Stealth on the run.

His Dark Blade opened cuts into the rat hide, but a quick Analyze told him the damage wouldn't be enough. He charged another Dark Blade, this time choosing to use it as a melee weapon. In the past, the melee option caused much more damage than the current iteration of the skill, at least on stronger opponents. Relying on his past experiences as a guide, he stayed on the ground and attacked the back leg of the towering creature.

He was right below the creature and strained his neck to look up, immediately averting his gaze when he saw the thing's *manhood* above him. He swung horizontally, keeping his wrists firm but springy. The blade bit into the wolf's skin and through its ligaments with ease before connecting with bone.

He felt the change in pressure through his hands and hinged his wrist while contracting his obliques. The torque of his body added power, and he drew his elbows toward his body to drag the blade through the limb. The resistance of bone relented as his technique won out.

His sword tore out the other side of the back leg, just below the hock. He noticed the weight of the wolf hinge the appendage on the skin and ligament that his sword hadn't managed to sever. If the amount of blood was any indication, his Dark aura had cauterized the wound. The blackness spread as the partially severed limb-stump fell off the foot and onto the grass below. He looked back up and caught an eyeful of the creature's package again.

The severed limb jerked up from the ground and the wolf howled in pain.

Rocky turned toward its head in time to see the balance between his initial skill and the wolf shift. The wolf's head and chest, no longer braced by its back foot, began to collapse— directly on top of him.

He cursed and sprinted around its back end. Liquid splattered on him, and he spat as some flew into his mouth. No, no, no. That couldn't be what he tasted. No matter how much he tried to deny it, his taste buds did not lie.

Oh, come on! I definitely didn't need a golden shower.

He clenched his mouth shut. He never wanted to taste that again. His original Dark Blade tore through the creature, finishing it off. The wolf's rear end went limp, and Rocky dove forward. Even with his incredible speed, the falling bulk clipped him.

The prickly rat skin of the soft stomach landed onto his legs, buttocks, and lower back. Blessedly, his upper body was free, and he dug his fingers into the earth to pull himself out.

He grunted in frustration as he checked his Health and Ether bars. The falling beast had halved his Health. His Ether was currently at ninety points but ticked to ninety-one as he watched. Unfortunately, his two active skills would significantly slow the regeneration, so he reluctantly released Stealth and Dark Cloak once his feet popped free.

He stood up, jogged away from the corpse on shaky legs, and assessed the battle. Sela and Zippo were engaged with a single rat-wolf to his left. He scanned his right, preparing to charge in that direction, as he downed a Health and Ether potion.

Epsilon, Omega, and Delta fought a rat-wolf, each one aided by the golems who had previously held the creatures back. He pumped his fist; the cavalry had arrived.

The other golems must be under the command of the Knights.

Two of the wolf creatures had only smaller golems for opponents, and Rocky charged one of them. He activated his two skills and the ranged assault on his target shifted to the other wolf being contained by smaller golems. The reaction speed of the ranged attackers told him someone here was in skillful command.

He used Analyze on one of the golems grappling that wolf.

Minion Golem
Journeyman-Fortifier
Level 35
Health Points: 1200 / 4500

Minion Golem? That was a very cool ability that he didn't know the Knights possessed. He fervently hoped it would speed up their current endeavors as he closed in with his target and distractedly used his Dark Blade with a triple charge. His mind was already playing through the rest of his day, rescuing more survivors.

His target leaped backward, out of the path of his strike. The Minion Golems strained in the same direction against the wolf and fell on their faces. The rat-wolf deked left and charged Rocky, its jaw opening wide. The two layers of the wolf's bottom teeth began to reciprocate. Rocky felt his sphincter clench and his muscles tighten.

He summoned his Shadow Clone nearly on top of himself and then released his Dark Cloak. The cloak hovered in the air, and Rocky sprinted away from his clone. As he left, a hand exited the shroud and pointed in his direction, middle finger extended.

Yeah, that's fair. I deserve that one.

The charging wolf didn't take long to close the distance. Once in range, it lunged, rotating its head and surrounding his clone with its teeth.

Rocky released another triple-charged Dark Blade at the creature's side. The skill connected with its body and toppled the beast. Rocky still felt his clone and mentally checked on it.

He caught a glimpse of his other self-sinking both daggers into the roof of the rat-wolf's mouth.

Definitely thought I was sacrificing the Clone. Way to go—me?

The hollow echo of a body hitting the earth reverberated up Rocky's legs as his skill careened over the prone creature and into the distance. The two golems, charging back into the fray, were met by a wall of phantasmal blades. He winced and murmured, "Oops" as they were torn into chunks of rubble.

The released Dark Blade hadn't passed by the wolf without dealing damage. The near-evisceration was evidence of that, but a quick Analyze told Rocky there was still work to do.

Rat-Wolf
Master-Shredder
Level 27
Health Points: 1300 / 7700

He was out of Ether and hesitated to use another Ether potion if he didn't have to. Closing the distance between himself and the creature, he lunged forward, punching his sword through its ribs trying to find the heart for a critical strike. The beast recoiled like a snake as his sword cut through, twisting its heavily damaged body to bring its back legs up to kick Rocky.

Both legs pistoned toward him, and he hugged himself close to the wolf's ribs, narrowly avoiding the first strike.

The wolf launched its body off the ground and away from Rocky. His sword squelched free of the wound. Before he could react, its hind legs retracted and punched forward. He fell to the ground, flattening himself into the grass as the wolf's hind leg clipped his shoulder and back. He screamed as a line of fire scorched him and a Bleeding debuff floated into his user interface.

Swallowing his scream, he shoved the pain aside, rolling through the grass. Mid-roll, the wolf's hind leg connected with his calf. The limb creaked and cracked as another debuff of a Broken Bone popped up on his interface bar. He swallowed back a scream, forcing himself to keep rolling to avoid the next blows. Each strike whistled past him and the disturbed air sped his rolling escape.

He checked his Ether bar—it was low—and he chose the Health Potion option as he sat up. Pain shot through his leg, and he bit down on his lip to avoid screaming as his stomach constricted. He tried to avoid looking at his foot, but he was pretty sure it should be facing forward.

Rocky palpated his calf and was glad to see that the bone hadn't broken through. Rocky clenched his teeth. Before drinking the Health Potion, he needed to correct his foot's position or it wouldn't heal right. He grabbed a nearby stick and put it between his teeth, then grabbed the leg and wrenched it, holding the bone and muscles in place. He bit down on the stick as he bellowed a soul-shaking scream. Dark spots clouded his vision, and he vomited.

Cold sweat broke out over his scorching skin, and he downed the Healing Potion, praying it would stay down. A cool wave of relief washed over him, and then his stomach bucked. Rocky swallowed the liquid that rose in his throat, the taste no longer pleasant—he couldn't afford to waste the potion.

Nauseous and dizzy, he forced himself to stand on one leg.

The wolf lay still, collapsed on its side, as a barrage of ranged attacks peppered the dying beast.

The survivors had come to his rescue.

Chapter Thirteen

Rocky monitored the clean-up of the battle, ready to jump in if the line faltered at all, but it hadn't. Sela and Zippo had finished off their target sometime during Rocky's botched fight with his own opponent, and had then joined the assault from range on the Batwing Bird.

Sela gave directions to Azoth, who skillfully disabled the creature's flight. At that point, Rocky used a Dark Blade to add his damage to the fray, mostly to ensure it didn't get back into the air. The Golem Knights quickly dispatched the final Rat-Wolves, with their comparable size and levels.

With the last beast vanquished, the survivors surrounded his group and the Golem Knights.

"Welcome back, Epsilon. Are these the survivors from Kingston?" Rocky asked, addressing the Golem Leader.

Epsilon nodded. "Some of the humans present are from other schools along our path, though the majority are from Kingston, yes. More survived there because of their ability to control golems—"

"That wasn't you guys?" asked Rocky.

Delta shook his head. "We can attempt to order our non-intelligent brothers around. However, the results haven't been optimal. I believe we are missing a requisite skill."

Rocky eyed the three surviving Minion Golems. He turned back to Epsilon, "If not you—then who?"

A young man stepped forward—unkempt hair that mimicked a bird's nest, dirty skin, and stained clothing. He was teenager skinny, with the accompanying coordination issues, and couldn't have been much older than Zippo.

This kid can take control of golems.

He used Analyze.

Adam Weatherbee

Apprentice Stone-Summoner
Level 21
Health Points: 90 / 90

The kid spoke up, his voice breaking with the telltale tones of puberty. "I'm Adam. I am the one who can control the golems. They lose levels when I claim them, but it has been less lately."

"Did you play video games a lot, Adam?" Zippo asked with interest.

The boy nodded eagerly, and he stood up straight. "Yeah! I am min-maxing in Intelligence and Wisdom... Wow, you are really strong! Journeyman rank—when did you get to rank up?"

"Teenagers, right?" said one of the older survivors, smiling at Adam and Zippo, who moved aside to talk excitedly. "My name is Garry. Can we keep traveling and talk as we journey?"

"Unfortunately, we have some other people to save in nearby villages. We will meet you back in the Territory shortly, though," Sela said. "Epsilon, think you can get them back safely? We really could use all of your help." She indicated the Knights, including Tao and Gamma, with the tilt of her chin.

"We will have this group back shortly." Epsilon held up a finger, emphasizing his next words. "We need to discuss our next actions with Tao and Gamma. I assume nothing has befallen my brothers?"

"They are just fine. They helped us defend the Grotto from an assault, and even met a dragon—they will tell you all about it when you arrive, I am sure," Rocky said, smiling reassuringly.

Omega hopped up and down, causing small quakes that trembled up Rocky's legs. In his typical surfer drawl, he said,

"Dude, they met a dragon! That's, like, totally epic. Did they save a princess as well?"

Delta shook his head, patting Omega's shoulder. The body contact put an end to the miniature hops, and Rocky's teeth were thankful. "That's statistically impossible in a world with so few monarchies. My guess is they …"

Rocky turned away from the conversation and assessed the corpses of the slain creatures. The meat on a single one of the monstrous creatures would be enough to feed the Territory for a few days—or Azoth for one lunch. Considering the state of their reserves, he wanted to get them back to his people. They would probably fit in his Bag of Holding, but he would collapse from the weight of just one of the creatures, even with the 90% weight reduction.

He shook his head and prepared to loot the bodies when he caught a Minion Golem shifting slightly from the corner of his eye. "Adam, how fast can the Minion Golems run?"

"Uhhh… well… probably pretty fast. I don't think they get tired." Adam moved closer and whispered, "I don't think they even breathe."

Rocky tilted his head, reconsidering the age of the young man. His heart warred between his growing fondness for the boy—he was so much like Zippo when Rocky had first met him—and his clinical brain shot ice through his veins.

How can he still seem so innocent? Do I dare risk him?

Adam looked over his shoulder at his three remaining golems. "After this last fight, I have to go collect more, too. I started this journey with fifteen."

Rocky hated himself but moved forward with his plan. He turned to Epsilon, interrupting the conversation between the golem and Sela. "Do you need Adam for this last bit of the journey, or can you make it back safely without him?"

"Adam has been valuable. However, the likelihood of another attack is very low. This area is known to be dominated by those birds and wolves hunting in tandem." Epsilon glanced around and shrugged. "I would assume all other predators in this area have been driven out by the tactics of these creatures. Plus, he only has three constructs left. Why do you ask?"

Epsilon's speech indicated it would be ok to 'borrow' the boy. Still, something in his voice didn't ring true. There was something he wasn't saying.

"I was thinking that his golems could run beneath Azoth and carry my bag of holding with these corpses." Rocky pointed at the creatures surrounding them. "Plus, we are heading off to save people from the non-sapient golems that are 'protecting' them."

Adam nodded excitedly and sized up Azoth, who was devouring the Batwing Bird. "I get to fly on that with you guys?"

The survivors, who had gotten used to the boy's Minions and owed their lives to them, weren't happy with the idea. People talked over each other, sharing their points of view. As the conversation finally shifted to grudging approval of the plan, Epsilon pulled Rocky and Sela aside.

It was a strange feeling to be metaphorically pulled aside by a creature that dwarfed them. Sela and Rocky jogged to match the stride of the Golem Knight Leader. Once they were a reasonable distance away, he turned to them, his face stony. "That boy may one day be able to create golems that are sapient. My two fellow Knights and I believe that he may be a key to our future survival, Rocky." Epsilon raised his whisper slightly and pointed a green finger at him. "Do not let any harm befall that young man."

Rocky swallowed and nodded at the warning. He waited for Epsilon to say more, but the golem remained silent, keeping his finger pointed at Rocky.

"He won't leave Azoth's back until the golems are defeated. I will convey to Azoth the importance of his life over ours. Does that appease you?" Sela offered. Under her breath, she murmured, "Like we would let him get hurt."

"You could always send Delta with us, if you want to keep Adam with you," said Rocky.

Epsilon shook his head and loosened his stiff stance, easing the tension in the air. "No, no. I apologize for my tone. I have spent a few nights in the boy's company and have grown unnaturally attached to the tiny thing."

Sela laughed. Epsilon shared his affronted look with Rocky, who shrugged.

Sela finally gained control of herself and waved a hand in a motion that seemed to placate Epsilon. "Humans call what you're feeling 'love', Epsilon. I am sorry, but it is funny to hear you being so paternal toward the young man."

The conversation ended shortly after that, with Epsilon questioning what Sela meant by paternal. She, of course, explained poorly, and Rocky stepped in, clarifying the phenomenon of parenthood and how the protective instinct could arise toward young offspring, even if the child wasn't your own or of your race.

Soon the parade of survivors was moving away from the Rocky's group as they went from carcass to carcass and looted.

Azoth and three Minion Golems followed Rocky. Behind him, the large creatures stomped along in unison with every tenth step of his. It was strange and surreal—he wasn't sure he'd ever get used to it.

Adam rode on Azoth's back, making occasional exclamations of delight as they progressed. The young man kept burrowing himself into the thick fur and feathers of the Chimera, and being the size that he was, the disparity was humorous enough. Add the fact that the kid could completely disappear into Azoth's fur—priceless. Everyone had a few hidden chuckles about it.

As Adam continued to hug the fluffy Azoth, Rocky asked, "Adam, how old are you, if you don't mind sharing?"

The boy buried his head in Azoth's fuzzy fur-feathers and said, "I'm ten and a half." Azoth sported one of the largest cat grins Rocky had ever seen. Rocky reached out and scratched his friend, who had instantly made the kid feel like he had a best friend.

He left the two new buddies to their shenanigans, reaching to touch the corpse of the rat-wolf he had first killed and thought 'loot.'

Rat-Hide Cloak
- **This cloak is exquisitely crafted and seems to be far more robust and durable than most other materials.**
  Quality: Good
  Enchantments: Locked

He put the item into his bag and then collected the entire corpse. The arm of the nearest Minion Golem twitched for a moment, then adjusted to the added weight, seeming unbothered by the addition of the third corpse.

He nodded in relief and considered the other three items the creatures had dropped. A few other corpses had dropped a piece of gear. They were all affixed with 'Rat-Hide' for a different part of the body. He secretly hoped that they had some sort of set property, like the Ring from Bam-Bam the Ogre. His mouth soured at the thought of Derik owning the other part of that set. He probably should invite the exiles back to the Grotto. Maybe without Derik.

He approached the bloody puddle and bones of what remained of Azoth's Batwing Bird meal. He gingerly touched the bones and received:

Rat-Hide Helm

- **This helm is exquisitely crafted and seems to be far more robust and durable than most other materials.**

  Quality: Good

  Enchantments: Locked

His mouth twisted as he inspected the stiffened helm. It looked like a rugby cap, and the thought of wearing the scratchy Rat-Hide on his head made him feel sick. This corpse also awarded him five Crystals.

Maybe I can award this armor to someone and buy myself an Ether-Tech helm.

He didn't pull the remains of the bird into his bag of holding. Instead, he jogged to inspect the two creatures that the Knights had downed. He received twenty more Crystals and a pair of boots from looting both of them. After placing one of the corpses into his bag, the other body refused to enter into the container.

He opened his notifications to find that the bag was full. That was an exciting development, and when they returned to the Grotto, he would have to empty everything to determine the approximate size of the space within. He was able to put the boots and Crystals inside, so he knew it had some space remaining, but not enough to add the monster's prodigious corpse.

Much to his disappointment, they left three corpses behind. Before leaving, Rocky removed a bird corpse and replaced it with a rat-wolf's larger, meatier one. Then the group of three mounted up on Azoth, joining Adam.

Sela spoke with Azoth, worried that the weight would bother him. However, the added weight of the boy hadn't phased the Chimera in the least. The real problem was with the available space to sit.

***

For the remainder of the journey, Sela sat in front of
Rocky in the saddle. She was pressed tightly to his chest, and his
arms wrapped over her to grip the tethering rope. He had once
given Sela a piggyback and found that distracting, and now his
brain wanted to categorize every sensation this new closeness
entailed.

When the group returned to the Grotto later that
afternoon, he wasn't sure if he was disappointed to dismount or
relieved. They had saved three of the towns from starvation, but
the fourth one had not needed help.

They arrived in Minden last, and Rocky immediately
knew something was different. From Azoth's back, the group
only found two golems circling the perimeter of the school.

There were several prone golem corpses, with hundreds
of holes peppered into their Bio-Armor, but a quick Analysis
confirmed they were dead.

The golden thread led them to a primary school. A rush
of relief flooded Rocky when he saw a man on the roof duck for
cover. He was pretty sure a flying lion would send him into
hiding as well. Rocky, Adam, Zippo, and Sela took down the two
remaining golems in short order after dismounting Azoth.

Adam's Minion Golems were left in the trees a fair ways
from the school. A few other schools had reacted poorly to the
constructs, even after Rocky's assurances. This time, having seen
survivors doing so well, he didn't want to be considered an
enemy.

Sela told Azoth to go hunt. His pet jumped into the air,
and Rocky yelled, "You better answer our call to come back this
time, Featherbrain."

"He says, 'Know you are, what is Azoth?'" Sela relayed
with a chuckle.

He had to crack a smile himself; he hadn't heard that one in a long time. The group cautiously moved to the front doors of the school, when a voice shouted, stopping the group in their tracks.

"That's far enough. We don't have any food or supplies for you to steal. I thank you for taking care of those golems, but I think you should move on now."

Rocky heard a weapon cock, the sign of a clear threat. Shading his eyes against the low evening sun, he looked up and found the barrel of a rifle leveled at his chest. He wondered if he could survive a bullet. Hadn't he survived much worse? This was not the time to find out.

"We are here to offer food and support. We have been saving people in nearby towns, but you folks don't seem to need it. You are the first group to take out any of the golems ringing the compound. At least, so far. Very impressive," Rocky said, raising his hands placatingly.

Doran Hetch
Apprentice-Sharpshooter
Level 24
Health Points 140 / 140

Doran hesitated before he safetied his rifle and pulled the muzzle up. Rocky breathed a soft sigh—he hadn't realized that he was holding his breath while the gun was pointed at him and his group.

"We can use food and water, for sure. Our supplies are running mighty low. I'll meet you in the cafeteria."

"You heard the man," Rocky said. Sela and Adam followed him toward the school doors. Rocky paused when Zippo didn't move to join them.

"Zippo?"

Rocky followed Zippo's gaze to a large number of freshly churched mounds of dirt. Graves. He counted sixty of them. These survivors weren't doing as well as he had thought.

They opened the doors and discovered the air inside the school wasn't rank and fetid, like others they had visited. As they made their way through the halls, following the signs to the cafeteria, Rocky noted signs of habitation, but no people. With each step, Rocky's shoulders inched upward, his muscles tightening.

They found two men with rifles in the cafeteria. One was Doran, and Rocky Analyzed the other.

Simon Hetch
Apprentice-Bullet Smith
Level 24
Health Points 190/190

The two men stood in front of a pantry door that, while depleted, still contained food. Something was off, and Rocky slowed his walk.

"Where is everyone?"

Both men looked at each other and Simon pointed toward the graves outside. "We buried them."

"What happened to them?" asked Rocky.

This time Doran answered, his voice just above a whisper, "We killed them."

Rocky wasn't sure he heard correctly. The sadness in the man's tone didn't match his statement. "What did you just say?" His anger was flaring white-hot.

Sela stepped in front of him and put a hand on his chest. "Stop right now. Let them tell their story."

"About two weeks back, the group realized we only had enough food left for a few days. We were on the verge of starving. So, we mustered the courage and attacked those golem creatures from inside the school." Doran sniffed and wiped his nose, tears streaming down his cheeks. "We couldn't do anything to them. There were forty-nine of us then, and even combined, our Skills just splashed against them. We had all been hunting and leveling together before they trapped us here. So, everyone was equal at around level twelve."

Simon picked up the explanation then. "You need to understand. We hadn't seen another human in a month and didn't even know how many of us still lived. We didn't think anyone was going to come to help us—"

Doran placed a hand on his brother's shoulder. "My brother and I killed them all, to save our supplies and last longer, but mostly—so we could get stronger Skills that might stand a chance of letting us escape."

Rocky's first thought was to kill them. He formed Dark Tidings into a menacing blade. The brothers leveled their rifles at him.

"Rocky, stop. Take a second to think. While they killed the others, they didn't really have a choice," said Sela.

Every emotion he had fired signals to his brain. He wasn't sure if it was his tangled Chidi or the proper reaction to the situation. "Sela, these men killed forty-seven people for their own gain. They buried them in graves just over there."

Both guns cocked. "You two, put your weapons down now. Or I will let him kill you both! You offer even the hint of a threat against anyone in this room, and any amnesty I have for you will evaporate. You have three seconds," Sela said. The guns lowered a heartbeat later.

"Good. Now, Rocky, I am not pleading their innocence. I am highlighting their necessity. Every other group we helped today was in a bad place. They couldn't have survived long without us. These two would have. When the option is life and death, some moral lines drawn in the sand need to be swept away on the tide." Sela laid a restraining hand on his forearm.

Forty-seven people. That was a rip current. "What, you want me to excuse their murders because they will survive because of them? That's like saying starvation gives someone carte blanche for murder!" Rocky screamed as rage boiled in his chest.

Sela pointed to the two men. "No. Don't lessen their suffering, Rocky. This isn't a city where a starving man can beg for food. This isn't safe. This is the wilderness. There was no help for these men. Make no mistake, they faced certain death."

He escalated the stakes in his mind. His teeth creaked from his straining jaws' pressure. If a human was attacked and fought back for fear of their life, the old world had a name for it. Self-defense. Did this situation fall under that umbrella?

No. It didn't. Did it land in a morally grey area?

Maybe on the very fringe. Rocky stared at Sela. She shrugged. "Weigh all of the factors. Death is final, and I don't think these men deserve it."

His stomach lurched. He hated that she made sense. Could he condemn people to death for something that they had needed to do?

He dropped a week's worth of rations onto the floor, then moved to pour some water into the sink. He turned to both men. "I won't condemn you to death, but I also won't claim what you did was right. You two have to live with that decision, not me. However, I am going to give you a week. Then I am going to send a patrol through here. If you two are still in this school or the area, they will have orders to try you for your actions. I don't ever want to see either of you again. Do you understand me?"

He didn't bother waiting for a reply. He gathered Adam and Zippo and stormed out of the school.

He felt a little less human as they flew away. In the early days, he would have immediately condemned the individuals to death.

***

The Kingston survivors had made it to the Grotto before them, which was cause for celebration.

Rocky opened his interface to check the current numbers of citizens within the Grotto and grinned. Sixty-three hundred and forty-two souls resided within Algonquin Valley—his Territory. That number would soon grow, as more and more survivors arrived.

He emptied his Bag of Holding, leaving only the Bottle of Gaia's Essence inside the Ethereal space. He was unsure of its worth, but he wasn't stupid enough to lack the understanding that it was immense. The contents of the bag surprised him, and he estimated its interior would hold goods in amounts roughly equivalent to the interior of the Guild Tent. He gazed up to the flapping fabric still speared atop the black-scaled tower.

Honestly, how do you get something like that down from way up there? We never spent much time in the observatory, but I bet that stupid tent blocks the view.

He methodically sorted through the corpses and contents from the bag, stowing the bodies in the Territorial Inventory and smiling at the thought that the butchers would be in for a surprise. He secretly wished he could hide in stealth near the Butcher's yard to see the reaction when the corpses were pulled out. They had probably never carved up something this big.

But a leader couldn't spend much time in such frivolous ways. He placed the Enchanter's pen, mortar, and pestle back into the bag, along with all the new gear.

With all of the organization out of the way, he checked his waiting notifications to find he had reached level eight. After a full day of questing and fighting, he couldn't believe that he had only managed a single level.

Come on. Did the system not see the size of those monsters? And their teeth? I had pee in my mouth, for Gaia's sake! That alone should be worth a level.

Rockland Barkclay Level 8

Class: Journeyman-Dark Chimera Knight

Level 3 Strategist

Class Skills: Dark Blade, Dark Mend, Soul Blade, Dark Cloak, Shadow Clone, Knight's Resolve, Knight's Quest

Health Points = 420/420

Dark Ether Pool = 280/280

You have 1 stat point and 0 skill points to distribute.

Stamina – 42 (Strength of Body +9) (+4 Stat V)

Strength – 44 (Strength of Arms +18) (+4 Stat V)

Agility – 51 (+4 Stat V)

Dexterity – 51 (+6) (+4 Stat V)

Intelligence – 28 (+4 Stat V)

Wisdom – 43 (+4 Stat V)

Charisma – 45 (+4 Stat V)

Luck – 12

Non-Class Combat Skills: Ether Cleanse - 10

Common Skills: Barter – 8, Camouflage – 7, Fall – 3 (+2), Tracker – 19

Profession Skills: Actor – 5, Cook – 2, Grooming – 6 (+3), Herbalist – 19, Miner – 1, Teacher – 20, Trader – 5

Moderate Skills

Non-Class Combat Skills: Combatant – 11, Ether Channels – 4 (+1), Ether Manipulation 5 (+1) , Stealth – 15 (+2), Swordsmanship – 14 (+5)

Common Skills: Analyze – 20 (+2), Endurance – 1 (+2), Perception –

12 (+1) Sneak – 19, Trance
Meditation – 4 (+2)
Profession Skills: Butcher – 1, Skinner – 1

The only good news with the slowdown in leveling was that his stats of Stamina, Strength, Wisdom and Charisma were approaching the breakthrough point. He shuddered as he considered going through that kind of pain—and humiliation—again. The issue there was how to best breakthrough in certain stats. From earlier conversations, he knew Stamina and Strength were paired, and Intelligence and Wisdom were also paired.

Charisma and Luck were paired, but they were spiritual stats and likely didn't cause the same physical 'breakthrough.' At least he hoped they didn't. One of the big issues on his stat page was the massive gap between his low Intelligence score and his Wisdom score, which was about to hit fifty points. Luckily, it appeared that his Enchantment boots counted toward the breakthrough point.

I can use that.

He decided to save his stat points for the moment so he could force the breakthrough when he wanted it. It was looking like he'd have to spend a lot of Crystals soon on gear that would force breakthroughs, to ensure he stayed in balance. Rocky broke into a cold sweat as he walked. Leveling mid-battle and receiving his assigned stat points could break him through and cause those convulsions at a very dangerous moment.

Okay, first goal is to ensure that never happens.

Rocky shook off his worries as he entered the Tower. He continued down the hallway toward the elevator to receive a few updates from Smith.

Smith, Sela, and the five Golem Knights were deep in discussion, secreted down a different hallway, when he arrived. His eyes narrowed. Why hadn't they waited for him? Why hadn't they told him they would meet?

He chased those thoughts away when he saw Sela.

"Rocky, the operators assigned to the monitors upstairs found the console that lists people who are still alive. Everyone wants—"

He was already running toward the elevator.

CHAPTER FOURTEEN

Rocky stood in the elevator, pushing the Operation Room button each time his heart lurched. His jaw was clenched and he was sweating like he had run a marathon—not the thirty feet to the elevator.

"Calm down, Rocky. Pushing the button won't speed up the Elevator." Sela said. She rubbed his back.

Rocky took in a deep lungful of air, then bit his tongue to stop himself from what came next. He was going to scream at her, and he knew she was just trying to help. She just needed to stop taking charge in every situation. Especially ones she didn't understand, like right now.

Also, an unfair assessment, which he recognized distantly. Stupid emotional web.

If only he didn't dread the end of the elevator ride. He needed answers to a question that had dogged him since Gaia hit reset. But he was afraid he might not like the answer he got.

You aren't angry with Sela. Just don't search their names. I'm better off not knowing—but I need the closure if they aren't still out there. Gahhh.

He clicked the up button like a machine gun.

The doors opened to the Control Room floor, and all but Rocky exited. Sweat dripped down his brow, and he tasted the salt of it in his mouth.

"You ready for this, Rockland?" Sela's eyes filled with tears that threatened to spill over.

No. The answer was definitely no. Still, her words successfully unstuck his feet from the ground, and he managed to place one foot in front of the other. His stomach clenched tight enough that he thought it was halfway up his throat. He licked his lips and tasted even more salt.

He scanned the room to find Smith standing near a station and looking back at him. Sela took his hand, and together, they walked over.

He knew that if he tried to speak a sentence, he would break. Then he would be crying, and they would never respect him as a leader.

"Barclay," he choked out. Sweat misted off his lips from the one word. He prayed that they would understand.

The woman at the computer typed in the surname he had given her. The results returned, and he was looking at a list of twenty individuals. None of them were named Nadine, Benoit, or Lacy.

He almost tipped into a dark place, one that would never release him once it sunk its fangs into him. Wait—his mother had kept her maiden name, and his sister had married—taking her husband's last name. He tried again, "Shealds," hoping for a better result.

Please be there. Please be there.

The woman typed in 'Shields' and he stopped her hand from hitting the search button. He reached over her shoulder to correct her spelling. His fingers left wet marks on the screen, and the woman wiped them away as he stepped back. He hadn't hit the enter key. He couldn't.

Sela squeezed his shoulder.

The screen populated, and this time, fourteen people were listed. He immediately saw his mother Nadine and his legs crumpled under him. He grabbed the table and his forearms left puddles on the surface. He held on for dear life, not wanting to slip. He read the whole entry. Name, Class, Rank, and Level. There was no location listed, and he had no way of knowing where she could be.

His stomach, still in his throat, did a somersault. Tears joined the sweat on his face. He nodded vigorously, trying to get his body to unclench his larynx. He had one more search to make. He wasn't able to speak. He released his death grip with one hand and reached past the woman. He typed in three letters. 'Obi.' This time, he hit enter and watched as names appeared on the screen.

Forty-two names scrolled across the screen, listed alphabetically, just like the last search. He scanned the alphabetical area Benoit should have been. No one named Benoit was registered. His second arm gripped the edge of the desk and he swayed. His arms slipped in the sweat and he collapsed.

His body convulsed, and he fought it. He had lost one of his loved ones, and it hurt. Benoit had been one of the good ones, a man who had come into his sister's life and brought joy. Rocky had loved him and considered him a true brother.

Sela knelt down and hugged him, hard. She whispered, "I am so sorry."

His eyes met Smith's. "Lacy?"

Smith jumped forward and scrolled down the list. "There is a Lacy here."

Sela hugged him, and he let the convulsions take him. His body jerked around like a fish in shallow water, completely beyond his control. He cried, in sorrow and in joy. Two of his family still lived.

Each beat of his heart solidified an iron core of resolve. "Two of them are alive, Sela," he said.

He would find them. They could be starving to death in one of a million schools out there, but he would find them.

CHAPTER FIFTEEN

Rocky finally got control of himself. He stood with Sela still hanging off his neck. She squeaked, and he softly disentangled her with a whispered, "Thank you."

He felt heat suffuse his cheeks and turned away. Back to the screen. He hadn't looked at the top of the screen during his initial rush. Now, he looked at it and saw the multiple tabs displayed for them to select.

- **Planetary Leaderboards**
- **Guild Leaderboards**
- **Hall of Fame**
- **Monster Compendium**
- **Atlantean News**
- **Search**

"Have you looked at any of these other tabs?" asked Rocky.

"I looked at each one briefly before realizing we could search names. Since then, there has been a non-stop request to check on loved ones," said the woman behind the desk.

"Would you mind?" he asked the woman at the computer station. There were so many things he needed to find out. First up, he needed to recruit other active combatants for the upcoming invasion. The outstanding question from Michabo twirled around in his head. With Sela in the room, he decided he'd wait to look that up when he was alone.

He sat down on the wood stump the woman had occupied and began clicking through the tabs.

He started with the Leaderboards and found that the names near the top were dominated by Master rank classes. The top forty names on the list almost all contained 'Mechano' in their class titles. The top two individuals were both Master rank and had Classes of Death Knight and Paladin, respectively. They both shared the same last name. Maybe they were related, like brothers or something?

The top leveled Mechano-Lord was named Ernest. Rocky felt his heart pound and his body flush with heat. Eight of the names on the grouping were greyed out. Included in that list was Corsair, the sadistic leader of Ottawa. Sela squeezed his shoulder again, and his skin broke out in goosebumps.

The list stretched to the top 100, and the next group of Journeyman ranks had no Mechano titled classes. That didn't mean too much, but it did say something. He scrolled and found Sela, Zippo, and himself listed in the nineties. They were all level eight after the day's events.

He clicked Guild Leaderboards next and found only 'Meliora' listed. The guild tent was expensive, and that likely meant people were opting to build the Guild Hall later. Still, the benefits he was currently seeing, like sharing escort quests, Etherience taxation, NPC leveling and more, were just so helpful. Ninety-nine percent of the human population was missing out on those features, and Rocky's throat clenched. The human race needed to be stronger to repel The Guild Collective.

Another problem to add to his ongoing list.

He browsed through the other tabs quickly and didn't find any information in two of them—just more options to narrow the search parameters.

Hall of Fame had different areas to search through, but he didn't want to get into them with Sela present. Monster Compendium asked the user to define what type of monster they were attempting to find.

Atlantean News brimmed with archived Newspapers. The most recent edition had the headline "This is the End!"

He wanted to scan through that article and perhaps the other archived days that led up to whatever had happened. His curiosity would have to wait another day as a runner entered the room and placed a knowledge tablet on the station, complete with a list of searches. He glanced at it, stood up, and thanked the woman for allowing him to use the station.

Once she was seated again, the group moved away, and Rocky asked Smith, "Anything else to add?"

"Yes. We have been monitoring the satellite feed, and it is currently over South America. We have found some cities that seem to have cleared out the majority of golems and are collecting survivors to bring back to their Territory, like us. We also found some alarming—creatures." As he explained, he walked to the satellite station and nodded to the operator stationed there.

The screen zoomed in on a mountain. "Is it moving?" asked Sela.

Smith nodded. "It seems to be created from asphalt, and we have found quite a few of these monsters out there. Our current theory is that they are converted interstate highways and connected roads. If the Satellite sizing is correct, they seem to be on par with the Rocky Mountains."

Rocky gulped audibly and scanned all the faces in the Control Room. Every face was pale. Each pair of eyes pinned to Sela and Rocky. Was it comfort they wanted, or assurances that these things weren't a threat?

Rocky couldn't provide either, so he tapped the operator and motioned at the zoom out button. "Any good news, Smith?'

"Some of these other stations seem to tie into defenses for the Territory, Grotto, and Planet. However, since we have none of these, we aren't entirely sure. Finally, we have ensured that all escort quests have been shared with all guild members. On a side note, the military is currently cut in half to complete these requests. The council has asked that you and Sela attempt to find a ship. They don't want to spread our military too thin."

"They are scared to send out too much of the military?" asked Sela. "We are going to see Garnell in an hour. Right now, we are going to be taking an Elixir of Shortened Sleep. You should probably join us, Smith. At the shop, as well."

"We can likely handle it ourselves. I mean, Smith has quite a bit to do here," Rocky said.

Sela looked at Rocky pointedly. "It would be good to have a third person there, if nothing else, to confuse Amelia." Her look conveyed more than the words. She wanted Smith there for something else. Why wouldn't she just say it?

"Okay. I guess that's true," Rocky said. He would see how this played out.

Smith headed toward the elevator. "I will need to find someone to handle my post. Let me get Mr. Pips or Bart."

The group rode the elevator down, and Zippo hesitantly asked, "Can I come with you three into the shop as well?"

Rocky nodded 'yes' as Sela shook her head 'no'. If Sela was going to bring Smith. Rocky was going to bring Zippo.

Rocky spoke quickly. "Both of you need to find a disguise to wear into the shop that hides your body and face. You aren't to speak until we have a private room. Do you understand?"

Sela raised a questioning eyebrow. He shrugged at her as Zippo began bouncing on his toes. Rocky couldn't fill the fatherly role that Zippo needed. Joe had done that for him before he died. Now Rocky saw Smith and the boy bonding, and he hoped this would strengthen that connection.

Zippo saw their unspoken conversation. "Don't worry, guys. I got this."

Both Smith and Zippo split off on the ground floor. Sela and Rocky approached the Golem Knights, hoping they weren't interrupting a personal meeting. Epsilon motioned to Gamma and Tao, who opened the circle, making it inclusive instead of closed-off.

"Glad to see you are back safely, Rockland, Selaphelia." Epsilon greeted them with a nod of the head. Rocky was surprised to hear the proper pronunciation of Sela's name. He would have to work on it himself if Epsilon was going to show him up.

"Adam has returned with the group you brought in. We have a meeting in the shop, but we wanted to check in and discover your plans moving forward."

Epsilon looked to his fellow warriors. Each Knight nodded—they were ready to take anything on.

With the last member's acknowledgement, Epsilon said, "We wish to help with the surrounding villages, but we think that there is another way." He stared intently at both of them, taking a deep breath and explaining, "We think we should attempt the larger towns as a group. By targeting large towns, the Knights would stay together. We also think that, in this way, you may find additional Territories."

"You said you couldn't capture Territories? Why the change of heart?" Sela asked. She never gave Rocky a second to get his own question in.

"Logically, we have assumed Gaia did not want us to capture Territories. We also believe we cannot hold them. However, the predicament of finding humans and needing to escort them all back to one place is not going to be easy. Having multiple Territories under your control will make the task far easier" said Delta.

The return of Smith with Bart in tow signaled the conversation's end.

"We will talk about this more tomorrow morning," said Rocky.

Bart was complaining about having to do more work, and Smith expertly countered every point. Zippo sprinted toward them. wearing a blanket like a robe. The front of the quilt shadowed his face. "Go take your Elixir of Shortened Sleep and put your blanket back on your bed, you goof," said Rocky.

He chuckled at the boy's antics before turning to Smith. "Is yours just as bad?"

Smith bared his teeth and pulled on his collar.

CHAPTER SIXTEEN

After waking up from the Elixir of Shortened Sleep, Rocky, Sela, Zippo, and Smith made their way to the shop.

Garnell was momentarily confused when four kimono-garbed, fox-masked Beastfolk appeared, but a casual hand gesture from Rocky had put him at ease.

The trader invited the four of them and their disguises into the more expensive sales room.

Rocky liked this room a lot better. Mesh backed chairs surrounded a beautifully polished table. The smell of wood and leather dominated the room. But how much of that was real?

They were in the shop, after all. Just projected images.

Sela got down to some business while they waited for Amelia to arrive. "This is Smith and Zippo... We are attempting to find the best transport ship available in the shop. Any ideas, Garnell?"

Garnell considered the question, and waited a long time before giving an answer. "The technology available in most shops is obsolete sell-offs. That doesn't mean I can't find ye something serviceable, but defensible?" He stroked his chin. "Ye are meeting with Amelia; ye may want to voice that question to her, since it is in her best interest to help your defense."

Smith shared a glance with Sela, and she nodded. Rocky did not understand the significance until Smith asked, "What does she know about transport ships?"

"The wee lady has a very unique class, and because of it—the lass is very up to date on technology. But it isn't my place to share her secrets with ye. Just like it is not my place to share yer secrets with her."

They continued to wait, and Rocky couldn't help but wonder if the Iridescent Kobold could truly help?

A tiny figure popped into the room and scampered onto a seat. Once the small rainbow snout poked above the table,

Amelia wasted no time. "What in the ninth tunnel has taken you all so long?" She glanced around the table.

"The fleet left going on a week ago and is deeply into the Etherless Void. Now, though, they have a bearing and are heading toward your planet at full speed. You have just over a year before they arrive. That's not even the bad news! With the beacon, they already have access, which allows them to control their constructs."

Rocky gritted his teeth and considered the leaderboard. At their first meeting, Amelia had mentioned Floridians. Unfortunately, where in Florida would be much harder to locate.

When we get back, I will tell the people watching the satellite to begin searching.

Amelia continued, "I have been keeping a close eye on their captain's logs. Early on, they sent out ships to check on planets as they passed—" she licked her snout, "—and they examined nine planets, all of them entirely devoid of life. Dahrix then set off bombs filled with poison gas on those planets—"

"I understand that this is news to you, and to the Guild Collective. However, without Ether, planets will die." Sela's voice snapped like a whip. "Please keep monitoring the situation, but I think the possibility of them finding a planet still alive will be more of a surprise. Especially with the length of time—we estimate for the Ether to have been missing."

"They speak," said Amelia. "The Guild Collective has run countless experiments, attempting to uncover the age of the Etherless Void. I would be extremely interested in how long your 'theories' estimate."

There was no doubt in Rocky's mind—that was a tone of condescension. The tension in the room shot up an octave.

"We are not estimating, I assure you," said Rocky, trying to stop the conversation before it devolved. Rocky knew just how sharp Sela's tongue could be. One more scathing remark from

Sela, and the discussion would surely amplify into a shouting match.

The fox mask that hid Sela's face glanced at him, and he couldn't tell what was going on behind it. He shrugged. She did this to him all the time. But he did consider—perhaps she had been about to respond calmly, after all.

"I have trouble believing those words." The iridescent Kobold glanced at Sela's form and added, "I apologize for my tone, but how could you be confident of your assessment? We know that it has been there for thousands of years, and I have never heard of a race that is long-lived at your reported low-levels."

"The existence of the Etherless Void dates further back than that. Have the Guilds never discovered mention of the Etherless Void in literature?"

Amelia eyed Sela up and down, sizing her up. Cautiously, she said, "Actually, the Guilds believe that they have the most extensive records of the Void. Their—my planet is the closest to the edge of the void. How could you possibly know more than they have gathered in thousands of years?"

Rocky again saw the storm coming, but this time chose to let the little Kobold suffer it. "You haven't asked the Martians or Humans about the Void, then?" Sela said scorn lacing the words.

Amelia's eyes went wide, and she glanced directly at Garnell. "Are you telling me that my theories about the Void stemming from the Humans or Martians was correct?"

Garnell shrugged and indicated the four who sat across the table. "Perhaps, if ye asked them that question…"

Amelia stared daggers at Garnell, then snapped her focus back to Sela. "What would you like in trade for more information?"

Sela remained silent, and as it stretched, Rocky felt more and more uncomfortable.

"We know that any help you offer us is also helping yourself…" As soon as he said it, he could feel satisfaction radiating from his Ancestral companion.

"I thought you said that this lizard had the knowledge we needed?" asked Smith.

"I thought we needed a ship from her?" asked Zippo.

The tension broke, and Amelia smiled at Zippo's form. Sela stood up and walked behind the young man. She whispered something in his ear, and Rocky couldn't be sure, but it seemed that the shoulders of his friend slightly drooped.

"Am I to take it that you don't have space-capable ships strong enough to repel the incoming invasion?" Amelia asked, tenting her scaly fingers together below her chin.

Sela sat back down and folded her hands. Amelia studied the human hands that protruded from the robes, and Rocky wondered if this was an intentional move by his guide.

"What we are truly looking for is a ship to study. We wish to know what to expect from the enemy," Sela said after a moment.

The Kobold studied Sela's long, intertwined fingers. "This, I can provide. My race is hiding deep underground, but we have the blueprints for every ship the Guild Collective has ever built or purchased."

"While blueprints are part of it, a ship or two that demonstrates the capabilities of the approaching fleet would save time," Rocky said.

"Do not worry about time. Maybe you didn't hear me earlier, but the beacon's coordinates indicate nearly the entire Nebula. It's actually hard to pinpoint the exact location of the signal. I would say you have at least a year to prepare. Likely more."

"Do you not have any ships to offer, then?" Sela stood up, ready to port out of the meeting.

Smith and Zippo followed her lead, and Rocky pushed his chair back.

"Yes, of course, we have some ships. I just figured you would rather build one yourself. If you wish to save time—I can understand that. A completed ship or multiple ships will cost you in trade," Amelia said, raising a hand to forestall them.

The conversation continued along this path, each group attempting to gain the upper hand in the negotiations. Sela and the others sat back down after a time. Finally, the terms of the agreement were laid out, and Sela removed her mask as part of a concession.

Amelia didn't seem as surprised by Sela's appearance after the negotiations. When the mask came down, she said, "This makes me more confident that you might know as much as you claim about the Etherless Void, human."

The agreement was for Rocky's Territory to work with Amelia and her people. They agreed to share information and attempt to destabilize the Guilds from two ends of conflict.

"This, and everything that follows, is shared in confidence." Sela paused to look at Garnell, who nodded. "We can probably discover the exact age of the Void once we are back to our Territory. However, I can guarantee it has been present for at least a billion years."

Seeing Amelia's mouth fall open was satisfying.

"I understand your skepticism, but the Planetary God we reside on is over 2 billion years old, according to the evidence. We will confirm this information as well. The Planetary Gods you claim eldest are but children to Gaia." Sela pulled out her Knowledge Tablet and pointed to it. "The ancient or dead languages on these devices were once commonly spoken in this Solar System."

"Is it true, then, that the Seraphim Seven, the Martian Hive, the Asgardians, and many other strong factions originated from the Void?" Amelia asked in amazement.

Rocky squeezed Sela's shoulder. "I can assure you at least some of those groups originated from this very planet."

Amelia clapped her hands excitedly, her greed on full display. "Is there any chance that they will come to your aid in this fight?"

"I don't think they are even aware of our return. I am unsure if this information will garner aid or destruction from said forces," Sela admitted.

Her old guild, Cathodiem, likely had some ties to the Seraphim Seven, if her reaction and his gut were any indication. The fact that her first thought wasn't to contact them spoke volumes of her recent discoveries.

Rocky needed to look further into Michabo's accusations.

"Now that I have agreed to purchase and provide you with a Shop Warehouse, a ship, and blueprints. What sort of fleet can you muster on your end?" Amelia demanded.

"That one ship will be the first of our fleet. We have a Territory and plans to capture many more in the upcoming days. We should be able to build some defenses and gather support before the invasion," Sela said.

Sela's words didn't appease Amelia's growing anger. "This is what you brought me? Then you stood by during this agreement. You Katydid!" She sneered at Garnell and transferred the look to Sela. "You four better have a good motive for this. Explain."

Rocky took the lead and was helped along by all attendees—including Zippo. Amelia asked many questions throughout the conversation and seemed truly impressed with the number of humans that had survived the apocalypse—and the number who had perished. She didn't entirely change her mood, but by the end of his story, she had at least considered their logic.

When they reached the end of the story, Amelia asked, "How many do you think can reach Master class or higher in the next year?"

Sela tilted her head back and forth and said, "I believe quite a few. According to the Planetary Leaderboards, two already exist, and at least forty approach 'The Grind.' If that's what we have in a month, I would guess there will even be a few who make Epic rank before the year is over."

"You have access to the Planetary System already?" Amelia stroked her snout. "That is certainly a development. If you could guarantee the participation of all those fighters, you would easily be a match for the Guilds' invasion force. They have one Epic rank, Darhix, with them, approximately forty thousand Master ranks, and at least two hundred thousand who are Journeyman and below."

She tapped her claws on the polished wood table. "They have brought with them a considerable amount of weaponry and ships, which will make your task extremely difficult. They also have the Mechano-Lord's conversion seeds, which can create instantaneous high-level troops for their cause."

The meeting continued for approximately an hour, and another time was scheduled for a follow-up. Amelia purchased the Guild Warehouse from Garnell, which paid for the use of the room. The Warehouse was another metal box the size of a refrigerator.

"Once you have this set up, I will sell you your ship for one Crystal. We both have some work to do. I will expect a progress report at the next meeting," said Amelia before she winked out of the room.

Rocky placed the metal box in his Bag of Holding. He removed his mask and said, "Thanks for all your help, Garnell. Everything you have heard here was in confidence, right?"

Garnell's mustache twitched. "I will have to share the news of the Ether returning to the Void. However, the return of yer planet will not escape me mouth. Ye have me word."

"When will you have to share that news?" asked Sela.

Garnell frowned and whispered, "Today." Then spoke louder, "They will hear within the week, anyway, of the Guild Collective fleet. I am sorry." He scratched his beard and said, "but Amelia shared this information as part of a separate agreement."

Rocky and the others abruptly arrived back in the Seed Shop. The room they occupied had enlarged itself to fit the four of them, creating a larger pie-shaped space. It was strange to think that their bodies just stood in this room the entire time— like coats on a hanger waiting for them to put them back on. He shivered.

The dark of night greeted them as they exited the structure. The only illumination in the Grotto came from the windows of the powered buildings.

Note to self—get some street lamps.

Victoria ran up to them. Saluting Smith, she said, "The council wishes to meet immediately; they are already waiting at the bonfire."

"Why at the bonfire?" asked Rocky.

"The golems are being included in the meeting."

Smith saluted Victoria, signaling her dismissal. Rocky moved to the side of the Seed Shop and placed the Shop Warehouse in a position opposite the Citizen Accessible Shop, and the structure started to grow. The sight of the Arbuckle expanding never got old for him or the others. Before they left for the meeting, they took a quick look through the new building.

The interior was nearly identical to most warehouses Rocky had seen in his lifetime. The major difference was the lack of workers within. However, the warehouses before the apocalypse had been moving in this automated direction. The door also had a security option to gain access, which only listed Sela and himself.

Once the building had finished expanding, the group made their way to the meeting site, and Zippo split off tiredly, mumbling about arranging food. The kid always needed something to eat, and Rocky had to agree with the sentiment. These meetings were bad enough, so eating would at least be some help. He hoped this one wouldn't last all night.

The council had prepared a substantial argument for why the golems and the military couldn't be absent simultaneously from the Grotto. When they heard about the destroyer class ship that would be arriving the following day, the argument was dropped.

Instead, the group discussed what areas needed to be freed first. North Bay was placed atop the list, followed by Toronto. The council hoped one of them would turn out to contain a Territory that would be conquerable.

Ottawa also became a hot topic, as the broken beacon was a constant reminder of an eventual threat.

The meeting finished in two hours, and they now had a plan for the next week. During the time spent freeing the prioritized areas, the ship would be taking Adam and small strike forces to clean up the small towns listed by the System-generated quests.

It was like a weight had lifted from his shoulders... right up until Bart suggested, "Perhaps we can use these Territorial Ether Points to create more ships faster?"

The rest of the council agreed and Rocky promised to look into it. His heart, however, was either frozen or beating so fast that it hurt. As soon as the meeting ended, he motioned Sela to follow him. He walked to a vastly empty expanse in the Grotto. He didn't want the news of Amber getting out. "Sela, we can't let them spend the Ether points. Otherwise, we will never save enough to resurrect Amber."

"Rockland, I know how you feel, but they don't know about Amber. So, of course, the most logical use of this resource is to raise up our defenses. I think there are other options to create defenses in the Grotto that we should be considering."

Rocky was nearly speechless. She had pushed for the connection, and now she was suggesting other uses for the Ether?

He tried again. "We need to come up with some believable story as to why we can't spend these points. I will not allow Amber to be sacrificed to the Spirit Realm."

"I am not suggesting we spend the points, Rockland. I am simply pointing out better uses of building time and resources that may be available. However, we cannot lie to them. Your suggestion of making something up is atrocious. Either we admit to them the decision we made, or we allow them to spend the points. Lying to hide a logical decision will only create larger problems."

Heat suffused every limb of his body. He closed his eyes and sucked air in through his nose. Trying to keep his mouth closed. Trying to avoid shouting. Sela had suggested the decision, even pushed for it. Michabo's words returned to his thoughts. Did Sela not want other strong women alive?

He opened his eyes, in control once again. "Sela, we have already omitted this information. That is lying, no matter how you spin it. Why aren't you willing to do anything to bring Amber back?"

Sela's mouth set into a firm line and she squared her shoulders. He couldn't help but take a step back from the storm brewing in her eyes. Her finger jabbed him in the chest, her fury penetrating through the layers of armor and Nanoweave, and he flinched.

After her second prod, she hissed, "Are you questioning my morals? Or questioning my loyalty?" She jabbed him again. "Omission is something a *true* leader must do, Rockland, and you must learn the lines you are pushing. An outright lie is a line that a leader should never cross. An omission can be rectified, but a lie will always remain a lie."

Her hand turned into a fist, and a tear traced its way down her cheek. "Without that connection to the Ethernet, how many would have died? And you are insinuating what? That I don't care about Amber?" She shot her fist into his chest and sobbed. "That I would dismiss her life so casually? You must think me a cold, unfeeling person. But I'm not surprised, after I practically throw myself at you, and you don't even notice, but this—perhaps it is you that is the callous and cold-blooded one."

Her words struck him harder than any physical attack she could have thrown. Then his brain played a montage of her taking the lead in situation after situation.

"You think *me* cold? Sela, I am trying so hard. One moment, you want me to be a leader, but then the next, you won't let me. You dismiss my input. You're holding meetings without me. Everyone always goes to you! Are you sure you want me to be a leader, or do you want that role for yourself? Make up your damn mind."

He clamped his mouth shut. His suspicions had just exploded out of him. He hadn't wanted to say all that.

Sela's face blanched and she stepped back. A tear traced down her cheek. She wiped it away. "I don't want you to be a leader, Rockland. These people need a leader. I thought you were it. But a leader can't just stand in front of people and demand the position. You need to earn it, something you haven't bothered to do yet."

"Earn it?" Rocky sputtered. "The system awarded me this Territory. I'm letting people stay here. To stay safe. You are here because I captured the Territory. I don't need your or anyone else's permission to be the leader of my own Territory."

She opened her hand, tears flowing down her cheek. Then she slapped him across the face. "How dare you! You just want me to be a tool. Do exactly as you say. I hoped you were better than that, Rockland. I hoped you saw me as something more."

The shock of her slap snapped him out of his stupidity. He stood there with his eyes closed, and he could feel Sela glaring at him. His head was spinning and cool tears ran down his burning cheeks. He had let his anger get the best of him. And not for the first time.

Eyes still closed, he opened his mouth and pleaded, "I am so sorry. I didn't mean—" His brain caught up to the conversation. He replayed her earlier words and his eyes flew open. "Wait, you threw yourself at me? You hope I see you as something more?"

"That's what you got from all of that?"

"You and I are related, Sela! You know, Ancestral guide and all?"

She scoffed. "We aren't even distantly related. Azrael was adopted into the Cathodiem Guild, and none of the nobility ever mixed with his line. Even if you were from my noble line of Selaphiel, it is common to marry within noble houses."

Rocky had only heard her admit they weren't related. He must have stood stunned for too long. By the time he regained the use of his primary brain, Sela had stormed off.

CHAPTER SEVENTEEN

Rocky hadn't felt like going back to his apartment in the Town Hall. There was too much to do. Contrary to the list of things he should be doing, though, he wandered at first, trying to come to terms with Sela's revelation.

If they weren't related in any way, did that change his feelings for her? Every part of him agreed that it did. He had been avoiding thinking of his feelings for her for so long. Now, he went through every interaction they ever had. From start to finish.

Her becoming his guide. Her laugh, when she played with Azoth. Her becoming his co-leader and gaining the druid class. Right up to her storming away.

Still, now the situation was muddy. He didn't know how to apologize to her. He fixated on that thought as he wandered, eventually weaving back through the tightly pressed buildings, then trudged back out into the open space still available to expand.

A black mound in the darkness made his mood tick up slightly. He triggered his Dark Cloak. He hadn't realized he was following his connection to the Chimera. Still, once his Dark Cloak increased his night vision, he could distinguish the massive sleeping form of Azoth.

He sat with his dozing friend and considered the future. From his vantage, he could see people moving around in the Longhouses. An upward head tilt allowed him to trace the lines of their newest tower and its spherical top. The Grotto was thriving, and tomorrow, the population would swell. It should have been a buoying thought, but the added responsibility made their other tasks all the more meaningful.

He pulled out the Enchanter's Kit. They needed to start being able to produce gear for themselves. As he turned the objects in his hand, he was reminded of his previous attempt.

And failure. What did he have that might add new information to this Enchanting problem?

A wave of euphoria flowed through his body as he remembered the locked gear. He pulled out the pieces of Rat-Hide gear and laid them out.

Slowing his breathing, he began his Meditation with ease. He studied the gear and found the typical patterns of swirling Ether he had observed in other Enchanted equipment.

He pulled the chest piece closer and studied the pattern. It was just like letters in an alphabet, but an alphabet he was only partially familiar with. Part of this pattern was definitely the Rune of Protection. However, the letter for Protection was more extensive and more stylized in some ways, while also linking to two other letters he didn't know.

Hesitantly, he reached out with a tendril of his own Ether and let it join the flow of the writing. He felt a phantasmal tug on his heart and almost released it, but soon, his Ether was following the path serenely. He could almost sense something, like a taste without substance. Like a sound without noise. A texture with no touch.

He allowed his Mediation to pour Ether into the channels of the gear, and the odd feeling grew. Then something began to crackle—almost fracture. He opened his eyes to inspect the equipment in the visual spectrum. It was similar to what he had seen Lingren do. Lingren had released the spell and let it work, and so Rocky let go of his external Ether. His pool dropped by one-hundred and sixty points, but the gear appeared to absorb it.

Congratulations! You have learned a new skill.
Enchanting
- **Enchanting is the study of runes and Ether flow. Many of the runes used in early Enchanting were found naturally in the wild. Each point in**

Enchanting increases the rune shaping of the individual by 1%.
Current level: Weak level 1.

He Analyzed the gear and was excited to find a change.

Rat-Hide Cloak
- **This cloak is exquisitely crafted and seems to be far stronger and durable than most other materials.**
  Ether Pool: Large
  Current Ether Pool: 01 / 110

Enchantments: 2 Locked, Protection V (40%)
Protection V (40%)
- **This protection Enchantment increases the gear's resistance to damage by forty percent on top of the material's inherent Ether protection.**

Find a shop or person capable of unlocking the gear to discover more.

He hadn't unlocked the entirety of the gear, and his elation dipped. He had to admit, he'd only studied the one Enchantment rune. He was confident that if he knew the other two, he could unlock the whole piece.

Not exactly a leap forward in Enchanting, but definitely a teachable step for citizens. His brain whirred with excitement from the discovery, and an idea began to take shape. His new enchanting skill seemed to hum, and he knew he was onto something.

He entered Meditation again and coerced a tendril of his internal Ether to coalesce. Opening the reservoir on the pen, he fed the tendril into the opening like it was ink. He pulled out a plain leather tunic and wrote the Protection rune onto the material. He continued to feed a stream of his Ether into the pen and watched it trail out the other side, much like using a ballpoint pen.

He felt his excitement rising as the letter seemed more solid. It even had a tube-like appearance, a thicker layer of Ether separating the interior from the exterior.

He finished with a bit of a flourish and released the tendril and Meditation as he opened his eyes. As he watched, the rune burned a perfectly black line into the tunic. It took longer than he expected, but it began to smolder and then catch fire. His head drooped as the euphoria fled. He carefully grabbed a corner and pulled the burning leather away from Azoth, carrying it over to a patch of rocky ground.

He returned to his previous state and watched the Ether tear the material apart. He was missing something, a medium that both adhered the Ether to the leather and protected it. What was he missing?

Something he could make with the mortar and pestle.

He meditated on the issue, and sighed as the Ether fire dwindled. His Ether began to escape the gear. He watched it float up into the air, and he was almost blinded by something in his peripheral vision.

As the tower glowed with a churning energy, his small patch of Ether dulled and was sucked into the spire.

Craning his neck, he walked toward the tower, continuing to Meditate as he followed the Ether's path. His Ether joined a spiral running down the outside of the tower before circling the dome languidly. He couldn't tell where it went after that, but he wanted to find out.

The doors opened automatically on his approach as he traced the lines of Ether converging onto the floor. The glowing lines ran in a large conduit down the center of the hallway. He followed the line to the mostly-vacant central Guild Hall, and the line began to spiral around the room.

The river traced the outer edge of the room, eventually joined by three other arteries. The spirals condensed, and the Ether within seemed to brighten and accelerate as the flow was obstructed. It reached its culmination point under the elevator shaft. Rocky watched with fascination as the energy flashed and almost disappeared.

Something pulsed up the tower and down into the ground simultaneously. He opened his Territory interface and climbed onto the elevator. The pulsing continued, almost like it was the Grotto's heartbeat.

He clicked the Control Room option, and the elevator doors closed. Each twentieth pulse seemed to add a Territorial Etherience to the funds available. Perhaps they could get Amber back faster. He continued to watch and calculate. The pulsing happened once every three to four seconds, and the extra tick of Territorial Etherience was every twentieth beat. Approximately one extra point every minute.

The doors opened to the empty Control Room floor. Smith must have sent his people home for the night. Rocky didn't exit the elevator and waited a moment. There. Right after the pulse below, the altar pulsed. He approached the place of power and waited. There it was again!

He started to feel nauseous as he saw the object continue to pulse in time with each beat from below. If one of the directions the energy translated was to his Territory, what was this other direction? Was Michabo receiving half of the tower's Etherience conversion of ambient Ether?

He placed his hand on the altar and said, "Michabo, are you there?"

A voice sounded inside Rocky's head. "Yes, we are here, Barkclay. You do realize that communicating like this takes Etherience, right?"

"Why is some of the tower diverting its Etherience to this altar?"

There was a pause this time before Michabo's response, "All places of power take a small supply of the Territory Etherience to sustain. The spirit realm has upkeep…"

Rocky snapped out of Meditation. "It seemed to exist all this time without any Etherience. Now it needs some of the Grotto's?"

The silence stretched before Michabo sighed mentally, a strange sensation to hear. "We had quite a store of energy. Resurrecting you and your three companions have exhausted that collection. Regardless, that is the function of this tower. We are only taking a portion of the extra Etherience, thanks to this fantastic filter."

Rocky's blood began to boil. Michabo had asked all of the Dungeon party to donate their Etherience. Even if it was at a poor conversion ratio of ten to one—he himself had donated more than they currently had in the Territory.

"I have work to do, Barkclay. Not everyone can stand around all day."

His nostrils flared at the insinuation and he screamed at the altar.

"Get back here, you bunny-eared jerk! I'm not done asking questions."

Michabo gave no indication that he had heard him. "Michabo, I need to understand what happened to all that Etherience we gave you. You said you had a huge store and used that for our resurrections. What about all the donated Etherience?"

Silence answered him.

His ears were so hot, he thought they might create their own solar gravity. He felt betrayed by the Native Spirit. There was something Michabo wasn't saying—something covert, perhaps even sinister.

Since he was already in the Control Room and he needed a distraction from his fuming rage, he chose to dive into another one of Michabo's claims. He found the right workstation and pulled up the Hall of Fame.

The screen changed, and in a prominent gold outline, a list of the top ten creatures to ever set foot on Gaia appeared.

Top Ten Highest-Level Individuals of All Time
1. **Zeus – Legendary – Level 76**
2. **Thor – Legendary – Level 75**
3. **Rudra – Legendary – Level 42**
4. **Ra – Legendary – Level 38**
5. **Buddha – Legendary – Level 32**
6. **Selapheliel – Legendary – Level 30**
7. **Uriel – Legendary – Level 29**
8. **Raphael – Legendary – Level 27**
9. **Azrael – Legendary – Level 4**
10. **Hercules – Epic – Level 99**

Each and every name seemed to be mythical in nature. He wondered if the stories of these powerful beings had outlived the disappearance of Ether, or if dug up relics recalled them from the annals of history.

Other sorting options existed, and he clicked on the filters to remove the males from the list. The list repopulated and he scratched his chin. The levels were significantly skewed, but there were Epic classes amongst them.

Top Ten of Highest-Level Females of All Time
1. **Athena – Epic – Level 92**
2. **Shiva – Epic – Level 92**
3. **Aphrodite – Epic – Level 72**
4. **Isis – Epic – Level 71**
5. **Freya – Epic – Level 52**
6. **Gabrielle – Epic – Level 12**
7. **Medusa – Master – Level 29**

Alarm bells sounded in his head. He clicked on the names displayed on the women's list. A date appeared for the time that the level was recorded. For Athena, it claimed, 'Time since last record: 2,005,738,138 orbits.'

He clicked through the list and noticed a distinct difference in times. All the women who were in the Epic ranks had been recorded nearly two billion years ago. All the women in the Master ranks hovered around the one-billion-year mark. It was hard for him to believe that not a single woman had grown into the high Master ranks in a billion years.

He scrolled back to the men's list. The powerful Legendary class individuals' records were demarked right around the same time. In fact, Azrael and Sela's last records were only a few million years apart. He wasn't sure, but he got the impression from Sela that Azrael had been much older than that.

That brought the Sela issue to the forefront of his mind. The conversation came full circle as he considered *omitting* this information from her. The decision would be easy, but he honestly didn't believe she could be part of whatever Michabo claimed. Whatever *that* was.

Rocky fooled around for a few more hours at the workstation before finally giving up. His eyes had begun to close, and a few times, he startled himself awake when his chin hit his chest. It was time to get back to his apartment.

He had gained new information, but it just added more questions. Plenty of women were listed as having successfully entered Master class in those billion years. Still, a vast number seemed to not have any record after level one.

He had also discovered that the top ten of all time had four individuals from the Cathodiem guild in his searches.

Selapheliel, Uriel, Raphael, and Azrael, were all part of the auspicious guild. They all had records that started two billion years ago, and newer recordings that dated only a billion years. Were they immortal? Or was the system mistaken?

He arrived at his apartment and chose to doze until the sun came up. He had already used an Elixir of Shortened Sleep, so he thought of it as a nap.

When he woke up, he would ask Sela.

CHAPTER EIGHTEEN

Rocky's eyes flew open. He was wide awake. He could only compare the feeling to memories of childhood—waking up on Christmas morning to brightly wrapped presents promising toys. Only today, he got a lifesize starship.

His bright mood soured at the memory of his two discoveries from the previous night and his failed Enchanting attempt. Deflated, he hopped out of bed and got into the shower. He stood under the hot water, hoping it would wash away some of his trepidation. His blood turned cold at the prospect of his conversation with Sela. Still, he knew he had to speak to her and hoped the hot water would warm him up to the task.

Opening the door to his apartment suite on the third floor, he tentatively knocked on Sela's door. The knock echoed inside, but no other sound came from within. After waiting half a minute, he left the Town Hall building to search for his guide elsewhere. As soon as he emerged from the building, the smell of food made his mouth water. He decided to look for Sela in the Mess Hall, and maybe get some breakfast while he was at it.

On his arrival, he scanned the tables and saw a few people he knew, scattered in pockets throughout the room. Sela sat at the center of a table, engaged in deep conversation with others. She was red in the face and doing a poor job of hiding her glare.

He joined the line for food and continued watching the exchanges. One of the individuals at the table directed his hands toward Sela and spoke animatedly. Sela opened her mouth and closed it again before slowly turning to someone else, her jaw clenched tighter, her face a little redder, and her eyes narrower. The vein in her forehead throbbed and grew larger with each response.

He was next to be served and focused his attention to the buffet. One of the cooks offered him some crispy meat, held up by tongs. He nodded, greedily remembering the last time he had eaten the 'bacon' substitute. "Could I have double?"

The cook laughed and gave him extra, saying, "It seems everyone's appetite is increasing. Are you sure I can't get you thirds of our rat bacon?"

Rocky's stomach flipped, but only for a second—it was still 'bacon' after all. At this point, he didn't care what he was eating, if these cooks could make it taste this good.

By the end of the buffet line, he was juggling two plates heaped with food. He was surprised to find something that looked like eggs in the mix today, and a sweet-smelling toast. The cooks had outdone themselves, attempting to create a breakfast similar to pre-Ether-wave standards. Rocky wondered if today was a bit of celebration for the return of food stores.

He was looking for a seat when he felt eyes on him. Sela was watching him. He glanced back in her direction and saw she was ready to explode. He chose to save the people around her. "Sela, we need to talk. Could you join me, please?"

She could blow up at him if she wanted. He deserved it anyway.

She nodded and disentangled herself, abandoning her empty plate at the table. They moved off to a private corner and sat back down.

"I am so sor—"

"Stop. Let's just leave it behind us. They gave you so much meat," Sela said as she snagged a piece for herself. Should he try again? Her throbbing vein returned.

Rocky decided to let it drop. He let out a half-hearted growl, and Sela forced a laugh before stuffing the bacon into her mouth.

Still chewing, she sighed. "Honestly, everyone thinks I have all the answers. Then when I do have an answer, some people want to keep reverting to, 'Make the Ether go away,' or, 'Can we go back to our previous way of life ever?' I honestly feel bad for those people. They won't ever truly fit into this world if they don't accept it."

Rocky batted away her hand as she went for another piece of 'bacon,' and she glared at him. Maybe he shouldn't poke the bear?

There was no denying she was right, and he hoped people would stop looking for ways out. If everyone pushed forward together, the future could be bright, but they definitely wouldn't have everyone—at least not immediately.

He wondered what sort of drain these non-contributors caused the Grotto. On the other hand, more people in the Territory meant more Territorial Etherience. So, for now, in the name of Amber, he let it slide.

He fended off another move she made for his toast, and said, "Rocky doesn't share food!" around a full bite. She laughed a little truer this time. He would give her the entire plate of food right now if that meant she would forgive him. However, he would settle for her being playful.

Maybe the best apology right now is to bring up my news.

He took a deep breath and steeled himself. "Michabo," he said, hoping to get the ball rolling. A lucky side effect occurred, and Sela stopped picking at his food. Her throbbing forehead vein returned and he forewent his next bite. "He told me a few things in the Spirit Realm, and we need to talk about them."

"He insinuated a few rather unpleasant things about my family, Rocky!" she shouted.

Rocky looked around abashedly and tried his best to reassure the people staring at them.

Pain and conflict. Those two emotions had become tied to Cathodiem as Sela discovered past secrets and possibly lies. He could understand her reaction.

The thing that hurt him more at this moment was the hope that shined in her tear-filled eyes. He assumed he would feel the same if such grievous accusations about his family existed, searching and hoping that there was some other explanation for any bad deeds.

To see her flushed face drain to white from one blink to the next made Rocky hesitate. His news might destroy that hope, and what little courage her playfulness had instilled quickly fled.

"Rocky, stop feeling bad for me and tell me. Please."

Tears welled in her eyes, and his knuckles cracked.

He filled his lungs. "The biggest thing he told me was that your guild was the enemy. I don't know what he meant. He was extremely vague. I think he was worried that you were part of something. He hinted at something else and asked me to question you about something. He wanted me to ask you how many Master Class women you knew in your lifetime?"

Sela flicked her eyes up and to the left. Recollection. Her mouth went from a straight line to a frown. She dropped her head. "I don't understand why that is important. I didn't know any, but only a few people can make it to Master class, and even fewer to higher ranks."

There was something about her head shake, though, that didn't appear to be denial. The action was more akin to a shiver and trying to remove the goosebumps it caused.

"Sela, there are lists of the highest leveled individuals, males, and females in the Tower. You are actually on the list for top ten strongest females—"

"See, that proves how few make it that high," Sela countered.

"Please, Sela, just let me say it all first. It will be easier for me, and then we can try to find the holes in it. There is more about Michabo to discuss. Okay?"

He continued before his mouth glued shut on him. "On those lists, there is a huge disparity. The entirety of the top ten, and possibly more, is male.

"That was strange. Stranger, though, was the huge number of women who died or vanished at level one in Master ranks. If the Master rank is like Journeyman, the Etherience needed from level one to two reverts to a smaller number than the last level of the previous rank."

Sela's face was ashen, and she breathed in small explosive bursts. He recognized the symptoms of shock, as he had seen it before on a fellow athlete who had ruptured their ACL. He pushed his plate across the table, stood up, and moved to stand behind her back, trying to massage her shoulders.

It was several minutes before she reached for some 'bacon,' and her action caused him to sigh in relief. He might have burst her bubble, but it hadn't been overfilled with hot air.

He continued the massage and talked to the back of her head, "That doesn't mean Cathodiem was involved in—"

Sela put her hand on his and patted it. "Rockland, I will be okay. I have been struggling with a question ever since I appeared to be your guide. I am still not entirely sure myself, but learning your Ether Cleanse skill makes me wonder how no one in my family knew of it. Why they didn't find someone in the EtherVerse that did?"

She turned around and motioned with her head for him to sit back down. She didn't return his plate, though, and he eyed it out of the corner of his eye as food disappeared. Sela continued talking in between bites. "I didn't tell you this, but the poison used was Chimera venom. I'm not even sure how the Martians came to possess a poison local to Gaia. While I was given a ton of medicines and seen by numerous healers, no one could cure it. All they did was prolong my suffering. I have honestly been considering testing Azoth's poison on someone after teaching them the Ether Cleanse skill. I don't know if I will actually do it, or if I just haven't captured an enemy that I can let die."

Rocky scratched his unruly hair and tried to think of a politically correct response, yet, he couldn't find one. But he didn't have to.

"Yeah, I know, not worth it. Also, a waste of the Chimera poison. I just want to confirm my suspicions, but this latest news kind of does that already. Is there anything else?" Sela asked.

He nodded and pulled his lips back. "I think Michabo is stealing a portion of the extra Territorial Etherience the Tower is generating. I am not certain if it is his doing, but I am absolutely sure half of the Etherience is going into the Altar."

Rocky motioned over his shoulder, attempting to get someone's attention. A cook rushed over and brought him some more food. Perfect.

Sela bit down with exaggerated force into a piece of bread. "Did it look like you could do anything to change it?"

He shook his head and munched on a piece of bacon, savoring the flavors.

"I don't trust this Michabo character. If he is a member of the Algonquin Guild, I was vastly misinformed of their strength. To own a place of power and an entire realm outside of reality..."

Sela stole his plate of food again, and he pursed his lips. He wanted to be upset but was impressed with the amount of food she was consuming. He turned around and motioned to the chef again. The man didn't look happy but brought another plate over. The conversation continued, and they discussed possibilities and their distrust of Michabo.

A bell Rocky hadn't heard before rung through the Territory, and he shot to his feet. The last time he had heard the static noise of a public announcement was from his high school days.

Smith's electronic voice filled the air. "Morning training begins in ten minutes; make your way to the courtyard." The man must have discovered a communications terminal in the tower.

Sela smiled and admired the scaled interior of the ceiling, "This is just like Atlantean Academy." Rocky hoped Sela was recalling good memories.

Perhaps, by the end of the day, we can have another Territory to add to this one. If not that, we will have saved the people of North Bay.

They stood up and added their four empty clay plates to a pile of dirty dishes. A disgruntled looking older man scrubbed the plates. Rocky stopped and asked, "Aren't you going to take a break for training?"

The older man gestured at the stacks of plates. "If I take a break, people won't be able to eat after training."

The man scrubbed each plate and utensil by hand in one sink, then dipped them into two rinsing sinks before stacking the clean plates on a nearby counter. Even a basic restaurant had a dishwashing machine. Still, post-apocalypse, they had lost some of the comforts of their previous life.

I am getting a Starship in a few hours. I think we can afford a dishwasher.

"The people who want to eat after training will just have to wait. Training is much more important. Get changed, and report to the square."

The dishwasher's stare bounced from Sela to the kitchen, and back. It reminded Rocky of a man who did not want to get fired from his job, and he Analyzed him.

Marcel Grey
Apprentice-Geologist
Level 13
Health Points: 110 / 110

"Marcel, is there a reason you are washing dishes when your class is a Geologist?" asked Rocky.

Marcel's mouth opened wide, but no sound emerged.

Sela looked at Rocky, and he just held up a hand, asking her to wait for the response. The last thing Marcel needed right now was someone else ordering him around.

"I need to be earning money. I can't just be a freeloader in this Territory. As much as some jobs are distasteful, someone has to do them, or they just won't get done."

He has a point.

"Very admirable, Marcel," said Rocky. He pointed to the dish pit. "We need everyone gaining strength. With so few humans left, there is going to come a time that a single strong individual may be the difference between slavery and freedom."

Marcel looked like a fish out of water, finally managing to squeeze some words out. "Who are you two?"

Zippo chose that moment to leave the kitchen in the back. Spotting Sela and Rocky, he exclaimed, "Let's go, guys! The two Territorial leaders can't be late for their scheduled training!"

Rocky grinned at Marcel and winked before following Zippo out of the Mess Hall.

***

Rocky and Sela arrived in the courtyard and found Smith waiting impatiently for them. He strode in their direction as soon as they were visible. Not even fully stopped in front of them, he launched into his plans. "I think we need to announce the tower and the possibility of searching for family members. I also believe we should let everyone know about the impending invasion. If we are transparent, it will motivate people to work hard."

Sela ran her hand through her long blonde hair.

Rocky opened his mouth to speak, remembered Sela's disdain for lying, and quickly clamped his mouth shut. In his mind, omission was also a form of lying, so he nodded his assent.

"You want me to make the announcement, don't you?" he asked.

Smith patted his back and expertly got Rocky's feet moving toward the much less 'makeshift' stage. Tao waited nearby, ready to guide morning training. The other four Knights were with him, and he wondered if the training would be led by the five of them today.

If he was honest, he didn't fully recall the brief announcements he made on stage. When he returned to Smith, Sela, and Zippo, he was sweating. The crowd was also cheering, "Algonquin! Algonquin!" into the morning air.

***

Smith clapped him on the back, "That was awesome, Rocky. Especially the part about 'fighting for every inch'!"

Ok, so I was inspired by an inspirational movie.

He remembered feeling tingles all over his shoulders the first time he had seen that particular scene. His team had often played a re-enactment over a boombox before games. While he was sure some in the crowd realized where the speech originated, it didn't change its meaning.

"This is so very different from the Silver Spires—I find myself wanting to see the Grotto's future," Sela said, musing almost to herself.

"Today, we will begin with combat training. Tao has informed me that you all know basic combat stance and readiness, so we can spend today's session discussing striking angles," Epsilon said.

For the next thirty minutes, the group, Rocky included, attempted to copy the moves the Knights demonstrated. Epsilon used Tao as an example, instructing the golem to punch or kick slowly, even pausing actions mid-strike. He pointed out blind spots the motion created, and attack angles opponents could use to capitalize on them.

Sela and Rocky paired up. As they sparred, she shared extra tips with Rocky, building on Epsilon's instructions. Many of the points she added were from his ongoing training with the Seraphim Sword. In thirty sweaty minutes, he learned just how much he had left to *discover*.

After Epsilon's session, Delta took over, guiding Meditation training and demonstrating a multitude of different circulatory patterns that one could practice with their internal Ether. "These patterns, if practiced often, can drastically increase your skills. It is said that each individual has a pattern that resonates most within them, but that may just be a myth."

After the training, Sela, Rocky, and a very excited Zippo made their way to the shop. It was time to get their first look at the starship they had purchased. They entered the shop in disguise again and made their way to Garnell's stall. He was with another customer but made some hand gestures, and a menu popped up. Rocky confirmed the transfer of one Crystal for the destroyer class ship, The Scourge.

Nothing happened.

He exited the shop and made his way back outside, trying to keep himself from fuming. Once they had reemerged, however, he stood stockstill, staring. The warehouse was no longer a rectangle. Instead, it had shifted into a wide frame that was left open to the air on both sides. The back end of a Starship extended away from the shop. It was so long that the engines were sitting mere inches away from a few parked tanks, near the military barracks. It was a little too close— two bent tank muzzles wedged under the engines groaned beneath the weight.

Damnit, I didn't expect it to be this big. I hope the tanks are still functional.

He backed away from the ship, attempting to take in the entirety of the construct. It reminded him of something from Starship Troopers. The sides were relatively boxy and straight, with multiple decks. At the aft of the ship, four humongous square tubes protruded. Two were above the ship, while the two below were what had bent the tanks. The front end of the vessel rounded slightly, with a bit of a boat hull tapering upward. He assumed that the front end of the ship housed the captain's deck.

He walked up to the front of the vessel and changed course when he saw something that looked like a doorway. On his approach, a notification popped up.

Welcome to the destroyer class ship, 'The Scourge.' As the owner of the warehouse, you have been granted access to the vessel. Would you like to enter?

~~Yes~~ | No | Read the Manual
You must read the manual and accept the terms and conditions before you are allowed to enter.

Oh, come on. Like anyone actually reads the manual.
Zippo saw the notification and sat down beside Rocky, "Maybe we can read it together?"

CHAPTER NINETEEN

Smith swapped in two fighter pilots to read the manual, and Rocky excused himself. To his surprise, Zippo stayed behind to read. It wasn't just the 'skimming to the end and clicking accept,' either. He was reading thoroughly and even taking notes on a Knowledge Tablet.

Rocky had yet to check on the status of the Crafter's Hall. Now that they no longer had an overcrowded housing situation, the builders were a little less harried.

He walked by the new buildings currently under construction, and found that two more Longhouses were going up, as well as what appeared to be a completed Crafter's Hall right beside the Mess Hall.

On his approach, a man wearing a safety helmet and a dirty dress shirt looked up and nodded before looking back to his plans.

Rocky Analyzed him.

Karl Keerdint
Apprentice-Engineer
Level 19
Health Points 290 / 290

Karl's health points were high, and he briefly wondered why. He decided that wasn't important.

Walking up to the man, Rocky asked, "Any idea what the hold up is on the Crafter's Hall? We need it—"

Karl gave him a side-eye sharp enough to cut him and went back to his plans. When Rocky made no move to leave, Karl looked at the building and sighed. "Just like I tell everyone else who asks," he gestured over to a group of people sitting in the grass. One person sewed leather together, and another worked with mortar and pestle.

Rocky rose up on his toes to see what was in the mortar—dried leaves ground down to powder. Was that what he needed?

"It will be finished when I am sure it isn't going to kill someone. Just because the roof is up doesn't mean it can withstand the forces you folks are going to put it through," said Karl.

For a moment, Rocky wasn't sure what he was insinuating, when a massive boom echoed from the circle of crafters. Rocky flinched and darted his eyes over the smoke-filled area. He stepped forward, but Karl put his arm out and shook his head. Had those crafters just killed themselves?

People exited the area one by one. Not one of them coughed. Instead, the smoke seemed to part around them, leaving clean air in a one-foot diameter around their skin.

One of the women, escaping the smoke, shouted, "Fennel, this is the fourth time today. Can you please go work away from the group? Just because we have our shields up doesn't mean it doesn't disturb our work."

Rocky looked to Karl, the dour man shook his head.

"Wait, are you not letting them in because they are a danger to the building?" asked Rocky as understanding dawned.

"Listen, I say when this building—" Karl paused as he took in Rocky's sword and combat gear. Clicking his tongue, the builder asked, "You aren't a Crafter, are you? Let me guess—you are this Leader I keep hearing about?"

Rocky nodded, and Karl's face grew thunderous.

"Follow me," he said.

A half-second ticked by before the man's harsh words registered. Rocky shook his head and jogged for a moment as he caught up with the Engineer.

They entered the building, and Karl pointed out each area and the problem with the current design.

"That there is supposed to be the Alchemy and Herbalist section. Fennel out there is mixing herbs and causing plumes of smoke." Karl pointed to a corner. "My boys have opened an exhaust pipe, but the exhaust fan hasn't been approved yet."

Rocky was secretly happy he wasn't the only person struggling with a mortar and pestle problem. He kept pace as Karl walked into another area. "This here is the Forge and Blacksmithing area. Once we move the forge and equipment in here, that is. Now, look up. Do you see any sprinkler systems in case of fires? The boys have roughed the pipes in, but we can't buy the tank or the sprinkler heads yet."

Each room had minor issues that Karl pointed out. Each solution would increase efficiency, safety, or production. In some cases, all three. Rocky hadn't heard about any of these problems at the town hall meetings. Actually, the last person he had heard speak to these issues had been—Derik?

Damnit. As much as I dislike him, I have to admit he does get things done.

Karl and Rocky returned to the entrance doors. Rocky pulled out fifty Crystals from his Bag of Holding. "Get everything you need, and make sure all the change gets returned to Smith. I will make sure the council is on top of this in the future."

Karl thanked him and put the Crystals into his pocket. He walked away—back straight, stiff legs, and stunted movements—like he was trying not to storm off. He didn't quite manage it and was obviously still upset.

Rocky walked into the clearing where the Council Meeting was taking place, and he was thankful they had started without him.

Smith, as the interim head of the military, was doing the final recap. "The first stage of the plan is to drop a quarter of the military, the Golem Knights, and Adam's Elites outside of North Bay. The A-Team will remain in the Grotto with the final quarter of the military. Once The Scourge has dropped off our assault team, it will complete each escort quest in the area. The return of the other half of our military forces from the surrounding towns will then give us the flexibility to bolster our assault, defend the Grotto, or attempt further survival quests from small cities."

So, Adam and his golems are coming with us now?

"To further bolster the Territory defense, the Exiles will be allowed back into the Grotto. Instead of hunting, they will perform community service and report to the military daily. Sela and I believe that they have redeemed themselves," Rocky chimed in.

Most of the council grew excited, and Meghan, the wife of an exiled member, stood up. "Thank you for allowing our loved ones to come home. I hope this is not too soon, but the highest citizen voted council member was Derik. Would he be allowed to join on his return or after his community service?"

Rocky sucked in a breath, his emotions all flaring together. He had just finished a similar thought but to have Derik's skill thrown in his face? He gave Meghan a withering stare and she shrunk back into her seat.

Sela placed a calming hand on his shoulder. He shook his head, clearing his stupid emotional turmoil, and forced a smile. "I am sorry, you caught me off guard. I believe Derik should be placed back on the council. Additionally, he will be in charge of the day-to-day needs of the Territory. His role is to bring those issues to the Council Meetings with suggested solutions." Smith nodded and smiled in relief. Rocky motioned for him to continue the meeting and sat back down.

It was mid-morning, and everyone had eaten already. The bonfire in the center of the clearing produced small wisps of smoke, and the sun had removed the dew from the grass. All in all, it was turning out to be a beautiful day.

Rocky turned his face up to the sun and basked in its warmth. The rays didn't feel as strong as a few weeks ago. He sighed and came back to reality. How long until winter arrived here?

We need to save as many people as possible before that happens.

A runner jogged over, interrupting the meeting, and waited outside the circle.

Smith dismissed the runner after he received the message. "The pilots have finished reading the manual. They have asked for five other operators as crew for the vessel. I must excuse myself at this time. Before I leave, my last report relates to the blueprints and the need for a shipbuilding yard. The council has been considering what the top priorities of the Territory and the world are. I want to put forward this project and a planetary defense grid as viable areas to spend Territorial Ether."

The crowd went silent, and Rocky knew he needed to tell them about Amber. This was the moment. He opened his mouth, but Sela beat him to it.

"That should conclude today's meeting. We have a lot of work ahead of us today, and as we move forward. When we meet next, we will hear more about the top priorities and make final decisions."

Rocky glared at his guide, not sure if she was attempting to omit the decision they had made. They had talked just this morning, and he bit back his gut reaction. Yelling at her wouldn't help trust. They would talk again soon, but he wouldn't approve a single point of Territorial Ether until then.

Zippo tapped him on the shoulder. "Let's go. I want to see the inside of the ship." The kid practically shouted while bouncing on his feet. His excitement was infectious, and as he walked with Rocky, Sela fell in step with them.

"Any idea where Azoth is this morning, Sela?"

She pointed toward the shop and warehouse building. Azoth was perched on top of the ship with one leg raised.

Really? Is he trying to mark the ship as his?

"He says 'ship stupid. Ship no talk. Azoth talk. Ship ugly metal."

It wasn't like pee was going to damage the metal. At least, Rocky hoped it wouldn't.

***

An hour later, Rocky and Sela were flying on Azoth's back on the way to North Bay. They would arrive there a few hours ahead of the main assault force. The pilots of the ship needed to run a few maneuvers and get the other five individuals up to speed. Zippo had insisted on being part of the inaugural flight of their new starship and had stayed behind.

If Azoth hadn't had a tantrum, we all could have been on the first flight.

Azoth hadn't wanted Rocky and Sela to fly any other way. It was touching that his friend wanted to be with them. Frustrating, but touching. Sela pointed out that someone should scout the area anyway.

North Bay hadn't been a large town. Rocky dredged his memory and guessed that it might have been nearing the fifty-thousand population mark before the wave of Ether. The possible saving grace was that the city had not one, but two, colleges practically side by side. As they approached, they could easily make out the structures of the schools from the air. It wasn't hard when a broad ring of golems of various sizes surrounded the buildings.

There were one hundred of the creatures, at least. He yelled to Sela over the wind. "There are at least three of those Basalt Golems; do you think they are leaders?"

Sela gripped his waist tighter and pulled herself close. "Let's go take a look, but my guess? Larger towns and cities had much higher probabilities of spawning leader class and sapient golems."

She must have mentally directed Azoth, as he gradually veered toward the schools. A few wingbeats later, Rocky received a notification.

You are entering a Territorial Zone of a powerful being. If you continue, it will be alerted to your presence. Depending on your intentions or its mood, you may be in danger.

He had seen this notification three times now in total, confirming that North Bay contained a Territory below. The next flashing notification was new to him, however.

The system has marked you as an owner of a starship. If the starship attacks or is too near a Territory, protections or drastic mutations may occur to increase the difficulty of the challenge.

Well, that settles the bombardment discussion.

He leaned out over Azoth's wing and scanned the terrain below them. It was a wide-open landscape, pockmarked by trees, stones, and tall grass. He couldn't see the Territorial Leader—the creature was either hidden, below ground, or—he jerked his neck upwards. Nothing was above them and he breathed a sigh of relief.

"Azoth says he can smell something, and his description isn't great. He claims, 'Smells like damp ground. Nests," Sela relayed as her arms tightened almost imperceptibly.

That would explain why the creature was hard to see from the sky. Sela, Azoth, and Rocky flew over the area once more and began their descent. A few people on the schools' rooftops scattered when they saw Azoth's winged form approaching. Seeing the human figures duck into the stairwells made him hopeful. They didn't seem to be in the dire straits that the small towns in the area had been.

Rocky called to Sela, "I don't want to land in a clearing where anyone could make a mistake and shoot Azoth. Do you think that the roof is safest?"

They angled toward the highest roof in the complex. "Don't shoot! We are here to help. Don't attack!" Rocky shouted the instant they touched down.

He slid off of Azoth's back, and Sela's feet thumped down beside him. He tapped Azoth twice, and the beast flew off into the air. Rocky figured Sela had explained the situation, but it was going to be much easier to talk to the survivors without his pet wanting to play or curiously sniff them.

No one came out of the door. Instead, it clanked shut. Rocky walked slowly toward the door with his arms above his head. Perhaps they hadn't heard him the first time. Once he was a bit closer to the door, he tried again. "We come to offer our aid and support. We are from a Territory south of you. We have brought food and water."

The door stayed shut and Rocky considered using Dark Blade to force the issue.

A nervous voice, muffled behind the door said "Could you please wait? We sent one of our scouts to inform the boss that people are here. If you attack, we have you surrounded."

Rocky entered a quick Meditation and scanned the immediate area using his Ether Manipulation. The kid was lying, and he felt their weak presence behind the door. Beside him, Sela circulated her Ether through her Channels in the pinwheel design they had learned earlier. Rocky smiled, seeing that she had chosen something new. He hadn't liked any of the new patterns as much as the flower petals.

He reconsidered breaking into the school. Sela had already stepped back, so he followed her lead, moving away from the door to wait. They weren't left long, as groups of twenty-something year olds flooded out from the door, carrying all kinds of makeshift weapons and gear. The vast majority sported hockey gear and wielded sticks.

He made a quick Analyze of a few and saw that they all had levels in the high teens of the Apprentice Rank. He was surprised—they were doing far better than he had expected.

A man in a suit walked onto the roof. He looked to be in his late thirties, maybe early forties. Rocky figured he had probably been a teacher or coach at the school. He quickly Analyzed the man.

Richard Sun
Apprentice-Trainer
Level 24
Health Points: 240 /240

"What makes you think we need your help?" Richard asked.

"The other survivors in the area have been near starving. They have desperately needed food and supplies. May I ask how you have managed to fare so well without removing the golems?"

"That is none of your business. We will continue to build our strength until we can defeat the local Territory." Richard squared his shoulders and raised his chin slightly.

The teenagers surrounding them seemed pretty healthy, but they didn't look clean or happy. He turned back to Richard and tried a new approach. "We already own a Territory nearby, and our starship is on its way to help everyone here escape to a place of safety and community. We have enough room—"

"We do not need charity. These boys and I have defended the people of Canadore and Nippissing. We will continue to do so, and you can take your offer of help back to where you came from."

Rocky had seen the nearby young adults shift from foot to foot, and some were still bouncing. "We have more than enough room, water, food and are currently trying to collect everyone from the surrounding villages and towns—"

"I said you should go." Richard snapped and stepped forward, his fists clenching and unclenching.

"We can search for lost families and friends using a computer program." It wasn't really a computer program, but that was the easiest and fastest way to make everyone understand. It was a bit of an oversell, but it wasn't completely untrue. More like an omission, like Sela had said.

One of the boys spoke up, "Richard, we could find out about your wife. We could find out about my brothers, my parents."

Richard's visage cracked and his eyes grew glassy. The man regarded Rocky warily and asked, "You aren't lying to us? Trying to take our Dungeon and supplies?"

"We are not lying," Sela reassured him. Every young man in the group instantly gave her their full attention—they weren't blind to her beauty. "Our ship will be here soon to pick you up. However, if you truly have a Dungeon, we would be interested in adding it to the Grotto and the two we already have."

Richard broke down, and a few of the kids hugged each other, removing their hockey helmets. The group looked relieved, like the final shot of the game was passed to the team's top scorer. They had done everything they could to create an opportunity, but now it could be left up to someone else to bring it home.

And he had committed to being that leader. To hold all that responsibility and withstand that pressure. For the briefest moment, he wished he could trade places.

"Yeah, we have a Dungeon. It's a bit of a nasty piece of work, though. It seems to be trying to trick us all the time. You progress through levels of the Dungeon. It's never the same puzzles or questions. Sometimes it gives you a puzzle that looks the same, but with a different answer. We have been trying only to farm the first few rooms for food and water, but a few more ambitious students thought they could get better things further in. We haven't seen—"

"This Dungeon always has questions? In each room?" Sela asked, intentionally interrupting what likely would have been saddening news.

Richard nodded, and she turned to Rocky, excitement gleaming in her eyes. "It's a puzzle Dungeon."

"Well, we have quite a bit of food and water we would like to share. Do you have an area where you all meet and eat?" Rocky continued her momentum. Keep them happy and get them back to the Territory. To safety. They could break down there and recover with the support they needed.

The hockey team escorted Sela and Rocky into Nippissing University. The hallways were barren and almost every classroom had been overtaken by makeshift beds and sleeping areas. The doors to the washrooms contained blockades of chairs and desks.

"In the middle of the night, people were often too lazy to go outside to relieve themselves. The blockades were an early decision that stopped us from having to flush the toilets manually by carrying up buckets of water, which we were running low on," said Richard.

How could people be so lazy as to use toilets that didn't work? Especially at the risk of others' lives. He considered what he would have done at the age of twenty if the world of luxuries he had always known suddenly vanished.

They followed Richard down a wide staircase that led to the second floor, following the signs for the cafeteria posted on the walls.

A thrum of voices echoed down the hallway as they drew nearer. The voices carried little enthusiasm, and Rocky thought of the schools and survivors in Ottawa. Surviving from day to day, but with no goal or future in mind. Just existing. When the doors opened, admitting the hockey-clad members of his escort, the conversation quieted. As Rocky and Sela entered the cafeteria behind them, silence blanketed the room.

Rocky stepped forward to speak, and people cleared out of his way quickly, almost scared by his clean appearance. Or maybe they were embarrassed by their dirty and bedraggled ones. He stepped into a clear area between all the tables. It looked like they used it for announcements often. Nearly everyone was in their late teens or early twenties. He hoped they weren't too old for a bit of a magic show.

He mentally selected a skid of rations and a large water tank filled with clean drinking water from his Bag of Holding. He summoned them onto the cleared area in front of him. The teenagers gasped. He was sure that it had looked like he had invoked the items from thin air.

He had their attention. Now, it was time to bring *them* home. "We are here to help. We have brought you food, water, and offer you a place in our community."

CHAPTER TWENTY

The arrival of the ship caused people to point into the sky and shout. A few teenagers ran away, even though they expected the arrival. Rocky had to admit that the sight was a bit disconcerting and not what he had expected. Instead of appearing on the distant horizon, it dropped through a sea of clouds directly above the roofs of the university.

On the bottom of the vessel, numerous small, noiseless booster engines were affixed. The two bottom engines, each one the size of a 747, pointed downward.

Rocky couldn't believe how quiet the ship was during its descent. He was directly underneath it, and it wasn't until the ship was within range of the roof that he heard a humming sound, which felt as if cotton balls were stuffed into his ears. Rocky tugged at his ears a few times, checking if they still worked.

The ship didn't land—it hovered. It wasn't small enough to touch down on the school grounds safely. Rocky spotted Azoth on board the ship, stalking back and forth, and he laughed.

Sela looked concerned but chuckled after a moment. Azoth supposedly wanted to try his claws against the metal. She had dissuaded his cat-like instincts—this time.

Adam and his team rode the Chimera down to the surface.

"We need to clear those golems if we want to land the ship." Adam handed Rocky and Sela a new earpiece each. "This one connects through the ship. There is a whole pile of these devices in the comms room."

Rocky placed the radio in his ear and heard Gamma say, "We can just jump down from this height."

"We await orders, Gamma. Do you think golems dropping out of a ship will be responded to well?" Epsilon retorted.

Omega's surfer drawl filled his ears. "I also totally don't want to be attacking our brothers. I get that they're dumb, but—"

"Selaphelia Ardensai here. Knights. Your comm is hot. We can all hear you. Over."

A bunch of grunts and what might have been shoving or light punches transmitted over the comms. A slight rocking in the ship accompanied the strange noises.

An unknown commanding voice came over the comms. "Captain here. Enough horseplay. You are rocking the entire ship. Over."

Rocky, who had agreed with Epsilon's first statement, smirked. The knights weren't as orderly and mature as they seemed. To him, it made them more human.

"Epsilon, here. Apologies, one of our numbers hasn't figured out these devices yet. Awaiting orders. Over"

Omega was the likely culprit—his voice had been the loudest during the first exchange. Rocky clicked his earpiece. "Let us handle the golems surrounding the complex first. Stand by as back up. Shoot—over."

Epsilon's voice dueled with Omega's. "Thank goodness—Roger that. Quiet down—I don't..." The ship shook again.

He turned to Adam and saw the kid smiling up at the ship. Omega could always be relied on to liven up the Knights. Rocky cleared his throat and got the young man's attention. "I am assuming your Minion Golems are up there as well?"

Adam nodded and held up two fingers. "I still have room for two more. I couldn't capture leaders in Kingston, but I'm hoping that 'Skill Level Insufficient' was because I didn't have five points in Construct Command."

Zippo, who had ridden Azoth over the golem's heads, walked over and pointed to a nearby Basalt Golem. "That one there is classified as a leader."

Anticipation rose within the group. If Adam could take over a Leader golem, then this would be a much simpler process. Adam stopped and placed his hands in a slightly spherical shape. Rocky hadn't seen Adam use his skill before and watched attentively. Blue energy welled forth from the boy's fingers, creating a slowly revolving strap, like a dog's leash. It even read "Rex" on one side.

"Rex was my dog. He..." said Adam.

Sorrow tinged his voice. Tears welled in his eyes, and Rocky placed a hand on Adam's shoulder. Sela had done the same, and their hands laid atop each other on the young man's back. His spell faltered slightly, then stabilized.

Adam released his skill, which expanded and wrapped around the neck of the Basalt Golem. He huffed and said, "This creature has control of too many nearby units to be taken." He looked away from a blank space in front of him that likely held a notification. "Looks like I can't take Leader golems."

"That's not what it said, Adam. Let's kill the units around this one, then try again," said Sela.

The tactic of firing from the safety of the school grounds wouldn't work on these golems. Richard explained that when they had tried in the past, the Leader golems sounded a wordless retreat. All of the golems then grouped up into a massive force a few hundred meters away.

The group strategized and chose to use Azoth to fly over the circular containment and attack from the outside. Rocky hoped that by forcing the groups to go around the schools, his modest attack force wouldn't have to face the one-hundred golems all at once.

"Selaphelia Ardensai. Be prepared to assist with a bombardment. Over," Sela said through her radio and received a quick confirmation. "Rockland, if possible, let's try to avoid killing this Leader. However, if not this first one, at least one of the three Basalt Golems."

Adam bounced up and down beside him. Sela had to know just as well as he did. Once combat started, it might not go the way they intended. At least they had the Golem Knights, Minion Golems, and a Starship as backup. He couldn't wait to see what his new toy could do.

Sela bent down and touched the earth below them. She started to sweat, and there was only one reason for that— she was setting something up below ground.

Azoth flew overhead, ready to engage the golems and coerce them toward the group. Sela stood up and nodded. Seeing his cue, Azoth dove down and landed on the head and neck of a smaller golem that had probably been someone's home.

His pet bit into the wood and the soil that covered the creature. Azoth's head whipped back and forth, and he began beating his mighty wings. The golem flew off of its feet and his pet released it, dropping it to the ground. The other golems reacted in near-perfect unison. The speed and coordinated reaction reminded him all too well of the battle in Pembroke early in the Apocalypse. This fight wasn't going to be easy.

Azoth hovered over the ground, at about a third-story level. He pumped his wings and backed away slowly as the golems charged him, stringing out and creating a triangle with the Basalt Golem at the peak. Sela chuckled and shook her head at his glance. He assumed Azoth was mentally commenting on the battle, and he wished he could hear his pet.

Sela and Zippo began to cast skills. Adam summoned another collar. Rocky charged his Dark Blade skill, and engaged Dark Cloak and Stealth. In the daytime, like now, the abilities wouldn't conceal him, but having both active drastically lowered the Ether costs.

The ground transformed into a swamp in front of the legs of the Basalt Golem. The creature sunk into the puddle, liquifying and melding into the swamp. Rocky was ecstatic until the marshy ground of Sela's skill paved over, sealing itself. The other golems ran across the swamp as if it had never been there, even though Zippo's Firestorm skill swirled nearby. The front line of Bio-Enhanced golems stormed forward and ran through the gathering cloud of carbon. The Basalt Golem and a significant number of the back group were caught, but at least ten of the golems made it through.

Rocky stepped forward and released his three charges in a horizontal swing. The three dark blades buzzed through the air, and it looked like the ten would be struck.

The lead golems stopped simultaneously. Five of them knelt and placed their hands onto the earth. Sela screamed as the golems stood back up. Thick pillars of sod and stone rose from the earth at the rise of their hands. Rocky's blades collided with the protective columns and began to screech.

Adam's collar landed on one of the golems, and it attacked the closest enemies. The remaining four instantly leaped onto the turncoat, pummeling it into the ground without hesitation.

In the distance, two Basalt Golems led the remaining constructs around the schools. Rocky had to decide right now—retreat, or bring everything they had.

He clicked his radio. "We need support. Fire at will."

The ship's laser ports slid open and blasts of lasers cratered the ground. Each time a beam struck; soil leaped into the air.

The golems were unfazed. They blackened in areas where the thick lasers struck. Many of the shots missed entirely, and Rocky couldn't help but wonder if the new crew member assigned to weapons was just too green.

The sizable rear bay door retracted and golems dropped from the sky. Omega shouted "Cowabunga, dudes!"

The creatures landed halfway between Rocky's group and Zippo's Firestorm, each landing accompanied by a boom and a spray of dirt. The Knights braced the impact with their knees, absorbing the brunt of the fall and staying atop the earth's crust.

The other golems that Adam had brought sunk anywhere from half to fully into the softer earth beneath them like lawn darts. It would have been comical if the situation wasn't so dire. At least the golems in the Firestorm should be destroyed.

Asphalt slunk from the Blighted area, and Sela shouted, "They have control of the earth." The tornado of fire came to an end, and golems rose from the now solid dirt, shaking off the hardened soil that had been a swamp moments before. A few charred and destroyed golem corpses stood like statues in the area of effect.

Unbelievable. They must have countered Sela's skill and used the soil as cover.

The Knights pulled some of the Minions free, which Adam directed to release others.

Over twenty enemy golems were still alive, and another seventy were coming fast, which made the decision for Rocky. He pressed his radio and shouted, "Rolling retreat! Keep their attention, but don't engage!"

Friendly golems made their way back to the group as the bombardment from the starship continued.

"The ship could pick up the survivors as we draw the golems' attention," Sela said. She sent the command out on her radio, using proper etiquette. He would have to make that second nature for himself, or larger scale battles would be impossible. The destroyer broke off and flew toward the back of the schools. None of the golems paid it any mind, and the ship had only downed two or three golems with its barrage.

Perhaps Amelia had given them a castoff ship. Rocky shook the thought from his mind. It wasn't the time to think about that. He pulled out a plasma grenade and lobbed it between the heavily scarred defense pillars. It exploded, and the somewhat hidden golems hugged closer for cover. They didn't close the gap, and a shiver flew up his spine.

They were going to wait for all of the units to mass. The group continued to fire occasional long-ranged spells while conserving Ether. They may need it soon, and they were only attempting to keep the attention of the golems.

The ship lowered out of sight behind the building, and he hoped the loading of the North Bay survivors would go speedily.

The two other Basalt Golems joined the first, and their troops spread out into a long row. Another shiver coursed through Rocky's body at the display of heightened intelligence of the mobs of golems.

An unspoken command was issued and the seventy-ish golems kicked off the ground in unison. The three leaders melted into puddles and flowed toward them like slithering snakes. Zippo shot a fireball at the approaching line, and one of the Basalt Golems formed a hand from its tube-like body and caught it. The Leader slammed its burning appendage into the ground as it continued its snaking advance.

"Knights, phalanx. Form up on Epsilon. Adam, have your golems fill out the sides. Humans to the interior. Steady retreat," Sela commanded.

The Knights nodded, and all but Delta ripped a nearby tree out of the ground, opting for distance weapons over their usual ones. Adam's Minions struggled to mimic the actions of the Knights. The strength difference between the Knights and Adam's controlled constructs was significant. Each one did eventually rip out a small nearby tree, if somewhat clumsily.

There was strategy in their formation. They could break most of the charge. But there was one glaring flaw. "Sela, I am useless here. Any skill I attempt is likely to hit an ally," Rocky said.

"You and Azoth can harry the edges."

"Be careful of the Basalt Golems; they can come right through this formation."

Sela smiled wickedly. "Oh, I know."

Rocky removed his Dark Cloak Skill and left Stealth engaged as he sprinted from the formation. Exiting from beneath Tao's legs, he pumped his legs as fast as he could, attempting to gain the edge of the enemy golem's charge. He wasn't going to make it. He pulled out two more plasma grenades and one gravity grenade, launching the latter first.

It went off a fair distance away from him and instantly slowed the edge of the approaching golems. He had thrown it a bit too far to disable them. He spat and kicked the ground at his mistake, rapidly tossing his two plasma grenades toward the same edge.

He dove, barely avoiding the charging Bio-Enhanced golem attempt at trampling him. He charged his Dark Blade and sent it humming at the backs of the five who had nearly run him over.

His only goal now was to try to break up the charge.

He withdrew another gravity grenade and launched it at the next group of five. He sighed as it went off and slowed another portion of the force. He took quick stock of his Ether. It was below half. Time to change roles. He checked his first targets and saw three still standing. Another four were missing legs and lying prone.

Ignoring them and those flattened or destroyed by his Dark Blade skill, he charged back toward the phalanx.

The Knights slammed the trees into the ground, and braced them with their back foot. The Minions followed the action a moment later and stopped the retreat just in time.

His ears rang and the ground shook as the remaining enemy golems struck the front of the phalanx in a resounding crash. Rocky prayed for the formation to hold.

Azoth's side circled back to the unprotected rear pocket of the phalanx triangle. Sela rose from a crouch and made a motion—shouting something, but he was too far away to hear. Zippo dual cast Firestorm and a Firewall. Rocky watched as the kid sunk to one knee from the effort, but he held the spells.

The Basalt Golems slithered through the legs of the Knights and attempted to form on top of pitfalls. Sela had strategically placed the traps just behind the Knights' line.

Rocky slashed through a golem on his way back into the phalanx just as Sela cast her Blight spell down into the pitfalls.

He ignored the Leader golems and ran to help Zippo. He had to deal with the threat of the circling golems as quickly as possible. The kid panted and paled. Rocky pulled two Ether Draughts from his bag, handing one to the young man and downing the other. Zippo fumbled with the top, and Rocky knelt and assisted him. "When I say release the spell, do it. Okay?"

He charged his Dark Blade. He stacked six before his Ether ran dry and his knees began to shake. He trusted the allies behind him to hold. He didn't have a choice—he was about to release everything he had. The twenty Bio-Enhanced golems behind Zippo's spells wouldn't die any other way. He released his skill, praying they wouldn't see the Dark Blades coming through the charcoal smoke. If they saw the strikes and erected earth pylons—the fight was over.

Just before they entered Zippo's spell, Rocky yelled, "Now!" and the noise, swirling wind, and grit, became grinding stone.

Rocky fell to his knee after his slash and glanced over his shoulder, rubbing his neck.

Half of his Territory's army fired laser rifles and tank turrets as they bore down on the backs of the onslaught of golems. The starship flew above them to provide support against any target that they had a clear line of fire for.

The end of the battle came swiftly. The fear, anticipation, and anxiety cut off in the blink of an eye. Zippo and Rocky looked at each other. Rocky assumed he looked just as pale and sweaty as the young man as they flopped onto their backs in the grass. His head felt like someone had taken a Louisville Slugger to it.

They both chuckled, but Rocky stopped abruptly as he remembered the Basalt Golems. He forced himself to roll over and took a swig of another Ether Draught, handing one to Zippo.

"What's wrong, Rock?"

Rocky waved his hand dismissively at his friend, conveying that it wasn't serious. Just an Ether Headache. He ambled slowly and unsteadily to stand beside Sela, who was staring down into the muddy pit.

"I think they are stuck for now," said Sela.

Adam bounced over. "Let me see if I can capture them now."

CHAPTER TWENTY-ONE

The military met up with Rocky's group and issued quick reports. Only half of the accompanying force would remain, and Victoria was in charge. The other half climbed back aboard the starship to oversee the remaining escort quests.

When Rocky pulled up his quest tab, and checked how many Escort quests the ship had to fulfill, he was elated. Twenty-five shared quests in total. Through the Guild, these quests were shared with all members. If they gave out the Etherience he was expecting, most of his populace would gain quite a few levels.

As soon as Adam had leashed all three Basalt Golems, a notification for North Bay's quest popped up, along with a twenty-sixth escort quest. Rocky quickly shared it through the guild functions.

Congratulations, you have completed a Chain Quest!
Preservation of Champion Life Quest
>> **Chain Party Quest – Atlantean Net Generated**
Save the North Bay Survivors I
- **Champions in North Bay are starving. While the golems are protecting them, they haven't been able to hunt for food. Bring them food and find a way to handle the situation.**
  Rewards:
2,253,000 (+337,950 Knight's Quest) Etherience
Survivors want to join your Territory
>> *Atlantean Statutes, Preservation of Life, Section XII*
--

>> **You have been offered a 2nd part in a Chain Quest!**
Preservation of Champion Life Quest
>> **Chain Quest – Atlantean Net Generated - Escort**
Save the North Bay Survivors II

- **Escort 90% of the survivors successfully back to your Territory. Adjustment to quest difficulty due to the quest group's access to a starship. Rewards:**

Etherience

New members of your Territory.

Atlantean Statutes, Preservation of Life, Section XII

Chain Quest (Change as per AC - 7.1f)

He did the math and assumed there were two thousand two hundred and fifty-three survivors in North Bay. Most survival quests had offered one thousand per individual Rocky rescued. He couldn't wait till the ship brought everyone to the Territory from the surrounding towns later today.

That quest alone had brought him halfway to level nine. Rocky smiled, hoping by the end of today, he would be at level ten and looking at his newest skills.

Adam had been standing and reading for too long, and Rocky tapped him on the shoulder. "Everything okay?"

The young man started and his Basalt Golems rippled. Rocky thought they might attack, but Adam's smile relaxed him. "I am good. I have a notification that I am trying to understand. Any idea what bonus hierarchy means?"

Rocky and Smith had recently looked into that very issue. Shortly after Smith's return, Rocky had promoted him to the highest rank he could, and had given him the pseudo-leadership role of the Military. Strategist level three hadn't opened new ranks, but it had revealed some hidden features. Rocky had taken his entire Leader page and transcribed it onto Smith's Knowledge Tablet. Together, they had figured out the dynamics of bonus hierarchy. Smith was likely still fiddling with the complexities of it.

Rocky asked to see Adam's screens to understand the teenage boy's question. By the looks of things, Adam's Leader Golems had upgraded his skill.

"From what I can tell, each person—or in your case, golem—has unique traits. For example—" Rocky pointed to Zippo, who had walked up, "—if a Mage based in Intelligence leads troops, they will likely boost those troops' spells." Rocky oscillated his hand to show it wasn't that simple. "They may also boost those troops' intelligence, or if they are a poor fit with the people under them, create debuffs."

Sela had been standing nearby, talking to Victoria. Out of the corner of his eye, he saw her motion for Victoria to stop. They walked over to join the conversation as he continued, "My guess is that you can now promote different types of golems to Leaders. They will then boost the golems under them in different ways."

Sela examined the Basalt Golems. "My feeling with these Basalt Golems is they will likely add either defense to your other golems, or Tactics. That would make the most sense, after the fight we just had." She made a quick appraisal of the tar-like golems. "Too bad they dropped down to low Journeyman ranks from the Master class they were at."

Adam pointed to each in turn. "It says that one adds Inherent Ether protection. What is that?" Not waiting for an answer, he moved to the next, "That one there says it grants a skill of Gaia's Defense. Any idea what that means? That—"

Sela jumped in to answer before he continued, "Slow down, Adam; we have all day. One at a time, alright?"

Adam flushed bright red and nodded.

"I think the first one might very well be why the lasers and ranged attacks didn't damage them as much. Inherent Ether is a body resistance against Ether-enhanced attacks and skills. The second one likely granted the skill for the pillars the golems conjured. I felt something tap into Gaia for a moment, which is also what canceled my Blight skill. What do you think, Rocky?"

He half shrugged. That assumption could be made, but she was better suited to make it.

Adam observed the gesture, and added the last bonus, exaggerating how slowly he spoke. "The last one there has combat maneuvers. Maybe that was why they were all so organized?"

The group nodded in affirmation to the young man, who bounced excitedly as he regarded his new constructs. Rocky motioned for everyone to begin making their way back to the school area. As soon as Adam took a step, the Golem Knights and all the Minion golems moved in unison. Rocky found the sight eerie. The Minions made sense, but Epsilon and his brothers?

They are watching this kid closely.

Zippo asked, "How many spots for leaders do you have?"

"Just one," Adam said.

"That's awesome. You can flip them into the leader position based on what you need," Zippo explained excitedly.

Rocky tuned out the rest of the conversation as he considered their next move. Some planning needed to happen before they went to attack the nearby Territory. Before Richard had left, Sela and Rocky asked him if he knew what resided inside. He answered that they always heard strange chirps and squeaks late at night. Still, other than random wildlife, they hadn't seen anything overtly dangerous.

Sela was chatting with Victoria again. As an actual tank class, Victoria may very well be capable of holding the attention of whatever creature resided inside the zone.

Maybe I can get her to tank the Puzzle Dungeon for us. I mean, the Grotto can always use more Dungeons.

He sidled over to the two women and received a look he didn't understand.

What? They look like I just walked in on them in the showers or something.

He felt his heart sink at the memory. He wished he would have taken advantage of the offer when it had stood.

He had screwed up and assumed that he and Sela were related. Now he felt like there might be a rift between them. Sela might have forgiven him for the argument last night, but that didn't mean she was still interested. What if he had blown his chance? He was pretty sure he liked Sela, but honestly hadn't had time to fully examine his feelings for the woman.

Sweating, Rocky realized he had blanked out. The two women stared at him, waiting for him to speak.

"I was thinking of challenging that Puzzle Dungeon when the party organizes for the attack…"

Idiot, stop blushing. Okay, don't stop—at least turn away, so they don't see it.

His action provoked a light giggle, and his head snapped back around. Who had it been? They wore identical innocent expressions.

His only way out was forward. "The group of you, Sela, Zippo, and myself, perhaps even Azoth, can head into the Dungeon. There will be a few hours before the attack on the Territory occurs."

"I saw you down a few Elixirs during that fight already. Isn't the plan to attack Toronta tomorrow?"

"Toronto. And yes. But I think bringing in another Dungeon for the Territory's growth will be a good thing. Or leaving the Dungeon to defend this Territory, perhaps?"

Victoria looked lost, probably unsure of what her opinion was worth. "I can't tank the Dungeon, Rocky. I am in charge of the military here."

"This Territory is close to Algonquin already. We don't need it. Once you capture it, just convert it to a Territorial Sphere and add it to the Grotto," Sela said.

Rocky winced at her tone. "What? Can you collapse Territories?"

Sela looked at him as if he was dumb. "Of course, you can. You don't want Territories all over the place. How would you defend them?"

Between clenched teeth, he said, "There is no downside to this?"

The group entered the school zone. "Well, you lose some of the Etherience of the zone, just like if you capture a Dungeon Core. It can't take all of its energy with it. However, this is a huge reason for interplanetary wars as well. Armies would capture spheres as they moved, keeping only strategic positions. Those spheres were often loaded onto ships and brought back home. Didn't I explain this?" Sela asked, puzzlement furrowing her brow.

He pointed a finger at her. "No, you didn't. You alluded to wars for Planetary Essence. You never mentioned how."

She shrugged. "Well, how else do you suggest capturing Essence and Etherience?"

He pointed to his Bag of Holding. Sela's eyes widened comically. She guffawed at him, and he felt childish. How was he supposed to know that the Bottle of Gaia's Essence wasn't the typical capturing method?

***

A rushed meal and a scant fifteen minutes later, Rocky stood in the entryway of the Dungeon.

This Dungeon, like many other wild Dungeons, didn't have an entrance large enough for Azoth. Rocky assumed that it was a measure against huge Master class creatures or higher from entering.

Most Dungeons he had fought to date were seriously under-leveled compared to the evolved mobs. He took a deep breath.

"Everyone ready?" Rocky asked. The group gave varying levels of consent. Zippo and Adam cheered and gave each other high fives.

He had been against bringing Adam with him on this delve, but the boy had pouted when Rocky had told him, 'No,' and he'd had no choice but to melt and relent.

The Golem Knights had stepped in on Adam's behalf. They insisted the boy join him, even though they wanted the boy to be out of harm's way. Adam couldn't bring his massive golems, and that worried Rocky.

What is their fixation with this kid? They want him to get stronger but also to be protected. That's a tight line to walk.

He glanced at Adam, who was currently enthralled by Zippo's slightly rosy story about Maximus, the Arena Dungeon. Rocky recalled the events in a very different light. Unbidden memories of all the lost survivors and the subsequent zombies... just thinking about the undead made his skin crawl.

The boys stopped talking when they reached the entrance to the Science Building—the entrance to the Dungeon. Richard had warned them that each room was a puzzle that needed to be solved. Passing the problem rewarded the group with a loot basket. Failing the puzzle would release mobs into the room. The Dungeon escalated the strength and number of the mobs based on the number of failures.

I should have asked what type of mobs were in here. Should I put this off?

Rocky had always enjoyed a good puzzle, but he wasn't sure how he would fare when the stakes were high. He would likely need to rely on Sela's judgment, as she had experienced Puzzle Dungeons in the past.

"You ready to head in?" Sela asked.

If she wasn't worried, then he probably didn't need to be.

She turned away and opened the door before he could answer.

Guess it was a rhetorical question.

The two boys followed her.

"See you in a bit, buddy." Rocky gave the Chimera plenty of head scratches. Azoth had no chance of fitting into a standard sized human enclosure. If this Dungeon agreed, they would hopefully be able to add it to the Grotto and maybe make it larger.

Welcome to the "Philosopher's Conundrum"
You have entered in a group of four, suggested group size 5-10.
Good luck!
Level: Unknown
Age: 54 Days
Best time: N/A
Clears: 0
Ether Concentration: Moderate
You can exit this Dungeon at any time. Simply leave the way you came in.

He looked around and immediately thought of high school science class. Beakers, bunsen burners, test tubes, and copious shelves filled with chemicals lined the room. His eyes searched the room for the puzzle.

Zippo called. "Create the element of life."

Rocky found the clue scrawled on a chalkboard that Zippo had read from.

Well, that was straightforward. Water. But how would he make water from the chemicals in front of him? Rocky scanned the shelves and tanks. A hydrogen tank and oxygen tank stood in the corner of the room. He had the necessary components for creating water.

He couldn't recall how to combine those elements to create water. Did he need cold air? Once the water evaporated, the coolness of the stratosphere created clouds that rained the water back down. That didn't sound right—steam didn't break up into separate atoms. It was merely water changing states.

"Anyone know how to make water?"

Everyone shook their heads, and Rocky ran his hand through his hair. He took a deep breath and tilted his head back.

Phosphorescent lights and pipes ran along the ceiling. The classroom didn't have faucets in it, which would be a huge safety issue in a real laboratory. Some of the pipes reached the counter spaces and fed the lit bunsen burners. A fire suppression pipe ran down the center of the room. Not all of the tubes were for gas. He followed the pipe with his eyes, stopping at the joint where it connected to a sprinkler. There was nothing under the sprinkler, and it was too high up to hold a bunsen burner near the heat-sensitive device. Even if he stood on a chair, there was no way to reach it.

"Zippo, create a Fireball near that Safety Mechanism."

Right, fire mage.

The heat of the Fireball broke the mercury with a click. All the furniture in the room sunk into the floor. It was eerie, almost like they had been standing in an illusion. Rocky vowed to touch something in the next area to ensure it was real. Over in a corner, a woven basket appeared, filled with what looked like a leg of meat that could feed 100 people. Or provide Azoth with a snack.

He wondered if the Dungeon created items that the survivors needed. It would make a great deal of sense. Dungeons required challengers that they could leech off and attempt to kill. If the Dungeon created loot to lure people in farther, it would have more opportunities to do both.

If all puzzles are going to be that easy, though...

Rocky summoned the haunch and basket into his Bag of Holding and then followed the group into the next room. The room was a long hallway.

Adam was the first to spot the clue. "The more you take, the more you leave behind. What am I?"

"Footsteps. The answer is footsteps, but how do we use that?" said Rocky.

Sela pointed up at a counter midway down the hallway. The number Twenty was displayed and counted up a few ticks. Zippo and Adam moved around, examining the walls.

"Both of you stop for a second," said Rocky.

The counter stopped moving up the moment the boys stilled.

"The more you leave behind," he mused to himself. "Zippo, take a step backward."

The young man complied and the counter dropped down to twenty-three.

Rocky clapped his hands together. "We need to cross this hallway to the door and have the counter at zero. Sela and Adam will walk forwards, while Zippo and I will walk in the same direction but backwards. As we near the door, we will adjust as needed."

They cleared the room with relative ease and another basket appeared. This one had four glass bottles, filled with a transparent liquid. He sniffed the contents. "No scent." He poured some on his finger and tasted the liquid. "Definitely water."

The others gave him strange looks that indicated they had already assumed that.

Maybe I am a bit paranoid. Have they never heard the saying, 'don't take candy from strange dungeons'?

He gathered the basket and the bottles into his Bag of Holding, and the group continued.

The rooms that followed were all relatively simple, and the group continued to gather food and water. The tenth to the eleventh challenge required them to climb a staircase and enter a door on the 'second floor.' The room they entered didn't contain a written clue, or at least no one saw the hint they had grown accustomed to finding.

Coming up empty, Rocky took another look around the room. Crates. Nothing but crates stacked haphazardly. The same phosphorescent strip lights lined the ceiling as they had the previous chambers. The floor contained a checkered black and white tile pattern. Four of the checkers were slightly sunken holes. He walked over to one and spied a symbol etched into the simple grey bottom of the depression. The symbol represented fire to him, and he glanced at the crates. On the nearest box was a symbol that looked like a wave of water.

Right out of a video game.

"Match the boxes to the symbols?" asked Sela.

Zippo and Adam jumped into action, figuring out what each sunken pit contained. They soon called out, "Earth, Water, and Air."

The amount of food gathered thus far on the first level would barely feed a portion of the North Bay survivors for a single day. Based on the gaunt look of those survivors, he had expected this level to ramp up in difficulty.

Guess not.

They moved the crates to the corresponding symbols on the tiles. They neatly stacked the rest of the containers until each area held three vertical boxes. The lighting turned red and the crates sunk out of sight.

The ominous red light was a first, and he worried they had messed up the puzzle. A wall slid into the ceiling and revealed five stone statues. He wasn't sure what to make of it.

The statues drew an assortment of weapons and advanced. Now, he was sure they had failed.

He Analyzed one of the stone combatants.

Gargoyle
Apprentice-Axman
Level 22
Health Points 230 / 230

He stepped forward and shot out a single charge of his Dark Blade ability. He was beginning to feel like a button masher with an individual skill to his name. He clenched his jaw, hoping that his next tier would open up some new combat options. Right now, he only had his clone and the Dark Blade Skills as offensive options. His new class of Chimera Knight was rather disappointing, especially when Azoth couldn't be with him.

The statue wielded a sword, forming a slab of stone onto its forearm. It knelt and angled its stone shield. Rocky's Dark Blade bounced off the protection and deflected diagonally toward the ceiling, where it screeched in protest as it dug into the steel supports.

He cursed at the ease with which the creatures countered his skill. He used Shadow Clone and his second self popped into existence and shook its finger at him. He had forgotten to use the ability during the battle outside and it felt like this was his scolding. Finger still waggling, his second self disappeared in Stealth.

Sela took no notice and waded forward, engaging two of the creatures. Adam backed up and started casting his leash. Zippo threw fireballs at a spear-wielding gargoyle. It formed a buckler and deflected them up and away, just like Rocky's ranged ability.

Rocky rushed forward, and a swinging ax greeted him. He planted his front foot hard and leaned back, swaying out of the path of the half-moon blade. Stepping forward again into the opening, he raised his sword and chopped down. The blow cracked the stone of the Axman's demonic cranium and bounced off. Rocky dove forward as the ax reversed direction and speed toward him.

Back on his feet, he charged his blade with his skill, holding it on the edge and causing the black steel to grow darker. He brought the blade up to block a strike from the sword and shield-wielding Gargoyle.

Blocking was a mistake.

Rocky's arm crumpled under the strength of the attack, and he almost lost his sword. His block was partially effective, saving his life. Instead of the blade cutting deeply into his chest, it deflected just enough to cut into his pectoral muscles. He cried out as the thick sword tore him open.

A bleeding and fracture debuff floated up to his status bar, and he swore. The two creatures advanced, and he used a double Dark Mend on himself as he backpedaled away. These things were ridiculously powerful. His coated blade had barely cut the dense stone.

There was no time to admire what little damage he doled out. A massive hammer smashed through the sword wielder. As the creature broke into three large chunks, one of its brethren stood behind it, brandishing a two-handed war mace.

The ax wielder attempted to engage the traitor gargoyle, But Rocky's shadow clone leaped onto the ax-swinging Gargoyle's back, unbalancing it and changing its blow into a faceplant.

His clone jumped off the Gargoyle as the warhammer rose and fell, dispatching another creature. Within moments, the battle ended, and Rocky pulled up his party's display. He wasn't the only one missing health—Sela had also taken a few hits.

She was doubled over and panting. Rocky's Ether was low, but he managed to cast a double stack of Dark Mend on her as well. They decided to wait to regenerate all resources before the next room. The spell congealed onto her stomach, and as it dulled the pain, she looked up at him thankfully. Her stomach didn't have a noticeable wound, but her hardened armor displayed spiderweb cracks. She pointed at the hammer golem. She had taken a blow, before Adam gained control of it.

No door to another room opened when the last mob died, and he asked two questions to his sweaty group. "Where is the door, and why was that considered a failure?"

"We only saw one symbol on each box, right?" asked Zippo. The group all nodded, remembering each crate they had moved around. "I feel like we should have placed the symbols in the corresponding direction to the floor symbols, and facedown to match."

That would make sense. I should have thought of that.

Still, that was only their first failure, and the mobs might have killed them, if it wasn't for Adam. How had the survivors beaten these things? Did the dungeon scale its challenges based on opponent strength?

Adam pointed to his leashed mob. "I think the door hasn't appeared because this thing is still alive."

Dang, I would have liked to have that along for the rest of the Dungeon.

He turned to Adam and asked, "Can you make it put down that hammer?" The creature placed the weapon on the floor, standing on its square top. Rocky walked over and attempted to lift the substantial stone. He strained and barely managed to get it off the floor tiles.

He wasn't sure he'd be able to pick up the weapon if he set it down. He spun and the momentum raised the head of the hammer until it was parallel to his shoulders. His hands strained to hold the weight. He had to do something quickly, before the hammer got out of control. He shifted his feet and maneuvered the weapon, crashing directly into Adam's pet.

As soon as the hammer made contact, Rocky released it and the creature crumbled. Their reward appeared—a basket and a door to the next room. A small statue laid in the basket instead of food. The figurine replicated the five Gargoyles.

Rocky relegated the basket to the safety of his bag and flipped over the statue to find an ominous number one sunken into the base of the piece.

CHAPTER TWENTY-TWO

Rocky paused in the stairwell to the Dungeon's third level. His squad had taken a beating. His armor—cracked and torn—had seen better days. Sela looked confident, even though she sported a nearly destroyed chest piece. Zippo looked drained and pale, and Adam was breathing hard while sweating buckets.

They had failed two more times on the second level. Each failure increased the difficulty by upping the number of gargoyles by one. Bringing Adam along on this run had saved them numerous times.

They had figured out a few other tactics that worked. They couldn't rely on Adam forever. Rocky used his Dark Blade's charged edge on his Soul Blade to hold back one or two of the gargoyles. Sela's Dark Vine skill had also proved useful—at least for holding two of the creatures at bay. Each of the gargoyles moved at a glacial pace and relied on close range. He didn't like to admit it, but that was probably the main reason they were able to dispatch them.

A sense of foreboding slithered down the stairs. Whether the boss resided above, or stronger mobs, it didn't matter. The group had barely survived the second level. He sat down and joined the others as each waited for their Ether and Health to regenerate. His gear had a low Ether pool. "Sela, if the pool runs out on the armor, does it fall apart?"

"It won't fall apart as long as the material isn't in such bad shape that it structurally has to. The Enchantments will stop working, and the armor's inherent Ether will be gone. Even if you were wearing a piece of Eternium, at that point, you would only be counting on the inherent material strength versus an Ether-charged blow."

"Do you think there will be more puzzles above or a boss fight?"

Sela shrugged. "It could be either. There used to be a similar practice Dungeon at the Atlantean Academy. We were always told the instructors set it up, but now I think it was a Territorial Dungeon. That Dungeon had a difficult puzzle for its finale. If you got it wrong, though, no mobs attacked you—so, maybe it was set up by instructors."

"When in the Apep Dungeon, you thought it might be a puzzle Dungeon because of the traps. How come this one hasn't had any traps?"

"Each Dungeon is as different as each person you have ever met. Just look at Maximus and LFD."

Each of the Dungeons had vastly different personalities. The next floor could be more puzzles, a boss room or one big mystery. At least they hadn't taken too long to clear the twenty puzzles so far. He stood up and brushed himself off. "Shall we?"

They ascended the stairs and entered a chamber as vast as a football field. The floor was open, with a few concrete pillars interspersed for structural support. Sunlight streamed from the windows, no matter the direction he looked in. He took a deep, relaxing breath. He needed his mind to be clear. Focused.

A golden Sphynx statue loomed over them from ten meters away. He glanced at his group to find everyone transfixed. He wondered if they felt the waves of the statue's ominous vibe the way he did.

He used Analyze.

Golden Sphynx
Journeyman-Riddler
Level 43
Health Points 1400 / 1400

He gulped nervously and whispered, "Do we have to fight it?"

"A Sphynx usually asks a question that you must answer correctly. If you answer incorrectly, it will attack. Maybe send your clone in first?" said Sela.

Rocky mentally commanded his second self to exit Stealth and approach the Sphynx. His clone appeared beside him a moment later and rolled its dark eyes. Giving the entire group the finger, it approached the Sphynx.

His clone was crushed under one of the front paws of the creature. It happened so quickly that he almost missed it. A crash of stone on stone sounded as his clone turned to smoke, and the golden foot hit the concrete floor. It opened its mouth and spoke, "No constructs will be allowed to answer the riddle. Approach, or stay distant and provoke my ire."

Swallowing hard, Rocky edged forward. The others fell in behind him, mirroring his unease. Once they were a few feet away, the Sphynx smiled, rivaling the Cheshire cat's sly grin.

"Good. Now answer me this: What eight-letter word can have a letter taken away, and it still makes a word. Take another letter away, and it still makes a word. Keep on doing that until you have one letter left. What is each word?"

Rocky had never heard this one before. He looked to the group and saw each face looking back at him. Okay—they didn't have the answer either. He groaned and kicked his brain into gear. The one-letter word had to be a vowel. So, either A or I, as they were the only single letter words in the English language. He hoped the Sphynx wasn't using trickery, since it didn't specify the language.

He moved to two letters, and again both A and I could work. 'As' and 'an', or 'Is' and 'in'. He was sure more combinations existed, but when he considered 'in,' something tickled his mind. 'In' was in plenty of words ending in -ing.

He decided he would keep going with 'in.'

The Sphynx interrupted his train of thought. "I will give you ten minutes to correctly answer the riddle."

His pulse throbbed as his heart beat faster. He swore inwardly. He couldn't do this alone and so he explained his logic to the group. The others began tossing out three-letter words.

"Bin ... Gin ... Vin ... Fin ... Sin—"

"Of those words we have been saying, 'sin' can become 'sing,' which fits with the 'ing' theory." He babbled and glanced at the Sphynx, hoping for a hint or clue in its expression. Instead, it cleaned its forepaw, sharp golden teeth glinting in the sunlight. The cat's stone tongue scraped over its paw, the grating sound worming its way into his ears and driving him to rush.

Damnit, calm down. Keep going.

"We need a five-letter word now. I think adding more consonants is better than adding vowels. So the next word can be 'swing' or 'sting.' 'Swing,' I can't add another letter; can I add something to 'sting'?"

"Five minutes left. I may have to invite my first visitors to be my dinner."

Rocky was sweating like he had just played a full forty-eight minutes on the basketball court.

"'String', and then 'stringy', maybe?" Sela offered, successfully reminding him to stay on track.

He nodded, seeing 'string' but backtracked because 'stringy' had no way of adding letters. It also contained seven letters and they needed eight. Sweat dripped down his face. He wracked his brain but couldn't think of another word that included 'string'. Maybe he had to go back to 'sting' or even 'sing'.

"We might have to go back." Rocky said and the group backtracked all the way to 'sing.'

"Two minutes remaining. I wonder what humans taste like."

Rocky took a stuttering breath and pulled his sword. He needed to be ready if this turned into a fight.

He was out of ideas. He looked around to see if anyone else had any ideas. Silence. Everyone stared at him.

"'Staring,' that's the next word from 'string!'" The group, who had begun settling into combat stances, jumped at his shout.

Adam whispered something, and Rocky didn't hear it. He stared at the kid. "What?"

Adam gulped, shrinking under Rocky's tone. Zippo threw Rocky a look that told him his tone was unnecessary. "He said, 'starting.' Not sure why we don't just kill—"

That was it!

Rocky shouted at the Sphynx, "Starting, Staring, String, Sting, Sing, Sin, In, and I!"

The golden creature smiled and displayed its sharp teeth. Its claws unsheathed from its padded feline feet, and its wings opened wide on its back, scraping the ceiling.

Rocky tensed his muscles and placed a second shaking hand onto his sword. But the Sphynx was only stretching. A full set of golden-colored plate armor glistened within a basket that materialized next to the Golden Cat-Creature.

Congratulations! You have completed the "Philosopher's Conundrum."

> **Bonus:**
>> **For the first completion of the Dungeon, your group has been awarded 430,000 personal Etherience per party member.**

The Dungeon has been classified as a Level 43 zone.

2,001,133 Etherience remaining until level 9.

He smiled at the prompt, and the relief of completing the Dungeon washed over him. Adam had been their saving grace. Without him, the high-level Dungeon would have been impossible. A single failure probably would have cost the group their lives.

"Is a level forty-three Dungeon ranked for total levels or current rank?" Rocky asked.

"Dungeon level classifications are slightly unusual. People argued for years over whether it is a combination of levels from all ranks, or just your current level. Honestly, my opinion is that the system just ranks the mobs and boss levels on strength. Since I have never seen a level forty-three Apprentice, this Dungeon is for Journeyman Ranks."

Rocky nodded and Analyzed the prized gear. His eyes bugged out; nestled within the basket was a set of five items—a chest guard, leggings, boots, gauntlets, and a helm. They were all titled The Golden Defender and locked. A set would be a lot better than one strong piece of armor, like the Bone Breastplate he had given to Victoria.

Rocky stored it away and addressed the Sphynx. "Are you the Dungeon?"

The Sphynx shook its head.

Rocky tried again. "Could we speak to the Dungeon?"

The Sphynx stood up and moved to the far side of the building, like a cat that lost interest and went to sun itself.

A computerized voice asked "Do you have a complaint about the loot?"

Rocky jumped, landed, and spun, finding only an empty floor where the Sphynx had stood moments ago. Selecting a random location on the ground to focus on, he cleared his throat. "No, the loot is amazing. I am hoping to recruit you."

"Of course, the loot is amazing. For the first clear, Dungeons are forced to increase the rarity. What do you mean, 'recruit me'?"

"We require Territorial Dungeons, and you could be our third, if you agree to our terms."

"Do you have a copy of your terms with you?"

The conversation became extremely one-sided after that. Rocky talked, and the Dungeon remained silent. He wasn't even sure if it was listening.

"Leave now. I will give you my answer in a day. I wish to discuss this with my Sphynx."

Does that count as talking to yourself?

The Dungeon opened a stairwell that led to a hidden door and a path out of the science building. Rocky was breathing fresh air again. It was time to see what the military had discovered in the Territory. His screen lit up with notifications.

Congratulations, you have completed a Chain Quest! Preservation of Champion Life Quest

Chain Party Quest – Atlantean Net Generated Save the McDougall Survivors II

- **Escort 50% of the survivors successfully back to your Territory. This quest difficulty has been adjusted due to distance to Territory. Approximately 100 miles (160 km) Rewards: 299,000 (+39,000 Knight's Quest) Etherience 260 new Territorial Citizens.**

Atlantean Statutes, Preservation of Life, Section XII
Invite new citizens to join Meliora?
<Yes> | No

He clicked the 'yes' button in excitement. Nothing happened, and he shrugged at Sela, assuming something had occurred with the new citizens. All his notices were for escort quests, and he clicked the summarize button.

Congratulations, you have completed 25 Chain Quests!
   Rewards:
   3,118,000 (+467,700 Knight's Quest) Etherience
   3,118 New Territorial Citizens.

--

Congratulations! You have reached level 9. You have been awarded 1 stat point and 1 skill point.
   9,031,413 Etherience remaining till level 10.

As they walked, Rocky sunk his Skill Point into Knight's Quest. The amount of extra Etherience he received confirmed his earlier choice and made him feel slightly better about his offensive skill stagnation.

His party was in good spirits when they rounded the corner and caught a glimpse of the command center.

The calm planning center they had left was now a beehive of activity, and Rocky didn't know if that was normal. Sela jogged toward the Operations Area, and Rocky followed her lead. Adam and Zippo continued to babble as they ran, and the normalcy of their actions calmed his nerves slightly. What was going on?

Victoria motioned for them to stand off to the side. The crackle of the radio was all he heard, but no communications. The hum of white noise clashed with the utter stillness of the command area, making it all the louder. The beehive they had jogged toward had frozen.

"Scout fourteen. False alarm—the creature in question Analyzes as a Master Class, but not a territorial leader. Resuming scouting mission. Over."

The collective sigh of held breaths hung in the air as the radio hummed to life. Each scout sounded off, reporting in their situations. Rocky heard twenty scouts in total. The Operations Tent exploded in excited murmurs about levels and where to place skill points or stats.

Victoria walked over, grinning, and asked, "How did the Dungeon run go? Any luck recruiting it?" She pointed around at the group. "As you can see, Meliora members are pretty excited about the free Etherience!"

Rocky looked around and smiled. They had needed this win, and with the new Guild Dome and accompanying Tower, he was sure they would be able to find housing for everyone, especially if they used the Starship to get the Guild Tent down.

"It went as well as could be expected. The mobs were powerful, and we luckily didn't have to engage the final boss. We will find out tomorrow if the Dungeon wishes to agree to our terms. We got a nice set of gear for being the first to clear—might even be good for a tank." He winked at Victoria and caught Sela glowering at him.

What did I do?

Victoria was excited at the prospect of new gear. Rocky was equally jubilant to have a tank with proper equipment in his Territory. In all the video games he had played, a durable tank helped protect lower-leveled players more than any other class—besides a good healer. He would have to figure out if there was an unselfish healer back in the Grotto. He hadn't liked Gaston very much.

"Scout two. This is the fifth burrow I have come across. Is anyone else finding numerous warrens or dug holes? Over."

Each scout reported in, confirming the report of the second scout. Rocky had a skill that was perfect for scouting high-risk areas. He summoned his Shadow Clone, and it billowed into existence, waving its hands in front of its body, as if to say, 'No, I will not do this.'

"I thought I was braver than this." Rocky said to no one in particular.

Sela laughed, and he wasn't sure if he had made a joke, or if she was making a statement. He pointed toward the

Territory grounds, and his clone sneered at him before sprinting away. A few steps in, the shadowy form vanished from sight.

He sat down and told the group, "I will go explore those caverns with my clone. Sit tight." Once his explanation left his mouth, he entered Meditation and looked through the eyes of his second self.

The clone charged in with remarkable speed, considering it only gained fifty percent of his stats. He assumed his breakthrough in Agility and Dexterity was affecting it. If nothing else, the power of his clone spoke to his growth.

Sparsely spread trees flashed by, and he received the Territorial notification. He was surprised that his clone triggered an announcement, and that he saw the notice through its eyes. He closed it on the run, but the next notice made him freeze.

Due to the proximity of your starship, mutations have occurred with the local leader of the Territory!

Rocky conveyed this information to the group and focused on his clone.

A hundred meters further, one of the warrens loomed up from the overgrown grass and tree roots. Its cavernous mouth with its dangling vegetation and freshly churned look, making Rocky's clone shudder.

His clone stepped over the threshold and he had a split-second of regret. Using the Skill in this way always felt a little masochistic, but he forced down the thought.

Using many of his learned skills, Sneak, Stealth, and the clone's inherent Dark Vision, he made his way deeper into the underground space. The tunnel wasn't wide, and Rocky believed it might be a giant insect nest, even though he didn't see the usual signs. Most insects would have active members outside the nest.

The tunnel wound through the earth, leading him onward, and his limited vision decreased as less sunlight was available for his Dark Vision to pull on. Still, his clone had a ten-foot radius of view.

His tunnel joined a slightly larger branch, and he deliberated which direction to take. Kneeling, he attempted to determine which one led deeper underground and which one headed back to the surface. It was subtle, but the right side seemed to slightly fall away. Once his clone was on that path, the angle of descent picked up quickly. It was the right direction.

A few steps later, and the path dropped off in a quick forty-five-degree angle. His clone's cone of vision had decreased again to five feet. He strained his ears to pick up a sound—any sound—that would give him a hint regarding what lay ahead.

He moved his clone to the wall and crept carefully, trying not to disturb the loose dirt and stones. At the bottom of the depression, he found himself looking back up an incline that escalated to a purely vertical ascent. He relayed the layout in cool detachment and ordered his clone to scale the wall using daggers.

His clone made it look easy as it rose to the top of the loose dirt. The daggers served as footholds, and his invisible head peeked over the top of the escarpment. Even in his relatively emotionless headspace, a stab of fear shot through him. Scales as big as small cars greeted him, not more than three feet from his limited vision.

Something felt off. He looked up over the round back of the scales and glimpsed claw marks and bite impressions coating the creature's body. He used Analyze.

Terror Snake
Master-Constrictor
Level 13
Health points 0 / 2300

Dead

At first, he was relieved. But he couldn't push the image out of his mind that whatever had killed this mile-long snake was the real threat. Chitter and squeals reached his ears. Far too close. His clone whipped around and encountered a furry face, beady eyes, and a mouth full of sharp teeth. Rocky jumped to his feet, startling himself out of Meditation.

He shook his head, his cheeks making the sound of a motorboat. Shuddering, he said, "It was a—ferret?"

CHAPTER TWENTY-THREE

Rocky stood in front of an entrance that was far larger than the one his clone had entered. Sela had scanned the area and determined that this was the main tunnel that had led to the snake's corpse.

The group entered the Territory, and a notification informed the Golem Knights that they were unable to capture Territories. According to Epsilon, they were not allowed to damage the Leaders, or the Territory would become uncapturable until a new Leader spawned. That was one colossal wrench in the mechanism.

The army needed to change their plans. Victoria had hoped to use them as the vanguard in the upcoming assault. Now, she was going to play that role, alongside Adam's golems, and Rocky wasn't sure it would work. The Knights stood ready to bail them out of trouble, should the creature prove far too powerful for them alone.

The ground trembled again as Sela used her skill and collapsed another branch tunnel. She had already made a near-complete round of the Territory on foot, collapsing underground branches, and the ferret still hadn't shown itself.

In the time it had taken her to make her rounds, the military, tanks, and golems had felled numerous trees, and the Knights had stacked the wood near the entrance. Following Victoria's instructions, Sela left small air holes through the collapses so that smoke could travel into the tunnels.

A group of thirteen people stood ready to work at Zippo's command, all of whom had a fire spell or wind spell. Both were crucial to set the pyre ablaze and push the smoke into the nest. If the smoke forced the creature out of the earth, they would have a fighting chance.

Sela collapsed a final tunnel and stood up shakily. "I am done, but would like a few minutes to catch my breath."

When Sela signaled, the 'Fire Brigade'—Rocky came up with the name in the moment—began to cast. Within seconds, thick white smoke flowed into the tunnels, and the felled trees popped and crackled like kindling. The scope of the spellcasters' power was scary.

Perhaps resistance to elements is much better than I gave it credit.

Sela clicked her earpiece. "Selaphelia. Movement in the tunnels. Get ready. Over."

A small portion of the military waited behind them. At first, they were going to stack all of their forces at this one entrance, but Sela pointed out that a ferret could dig new tunnels or re-excavate the collapsed ones. A contingent of the stationed military was to warn them if the creature exited elsewhere while attempting to hold it still until the heavy hitters came running. Sela would be able to give them some advance notice if the animal chose a different tunnel.

"Thor's hammer!" Sela exclaimed and turned to look at Rocky as her face paled. "The footfalls of one creature just turned into three. Two tunnels are being dug simultaneously, and something is coming straight for us."

"Explosive pinecones." Rocky swore—heard what he had said, and tamped down his anger at the system. He was sick of its censorship but now was not the time. "Sela, that must be the mutations. Can you guide Azoth to one and fly to another?"

She made a face that told him she wasn't sure. He jumped on Azoth's back and shouted, "At least try. I don't want to leave any of the groups without support." Sela nodded, and Azoth back-winged furiously, adding his gusts to that of the casters.

Rocky clicked his earpiece. "Rocky here. Adam, Zippo, and Victoria, cover this entrance. If any group dispatches an enemy, help the others." He forgot to say over and didn't bother correcting himself. Of the two errors that were rattling in his mind, the radio etiquette issue was secondary. How had he been stupid enough to assume only one powerful enemy creature was below?

Now, his false assumption endangered his military and his friends.

Damn, damn, damn. Maybe, Azoth and I can take down our enemy quickly. Sela is going to be entirely by herself—do I help her first, or Zippo and Victoria?

Azoth stayed aloft, circling the area in scouting patterns. From the sky, it was easy to distinguish the exits. A trickle of white smoke leaked from each, creating small streams of cloud-like white rising into the sky all over the Territory.

Rocky glanced down. Tao ran along through the sparse trees, following Azoth's flight. At least they had the backup plan.

Azoth dove, and Rocky white-knuckled the saddle. Not being able to hear his pet was making it extremely difficult to prepare for these moments.

What had Azoth reacted to?

Fighting against the forces of the descent, Rocky tried to search the ground as wind buffeted his head. It proved to be impossible to get a good view of anything other than the sweeping landscape. He would have to trust that Azoth knew what he was doing. He tucked into Azoth's back as deeply as he could and held on for the ride.

Objects whooshed by him, and the noise alerted him to their low altitude and impending collision. He took a deep breath before the air was ejected from his lungs. Azoth must not have struck squarely because, while most of the momentum of the flight dumped, not all of it. There was a jarring half-stop, followed by a slow coast to a halt.

Rocky rolled out of the saddle. Something hissed and barked. He managed to orient himself as Azoth closed his wings before getting broadsided by a long, brown ball of fur. A boom reverberated out from the impact, and Rocky winced at the sheer force behind the blow. The two became a rolling mess, and he couldn't distinguish where the furry ferret ended and the black feathers began.

The posted military, with accompanying tanks, moved forward in formation.

His radio crackled and the steady beat of "Contact. Contact. Contact," filled his ears.

He ground his teeth—the other three enemies must have exited in near unison. They had to defeat their creature quickly if they wanted a chance to survive. Or should he order the knights to engage?

Rocky needed to separate Azoth from the ferret, or he and the nearby military would be useless. He used a quadruple stack of Dark Mend on his pet and summoned his Shadow Clone, exhausting the majority of his Ether in a single moment. He chugged an Ether Draught and gained the Debuff for excessive use.

His clone arrived, facing away from him toward the fight. Rocky ignored the full moon in the middle of the day and ran to assist the tangled ball of flying feathers. He managed to get approximately ten feet away before he entered Stealth. Closing in, he tried his best to time his strike properly and thrust his weapon at a patch of brown fur.

The tip of his sword scored home and ripped back out, thanks to the momentum of the tumble. The ferret didn't react at all, and he assumed that his sword felt similar to Azoth's claws or teeth.

How could he disentangle the two?

His clone exited Stealth and ran its two daggers down the ferret's side before being flattened beneath it. The ferret squealed, and Rocky hoped that stacking damage would be enough. He struck at the ferret at every opportunity. The vicious boss reached its pain threshold and kicked off of Azoth, rolling away.

The kick launched Azoth backward, and he collided with a tree. The spruce groaned and splintered as it crumpled away from the impact. Silence reigned for a moment, and then the ground shook with the thump of the felled tree.

Azoth rose to his feet and shook himself. Even with the stacked Dark Mends, his pet looked rough. His tail was broken, and he seemed hesitant to place weight on one of his back-lizard claws.

Rocky turned back to the ferret. Red blood covered its fur, and it radiated menace and outrage. The military opened fire, stopping the beast from engaging Rocky and Azoth for a second round. Rocky charged at it and Analyzed the boss on the run.

Podo
Mutation 2
Master-Beast
Level 42
Health Points 2100 / 3340
Territorial Leader

The creature's damage mounted and its wounds continued to bleed health as more ionized bolts struck. The beast crouched low, preparing for Rocky's attack. It curled its tail around its body, reducing the effectiveness of the military's strikes. Rocky sneered and channeled his frustration into a loud war cry.

His scream was more for show than a declaration of battle. The longer he held its attention, the more bolts would meet their target. He stopped short and set up in his Seraphim Sword stance.

The ferret shifted its attention to the military.

"No. None of that!" Rocky screamed, stepping forward and slashing out. His sword connected with the black wet nose of the ferret. The blow was akin to a paper cut, but it drew its attention back to Rocky. He engaged Dark Cloak and stepped back into his neutral stance.

The ferret took a single step and attempted a circling maneuver. He stepped into its path, slashing it again. The creature flinched and hissed at him.

This tactic wouldn't last long, but it didn't have to. Rocky chugged another Ether Draught and added another stack to his Debuff.

With the new Ether, he stacked his sword with Dark Blade and held it on the edge as he continued distracting the beast. Azoth limped over and roared at the ferret. Its attention diverted for a moment, and Rocky caught it with another slash, leaving behind a trail of Dark Smoke in its light wound.

The ferret bunched its legs and focused on Rocky.

He fought against his urge to curl in on himself, and instead held his sword form and swallowed his nerves. He checked his Ether pool. The creature pushed off the ground, and he performed a rising strike, releasing the four stacks of Dark Blade.

Be enough.

The vertical slashes collided with the beast's snout, pushing it back and eliciting a screech. The blades didn't have the power to bisect the Territorial Leader. Still, they ripped away fur and skin, causing a mist of blood as the shrieking rage of the rat-like creature intensified. The ferret's back claws held, faltered, and finally lost to the spectral blades.

The creature slid backward slowly at first and then sped up until its back collided with a tree. Rocky relaxed his stance as his blades, and the continued barrage from the military, finally dropped the creature. Once it died, its inherent Ether fled, and his blades flew through the corpse, the tree, and hummed away in a swathe of destruction.

Rocky wanted to sit down and rest, but he couldn't. He clicked his radio. "Rocky here. One down. Report in."

He pulled two Health Potions from his Bag and walked over to Azoth. "Head up, buddy." He poured both into Azoth's maw. Some of the potion leaked out, but he managed to send most of the liquid down his throat. Azoth wouldn't be flying soon, but the potions would help realign the bones in his wings.

"Main force. Engaged." It was the only radio response he received, and his stomach dropped. He checked his party screen. Zippo, Victoria, and Adam's health were doing well. Sela was alive, but her health was dangerously low, sitting just below half.

"We're going to Sela." He hoped his pet got the message and could sense Sela like he could sense Rocky. "Tao, you're with us. Is one of your brothers already with Sela's group?" Azoth took a moment to orient himself and then began to run.

Tao nodded as he shouldered his sword and sprinted after Azoth. At least he could radio to one of the Knights to save Sela if he couldn't make it in time.

"Go help the main force," he shouted over his shoulder at the military.

Azoth had grown larger still and was nearing three quarters the size of his mother, Skandranon. It usually wasn't this apparent, but running beside Tao, the size increase was evident. Azoth raced directly through a tree in front of him.

Rocky dodged around the fallen trees and splintered wood as best he could.

They sprinted for a few minutes, and he continually glanced at Sela's health bar. It remained steady and Rocky hoped that was a good sign.

The sound of ionized tank fire and angry squeaking was the first sign of combat. Azoth blew up a tree, and through the wood shards, Rocky saw the battle.

Sela was in her raven form and dove at the ferret, dragging her claws through its fur. The ferret attempted to tear the military apart while simultaneously keeping an eye on the large raven. The strewn bodies wearing military fatigues told him it was having some success.

His mind fuzzed, and he bellowed a war cry. He wasn't sure if he knew any of the dead, but these were his people.

As he entered range, he Analyzed the second ferret.

Kodo
Mutation 1
Master-Beast
Level 42
Health Points 1400 / 3340
Territorial Leader

Rocky poured another Ether Elixir down his throat and screamed in anguish as he began using his Pool. He entered Stealth on the run and increased his speed. His vision narrowed as he charged the edge of his Soul Blade with the Dark Blade skill. He had likely used too much Ether in the last few days, and he was bearing the brunt of that now. Darkness closed in as he fully bottomed out his Ether Pool. He bit his lip hard and tasted blood.

The self-inflicted pain pushed back the black.

Rocky approached undetected. The beast was too distracted by Sela and the military to notice him. He jumped at the ferret's exposed side, leading with his sword, While Azoth attacked its head. They made contact with the beast.

Rocky's sword sunk into its flesh to the hilt. The collision, paired with the strain on his brain, overtook his will. A spike of intense pain tore through his mind, and he released his Dark Blade skill. He had just enough time to register a different effect than usual.

The darkness, moments before confined to the edge of his vision, closed in sharply. His eyes rolled up, and he crumpled into the side of the ferret like a fly hitting a windshield.

CHAPTER TWENTY-FOUR

He groggily opened his eyes to see Azoth staring down on him. His pet curled up around him, enveloping him in walls of feather-fur. The last thing he remembered was pain, and then darkness. He glanced hurriedly around, searching for a threat.

He seemed to be alone and the radio was silent.

He clicked the earpiece, and asked, "Rock here. Report?"

He sat up and almost jumped out of his skin. Tao sat nearby, cross-legged and Meditating. "That was quite the attack, young Knight."

Is he referring to my new class?

Sela's voice came through his earpiece. "Selaphelia Ardensai here. All three bosses are vanquished, Rocky. Just cleaning up and healing the wounded. How is your Ether? Over."

He clicked the button and released it three times, notifying Sela to change over to the third channel on the device. He changed his channels and said, "It is back close to full, but I have a debuff called 'Raw Ether Channels' that is decreasing the total Ether Pool significantly. Plus, I have a splitting headache. How did we do?"

"The fight went worst in my sector. I couldn't face the creature head-on in my cat form. It was too fast. I chose to try to hold its attention as a raven. The only reason it wasn't a complete disaster was my Leadership Aura. It was a good thing you and Azoth arrived when you did. Victoria's group had minimal casualties, mainly due to Adam's newest golems. Their ferret was the strongest of the three we faced. So, I would say it was the primary Leader and their fight went very well. Can you check that area for any survivors we missed, and loot the corpse?"

Sadness swept over his heart, and he forced himself to rise, despite his pounding headache. "Affirmative." He and Azoth began hunting for survivors. He found four dead bodies, three disabled tanks, and one badly wounded survivor. He used a double-stacked Dark Mend to stabilize the woman and forced a Health Potion into her mouth. The use of Ether made him feel sick, and the timer on his Debuff jumped back up. Rocky massaged the woman's throat to ensure she swallowed the potion. The paleness of her face gained a couple of healthy shades back, and he breathed a sigh of relief.

He moved to loot the ferret's corpse and heard a knock coming from one of the tanks. He sprinted over and found the dented hatch of the tank unserviceable, no matter how hard he pulled on it. He scrambled atop it. Someone shouted from within, and he could just barely make out pleas for help.

"Get back from the hatch." He used his sword to shear through the metal. He changed its shape to that of a can opener and worked it back and forth to pry the edges apart. Once the destroyed locking mechanism was free, he opened the lid, and a scared-looking young man stared at him. "Let's get you out of there." He held out his hand.

The youth took it, and together they checked the other tanks for any signs of trapped personnel. The hatches weren't fused, and when they opened the other three tanks, they found the interiors empty. Rocky dropped his shoulders in relief and returned to the ferret corpse.

The creature had a large hole punched right through its body, and light was visible down the channel it created. He studied the puncture wound and moved to the other side of the corpse. A tree stood in the same line of view, also pierced. Recalling the last moments of consciousness, he thought that perhaps this was from his Dark Blade. The energy had released, and he had used a thrust attack. He would have to test it later.

He placed his hand on the creature and thought 'loot.'

Ten Crystallized Ether and a jacket, which was made of dark leather, appeared in his hands. The jacket had a beautiful fur-lined collar and hood. The coat was strangely 'in fashion,' at least what little Rocky knew of recent fashion trends.

He Analyzed the item.

Kodo's Jacket
- **This jacket is lined with the Fur of the Territorial Leader Kodo and looks quite warm.**
  Quality: Excellent
  Enchantments: Locked

The prompt made him think of the upcoming winter, and what that might mean for people in his Territory. At least the Crafter's Hall was finished now. Perhaps if there was an Enchantment that kept gear warmer, he could learn it before the first snows fell. His mood soured as he remembered his recent failures in Enchanting.

Discouraged, he scanned through his notifications.

Congratulations! You have reached Territory Leader level 5. You have been awarded 2 Leader Skill Points.
--
Congratulations, you and your party have successfully conquered a new Territory.
The Nest has been captured due to the death of all three leaders. Would you like to take ownership of the new Territory?
Yes | <No>
Would you like to place the Territory onto the Market?
Yes | <No>
Would you like to condense the Territory into a Territorial Sphere?
Warning! A transfer of this sort will sustain losses.

<Yes> | No

Rocky selected yes to the last question. Sela had mentioned that this was the option he should choose. He hoped he could place the Territory where it was needed or, worst case, add it to his. He had just discovered another way to increase his and Sela's Leadership Class levels. This flipped his emotions and Rocky swore again to keep working on his strange 'Chidi.'

Azoth and Rocky made their way back through the forest, following the clear trail of destroyed trees that Azoth had plowed through. When they made it to the first corpse they had downed, he looted it and received a pile of ten Crystals and a pair of boots.

The boots were of the same Dark Leather and had a fur-lined rim at the top of the ankle-high gear. He Analyzed this item as well.

Podo's Boots
- **These boots are lined with the Fur of the Territorial Leader Podo and look quite warm.**
  Quality: Excellent
  Enchantments: Locked

He assumed the last piece of gear would be pants or a pair of gloves. He grew excited about the prospect of having two sets of equipment. The one from the Puzzle Dungeon and this set from Territorial Leaders. His last collection of gear from Skandranon had been mighty.

He doubted he would be wearing the fur-lined gear, though, unless it was a near-perfect fit for his build. There was something about the style that made him think it would be near impossible for him to pull it off. He mounted atop Azoth, and the Chimera made a quick flight to the main force.

Clean up from the battle had begun, and the military butchered the corpse of the ferret. His heart sank when he saw the line of ten corpses, laid out and ready for transport back to the Grotto. This was the first time his people would be able to return the bodies to the grieving. But they didn't have room for a cemetery in the Grotto.

Perhaps we can give the corpses to the Dungeons? I doubt people will like that suggestion, though.

When Azoth landed, Zippo and Adam rushed over to greet the big bird-brain. His pet rolled around to allow them access to harder to reach areas. The silly antics, as usual, brightened his mood, and he went in search of Sela after telling the young men, "Don't *spoil* him too much."

Sela was treating some of the wounded with bandages. Upon his arrival, she demanded his Bag of Holding and poured potions down a few throats. "Honestly, combat classers should always have one potion on hand. It's common sense."

Once the severe cases were on the mend, thanks to some liberally applied potions and some sparing Dark Mends—his head still felt like the anvil a forge hammer had used too much—Rocky and Sela moved aside to discuss the day.

"Azoth says, 'Azoth deserve spoiled food. Who else eat if not Azoth?'" Sela looked at him curiously after she finished and he explained where the comment must have originated. They both laughed, partly because it amused them, but her laugh sounded slightly forced. Perhaps his mirth was forced somewhat as well. He could feel a great sense of relief from having survived the encounter, and he knew he needed to release the tension.

Feeling loose and relaxed, Rocky held up the brightly glowing blue sphere.

"So, you *were* listening to me," Sela said.

"What would the Market have done?"

"Mercenaries and pirates usually used the Market. There was an entire industry that existed to ravage new planets or burgeoning young Territories. The bands of mercenaries used the Market to make a very bloody, but lucrative, living."

"What are all the options for this sphere? A larger Territory doesn't seem worth an entire Market centered on this object."

Sela snapped her fingers. "I think you are missing some of the minutiae of Territories. Territories are usually higher density areas of Ether. Right now, on Gaia, that might not appear to be the case, due to the huge levels of Ether spread across the entire planet. However, more area in a Territory allows the owner to increase the Territorial Etherience stores faster, reach higher Territory levels, Leader Levels, and adds safety to areas surrounding it."

She made a broad gesture with her hands. "While the inside of a Territory is safe, the edges of a Territory also gain a layer of protection from their proximity. Normally, to increase the Ether inside the Territory, it pulls it from just outside the zone. Powerful creatures can feel the slightly lower Ether levels in the environment and move farther away from Territory edges. During my time, there were so many Territories in existence that there were few places on Gaia considered unruly. On the Pangaea, you could only go far north or very far south to encounter untamed lands—"

A voice crackled over the radio. "Scourge Captain here. Finished all drop offs. Ready for extraction? Over."

Someone, perhaps Victoria, answered, and a response ETA of fifteen minutes relayed back from The Scourge. Rocky pointed to the sphere. "I can't convert this straight to Territorial Etherience then?"

Sela shook her head. "Unfortunately, not. You are more playing the long game with these orbs. There will be other options, and we will go through them when you ground it in the Grotto. The other choice is also something to consider. With an orb like this, you can choose a location and establish a Territory.

This was of great use during expeditions upon hostile planets. For us, it may be worth it to establish somewhere more central?"

He considered that option. Placing a Territory centrally to groups of survivors had its appeal. If they were to capture an area in each Canadian province, then they could perhaps save more. He shook his head after a moment's consideration, "We know that Territories already exist and are capturable. I think we can assume that we will find additional Territories that are near enough to an area that we could make it work. The issue will probably be finding the time to capture them."

"I, too, would like to save everyone, Rockland. But it may be impossible. It will likely spread us far too thinly. I suggest we capture Territories closer together and ferry survivors back to them. It may not be ideal, but in the long run, we will have a stronger fortified position."

His emotions flared, dominated as always by anger. He forced down his initial reaction and considered why he was upset, attempting to separate his emotional turmoil. It didn't take long to find the actual culprit—his family, which he had been trying not to dwell on recently.

They were alive and out there somewhere. Rocky needed to find them, and right now, a part of him wanted to just search places, one at a time, until he did.

"Your family?" Sela asked. Her soft voice suggested that she understood.

His voice trembled a bit. "Yeah, I just don't know how else to find them, Sela. What if they are dying right now?"

She hugged him tightly, and he leaned into her embrace. The moment lasted for a gloriously long time and drew a few eyes from army members. He let go, feeling embarrassed for a reason he couldn't place. He smiled at Sela and mumbled something that could have been a thank you.

A young runner stood nearby, holding the last piece of looted gear from the ferrets and the Crystalized Ether. Rocky

accepted them and studied the hideous fur-lined cloak,
Analyzing it in the process.

Pan's Cloak
- **This Cloak is lined with the Fur of the
  Territorial Leader Pan and looks quite warm.
  Quality: Superb
  Enchantments: Locked**

He used the rest of the time until retrieval on attempting
to unlock any Enchantment on the pieces of gear he had
captured. To his frustration, other than Protection, he wasn't
able to identify anything.

On the flight back to the Territory, he contemplated the
Enchanter's pen. He knew he needed to use the mortar and
pestle to make some sort of ink for the pen, but what material he
should use was anyone's guess.

Upon his return, he asked Smith for herb choices, and
the latter provided him with five different options.

***

He looked at the five pieces of ruined gear as Sela stood
nearby, shaking her head. She had pointed out earlier that
regular ink made from herbs wasn't going to work.

"You need something that can hold the Ether. Right
now, it is leaking in all directions, causing the leather to burn up,
and the Enchantment to fade. Can we go identify the rest of the
gear now?"

They entered the shop to find out what type of gear they
might be able to dole out to their citizens at the celebration that
evening. Their population had grown by over three thousand,
and Sela again suggested a welcoming ceremony. She pointed

out that they could reward Victoria with gear in front of everyone at the party to increase morale.

They had decided to postpone the trip to save Toronto by a day. After the attack on North Bay's Territory, far too many people had Elixir Debuffs that needed to clear. That had been his main argument against the celebration tonight, until Sela pointed out the error in his judgment. Trying to save everyone faster was likely to get them killed.

Plus, she is right that the new citizens need to feel welcome and appreciated.

***

His visit with Lingren was relatively quick—the man did not want to be seen with Beastfolk at his stall. Sela's previous antics, while gaining them a discount on their current gear, hadn't been forgotten. Lingren, cold and business-like, unlocked the gear at his quoted price. Rocky observed him closely, hoping to discover tricks in his method. But there wasn't anything he could identify as unique. Lingren probably simply knew far more glyphs than he did.

They stopped to pick up a large amount of alcohol for the celebration that night, taking a moment to chat with Garnell and schedule a meeting with Amelia. Since they were taking the day off tomorrow, they might as well get it out of the way.

***

That evening, Rocky stood behind the stage as people gathered to hear him and Sela speak. He searched for Smith, remembering another friend standing in his position at the last celebration they had thrown. Joe had supported him when he had been nervous at his first speech to the Grotto. He no longer felt those nerves. Too much had happened since then for him to feel anything other than sad.

He looked over at the gear and Analyzed it one more time, seriously considering changing his class to a tank.

Sphynx's Golden Breastplate
Ether Pool: Moderate
Current Ether Pool: 56 / 90
Enchantments: Protection V (49%), Stamina V (+10)
--

Sphynx's Golden Plate Leggings
Ether Pool: Moderate
Current Ether Pool: 55 / 90
Enchantments: Protection V (45%), Stamina V (+10)
--

Sphynx's Golden Plate Gauntlets
Ether Pool: Moderate
Current Ether Pool: 51 / 70
Enchantments: Protection V (38%), Stamina II (+2), Strength II (+2)
--

Sphynx's Golden Plate Helm
Ether Pool: Moderate
Current Ether Pool: 59 / 75
Enchantments: Protection V (57%), Stamina I (+1), Vision I
Vision I

- **This Enchantment makes the helm translucent for the wearer, creating an unobstructed view in the front-facing direction.**

--

Sphynx's Golden Sabatons
Ether Pool: Moderate
Current Ether Pool: 47 / 70
Enchantments: Protection V (19%), Inertial Increase V (50%)

Inertial Increase

- This Enchantment increases the force required to break the wearer's inertia, making it harder to knock them down.

Rocky studied this set's Glyphs for a few hours, drawing them out into his Knowledge Tablet. The increase to his Enchanting skill and unlocking skill probably signified it was a good idea. The other set of gear from the ferrets was better quality, but it had some strange Enchantments.

Kodo's Jacket

> Ether Pool: Large
>
> Current Ether Pool: 110 / 130

Enchantments: Speed of the Ferret (+10 to Agility and Dexterity), Ferret's Uncontrollable Curiosity

Speed of the Ferret

- This Enchantment increases the Agility and Dexterity of the wearer. Unfortunately, this Enchantment comes with a side effect. Ferret's Uncontrollable Curiosity always accompanies Speed of the Ferret.

Ferret's Uncontrollable Curiosity

- This Enchantment forces the wearer to complete random quests for no reward. If these quests remain unfinished, a random negative debuff will sprout.

--

Podo's Boots

> Ether Pool: Large
>
> Current Ether Pool: 90 / 100

Enchantments: Fleet Footed Ferret (+10 Dexterity, Agility, Stealth and Sneak), Fabulous

Fleet Footed Ferret

- **The wearer gains the Fleet Footed Ferret Enchant. This will increase Dexterity, Agility, Stealth and Sneak by 10, but comes with the Fabulous Enchant.**

Fabulous

- **The wearer of these boots must always look their best. If their looks are verbally scrutinized, these boots will fall apart in shame.**

--

Pan's Cloak

> **Ether Pool: Massive**
> **Current Ether Pool: 150 / 200**

Enchantments: Billow, Deflect V

Billow

- **This Enchantment allows the cloak to move on its own, even on a windless day. Sometimes this is quite uncomfortable, as the mantle can discover nonexistent gale-force winds.**

Deflect V

- **This Enchantment will cause a strike that would normally impact the wearer to be deflected by the item. Per rotation, this Enchantment can only function five times and will dampen the blow by a maximum of 50%.**

They were going to offer the cloak to Victoria, but they wanted to allow her to decide. He wasn't sure how often the cloak would choose to pull the wearer off their feet. Sela had told him that this type of gear wasn't prevalent, but it existed. People called it 'cursed regalia' and sold it to an Enchanter if it had a decent-sized Ether pool. Enchanters could remove the current Enchantments and add other more reliable ones. Rocky hoped that he could perhaps use the other two pieces in the future to make something more useful.

"Ready to go welcome the new members to the Territory and Guild?" his guide asked.

He nodded, and together, they made their way onto the stage as the buzzing crowd grew silent.

CHAPTER TWENTY-FIVE

The noise from small pockets of celebration rang out from many directions. Right now, though, he had pulled someone aside that he had meant to have a talk with for a long time. The other partygoers around the bonfire looked concerned and worried at Rocky's choice. He wouldn't kill Derik. Probably.

Once they were far enough away from the crowds, Rocky asked, "What has been your problem with me, Derik?" The few drinks Rocky had consumed had loosened him up just enough to be extremely blunt.

"We were running for our lives, Rocky. Then, out of nowhere, you came and saved us, claimed the land we stood on, and left us here." His voice grew more agitated. "You ordered Selaphelia to return, and she taught us more about this world. You keep bringing more people here and dumping them on others, but what have you personally done to help any of them?"

Rocky wasn't sure what Derik was trying to tell him. Was he upset that Rocky had saved them? He doubted that. He tried answering the final question Derik had voiced. His buzzing mind finally picked out the string he believed Derik was on.

"Derik, you're upset that I am not teaching people how to survive in this world?" The man sneered at him, and Rocky took that as an affirmative. Well, that made for an unusual opinion. Derik had assumed Rocky was withholding information from other survivors?

"I think we have a misunderstanding, Derik. I only know as much about this world, and possibly less than, anyone else in the Grotto. Sela is my Ancestral guide, and I feel like I am pulling teeth with her sometimes to find out anything." He looked over to Sela, who was laughing heartily at something Smith had just said.

In that moment, talking about her and seeing her enjoying the company of another, he felt his heart sink. Maybe alcohol wasn't the best option.

He swallowed the lump in his throat and pointed at her and then himself, "The only reason she is with me is because of this Territory. And I had no idea what I was doing when I captured Algonquin Valley. I was headed to my car, and then on to Ottawa, when I accidentally entered this place.

"My only wish since the start of this whole mess has been to save my family. Anything you think I have, any benefits or bonuses I earned—I would trade it all for them to be with me."

Derik's eyes widened, and his mouth fell open before he snapped it shut. "The rumors about the fight between a massive Chimera and the Wolves you got the meat from is true, then?"

Rocky nodded. Fond memories of Azoth swirled in his mind, along with the colon-clenching recall of the battle. "Derik, I really want to get over whatever is between us—but I am going to leave again. I don't know when, and I can't say for how long. As soon as I find out where my family is, I will be like this ale after a good toast." He drank his Cuppa Macht leaf to the bottom to make his point sink home.

Derik clenched his jaw and emotions played over that man's face before he got control of himself and sipped his drink.

"Rocky, you don't think that other people in this Grotto have family that they wish they could save? You think I wouldn't be long gone if I had the strength to survive on my own?" He squeezed his own Cuppa Macht leaf slowly, bending it as he spoke—wine first rising, and then flowing over the top of the container. Derik crumpled the cup in his fist. "Not many people have the strength you have accumulated, and you are going to chase ghosts with it. That's selfish and irresponsible."

Every emotion flared to life inside Rocky, and he seriously considered killing Derik. Maybe Derik wasn't close with his family; perhaps they had died years before the Apocalypse.

Rocky didn't care what the man's story was in that instance. He knew his family was alive, and he would find—

Hold up. Derik probably doesn't know about the search function.

Rocky withdrew into Meditation and felt his emotional response shift outside of himself. Choosing to enter Meditation would allow him to respond calmly to Derik, instead of yelling at him. "Derik, I know I won't be chasing ghosts. My family is alive and waiting for me." The man's face reddened, and he knew Derik was about to explode in anger. "That massive Tower you couldn't hope to miss—it has an upload to the EtherNet. Through it, you can search for the names of people and see if they still live. My sister and mother were on that list."

Derik's face went from filled with blood to deathly white. Detached Rocky watched the man collapse onto his butt. Derik no longer looked at him, his eyes wild and his mouth forming words with no sounds. Rocky pulled up his interface and granted access to the elevator for twenty-four hours. He exited Meditation; his own emotional response having flamed out after the man crumpled.

Rocky knelt down and placed a hand on Derik's shoulder. "I have granted you access to the elevator and the control room for twenty-four hours. Since we made the announcement, the exil—" Rocky stumbled as he tried not to bring up Derik's exile, "— you missed. There is a rotating shift in the control room. Ask the tech on duty to search for your family. Once you have done that, come find me. As much as I dislike admitting it, we need your expertise to organize a great deal."

Derik rose on shaky legs to stumble-run toward the tower. Rocky hoped he found good news, but felt slightly torn as his goodwill fought his dislike of the man. He glanced forlornly back at the fire and festivities—his energy from before the conversation had dried up. It had taken everything Rocky had within himself to respond kindly. And not kill that ungrateful little...

In his current emotional state, he doubted anyone would want his company. He walked away into the night.

He had no destination in mind and walked mindlessly among the Dragon Scale Buildings of his Territory, looking at them but not seeing them. Derik's accusations still stung. What had he done for the people here? He took solace in all the buildings and people he passed—he had brought these survivors here, and that was more than he had done for his own family.

Derik's words had cut him, even while in Meditation. A deep part of Rocky knew what he had refused to admit to himself. Finding his family would only be the start. Would bringing them to this Territory even be safe?

He glanced at the destroyer hovering a few inches off the ground in the unused western portion of the Grotto. They had one ship, blueprints, and time—matched against a terrifying enemy. An enemy that wanted the genocide of all of humanity to pave the way for their control. He tried to be optimistic, but that was hard. Realistically, bringing his family here would just place them on the frontlines of the upcoming battle.

So now are you suggesting doing nothing? Leaving them to fend for themselves?

His inner drive sparked, and he peered around, eyes refreshed. This was only the start. In a single month, he had created a place for people to survive and grow. They had a year, and they would be the frontline of the coming battle—but they would be the bulwark. His family would be with him in this Grotto when they repelled the Guild Collective invasion.

He had an intense need to be doing something toward reaching that goal. His mind buzzed, searching for the best way he could contribute. Enchanting was what the people of his Grotto and his adventuring party needed most. But he'd failed at that—more than once. They couldn't afford gear for everyone, but if they could Enchant their gear... he had to keep trying.

He sat down and pulled out his Enchanting pen, mortar, and pestle. After the first failure of the prepared inks boiling away on the clothing, Smith had suggested some herbs and barks that could be powdered. He hadn't heard of the first herb, dried Mageleaf. Smith claimed it was a new specimen of plant that relied on Ether to grow.

He converted his sword into a sharp paring knife and cut the thin silver leaf into small pieces. With his Pestle, he ground those pieces until the dried leaf became silver powder. He added each section until he converted the entire three-foot length of the dried leaf into dust. He upended the bowl and tapped the last clinging traces into the reservoir of the pen.

Congratulations! You have learned a new skill. Alchemy
- **The first step in alchemy is learning to prepare your ingredients.**

Current level: Weak Alchemist level 1.

He pulled out a piece of leather armor and entered his Meditation. Like last time, he connected an internal Ether channel to the pen and tried drawing the runes on the leather.

The cap on the back of the pen shot off, as the 'ink' blackened and smoked. The pen was scalding hot, and the silvery ink sparked like a firework. Rocky dropped the pen as the burning pain seared his hand, even through Meditation. He watched in horror as the pen continued its impression of a roman candle.

I can't afford another one, if this one breaks.

The reaction finally died out, and he shook his hand as if to flick the pain away. Rocky waited for his Dark Mend skill to heal the damage to his hand, then tried the other two plants Smith had given him, Kingsbraid and Fernicular—both of which only grew now that Ether had returned. He was smart enough not to hold the pen on the second two attempts. Both failed and created amusing displays of something on par with a massive sparkler.

He had performed his Enchanting experimentation in the completely barren field on the western side of the Grotto. To his embarrassment and grudging amusement, the next two explosions drew 'ooooo's' and 'ahhhhhs' from the festival. At least he had unintentionally made someone's night.

In some video games, Enchanters needed to break down other Enchantments to gain materials. Rocky pulled out the Cursed Regalia and began examining it while Meditating. He found something linking the magic to the article, but like other gear that was dropped by Dungeons or the world spawns, it wasn't as obvious. It almost appeared that the medium holding the Enchantment was woven into the material.

He turned the chest piece over in his hands multiple times, trying to find a starting point. The attaching glyphs didn't seem to have a starting or endpoint, instead seeming to loop in on each other. He examined the connection with the Ether Pool, and found two seamless transitions entering and exiting the bright blue ball.

At the bottom of the Ether Pool was a small bump. He created a thread of his Ether and prodded at it. Nothing happened. He enveloped it and instantly felt subtleties in it that he hadn't been able to see with his mind's eye. It was a very intricate knot, perhaps even a very tightly woven spiral of some sort.

The threads of the weaving were so tiny that he thought he could sense hundreds, if not thousands, of them. He continued feeling his way along the Enchantments, tracing the pool, and then the glyphs before his Ether Thread showed him an apparent connection between the two glyphs.

He felt the two ends of the glyphs and the mental welding point between them. Taking a deep breath, he made his mental thread of Ether thinner and sharper. With the utmost care, he began to try to sever that point. It was like trying to cut through steel with a butter knife, and in his interface, he saw his Ether dropping, but he also felt some minuscule progress.

Just before his Ether ran dry, the bond snapped. Then like a snake turning to dust, the glyphs reversed flow and pulled themselves back into the pool of Ether. He waited for something else to happen, for a notification to pop up, but all he held now was a fur-lined Tunic that contained an Ether pool.

He checked his character screen, and he had gained a few levels in Enchanting. No magic medium appeared from 'disenchanting' the piece of gear. He exited Meditation, feeling the sweat and cold night air he hadn't noticed before. He threw the piece of equipment into his Bag of Holding carelessly and fell backward, his back meeting the soft soil. He stared at the night sky from the grass, breathing heavily.

"How the hell am I supposed to discover the secret to Enchanting? Why won't someone in the shop just give me a hint?" He spoke to the universe as his feelings of failure swarmed over him. He couldn't even accomplish the one task he knew would help his people.

Popeye's Disproportionate Biceps.

The strange swear replacement inside of his head elicited a laugh. He sat back up and shook his head. He would try Enchanting again after he had a full night's sleep and wasn't so abysmally tired. Or affected by alcohol. He considered returning to the festivities but wasn't in the right mood. The fresh night air left him with an intense desire for a blistering hot shower.

He levered himself to his feet, picked up his Enchanting materials, and made his way back to his apartment. Perhaps there was some sort of hint inside of the Knowledge Tablet. Sela claimed that she didn't know the first thing about the profession. She also insisted no one would share this knowledge with him.

Perhaps he could ask some of the Montessori volunteers to look specifically for this tidbit.

It's worth a shot.

He opened his door on the third floor and stripped out of his cracked armor. He didn't even bother to hang it up on the rack. He was in the mood for only one thing.

He turned on the shower and pulled off the Nanoweave Under armor. The rising steam of the water made him happy, and he climbed into the deluge. As he cleaned himself, he noticed again that his hair could use a cut. It might even be long enough to put up in a bun. For now, that might be the better solution, as he didn't know of any hairdressers in the Grotto.

An insistent knock rattled his door, and he jumped. He ran from the shower and grabbed one of the fluffy towels he had purchased. He wrapped it around himself and flung open his door. Sela stood there, hand raised to knock again. She took in his wet hair, bare chest, and hastily wrapped towel.

Her face flushed bright red. "You can't just leave the party. One second you were talking to Derik, and the next you were just gone. I was looking all over for you."

Relief flooded over him, and he relaxed. Nothing serious had happened. The feeling of euphoria spread, and he joked, "Well, here I am. Call off the search."

She pointed at him, her mouth moving but no words forming. She advanced on him, poking him with a single finger in his solar plexus. He flinched back as she continued jabbing her finger with each word, "You—aren't—funny. What—if—something—had—happened—to you? What if you killed Derik?"

Her prodding had pushed him back to the doorway of his still running shower. Rubbing his chest with his free hand, he laughed. "Sela, that hurt. It's okay, see—" he raised his hand to point at the shower, "—I just wanted to take a long shower, and Derik is alive; at least, as far as the last I saw of him."

Sela bit her lip. Something about the action made his breath catch, and unlike in the past, he took the opportunity. He leaned in and kissed her.

She jerked, and he thought he had misinterpreted the moment. Then she kissed him back, discarding her cracked chest piece and throwing it on the ground to join his.

Wearing only her Under Armor, she gazed intensely at him, eyes half-lidded, and whispered, "A shower sounds perfect!"

Chapter Twenty-Six

Rocky woke up the next morning with the most beautiful silhouette wrapped in a white sheet beside him. He considered waking up to this view every morning and a goofy smile spread.

The ecstasy was followed quickly by a wave of terror. He had a habit of falling in love immediately, and that was often to his detriment. A female 'friend' had put it best, telling Rocky, "You mistake lust for love, dummy."

His heart beat faster and faster. He knew Sela well, but he didn't know what sort of customs surrounded relationships during her lifetime. For all he knew, this was a casual occurrence for the woman, and yet and here he was, already planning more of such events. His nerves were at war, and his stomach roiled with contradictory feelings.

His stomach growled, causing Sela to wake up and stretch. The smile she wore when she looked at him quelled his nerves. His cheeks hurt from the return of his goofy grin. The pain reminded him how much he had laughed and smiled with the woman the previous night, and just how great everything had been.

Sela put her head on his chest. "Are you as hungry as I am?"

He tried not to laugh but couldn't manage it. "Ow, don't make me laugh anymore. I think we overdid it last night." He went against his own words with a bellowing laugh. "Ha—ow, yes, I am starving. Would you be game for another shower and breakfast?"

Her tight squeeze of his chest was all the answer he needed, and he got up to turn on the taps.

A good chunk of the morning later, and far hungrier, they finally escaped the room. On his way out of the City Hall, he looked up to the mounted clock. It was only nine in the morning, and they had a busy day of meetings in front of them.

They walked by the area that served as the starship's usual resting place. It wasn't there, and he assumed it was already out collecting more survivors from surrounding areas.

The previous night, they had discovered that the ship could reach anywhere on the planet in under an hour. Short distances were less efficient because of the time to speed up and slow down the destroyer's momentum. The Council had subsequently ordered the ship to be on rescue and escort quests.

Rocky and Sela agreed. Each citizen gained some Etherience for each quest completed, and each new survivor added would increase the productivity of the area. With the rooms in the Guild Hall, they had more than ten thousand spaces available for housing. That wouldn't mean much at the current growth rate, but at least for now, they had spare vacancies and were working to construct more. They had three more yet unassigned Longhouses, and if desperate, the soon to be recovered Guild Tent.

Breakfast became a large table affair with the parade of people stopping by to speak with them. Smith wanted to finalize the military rankings from Rocky's Leadership class. With the conquering of the nearby Territory, he and Sela had both gained a few levels to those special classes. He was now able to promote actual Military Leaders. Finally. There was a downside to those promotions. If his military leaders were killed, he could, in theory, lose the Territory.

The good news was that Sela believed, in their situation, the Territory would need both of their class conditions satisfied to lose the Grotto. Victoria received Colonel under Smith's rank of Brigadier-General. There were three higher ranks in the options Rocky had yet to unlock—Major-General, Lieutenant-General, and General. The information for opening these wasn't available yet either. By unlocking Brigadier-General, each rank below now had space for five individuals. He had appointed Smith as the sole Brigadier-General.

Smith, like Sela and Rocky, received two additional stats per level for his new role. Rocky assumed the next three ranks would grant the same. They desperately wanted to unlock them. Victoria's rank gave her one stat point per level, and it allowed her to choose between Strength and Stamina.

Smith suggested Derik for one of the spots of Major, as it gave the same one stat to Intellect or Wisdom per level. He inserted Zippo into that rank as well, bumping a member he didn't know. That member shifted up to Lieutenant-Colonel, which allowed individuals to choose between Charisma and Stamina each level. Smith left, promising to promote the lower ranks himself. Rocky's increased Leadership level also meant that the entirety of the military fit under the system ranks. This was a significant boost for their fighting forces, and it couldn't have come at a better time.

A group of women sat down at the table, glaring at Rocky. The first woman to sit pointed a finger at him. "You will put the new Territory points into increased growth speed."

Rocky didn't fully understand what the woman wanted. Sela whispered, "Growth Boost," toward the speaker, and she corrected herself. That was when it all clicked. These women wanted him to place the skill points the Territory had gained into increasing pregnancy speed and the growth rate of children.

"But isn't that terrifying? Children fully grown by the age of eight. And your pregnancies taking three months."

The other women in the mob rolled their eyes. The same woman spoke again. "We are all pregnant already, and there are many others. I speak for all of us when I say we want our children to be stronger as soon as possible. Do not presume to know what a pregnant woman wants."

He clicked his mouth closed. "That's why I didn't put the points there in the first place. I didn't want to make that choice—"

"And in doing so, you made that choice for us! Now, I am telling you to make it right. Our children," the woman raised her hand to include the entire Mess Hall, "need to be the number-one consideration. Or what is the point of all this?"

Originally, he had wanted to put points there anyway. "Sorry for making the assumptions I did. I completely agree, and with your approval…"

He opened his Territory Skill screen for the women to witness, and checked the level and available points.

He skipped to the last notification for his Territory. After the Crafter's Hall was completed, he knew the Territory had leveled, but he hadn't had time to check on its current level.

Congratulations!

- **You have reached all the criteria to increase your settlement level—currently level nine, Town.**

To reach level ten, create a Marketplace, reach a population of twenty-five hundred and ensure there is housing for fifty percent of your citizens.

He had leveled up five times—the prerequisite building needed as a bottleneck already existed. Algonquin Grotto was far above the population to level again, and he made a mental note to ask Karl to build a Marketplace.

Territorial Skill Tree
Skill Points available: 0
All skills will affect any and all Territories owned by the same leaders. Skill points are awarded at 5 per level, in most cases. To discover more, level up and capture additional Territories.

Skills

Stat Boost

- **While individuals reside within the boundary of this Territory, all stats will be increased by x, where x is the number of skill points in this skill.**

0 / 50

At fifty skill points, the skill will upgrade.

Resource Boost

- **Every resource that spawns within your Territory will give x% more when collected, where x is the number of skill points in this skill.**

20 / 50

At fifty skill points, the skill will upgrade.

Etherience Boost

- **All individuals who gain Etherience within your Territory will be awarded x% more, where x is the number of skill points in this skill.**

0 / 50

At fifty skill points, the skill will upgrade.

Growth Boost

- **All women will carry to full term faster by a factor of x%. All children will grow x% faster to maturity, where x is the number of skill points in this skill.**

<25> / 50

At fifty skill points, the skill will upgrade.

He placed the twenty-five points to Growth Boost and clicked accept.

The woman leading the group pointed at him. "With the number of women getting pregnant right now, I suggest you put future points there as well."

Rocky gulped and glanced at the empty seat next to him. Sela had moved a small distance away, leaving him to defend himself while she talked to Mr. Pips and Bart. They were grilling her on hunting practices and setting up fetch quests within the Guild Hall. It sounded like they wanted to know just how much Etherience per quest completed they should offer. Sela used some elementary math skills, access to the Guild Management page, and her experience to put them on the right path.

Three heaping plates of food and a few impromptu meetings later, he and Sela left to make their way to the Shop and meet with Amelia.

***

"I may have found a solution for the beacon," said Amelia and held up a tennis ball-sized metal sphere. "This will block the signal if you can get it close enough—"

"I don't see the—" said Sela.

"You didn't let me finish. I've discovered that Dahrix is already remoting into his creations."

"You are telling me that he is already controlling the people of Florida?"

Amelia nodded in response to his words.

Well, honey roasted peanuts.

"I don't think he is taking complete control yet. Just influencing decisions that the leadership makes."

"I am going to call back the Scourge—" Sela stood up, "—we need to take a trip to this Florida and try to convince the humans there of the danger."

Another interruption to their schedule and another meeting. With a possible hostile force.

Rocky raised a hand to stop her, but Sela had already vanished. More and more, she seemed to be taking charge and not consulting him. After last night, he knew she didn't mean anything by it, but he still wanted to talk about it. Heading to Florida could turn out disastrously.

"Amelia, can we pull you into a meeting to help convince them of the danger these guilds pose?" Rocky couldn't tell what the lizard was feeling, her face far too alien for him to read. "It would really help having someone attest to the crimes of the Guilds."

She looked to Garnell. Why did she seek his permission or support? They were from vastly different worlds.

Garnell nodded with a reassuring smile, and the tiny kobold swallowed before speaking. "I can do that. My Territory has access to three shops. The Aretrean Bazaar, The Fiscal Flats, and the Global Warehouse. Garnell has a fellow Gelthisarian salesman within each."

Ah, that must have been the reason she had looked to him.

Garnell cleared his throat. "If ye find them, they will alert me, and I can transfer all the individuals to this location. However, if the Flow Ridians don't have access to one of those shops, you will need to bring them to your Territory."

Rocky shook his head, unwilling to compromise his position just yet. Especially to the potential threat that the converted and possibly controlled Floridians posed. He purchased the orb for a Diamond Chip, left the meeting, and paid a reluctant five Crystals because they hadn't bought enough.

Sela had gathered a good portion of the Council just outside of the Shop. They spoke over each other and Sela shouted over them.

"That is enough!" Silence took hold at Rocky's booming voice. He lowered his voice and said, "Let's move this meeting to City Hall."

The group wasn't the first to arrive in the meeting room, and Rocky scrutinized Derik's seated form. How had the man heard about the meeting fast enough to arrive here? Derik stood and addressed the group. "I would like to petition the council to allow me to sit in and add my thoughts to the meeting."

The Council exploded with excitement and ran to greet the man. Rocky didn't get the opportunity to deny the request.

Derik looked at him and nodded. His usual hostility was absent, and a surge of hope coursed through Rocky.

The Council sat down and discussed whether they should take the meeting.

"This is not a discussion if, but a discussion of how. Establishing contact is a must if we have any hope of dissuading them from their current course. Right now, we need to choose the least aggressive method of approach," Rocky said.

A few people protested his statement, until Sela and Derik stood up at the same time.

"I agree with our Leaders. However, I don't believe a starship arriving at their Territory or Area of Safety will be a good option. Do we know where they are in Florida?" asked Derik.

Oh, yeah, right; Florida is a pretty big patch of land, isn't it.

They had kind of forgotten about that detail—they were too stunned by the severity of the news. Rocky gave Smith a knowing look—they had a Satellite—and Smith called for a runner.

"I suggest we fly a diplomatic party to the area of Florida but do not cross the state line. Azoth can carry Rockland and one other to search the state for human settlements. Sela can fly on her own, I believe?" said Derik.

The Council nodded along, and Derik continued, "Let us nominate the last member to accompany the group, and then I move for a vote."

Derik's expertise in a council environment humbled Rocky. He looked at Smith, who gave him a thumbs up.

Whatever the reason for Derik's change in attitude, he was pleased to have his support. At least for now.

The Council voted unanimously on Derik accompanying Rocky on the mission. He pictured having Derik's arms wrapped around him—he shuddered—and answering his incessant questions. Azoth could carry four now, if two of them were children. Rocky assumed three adults would be fine. Maybe Sela could act as a buffer. But he didn't like the idea of Derik's arms around her either.

The runner returned, delivered his message, and Smith stood up. "It seems that their compound is pretty obvious. From what my subordinate just reported, there is a large Port that remains unconverted to golems. It's visible from Satellite, as it is the only surviving infrastructure for miles. Supposedly they have massive gas tanks and an entire fleet of off-road vehicles."

The Council went up to the Control Room, and they studied the Port and its exact location. One of the techs said, "It's Port Everglades, in Fort Lauderdale. I used to own a timeshare down there to escape winter."

The group adjusted the plan. The Port was far to the South, within the old borders of what had been the State of Florida. The starship would fly them out over the water and stay at altitude during the entire exchange. The group wasn't sure what sort of wildlife the oceans now hosted, and they were absolutely sure they didn't want to find out.

***

The hum of the Ether Engines signaled the return of the ship and the start of the diplomatic mission. Landing the ship took an additional fifteen minutes. Still, with the entire Council, and Rocky's group loading up, it was necessary. The flight to the drop-off zone took only ten, further highlighting the ship's limitations. They needed drop ships.

It was surreal to think that they could travel anywhere on Gaia in such a short time. The mysteries of the world had grown, yet the distance itself seemed to shrink.

Hovering high above the undulating ocean, Rocky tried to spot any creatures in the water. The waves seemed to go on forever in one direction. Far in the distance, in the opposite direction, he could just make out a landmass through the clouds. He was sure that landmass contained the Port.

They left through a side dock in the ship, which displayed a greenlit LED titled Atmosphere—only when the LED was illuminated would the button under it open the doors. Rocky and Derik climbed onto Azoth and tied themselves into the saddle. Derik seemed as uncomfortable with the situation as Rocky, and somehow, that made him feel slightly better.

They weren't entirely on the other side of whatever problems they had with each other, but they were both willing to grudgingly put up with the other. This rang with more humanity to Rocky, at least more than the political posturing Derik had been putting on in the meeting room. Rocky wasn't sure he would ever trust Derik completely.

"Thank you for telling me about my family. My eldest daughter and horrid ex-wife are still alive out there— somewhere."

Rocky navigated his tabs and gave Derik control over the Territorial Jobs. Rocky had been putting off the onerous chore and was glad to hand it over to the man. It was honestly more punishment than promotion. At least that's what Rocky told himself as he patted Azoth, signaling his pet to fly.

"What's this—ahhh!"

Azoth launched himself out of the dock, and the whipping wind cut off any further discussions. He could have used the radio, but Derik was too busy screaming to listen. Rocky grinned.

Sela, in her raven form, leveled out beside them. Rocky enjoyed a relatively steady flight from Azoth, as the Chimera coasted more than flew toward Florida. Large groups of flying white birds appeared along the coastline. They looked tiny from this distance but he was willing to bet they had mutated due to the two waves of Ether. If he had to guess, they were probably seagulls. He gulped and looked back at his ship; a flock of that many mutated seagulls could easily overwhelm them.

Not one to be shown up, it seemed like the ocean wanted to compete with the sky. As the water grew shallower, there were definite signs of wildlife within its depths. Fish the size of killer whales meandered through the water. A large shadow, which dwarfed the fish, shot out from the dark blue. It was some sort of enormous crocodile dinosaur hybrid, and it attempted to snag one of the killer whale-sized creatures. It missed its first attack, and a life or death chase ensued.

Just when he thought the crocodile creature would capture its prey, it jerked to a stop. Derik tensed behind him in the saddle. The enormous crocodile convulsed, undulating and frothing the water. The sea became murky and try as he might, Rocky couldn't distinguish what had just happened. Azoth coasted on, and the Port came into view, demarcated by standing cranes and white gas tanks.

I wonder just how much Gas—Gaia's Essence—they are holding?

Double-barreled turrets faced the ocean, and a few seconds later, the turrets were all riveted on Azoth's approaching form. Sela must have ordered Azoth to stop and hover in place as the gentle coasting ride ended, and Azoth began to pump his mighty wings. Derik and Rocky were bumped up and down in the saddle for the next five minutes as Sela's raven form dove toward the coast. When she landed, she transformed into a human, and men with assorted weaponry surrounded her.

They didn't immediately open fire, and Rocky marked a point in the Floridians' favor. Azoth dove toward the group a few minutes later. As soon as they landed, Derik and Rocky untied themselves and slid from the saddle. Efficient men with assorted weapons quickly surrounded both of them as well.

One man stepped forward, and Rocky used Analyze.

Dmitri Gausse
Apprentice-Mobster
Level 18
Health Points 175 / 175

"We will bring with us, send pet away. Show us, mean port no harm," said Dmitri.

Rocky turned to Azoth and gave his friend some scratches. He didn't bother communicating the request, as Azoth had heard it. Azoth gave him a head bump, took a running start, and used a few wing beats to jump into the air.

Dmitri sighed. "That is awesome pet. You tell me how you get this, yes?"

CHAPTER TWENTY-SEVEN

Dmitri turned out to be a friendly and talkative individual. He and a large group had been henchmen for the mob and were stationed at the Port the night the first wave had struck. When the twenty-four hours elapsed, or one rotation of Gaia, some ships, vehicles, and equipment had changed into golems. The 'Dockmaster,' which Dmitri said as if it was a title, owned the majority of the Port.

As they passed groups of people, Dmitri gave warm greetings in multiple languages and then explained who they were to Rocky. "They are US Marines. Station on boat and major reason Port stay safe. Another reason is—" he pointed at himself and the guards around him, "—Russian mafia. Between us, many weapons. Though people still dying. Dockmaster, take charge and get better, but now we safe. No one dies in long time. No one starve." He looked toward a building surrounded by guards, and sighed. Rocky waited for the man to turn that direction but he never did.

"Are we going to see the Dockmaster now?" Rocky asked as he channeled as much diplomacy as he could muster.

Dmitri nodded. "Yes, he is waiting, meet you. Want meet people we not have to rescue and bring here." He pointed at his ear and showed off a skin-colored radio transmitter. Derik and Sela smiled, and Rocky tried not to chuckle at Dmitri's openness. The other 'mobsters' around them didn't react. Perhaps it wasn't supposed to be a secret.

They approached a large blue warehouse that was covered with chipped paint and rust spots on sheet metal. It had seen better days, but it was large enough to house the entire population of Rocky's Territory.

"How many people do you have here?" Rocky asked.

"Two-ten thousand," Dmitri responded, a tinge of pride in his voice.

Rocky took it to mean twenty thousand. He frowned and looked around again. The warehouse wouldn't fit that many, and he wondered where the rest were staying.

He had believed his Territory was doing well, but hearing that another group was nearly double the size of Algonquin Grotto made him feel inadequate. Based on Dmitri's stories, he could easily guess the reason behind the larger size of the Port. They had an abundance of weapons, probably shop access, and people willing to go out early after the first wave. He recalled how well Ottawa had been doing, despite Corsair's ulterior motives. Getting early access to a shop was definitely a boon.

I just hope this Dockmaster isn't anywhere near as diabolical as Corsair.

The warehouse contained row upon row of crates converted into households. The upper levels of the containers had rope ladders or stairs made from debris. Each container provided yet another level of privacy for the people staying within. Even with all the crates, many people camped out on the concrete floor. People stared as they walked by, and whispers broke out in their wake. The group's clean appearances, armor, and lack of visible weapons inspired constant hushed chatter as Floridian survivors followed the escort.

Dmitri stopped talking and grew serious as they approached an open metal staircase. Two men in military fatigues guarded the bottom. Dmitri nodded to the men and led Rocky's group up the stairs. One lone figure kept watch at the top of the stairwell. Rocky's stomach clenched as the dull, black accenting metal came into view. Mechano-Lord.

Dmitri passed Rocky off to the man and whispered, "You find Dmitri before leave. Introduce Dmitri to pet Azoth."

Rocky found himself liking the man more and more. He shook Dmitri's hand and allowed the Mechanoid human to lead the way into an office near the roof of the warehouse. The office was just a single windowed room surrounded by more sheet metal. The Mechanoid opened the door, revealing a robotic-man behind a desk, flipping through the pages of his Knowledge Tablet.

Dockmaster (Ernest Ford)
Level 49
Master-Mechanoid
Health Points 1510/1510

The man's head jerked up when the door opened, and his two human eyes met Rocky, Sela, and Derik's in turn. It was an eerie sight. The man's entire face was some sort of coppery metal. The eyes were the one piece that seemed human—that, and strangely, the palms and fingers of his hands, like he was wearing a pair of skin gloves. Rocky forced down a shudder and stepped into the room.

The man nodded to his guard, and the door closed behind them. His face cracked into a wide robotic smile as he took in the group standing before him. The action humanized him, and Rocky's unease vanished.

"It is good to see others who have found a way to survive. Please, sit. Can I get you some water or food?" asked the Dockmaster.

"No, thank you, Ernest. We have our own, and I believe your food is mostly claimed if the figures on the Knowledge Tablet are accurate," said Sela.

Ernest smiled again. "No one has called me Ernest since the Turn." He glanced back at the Tablet. "Do not fear for our health, however. While you are correct, we aren't starving, but we try to bring in the right amount of food for each day. We have some refrigerators and deep freezers, but nowhere near enough to hold food for more than a day."

Rocky's guilt sparked as he thought about his Territorial Storage. He assumed the Floridians knew about Territories already, thanks to their patrons.

"That is very good to hear. We have a starship, which I am sure you have seen, and we may be able to offer aid if you ever need it," said Derik.

Ernest's head snapped around inhumanly fast. He smiled at the mention of the ship. "Yes, we saw the ship when you arrived. I will admit, we initially thought our saviors, the Mechano-Lords, had arrived, even though they said it would be quite a while to travel here."

Rocky grimaced at the reverence. "What have these Mechano-Lords told you so far?"

Ernest tilted his mechanical neck and narrowed his human eyes in concentration. "Not much, actually. They wish to find new areas to explore and set up outposts. At first, we were skeptical, until they began teaching us about the EtherVerse, as they call it." He pointed at the Tablet and his mechanical body. "These are but a few of the benefits they have bestowed upon us. I would like to say we would have made it without them, but we were barely scraping by from day to day, surrounded by encroaching monsters."

From his tone, Rocky could tell it hadn't been a natural choice for the man. He knew that weight of responsibility—and what it could push a man to do. How could he tell the man that his saviors were, in fact, conquerors?

"I was going to mention as well that we could—" said Derik.

Ernest's suspicious glare forced Derik to mumble to a stop. Rocky assumed it was Derik's tone, which was very polite, but also very political.

How had the Mechano-Lords managed to convince someone so instantly suspicious?

"I want to know the actual reason you are here. That starship out there says you don't need anything from us, except for maybe the gasoline. However, I am not an idiot. Gasoline doesn't fuel that boat, and while it is valuable to the Mechano-Lords and the Guild Collective they represent, it isn't worth a trip from humans who know what it is."

Rocky was unsure that he could break the news lightly, so he looked over to Sela.

"The Mechano-Lords want to come here and commit genocide, take over the planet, and plunder as much as they can," Sela said bluntly.

Rocky stared at her, his mouth agape.

Good thing you eased him into it, Sela. Wouldn't want to shock the guy.

"Dahrix said you would say something along those lines." He held up a hand to stop any rebuttal, even though one hadn't been forthcoming. "You will notice I am not saying you're lying. However, do you have any proof of your claims?"

"We have someone willing to tell you all about the atrocities they have committed on the planet of Helion Prime. And we had to fight and destroy a group of murdering psychopaths that Dahrix had sponsored before you."

Ernest's mechanical eyebrows rose. "Where is this witness to the Mechano-Lord's oppression and genocide?"

The Dockmaster had access to the Fiscal Flats and even knew of a Gelthisarian tradesman. Rocky needed to describe the Karacy race as dwarven before Ernest nodded knowingly. The suspicious man was more than happy to get to the bottom of the accusations.

Despite Derik's protest, Ernest sent a runner to notify the Mechano-Lords of the meeting. "Both parties should be there to defend themselves. Look at it from my point of view. Dahrix claims you are the psychopaths that want to take over the entire continent. That you killed one of his previous vassals in this pursuit, and you claim that Dahrix wants to take over the entire world."

Rocky looked at Sela and Derik—they both wore expressions that likely mirrored his own. That was quite the lie, but an effective one. Rocky considered ways to counter the claim. He could bring Ernest to the Grotto and have his people attest to his actions in Ottawa. If Amelia Nanospark was telling the truth, Dahrix would then know the location of his Territory and remote into his constructs here in Florida to attack.

He might even have other groups in any number of areas around the globe.

Amelia hadn't mentioned others yet, but no matter what, he wouldn't be giving away his Territory's location.

***

Ernest entered the Arbuckle shop sphere separately from Sela, Derik, and Rocky. Thinking back to all the times he had exited first to find Sela defenseless, Rocky's respect for the half-man's forethought grew.

Their group of three phased into the shop. Rocky expected an extensive bazaar and stared in partial horror at the new surroundings. It was a damn mall. Storefronts displayed advertisements, stairs, elevators, and escalators all leading to the next floor. He stood next to a kiosk that neatly listed all of the stores under categories, like weapons, armor, elixirs, materials, Enchantments, and more.

Like all malls, this place teemed with people. So many different races phased through each other, and for a moment, it was like watching a science fiction or fantasy movie.

"The Dwarven shop is on the third floor. Follow me."

Ernest ushered them into the shop and they vanished into a private meeting room. The Karacy tending the shop wasn't in the space. Instead, Garnell waved quietly from his seat away from the table. Rocky chose one of the mesh-backed office chairs. Derik and Sela sat on either side of him. His nerves were on high alert, and he absently half-spun in his chair. Sela gripped his armrest to hold it in place, preventing him from twirling further.

He rested his hands, fingers laced, on the table. The coolness of the glass tabletop calmed him. Ernest sat at the head of the table and silence blanketed the room.

Dmitri phased into the meeting room. "Dockmaster, I join speaking, yes?"

Ernest blinked at the man and nodded. He addressed Garnell, "Are you this witness that can attest to the crimes of the Mechano-Lords or the Guild Collective?"

Garnell frowned at the man's tone. "No, not I. I am just an intermediary. I, by the laws of me guild and people, cannot become involved in these matters."

Dahrix was the first to arrive. A shot of adrenaline coursed through Rocky's body and he jumped to his feet.

The creature looked so similar to Corsair. It terrified him. There was the obvious difference in color, but after that, the smoky white stress lines in his metal body reminded Rocky of Damascus steel. His eyes' blood-red orbs glowed with hatred. He had a metallic face like Ernest, but it had no humanity left to reflect. This creature was nothing but cold steel.

Ernest rose and nodded at Dahrix. Ernest didn't wear the smile he had displayed when Rocky's group had first arrived in the warehouse. Rocky hoped that was a good sign.

Dahrix returned the nod and sat beside the man, studying Rocky, Sela, and Derik on the other side of the table. He ignored Garnell.

Dahrix's voice boomed. "These are the combatants who defeated my vassal? They appear too weak and innocent to have been so devious."

The arms of the chair creaked under the pressure of Rocky's tightening fingers. Not two minutes in, and this creature offended them while simultaneously undermining their position. He clacked his jaw shut as hot anger flushed his face. He'd had opponents like him on the basketball court, and he wasn't going to rise to the bait.

Derik clicked his tongue and shook his head.

Sela placed her hands on the table and stood. "Do you claim your extensive fleet of starships is coming to protect humanity?"

Ernest wore an unreadable expression. If Rocky was to hazard a guess, Ernest hadn't known about the fleet—or thought a small force was traveling to the planet.

"What fleet do you speak of?"

Dahrix was smart. He knew it would be impossible for them to prove this.

Sela sat down and smiled at Rocky. Her smirk said, 'The seed is planted.'

They sat in silence for a few minutes before an iridescent Kobold popped into the room. Amelia whispered. "Sorry, I am late. I had some things to take care of at home." She glared at Dahrix as she took her seat at the foot of the glass table.

Once she was seated, Ernest cleared his throat, which seemed like a pointless gesture for a robot. "Hello. I am told that you have some information you wish to share with me regarding the Guild Collective and, more specifically, the Mechano-Lords," he said.

Dahrix watched Amelia very closely. He seemed to have no room to pay attention to anyone else. It was as if his computer, or brain, or whatever resided in his head, was overloaded by the Kobold's very appearance.

"The Guild Collective wants nothing more than to establish your planet as a colony. They have done so numerous times already. They only succeeded in truly capturing a single one. Helion Prime. Because they feared uprising, they massacred every living sapient on the planet when they arrived," Amelia said.

Ernest listened as she outlined what she had already told Rocky and Sela. Derik listened with rapt attention, his face morphing to horror at her firsthand account of the Guild's deeds.

Dahrix remained silent through the entire process. At first, Rocky viewed it as a good sign, until he saw the robotic eyes look away entirely. Was that unconcern?

Ernest shifted his chair further away from Dahrix as Amelia continued speaking.

Dmitri remained silent and his look of terror spoke for him. Amelia finished the last of her emotional tirade and sat down. Rocky hadn't realized she had been standing on her chair to begin with, as her height hadn't changed.

After a few tense heartbeats, the Mechano-Lord spoke, "You claim that we have wronged your people, and have twisted the truth." He looked at Ernest and shrugged. "We have in the past helped other new planets, much in the same way that we are now helping yours. After they are safe, we create terms of alliance and trade before leaving."

Dahrix smiled and a chill swept over Rocky's heart. "I have with me an entire documented list of every race we have helped. On that list, you will find no mention of Iridescent Kobolds. In fact, I have never seen one of your kind in person until now, little lady. So, I would like to ask you, or our esteemed host—who exactly are you?"

His glare, when accompanied by his grin, made Rocky's skin crawl. Amelia's scales dimmed by the tiniest of margins.

What in the world is going on?

"I can confirm that her race isn't Koboldian. I will not reveal her heritage to the room, however—" said Garnell.

Ernest shot to his feet. "You come here in the guise of a cute creature to gain my sympathy?" He looked at Rocky, Sela, and Derik, "What is this? A play on the humanity of others, since you have none of your own?"

Rocky stared at the glass table, at his leather pants beneath it. A part of him understood Ernest's tone. Why would she keep her heritage a secret, and what did it mean? Was she lying about more than that?

"They didn't know you weren't a Kobold either. Reveal yourself, deceiver!" Ernest's tone changed. It was subtle, but the emotions that laced his voice before were absent.

Amelia licked her teeth and pointed at Dahrix. "If he leaves the meeting, I will remove my guise. I cannot reveal myself for fear of that monster."

Dahrix stood and spoke, "Ernest, we will make all due haste to your location. If you can hold out long enough, we will aid in this fight. My only caution after meeting the players is not to let them capture more ground or recruit allies." The monster came off as the white knight—he had played them beautifully.

Ernest nodded, and Dahrix phased out of the meeting room.

"Amelia, ye do not need to do this. Think about this," said Garnell.

She shook her head and stood, moving to a corner. She whispered, "I know the risk. I am all in, Garnell."

Then in an instant, she changed. In the place of a tiny kobold stood a creature from a nightmare. She had black, chitinous skin, and skeletal wings adorned her back. Her dark black glossy claws were almost as sharp as her teeth. Elongated and deadly fangs dominated her deadly mouth.

Rocky stared in horror, as did everyone else in the room. Except Garnell.

"My race was the trueborn of Helion Prime. My story is a firsthand retelling. Do not allow them to fool you," Amelia said.

"Why did you keep this from us?" Rocky asked.

"How could you let us believe?" Sela pointed at Garnell.

Derik just sputtered at the creature that had transformed before him. Ernest crossed himself.

Dmitri was the only one who stayed sitting through the entire event. His eyes were unfocused and filled with tears. He was in another place, another time, maybe.

Rocky turned to Amelia. "How could you keep this from us?"

A tear ran down Amelia's cheek. "Because I knew how you'd react. How everyone reacts. Others see us as less than them, as inherently evil. So, who cares if they kill my people, right?"

Her statement left him torn. Did her appearance change the story and truth? No, it didn't. At least it shouldn't. But looking at Ernest, it did. Ernest pointed at them and blinked out of the shop.

Amelia's skeletal wings drooped behind her. Before anyone could say anything, she left.

"Garnell, I—" said Rocky.

Garnell shook his head. "Ye believe appearance carries so much weight—it makes me think less of ye."

Rocky hunched his shoulders, his arms limp at his sides. "Garnell, will you receive any blowback from this? I assume Amelia just gave away her rebellion?"

Garnell held up both hands. "Gelthisar is a unified planet of allied guilds. There is no chance of anyone, other than the other Elder Planets, threatening us. Amelia, on the other mitt, has now entirely thrown her lot in with ye, and ye just scorned her for her appearance."

Rocky glanced at Dmitri's seat and found it empty. It was just them and Garnell.

Did Amelia's appearance matter? Was he that hollow? No, definitely not. The only part that bothered him was the way it had been revealed. The way he *let* Dahrix use it against them.

CHAPTER TWENTY-EIGHT

Sela, Rocky, and Derik stood in the pie-shaped metal room of the seed shop for Fiscal Flats.

"If ye believe that the way a person looks makes a monster, then methinks ye haven't seen true monsters." Garnell's parting words rattled around in his head. He was right. And that was why it stung. What Garnell must think of him. And Amelia. He wished Amelia had trusted them with her secret sooner. So why hadn't she? He must've made her feel like she couldn't trust them. Couldn't trust *him*. A fine leader he was turning out to be.

Amelia had just revealed herself to a puppet of Dahrix. Ernest. She and her people were committed to this. She hadn't revealed her race in front of Dahrix himself, but knowingly revealed the information to her enemy.

Rocky closed his eyes. He worried about Amelia. He didn't care what she looked like, and if others did, he would try his best to correct them. Right now, they were dealing with her secret. Not her. He couldn't help but be upset with her choice to hide it.

Sela nudged him. The longer they waited, the more time they gave a possible hostile enemy to gather outside.

He didn't want to start a fight here. These people weren't the enemy, and he couldn't—wouldn't—attack them, unless he had no other choice. "Let me go out first. If they attack, I have the best chance of surviving." He clicked his earpiece radio, connecting him with The Scourge. "Stand by for possible hostile actions."

Sela nodded grimly.

"I may be able to create a portal and carry more than one of us from this room," Derik said.

Sela's eyes flew open. "No, that is not going to work. Derik, it is a horrible idea to try to use a spatial skill inside of a shop dome. The Enchantments on the Arbuckle often respond and interfere with such spells."

Rocky patted the man on the back and stepped up to the wall. At his touch, a door opened, and he exited.

They were surrounded.

At least fifty Mechanoid Humans encircled his group's door to the shop dome, and behind them, row upon row of citizens. Ernest stood a few feet in front of the ring.

"This man—" Ernest pointed at Rocky, "—has attempted to deceive us." The jeer of the crowd behind the shop alerted Rocky to an even larger presence.

Sela and Derik exited behind Rocky.

Rocky held up his hands and shouted, "We did not come here to fight or deceive. We came to talk." People gasped in the crowd, and Rocky looked around to find the cause. His starship slowly inched closer to the Port. A haze occluded the ship, indicating a shield or an effect that distorted the air.

"They came to talk. Then why do they need a ship?" Ernest didn't sound like himself. There was something about his voice. Rocky's eyebrows knit together.

Ernest glared at him, a red light of hate shining from his human eyes. He didn't remember the red in Ernest's eyes before, but it might have just been the sun's reflection. But his eyes had changed so fast.

Ernest turned back to the crowd. "I do not wish to hurt these humans. However, if I let them go, they will only come back to invade us later. They know where we live—" he pointed at the ship, "—and that ship can come at any time."

Derik tried to speak, but even Rocky couldn't hear the man over the deafening reaction of the crowd. The noise cut off sharply as The Scourge continued its steady approach.

A heavily accented voice drew his attention. Dmitri stood in front of a large contingent of dangerous-looking men. "These people come here—talk. They not attack, only talk.

Ernest, you say protect humans, but now want to attack first outside humans that find us."

The crowd hummed at Dmitri's revelation. "I was in shop. They as shock as you."

Ernest glowered at Dmitri, his eyes flashing red again. "A demon, Dmitri. They brought a *demon* to testify against Dahrix. They wanted us to turn against the only people who were coming to help us."

Rocky narrowed his eyes. Ernest seemed to be acting strangely. The man had every right to be worried, but this angry? Was it the appearance of Amelia that disturbed him so much? Was he highly religious?

"Just because she looks a certain way does not make—"

"You say that, but what was your real intention coming here? What did you hope to gain?" said Ernest, spittle flying from his mouth.

Sela shouted, "Allies; we wished to gain an ally against future invasions. We wanted you to turn off the beacon—"

Ernest clapped his hands, creating a soundwave that silenced the crowd, Sela and Dmitri. "By their own admission, they came here to stop our saviors from coming. They wanted to shut off our only hope!"

The crowd jeered and booed again, stoked by Ernest's words.

One of the Mechanoid Humans stepped forward, "Dockmaster, they are just talking. I believe as Dmitri does—" He stopped speaking mid-sentence and retreated into line.

What had just happened?

Dmitri looked between Ernest and the retreating man. Then he sneered, "Ernest, what evidence you have that they invade?"

Ernest scowled at Dmitri, but he didn't shrink back. Those behind him gripped their weapons tighter.

Ernest attempted a smile, but it wasn't even close to human. Not at all like his fatherly smile of that morning. "Dmitri, when they come back to attack us, will you and your men protect the people from that?" He indicated the starship.

"I will protect people from any threat. These people are not threat. If they want attack, they would do without talk. Evil men no talk, just action."

Ernest clenched his mechanical jaw, the metal creaking in the silence. "On your head, be it then, fool." He walked purposefully toward Rocky, Sela, and Derik.

Once he was right in front of them, he whispered, "I will find your little Kobold wannabe. I did not know we had left any of them alive. I must thank you for that." His eyes were bright red.

Dahrix.

Rocky's posture stiffened, and a coldness spread from his core. But how could—he was—the beacon allowed this much control?

He raised his voice for the crowd. "We know you are from the north. If you come south in any way, I will take it as an act of war. That is your only warning."

Ernest shot up from the ground, flying away.

Rocky looked to Dmitri and nodded in gratitude for the man's support.

The crowd's buzzing over what had happened quickly morphed to gasps and a few shrieks as Azoth landed.

The pet looked around nervously but allowed Derik and Rocky to mount up.

Dmitri came forward. "I pet bird?" He moved forward, not waiting for an answer, and rubbed Azoth's neck. "Ernest, not same. Do not go straight home. He likely follow you. Be careful."

Rocky whispered. "Do you want to come with us, Dmitri?"

"No, we stay. People need us here. People need you back home, yes? Good luck—next time you tell me about beauty here, ya?"

"Hopefully, we meet again, my friend. And thank you." He held out his hand to shake. Dmitri took it and looked shocked for a split second. Rocky pulled him in close. "Take this. If you get it close to the beacon, it will disrupt the control Dahrix has on the robots. It may save your life."

Dmitri pulled back; the shock erased from his face. He nodded once, smirked, and walked away.

Azoth made a running start and jumped into the air, pumping his wings as Rocky engaged his earpiece radio. "We are coming back. Stand down shields and open hatch."

As soon as they landed onboard, Sela ordered the ship to fly south instead of north. If they could circle the planet once, they should lose anything following them. At least, Rocky hoped so.

Derik asked Rocky, "What do we do now?"

"I don't know, Derik. In Ottawa, Corsair was killing people, otherwise I probably never would have attacked him. Here..." he ran his hand over his sweaty forehead and into his hair. "Here, they are protecting and providing for all those people. If we disturb the balance, Dahrix will retaliate in a way that hurts as many humans as possible."

Sela said, "Did anyone get eyes on the beacon?"

No one answered.

"We can try to have the satellite team pinpoint it. Perhaps we can sabotage the beacon only?" said Sela.

"I gave the disruption device to Dmitri." Everyone looked at him, stunned. "They already have a bearing on the planet. Now the beacon lets them control people stupid enough to accept the mechanical hybrid class. Dmitri is our best chance to get the device close to the beacon."

The trip back to their Territory took three hours. They took the southern route and stopped over the frigid waters of Antarctica for an hour. The starship, designed for space exploration and well-built to handle the cold, kept them warm. They hoped that any following individuals, mechanical or otherwise, would not be able to survive the frigid temperatures.

As a last measure of safety, the pilots ascended into space. Rocky, glued to the window for the remainder of the trip, studied the beautiful blue sphere of the Earth. Hollywood movies didn't do it justice, and most of those movies made the scene unforgettable. Looking down on the real view himself, Rocky was unreservedly amazed. Somewhere in that sphere was his family, and he was going to find them.

He had imagined the ascent and descent from space differently. The Scourge made it seem like a simple elevator ride. Sure, there were some bumps and shakes, but it was akin to minor turbulence. The technology of the EtherVerse was far superior to what humans had reached with their technological innovations.

Once the ship landed, Rocky, Sela, and Derik decided to allow it to return to its previous mission of ferrying survivors. They stipulated that the pilots were to come in super-orbital and hover below five thousand feet, in hopes of reducing the visibility of the starship from range. It wasn't a perfect solution, but he wouldn't willingly let people die because of Dahrix.

An emergency council meeting followed, and after hours of talks, everyone left frustrated. There was no easy solution to this problem. Any action they took would inevitably bring backlash. In the end, they chose to continue growing and building their Territory, gaining allies and preparing for the inevitable invasion. Still, the decision left a sour taste in everyone's mouth.

Sela and Rocky exited the council meeting and met Zippo and Smith for dinner. They didn't converse much but enjoyed each other's company as they ate their meal. Only Zippo seemed inclined to speak, and then only because he wanted to hypothesize about the meal. "I think this meat is marinated. I think that is Mage Leaf, Chives, Mint—Coffee? Wow, this is good; right, guys? I think I am going to go chat with the chef."

Smith smiled at them both, "I would also like to discuss some things with the chef. Thank you for the company."

Sela and Rocky suddenly found themselves alone. It was late at night, and tension hung in the air. At least Rocky could feel something, like an unspoken question. The moment grew uncomfortable, and Rocky could no longer take the silence. "Do you think you could help me with an experiment?"

"Another Enchanting experiment?"

"I can't seem to figure out how to hold the Enchantment in place. I need something to both hold the power and buffer it from the material. The concentrated Ether channels burn it up, otherwise."

"Didn't you manage to collapse the Enchantments on the ferret gear?"

"I think that gear would hold any Enchantment I try. There is something different about the material it is made of, like it already has the medium inside."

They put their plates onto the waste station and left together, continuing to hypothesize about mediums that might work. They considered ores first. Rocky pulled out the piece of Enchanted gear he had purchased from the shop. They both scrutinized it. Even using an Ether Thread, no metal existed on the cheap leather jerkin. Sighing, he pointed to the small sparkles that were visible to his Ether Manipulation. "This here is the medium, but I have absolutely no idea what that is."

Sela shrugged. "Want to try to cut open the ferret boots and see what makes it different?"

Rocky nodded, and they made their way to an open field to experiment.

Rocky and Sela had been over every inch of the leather gear, in both the visible and Ether spectrum. There was nothing discernibly different, nothing that they could feel or see, at least.

He was reluctant to destroy it, but one Enchanted piece of gear would do very little. Discovering the secret to Enchanting could be the pivot to victory.

Rocky cut the leather boot with Dark Tidings. "Look at the Ether Pool."

"It's leaking out, creating forking, random channels, but why isn't it destroying the material as it moves through it?"

Rocky studied the exposed material and found a subtle difference. Those same sparkles were interwoven with the leather. The leaking Ether moved randomly through the destroyed item, but anywhere it went, it took a path through the medium. Almost like a conduit for electricity—the path of least resistance. Maybe.

They spent an hour on the destroyed boots, trying to discover the medium and coming up empty. They tried cutting out the sparkles, but whatever they were was either destroyed in the process or had retracted into the Ether pool They finally gave up on the Enchanting for the evening, after several unsuccessful attempts.

He slammed the shredded boots into his Bag of Holding and pulled out the Territorial Sphere. "Any idea how to use this?" He hoped to do something productive after banging their collective heads against the wall for hours.

"I am pretty sure you just touch it to the ground. However, I usually handed the captured spheres to others. Just try it."

Rocky placed the sphere on the ground. A notification popped into his vision.

Would you like to assimilate Small Territorial Sphere into Algonquin Valley?

<Yes> | No

Sphere will increase Territorial size by 10%.

Sphere offers a secondary option. Would you like to:

- **add 10 points to Territorial Skill Points?**

<Yes> | No

- **add 10,000,000 Etherience to Leaders' personal Classes?**

Yes | <No>

- **add 2 levels to Leadership Classes?**

Yes | <No>

For additional secondary options, find higher grade Territorial Spheres to convert.

Rocky and Sela stared at the prompt. They spoke over each other in their excitement. They looked at the options in their Leadership Classes. They had already explored the Territorial Skill after the pregnant women's rebellion. They had agreed that Growth Boost was their first to fifty.

Leadership Class
Strategist Level 5
Skill Tree
Current Skill Points to Assign: 4

<u>Skills</u>

<u>Production</u>

- **Production will increase the amount of material dropped by monsters who die inside your Territory Borders. In addition, this will slightly increase the rate that your profession skills increase.**

1/5

More skill points increase effects. Five skill points needed to unlock subsequent skills in the tree.

Army

- The army will increase the combat skill gains of individuals when you are leading large raids. This will also slightly increase the speed of your personal combat skill gains.

0/5

More skill points increase effects. Five skill points needed to unlock subsequent skills in the tree.

Enlightened

- Enlightened will increase your popularity amongst the people for the good decisions you make. It will also slightly mitigate the anger toward you when you make bad decisions.

0/5

More skill points increase effects. Five skill points needed to unlock subsequent skills in the tree.

Adventurer

- Adventurer will increase you and your party's Etherience gains slightly when you are fighting together. Inside Cardinal Dungeons, this effect is doubled. Inside other areas of interest or non-Cardinal Dungeons, this effect is increased by fifty percent.

0/5

More skill points increase effects. Five skill points needed to unlock subsequent skills in the tree.

Rocky and Sela looked at their Leadership Trees. Sela's would add some functionality, mostly during combat, but only when she was present. Rocky's Strategist class would add to the entire Territory, and perhaps even unlock higher levels in the military ranks. As they considered, he placed his four free skill points into Production toward that end.

They continued to discuss the best use for the sphere. Azoth joined them, and they gave him loving scratches as they considered the options.

The contact and closeness of his pet lessened his frustration. They had failed at Enchanting, he still had no idea where his family was, and he couldn't talk to Azoth. Rocky considered screaming into the night sky. He accidentally clenched his hand in his friend's feathers, and Azoth growled. He let go and gave him an extra scratch as an apology.

"Alright, so the ten million Etherience will bring us both to level ten. Ten Territory skill points will increase the growth of young children and the pregnancy rates of their mothers. That should keep the ladies happy. Two Leadership Levels will increase resources and your ability to intimidate creatures and people. Maybe offer higher military ranks, but we doubt it?" said Rocky.

"That sums it up. My vote is for personal Etherience. We are going to be capturing more Territories in the future, and being higher levels should help with that. The stronger we are, the better for everyone. We can always start adding to other areas later."

It was selfish, but it was also the fastest way to grow the Territory. As long as they both survived, that is. The stronger he and Sela were, the more quickly they could capture Territories, and the more people they could save. Like his family.

His mood bottomed out, and he didn't know how to pull himself out of it.

Sela leaned in and whispered, "Do you think it is about time for a hot shower?"

They walked back to the Town Hall and their apartments, laughing and joking along the way. The unknown heaviness in the air vanished.

CHAPTER TWENTY-NINE

The hum of activity outside the Town Hall woke Rocky far too early after a late night. Sela was curled up next to him, using her pillows as earmuffs instead of waking up. At least he wasn't the only one. He decided to get out of bed—the Territory was preparing for Toronto.

He checked his interface. They had gained a few hundred citizens throughout the morning and previous night. This had bumped up his Etherience through the shared quests, and if this windfall continued, he was hopeful his Guild would have a good source of growth. They would run out of people to save eventually, but the fact that the ship was working around the clock was promising.

The return of the starship was the majority of the action. The rest of the buzz was likely the military mobilizing for the operation. From what he could tell, there were a few pockets of survivors within Toronto. The most concentrated area was in the downtown core, but there were quite a few survivors in what had once been the surrounding suburbs of the Golden Horseshoe. Most of the golems in the suburbs had been taken care of already. The individuals in those suburbs were struggling more because of the level gap between themselves and the wildlife. Golems still surrounded the downtown core and schools, however. Today, they planned to start from the outside and move slowly inward.

As the Territory readied for the journey to Toronto, Rocky mounted Azoth and flew north to find out the Puzzle Dungeon's answer to his offer.

He opened the front door and spoke into the Science Building. He didn't want the Dungeon to lock him in.

A smoky pink orb rose from the concrete just inside the door. The globe pulsed as it said, "We agree with the terms of the contract. However, before we sign, we would like to speak with your other two Dungeons. Can you accept this?"

Rocky picked up the Crystalized sphere, "Yes, I will have someone bring you to their entrances. If you choose not to stay after your conversation, I can bring you back here."

The orb vibrated in his hands. "We would prefer a new location if that occurs. This area has no more humans that we can sense."

That must have been the reason for the core's choice. If it needed creatures and humans to challenge its depth to gain strength, it wasn't going to get many this far north.

He agreed, and they made the short flight back to the Territory, where Rocky left the core near Maximus first. He wasn't sure LFD would make the best first impression, as the Little Friendly Dungeon seemed eccentric, even when compared to other cores.

***

Rocky joined Smith, Zippo, and Sela by the Military Barracks. He relayed his morning's activities to the group as a large group of people filed into the starship. Smith sent a runner to wait on the Dungeon core's conversation to finish and transfer the heart to LFD's entrance. If the Dungeon wished to remain, the runner would place it on the western Grotto wall.

"Smith has picked up all the quests he could find from this Toronto. There are quite a few, and I had to turn off my location guidance. Want me to share them with you, and show you how to adjust that setting?" said Sela.

Rocky agreed and found the setting as Sela instructed him. He discovered that he could toggle on one or multiple quest trackers under his quest tab. Smith shared a whopping three hundred and twelve quests with him. Toronto had a very large number of suburbs, named in the quest titles, most of which he'd never heard of.

They brought the Golem Knights, but planned to keep them in reserve. If they used the Master Class golems, survivors might see it as an invasion. The Knights would act as a safety net if another Territory existed in Toronto. The quests, picked up from the Atlantean Net, indicated a large number of groups in the Toronto area.

Arriving in Toronto in less than ten minutes, they hovered over a single building, and Rocky, Sela, and Zippo mounted Azoth and flew down. People stared at them with open-mouths from the school grounds and the roof. They were alive, not starving.

Rocky scanned the grounds and didn't see a single golem surrounding the school. As soon as they landed, the fifteen survivors happily joined his guild. Azoth ferried them back to the ship, further highlighting the need for some sort of dropship. Amelia could probably provide him with one. But he wasn't ready to face her yet.

If I am honest with myself, I still don't know where I fall on that issue.

The people ferried by his pet didn't look happy or comfortable to ride Azoth. Alright—from now on, they would land The Scourge. It wasn't like it saved time performing multiple trips on Azoth.

When Rocky landed on the next school, hostility greeted him. He analyzed the man training a shotgun on his group.

Viscilli Fairbanks
Apprentice-Warden
Level 19
Health Points 230 / 230

A few people peeked out at him, hovering in the doorway leading into the school.

Rocky held up his hands and called, "We mean no harm, Viscilli. We are only here to offer aid. Even if you do not wish to come with us, we can leave some food for you."

Viscilli growled at him and fired the shotgun. The slug left the barrel and impacted into Azoth's side. His pet roared in outrage, and a buff appeared on Rocky's interface.

He cursed and jumped at the man who was pumping the fore-end, bringing the next cartridge into place. Rocky could not cover the ten feet between the man and himself before the next shot.

He used Dark Cloak in anticipation. If nothing else, he hoped it would guide the next shot away from a vital area. Black vines burst from the roof and pulled the muzzle of Visicilli's weapon down. The next shot boomed out, and gravel flew in all directions. Rocky closed the distance and knocked the man out.

Azoth poised himself to kill and eat Viscilli, but Sela and Rocky managed to calm the Chimera down. Rocky cast Dark Mend on his pet, and once the wound healed, Azoth's bloodlust subsided. Slightly.

The people behind the door burst forth.

"Are you all okay?" asked Rocky.

Each individual was red in the face, and their eyes were wild. Some even had spittle and froth surrounding their mouths. He was thankful none of the people had weapons. They attacked Sela, Zippo, and himself with their fists.

"Do not kill them! Azoth, fly away now!" Rocky yelled.

Rocky and his group incapacitated everyone on the roof. This was eerie and far too familiar to Rocky. He looked over Viscilli first, spotting a glowing red handprint on the shooter, and gasped, "Snollygoster! I think we just found Frank."

What in the heck is a Snollygoster?

They placed the group of survivors, including the ten downstairs who hadn't participated in the attack, in cells aboard the starship. Rocky, found marks on all of them. Even the ones downstairs who appeared to be in control of themselves. He ordered the military to make them members of the guild, then teach them Ether Manipulation.

"You look like you are going to punch a hole in the ship. Calm down for a second, and let's discuss the options," said Sela.

He took a deep breath and closed his eyes for a minute, steadying his breath. "I just know that psychopath is headed toward the downtown core or a large group of survivors." He didn't have full control of his anger, and his voice shook

Sela looked at Zippo, and Victoria, outfitted in her golden armor and fur cape, who all stood in front of him. None of them seemed shocked or upset by his tone. He guessed they understood his rage at Frankie, the man who had controlled Corsair from the shadows for Apep. The man who was back to his devious ways.

"I went to school at York University. It is the closest option and likely to have the most survivors." Victoria motioned for them to follow her down the loading bay door. Once outside, she pointed in the direction of two golden threads. "York is that direction, and there are two schools on the path, plus a few more in the surroundings. Should we make those priorities?"

Sela gripped Rocky's arm hard, and he realized his jaw was painfully tight. He forced it to relax and opened his mouth wide to stretch it. He nodded his agreement.

Frank had also infected the next two schools. This time, they were more prepared and had flown ahead of the starship on Azoth. Victoria had joined Zippo and Rocky, riding the Chimera, while Sela returned to the ship for a time. Azoth didn't struggle at all with the armor-clad woman, but a sharing the ride with a plate-wearing individual was far from comfortable for anyone.

At the next school, Rocky had summoned his Shadow Clone as soon as they touched down. His second self had entered Stealth instantly. If Rocky hadn't felt the connection, he would have thought the skill hadn't worked. Zippo had used his Barrier skill, and Victoria had taken the lead.

This group of survivors had multiple handguns, shotguns, and even a few M3's. Azoth stood behind Zippo, and when they opened fire, the bullets pinged off the barrier spell in front of them.

Victoria raised an arm in front of her visor, and the bullets flattened themselves on the armor before dropping to the ground. The force and momentum of the shots died, absorbed by some skill of the tank.

One after another, the gunmen slumped to the ground. Rocky's clone flashed into view behind each one and ragdolling a target for a brief second before vanishing again. Fixated on Zippo, Azoth, and Victoria, none of the survivors noticed the Clone, until only two remained.

The two remaining gunmen ran dry on handgun ammo at the same time. They looked around; eyes wild. One of them spotted Rocky's clone as it drove a fist into the shooter's jaw. The other one pulled out a grenade as his friend collapsed.

Rocky sent a single Dark Blade stack at the man's arm. He had tracked the fighting and attempted to condense the attack, so as not to hit any of the fallen fighters. His blade sliced through the man's arm with ease, and continued to remove a large triangle out of the doorway. The concrete and metal door slid, as if in slow motion, and a section threatened to fall on three people lying unconscious beneath it. Victoria and Zippo made a motion and the sliding stopped.

"Hurry up and move those people. This thing is heavy," yelled Victoria.

Zippo is likely using his barrier skill again. What skill is Victoria helping with?

Rocky and his clone dragged the unconscious forms of the two men and one woman from under the debris. Rocky cast a double stack of Dark Mend on the screaming, armless man who had thrown the grenade. His screaming didn't lessen, but the wound closed over and stopped bleeding.

"Victoria, stay with them until the ship arrives. Zippo and Sela, with me. Let's clear inside."

They found four scared survivors, still in control of themselves, huddled together in a walk-in freezer. It had long since warmed to room temperature without power.

"Where did you get all the weapons? How long ago was Frank here?" asked Rocky.

None of them admitted to knowing Frank. The group stammered out responses to his questions, occasionally talking over each other.

"We have four police officers with us. They had raided their precinct right after waking up—Who is Frank?—The others grew more and more aggressive—they kept saying that we needed to go attack the University—Cecil came by and saved us from the golems—he said the nearby University was killing humans for food."

That was all Rocky needed to hear. He remembered Frank's ability to change his class name and assumed he had done the same with his name. The group had confirmed that they knew the Analyze skill.

Once the ship landed, he found out that the other school had been visited by a man named George, who had told them similar stories. Rocky's jaw tightened again, and he forced himself to relax it.

At least they had arrived early enough to save these people. The man's arm may not grow back, but it was better than blowing himself up.

They found eight more schools in the area. Frank hadn't visited three of them. Of the five remaining, three of the groups attacked them. Two schools had met a traveler within the last two days and were still cognizant. They were marked but hadn't yet succumbed to Frank's machinations.

He just hoped that Frank hadn't infiltrated their next stop—York University. If that happened, they were about to fly into something very different than a rescue.

Rocky vibrated with impatience as he discussed possible strategies to deal with potential large-scale defenses at the University with Victoria, Sela, and Zippo. "What if we bring the Golem Knights with us? They should easily be able to withstand all attacks, right?" Zippo asked.

"They would be able to withstand attacks, but there are two issues with that. First, that looks like an invasion of golems, which puts them against us, even if they aren't Frankie'd. Secondly, the Golem Knights can't respond to an attack without completely destroying the individuals doing the attacking. They are just too strong," Victoria said.

The same problem existed with bringing the military with them. There were just too many unknowns, and avoiding being labeled as hostile was prudent. Rocky chose to go with Victoria, Zippo, Sela, and Azoth.

The flight to the York University campus was interesting. It was a vast complex, and several of the educational buildings still stood, but because the University had also contained numerous residences, massive bare patches also existed. Likely the result of student housing converted to Golems.

The saving grace for the inhabitants seemed to be the campus size. While golems attempted to surround the space and 'protect' the humans inside, there were huge gaps between the skyscraper-sized creatures. Battle had marred the concrete, wooden, and earthy surfaces of some of the golems.

They landed on the Lillian Meighen Wright Centre, as indicated by the sign in front of the most central building that Rocky could see. Four two-person teams stood watch over the four cardinal directions on the roof. When one pair noticed the massive Chimera, a few ballistic shots rang out. Zippo flung up a prepared shield, causing the bullets to ricochet. Using his dual casting, he simultaneously shot a fireball into the air. They hoped this would signal the individuals to stop firing, but other groups had run over, and a few ionized bolts from laser weaponry joined the ballistics.

Zippo ignited his skill into a firework and shot off two more fireballs as sweat broke out on his forehead.

Worried for the young man, Rocky whispered, "Come on, get the message. Notice none of the fireballs are hurtling at you."

One of the later arrivals ran through the line, lowering the muzzles of the others, and Zippo sighed with relief. That same relief washed over Rocky's shoulders, raising goosebumps on his skin. First part completed successfully. He crossed his fingers, hoping the next would go as smoothly.

Azoth landed on the roof, and the weapons trained back up. The humans slid off his back with their hands raised, trying to look as non-threatening as possible.

One of the survivors yelled, "Who was setting off the fireworks? Our enemies are going to think we are fighting! You might have just instigated an attack."

"Umm, we are sorry—we were hoping to show you we meant no harm. What enemies?" asked Rocky.

CHAPTER THIRTY

Rocky and Sela stood in a large meeting room. They were the only ones standing, and were surrounded by strict-looking older men and women. The group of elders sat quietly at a hollow open square desk in leather business chairs. Dana Farth, former President of York University, took his position as head of the meeting and sat in the centre of the front table.

Within seconds of meeting each other, Dana Farth had instantly upset Rocky and Sela by insisting that they use his full name. He had further been the only person in the boardroom that spoke. Yes, an entire boardroom of smarmy executives still in charge of the survivors at York University. The fact that the highest level amongst them was eight spoke to how idiotic that notion was.

How can you lead people, if you don't even know what it was like outside?

"How do we know that you and your ship aren't with the other factions?" The white-haired mousy looking man, Dana Farth, asked for the third time.

Rocky ground his teeth together. "Wouldn't your enemies just bombard you from the sky with a weapon like that?"

Dana Farth was either senile or so paranoid that he kept hoping to catch Rocky in a lie.

At least he'd gleaned a bit of information from the exchanges, frustrating as they were. There were three factions within Toronto. One for each University—Ryerson, University of Toronto, and York. Multiple smaller factions resided within hospitals, local schools, and libraries, but the big three players were the extensive campuses of survivors. If he wasn't mistaken, they also were the most violent toward each other, and many of the smaller groups tried to avoid them.

Dana Farth constantly repeated himself, like a true politician, spewing empty words. It was painful to extract anything worthwhile from him, and Rocky had to string together the bits of information as best as he could. York was the weakest, or perhaps the least active in the conflicts. Damaged golems outside the campus walls suggested that other factions had attacked and failed. It was more likely that they avoided defeat through golem intervention. Sheer luck.

York held on by a tenuous thread instead of grabbing the one Rocky offered to escape this situation.

"Well, thanks to your firework display, an attack is likely already on route. The only way you can fix this problem is to provide support. Leave your starship here for a week—"

"A week!" Rocky exclaimed.

The next hour was far less exciting. The Board of Directors had tried to pull the 'go big and pare down' tactic of negotiations. Unfortunately for them, Sela was pretty good at this.

He exited the meeting hall, and looked for something to hit. Those old men were willing to be his allies? He was trying to save people, and if they didn't need his help—why would he leave his starship here? He found a concrete pillar.

Now my fist hurts.

Sela pointed at the door, her face flushed. "Those pompous politicians are trying to blackmail us? We can just leave at any time. We don't need to stay."

Twenty thousand people resided on campus. Rocky wanted to abandon the morons from the meeting. But he couldn't bring himself to abandon that many innocent lives, if an attack really was coming.

Additionally, the Board of Directors claimed they could convince Ryerson to ally with them—with Rocky's support. And Ryerson had even more survivors.

That was the real reason for them wanting the starship on display. It solidified their position, allowed them to bargain, and even collect some of the surrounding outliers. According to the discussions, they would advertise the ship as an escape to safety over the next week.

A Territory sat in the middle of the downtown core. It was situated where the Gardens Conservatory used to reside, and it complicated matters.

"It sounds like the University of Toronto is being aggressive in its expansion. I don't buy all the nonsense about an imminent attack, but I do think that the presence of the starship may entice small groups of survivors to come here. We can make quick night trips back to the Grotto for anyone who wants to join the Guild," said Rocky.

"Zippo has gone to check on their food stores, as well as spread the word about Algonquin Grotto. At least they are willing to let the Non-Power Classes leave to safety for the most part. Do you think we can capture this Territory?" Sela slowed down her walk, forcing the assigned guards to adjust their pace. She whispered, "I've got a feeling that the massive collection of exotic animals from that 'Zoo' is also a Territory, just that no one has gotten close enough yet."

The starship touched down as they exited the double doors into the courtyard. Most of their military exited. However, the silhouettes of the Golem Knights behind the military caused a problem. The shouts of fear and raised weapons surprised everyone, and Rocky ran forward with his hands raised high. "Don't fire! They are friendly!"

The ship's landing drew a massive crowd, and the Golem Knights stood frozen on the docking bay. He didn't think the basic weapons could have hurt them, even though no one fired. Rocky continued to walk forward, and Epsilon whispered, "We can't exit the ship—we are not permitted to enter designated learning areas. We will stay aboard for now." Everyone heard him, first because the entire crowd had gone silent, and secondly, when a three-to-four story converted building whispers, it's usually not as quiet as intended.

"Rocky? Rocky, is that you?" called a voice.

There was so much familiarity in that call—like the person had known him for years. He had grown accustomed to people calling his name—military runners, Sela, Zippo, and even Smith. Each one of those said his name uniquely. But this voice carried a tone he hadn't heard since before the first wave. He snapped his head around, heart leaping into his throat, searching for the person that matched the voice.

The crowd undulated as someone pushed their way through. His eyes followed the parting of the crowd, waiting for the individual to exit. A dark-haired, bearded man pushed his way to the front. The man's smile plucked at the strings of Rocky's heart. The man's thick eyebrows and unkempt beard surprised Rocky and his legs collapsed under him. His brother-in-law Benoit's smile wavered, and he jumped forward, loping to close the distance between them.

This couldn't be. The system hadn't listed the man. He had already assumed that he was dead. How could he be here? If he was here, was the rest of his family? Strength returned in a rush of adrenaline, and he shot to his feet, searching the crowd over Ben's fast-approaching head. When his eyes didn't find any more familiar faces, he glanced back at Ben. He drew to a stop in front of him and now wouldn't meet Rocky's eyes. Rocky pulled him into a hug. At first Ben was stiff, before he finally relaxed into the embrace.

After a brief moment, Benoit pushed away. "They flew separately, Rocky. They were going to visit New York for a day on the way back. I landed in Toronto and was going to take the train back later that night. Then the wave struck, and I thought it was all a dream …" His brother-in-law was nearly crying by the end of his recollection of the events.

Rocky grabbed his shoulders. "They are alive, Ben— this, I know." Ben met his eyes. "Yes, I have a way to find out if they are still alive, but I didn't know where. You say they are in New York?"

Ben's eyes narrowed. "You don't understand, Rocky. Humans are slaves in New York." Benoit pointed to the Golem Knights. "Golems are intelligent there, unfriendly."

The Knights were too far away to hear Benoit's words. Rocky considered telling them; they would want to go to New York right away.

"All the more reason to go there now, Ben. Wait... how do you know that? Did you go there?"

"No, of course, I didn't go there. I would have died or become a slave myself. A group of survivors escaped and managed to make it here. They told us what was going there."

Ben hadn't gone to New York the instant he had heard the news. Unbelievable. They were Ben's family too, and he didn't even try. That was his wife—Rocky's sister—didn't that mean anything to Ben? Rocky had gone to Ottawa to save them, risked his life more than once to find his family. He bit down hard, not wanting to say anything he would regret. Rocky's jaw creaked as he fought the urge to spit vitriol at his brother-in-law. His Dark Cloak swirled in his palms, restless.

Benoit's face flushed, and he lifted his chin. Rocky thought they were going to start screaming at each other.

"Who is this man, Rocky? His name is Daeric Nallo, and he is a Ranger?" asked Sela.

His name wasn't Daeric, but Rocky had heard it somewhere before. "You changed your name to your Dungeons and Dragons character. That's why we couldn't find you. Why would you go and do a thing like that? I thought you were dead. Dead!"

Ben shouted back, "I didn't know it actually changed my name. I thought this was all an elaborate dream at first. It was a strange option in the settings."

They screamed at each other for another ten minutes before they finally settled down.

"I am Selaphelia Ardensai, Rockland's Ancestor. What shall I call you?"

Benoit tilted his head and blinked, but responded without comment on the Ancestor. "Benoit or Ben is fine. How did you end up babysitting this oaf?"

Sela had the audacity to laugh at his brother-in-law's insult. "That's a long story, but it appears we have some time. Is there a place to eat around here?"

Rocky's anger flared anew. "Sela, we don't have time for that. We need to get to New York."

Sela frowned at him. "You know we have a satellite that can show us the state of this New York, right? Stop letting your emotions get away from you, and let's go have a look."

The group walked into the cockpit and used the remote station to zoom in on New York. It wasn't hard to spot, due to the large amount of—debris? From far away, the city still resembled a city. No buildings stood intact, but the road planning and districts still stretched out on-screen. Gravel filled the areas that had once held roads. Another zoom showed golems standing by as teams of humans used ropes to pull massive pieces of the rubble out.

The humans piled chunks of concrete, buses, and cars, creating a mountain of debris. A golem, that easily stood hundreds of stories tall, sat atop the heap as if it was a throne. Its hand was wrapped around a spear-like weapon. The sheer size and scope of this golem overwhelmed him, and he didn't think it could be defeated. He'd have to find another way to find his family. His mind pictured the interstate golems, and then the smoky apparitions Michabo produced.

That limp-eared jackrabbit could have warned me.

"Rocky, we can't just go in there. That thing can swat our ship from the sky, turn our entire army to a pool of blood, without standing up from that throne." Sela walked over and put a hand on his arm, but he pulled away. He felt betrayed.

She tried again. "Rocky, they aren't killing the humans. They must be feeding them, and there is a Red Quest issued to the golems by Gaia herself. Your family isn't exactly in danger."

Rocky shook his head and looked at Benoit. Benoit wouldn't meet his eyes. Another one too scared to act? No way.

"Do you think you can beat an area filled with enemies as strong or stronger than the Golem Knights?"

She tried again to place a hand on his shoulder, but he shifted away angrily. "Sela, a slave isn't a good thing. If they are slaves, I am not going to let them stay that way any longer than they already have."

"Benoit? Can you help me convince this idiot?" Sela said.

"She has a point, Rocky. Think about this. You're talking about a suicide mission. I mean, how do you plan to get in there?" Benoit responded.

He didn't have a plan. Maybe if he had better gear, but he had failed at Enchanting in all of his attempts. Perhaps if he had Bathilda, but she had left to scour the world clean of Nuclear radiation. He was a failure. He couldn't get anything right, and now his family would suffer because of him. He wasn't sure what was worse, not knowing where his family was, or knowing their location but unable to get to them.

Sela whispered, "What about Frank's activity here in Toronto? Are you going to let him take control of people and create an army of slaves again?"

"How can you ask me to choose between my family and survivors?" Even his 'girlfriend' was against him. Rocky couldn't take it anymore. He looked for an escape and saw Azoth enjoying some liberal pets from Zippo outside the ship. He rushed off the deck, out of the ship, and mounted up on his pet. "Let's get out of here."

***

Rocky returned to the Territory. He had wanted to fly right to New York, but he knew that Sela was telling the truth. He didn't want to listen to her position, but he had to admit she was usually right about these things. That was the most frustrating part. Wasn't she, his guide, his 'girlfriend'—shouldn't she support him in this? She should have helped him come up with a plan, not use emotional blackmail on him. Of course, he wanted to save the survivors from Frank. But why couldn't he do both?

And when she wasn't trying to stop him from finding his family, she was showing him up as a leader. Sela was more the leader of this Territory than he was. People came to her for answers before they even considered asking him. He could be standing right in front of them, and they'd still ask Sela first. Other than lucking into the Territory, what had he done for these people?

Derik's accusations looped in his head. What had he done for these people? He'd failed at Enchanting, incurred an invasion by Apothis, killed half of the escorted survivors, and not even found his family. His sole reason for building this place was to attract survivors, to find his family!

At least he knew where they were now.

But how was he supposed to save them? His Stealth Skill would drain through his Ether pool in seconds in a city of high-level golems.

If he went at night and used Dark Cloak in conjunction, he would be a bit better off. Then he would just need to find his family and get them out.

In theory, it was easy; in practice, not so much. New York City had been home to over eight million people. If the survival rate of around ten percent held, then the current population was eight hundred thousand. To find two people in eight hundred thousand wouldn't be an easy task, even without the golems to contend with.

Azoth paced beside Rocky, mirroring his frustrated motions. At least he still had one friend. He reached out and petted the bird-lion affectionately. Humans were clearly safe, to a degree, in New York. Sela was right about that. The first wave had hit nearly two months ago, and his family still lived.

Perhaps he could sneak in as one of the slaves. But how would he pull it off? What about the Golem Knights' search for other sapient golems?

He paced faster, weighing his options.

A runner approached, and he stopped pacing.

"Rocky! LFD says he is looking for you. We thought you were in Toronto, but we just received a transmission asking us to look for you here. Would you like us to send a message to the main team? Call a council meeting?"

Rocky shook his head and saluted the man before dismissing him. He managed to hold a neutral expression on his face until the man left. The council. They were probably planning on using the Territorial Ether for a high number of things. Sela had accused his plan of deceit, and he felt his anger bubbling. He hated that she was right, but also that she wouldn't own up to her part in that decision.

How could she not be willing to help me?

His anger continued to simmer, and he channeled it into every footfall as he jogged with Azoth to see LFD.

From his stylized entrance, LFD blurted, "I found the ring, Rocky. I dug through about …"

LFD continued to babble, and Rocky felt a spike of emotions. He went from anger to euphoria in the span of a second as tears welled in his eyes. He would be able to talk to Azoth again.

Out of the rock at the entrance to the tunnel, a silver ring rose to the surface. LFD was still babbling about finding the object, but Rocky hadn't been listening to his tales of exploration. He picked up the ring and Analyzed it.

Ring of Chaos Serpent
- **The Void God Apep created this ring. The wearer of this ring is the leader among other Cultists.**
  Quality: Superb
  Enchantments: Locked

CHAPTER THIRTY-ONE

Rocky's soul broke. He could almost hear the shards hit the ground. He stumbled mid-stride, tripping over his own misery. He reached out to the entrance support to steady himself and sagged against it. He threw the ring away from himself as tears ran down his cheeks. The accumulation of not having been able to talk to Azoth for so long, piled together with everything else, struck him like a forge hammer. Azoth shuffled over and nudged him. Rocky reached out and patted his pet. His friend. The only one that supported him for every idea, every adventure. Everything bubbled over, the final drop of water that overflows the glass. His friend was right there, right beside him. He just couldn't hear him.

"Was that not the ring you wanted?" asked LFD. Rocky barely noticed that LFD had stopped prattling about his pseudo-archeological dig for the ring.

Rocky shook his head. He had nothing left to give. His sadness slowly abated. The feeling hadn't disappeared, but he gained control over it. Hardened it. Resolved to act. He needed to do something for his family, but first, he needed to ensure his Territory would survive if he died.

"Please keep looking, LFD." He had no strength left to say more.

LFD whispered, "I will keep looking." His usual exuberance was gone, as if Rocky's sadness stifled it. He didn't have time to mollify the Dungeon.

Rocky walked to the Crafter's Hall, Azoth beside him. He continued to pet the fur-feathered beasty, more out of a need for his emotional support than for Azoth's enjoyment. The building was massive, and Azoth happily entered with him, sensing that Rocky needed him, or perhaps because he wanted more pets. The people inside stopped their work as the lion-bird entered. The Hall plunged into silence as Rocky and Azoth moved to an empty workbench. Some individuals turned back to their tasks, while others kept their eyes glued to the terrifying creature beside Rocky.

If he was leaving for New York on a possible one-way trip, he needed to leave a few things for the people of the Grotto. They would need a leader. A *true* leader. Sela, Smith, and the Council easily filled that role. Rocky grudgingly added Derik to that list.

The Grotto would need all of his Crystals, Gems, Marks and Chips. Rocky dumped all but one hundred Crystals into a private area of the Territorial Inventory. He added almost everything else from his Bag of Holding, leaving it practically empty. He kept the Bottle of Gaia's Essence, strangely attached to the rare drop he had acquired at the start of all this.

The Grotto would need the ability to Enchant their own gear. There were other higher forms of Enchanting that would still be locked—like Ether Technology. But for now, he could give them a starting point. It was absolutely essential for their continued growth.

Rocky looked down at the remnants of his Bag of Holding. A pile of one hundred Crystallized Ether looked pitifully small, compared to what he was leaving behind. Rocky shrugged. He wouldn't need it where he was going anyway.

In one hand, he held the Enchanter's pen, twirling the pestle handle around in his other palm before securing the device within the mortar. He planned to leave the Enchanting tools in the Territorial Inventory when he left, but first, he was determined to solve this problem. He placed the mortar and pestle on the table and turned to survey the room of crafters. Someone in this hall likely had the answer he needed.

Rocky tossed the pen back and forth between his two hands, contemplating each station. In the back of the shop, a smith worked the bellows of the forge, the noise of it absent. A second smith hammered away, behind the first. Still no clanging reached his ears, tempting him to investigate. However, this wasn't the time to indulge his curiosity.

He continued his scan of the room. A woman worked on tearing apart ragged t-shirts, sweaters and other assorted garments. The everyday wear was something he had gotten used to no longer seeing on people—at least not the people of the Grotto. Rocky remembered his own tattered clothing from his camping trip. He pulled the unuseable clothing out of his Bag of Holding and placed it on the ground. He had a sentimental attachment to the clothes of his former life—especially his Star Wars sweater. Yet, now that he had found a way for it to be reused, he would hand it over without hesitation. Rocky hoped that this seamstress and the many men and women working behind her would be able to keep his people clothed.

The leather workers toiled away, and while he was curious about their tools and methods, they had all they needed for now. The hunters all picked up skinning and placed the viable materials into the Territorial Inventory for the use of this group of crafters, and he assumed they used a solution or a skill to tan or dry the hides for use in their craft. He had purchased a stockpile of their wares from the guild funds. In a moment, he planned to Enchant some of that stockpile. Or destroy it.

Beyond the leather workers, a group of thirty to forty people read on Knowledge Tablets. If this was pre-apocalypse, he wouldn't have noticed. Back then, people were glued to their electronic devices. A few of the Montessori Teachers sat with the group. He Analyzed a member he didn't know.

Greta Hurd
Apprentice-Researcher
Level 19
Health Points 110 / 110

Sela had mentioned that a group of people were constantly working on researching new blueprints, techniques, and technologies. Rocky smiled and promised that if he somehow made it back to the Territory, he would take a more hands-on approach with this group. There might be a research page or building that worked like the video games he used to play.

His eyes finally landed on a group that could help him—the Alchemists and Herbalists section. Bundled plants and herbs littered nearly every surface of their workspace. Bunsen burners and glass apparatus occupied any free space. Smith had used them before for inks, and a few individuals worked away with a mortar and pestle. Their mortars and pestles were stone, and Rocky turned around to grab his diamond version of the device.

They were gone. So were the Crystals. He must have placed the item back in his Bag of Holding. He hadn't had his back turned for more than a moment, and no one could have snuck up on him—right? He checked, but the Bag of Holding didn't have the items within it.

Blood pumped through his ears, drowning out any noise in the Hall. He couldn't solve the problem if his tools were missing. Azoth tugged gently on his hand, and he ignored it. If someone had stolen the items, they must still be nearby. He activated Dark Cloak and checked the shadows, his vision now magically assisted. Another tug, this one much more violent, nearly took Rocky off his feet.

He looked down at his arm, wondering how Azoth was pulling so hard, without Rocky feeling the Chimera's sharp teeth. Azoth's fangs clenched around the Enchanter's pen.

"Azoth, drop it!"

Azoth let go and slunk away like a scolded doggo.

Rocky picked up the pen. Other than slobber, it was in perfect shape. Rocky breathed out in relief and looked to his pet. "Azoth, I'm sorry I—"

Something sparkly caught his eye under Azoth's stomach. "Azoth, move away from there. Please." His friend gave him puppy eyes, lowering his head to look up at Rocky. It almost made him laugh, but then he stood straighter. He stepped forward and Azoth relented, moving away from the pile of Crystals, mortar, and pestle he had procured.

He had completely forgotten his pet's obsession with shiny objects. Azoth was worse than a crow. The Chimera used to steal Zippo's first staff because the top had some sort of gem inside.

Rocky bent down and placed all the Crystals back into his Bag of Holding.

Note to self, don't leave piles of Crystals near the birdbrain.

Rocky picked up the mortar, and something moved within it. He sighed. Azoth had likely slobbered inside of it. He inspected it to assess the damage. But it wasn't slobber. Somehow a Crystal had fallen into the bowl. Rocky moved to place it in his Bag and stopped. It was broken in half. But how? He had tried to break it in the past but it had been impossible. The glowing blue Crystal palm-sized snowflake was far sturdier than it looked.

He stared at the palm-sized Crystal that had cracked in half. He brought the mortar up to his eye and peered through the thick diamond side. Grains of blue-tinged sand slid around within its bowl.

Rocky experimentally placed the pestle atop the Crystal. He applied a bit of pressure, and the Crystal cracked further, the half becoming four smaller chips. He worked the device until he was left with shining blue sand. Even without his Ether Sight, he was relatively sure this was the answer. He compared the Mortar and its contents in Meditation. They were an exact match for the tiny sparkles he had seen on the surface of the Enchanted gear.

He uncapped the pen as Azoth slunk back toward him. He pointed at his pet and laughed, "No, Azoth. Go lay down, or hunt, or something. Leave me in peace." He softened the blow by scratching Azoth vigorously. He kissed him on the forehead. "Thank you, buddy."

Azoth jogged from the Crafters' Hall and people dove out his way. "Sorry about that, everyone."

He couldn't wait a second longer and turned back to his workbench to Analyze the Crystal dust.

Crushed Ether
- **Crushed Ether has the ability to hold limited amounts of Ether, but has no value to most of the EtherVerse. It maintains much of its strength from its Crystallized version, and can be used in certain crafting endeavors.**

He pulled out his tablet and wrote what he read in it, along with the way to obtain Crushed Ether. If he was right, this material could be used in all forms of crafting. Perhaps smiths could combine it with metals, tailors with cloth, leatherworkers with hides, alchemists with potions, and enchanters with gear. This would be expensive for his people. No wonder Enchanted gear was costly.

He carefully upended the Crushed Ether into the Pen. He pulled out a piece of leather and drew the Rune of Protection on it. After the first line, he removed the pen from the mark he had just made. Other than a slight indent from the Pen's tip, the material carried no Crystal.

My excitement has gotten the better of me.

He entered Meditation and created an Ether Thread. He connected it with the pen, and the stylus cooled drastically in his palm. The crushed Ether glowed to his Ether Sight, and he drew the Rune of Protection again. A beautiful Ether Channel, suffused with tiny glowing stars, followed his stroke.

He finished the symbol and almost lifted the stylus before looping it back on itself. Sweat pricked his forehead, and he rested his stylus on the leather for a moment, surveying his work. It wasn't pretty. He had been slower in certain areas, faster in others, and the symbol had thick and thin portions.

The Pen dripped where he had left it and the blotch it created grew larger. He pulled it off and cut off his Ether Channel from the Pen. As soon as he finished, the gear flashed in his Ether Sight, almost blinding him. When he looked back, the sloppy rune stared back.

He exited Meditation and looked at the Leather in the normal spectrum. It wasn't blackening—yet. He Analyzed it.

Leather Tunic of Protection
- **This tunic was made from basic grade leather, and has a poor Ether pool absorption pattern. Likely this object will never recharge after the pool is exhausted.**
    Ether Pool: Tiny
    Current Ether Pool: 10/10
Enchantments: Sloppy Protection I (5%)

Okay, it was a piece of junk. But Rocky had never been more excited by an item to date. He pumped his fists up into the air and shouted, "I did it!"

Everyone in Crafters' Hall applauded. It didn't last long—five seconds at most—a polite tradition, but it still felt good.

For a moment, he was surprised no one came over to see what he had done, but they were all likely working toward crafting breakthroughs of their own. They didn't have time to inspect each breakthrough.

Rocky enjoyed his celebration for a few more moments before examining the gear. The note about the poor absorption pattern was troublesome.

He entered back into Ether Sight through Meditation and examined his rune. His embarrassment grew when he used a thread of Ether to trace his rune. The edges of the lines were wavy, and many weren't straight. He was surprised the Enchantment held, but assumed that all of his former 'practice' helped him. Slightly. Plus, his skill in Enchanting.

His large blotch at the beginning-come-end-of the rune had actually become the Ether pool. His Ether Thread examined the pool and found a tail on it. He remembered the knots or spirals he found on other pools and winced. When he pulled his Pen away, it had created this tail. He exited his Ether Sight and looked at the pen in his hand. He pretended to pull it away while spinning the tip in circles, practicing a spiral. He moved his hand in a small figure eight, and considered that it may create a knot, but only if he pulled the thread through.

He continued to work on piece after piece, keeping careful notes in his Knowledge Tablet. He would tell others about his findings and wanted the map to be as clear as possible. Rocky studied all the gear he held and did his best to draw the complex runes onto the tablet. He tried to describe how to join the symbols. The highest-level Enchantment was always a bigger symbol and had to come first in the order of script. If the Enchantments were of the same level, they dominated a similar space.

Congratulations! You have learned a new skill.
Penmanship
- **The ability to create legible script. Each point in this skill increases hand stability with a writing utensil by 5%.**

Current rank: Weak level 1.
--

Congratulations! You have learned a new skill.
Artistry

- **The ability to make beautiful pieces of art. Art can take many shapes, and an Artist can capture them all. Each point increases the user's Artistic Creativity by 1%.**

Current rank: Weak level 1.

It was clear that his 'Penmanship' and 'Artistry' would need to improve right alongside Enchanting if his people were going to get better at this.

Rocky stopped, as he had no more Crystals left in his bag. During his experiments, he had created a set of gear with Protection and +1 Strength on the gloves, tunic, leggings, and boots. He looked outside and found it was already dark.

I think I got a little carried away. One hundred Crystals gone in a few hours.

He glanced back at his workstation, strewn with gear, and he swept the set into the Territorial Inventory. Smith or Sela would find a use for it. He checked his skill page and found Enchanting ready to rank up.

Enchanting
- **Enchanting is the study of runes and Ether flow. Many of the runes used in early Enchanting were found naturally in the wild.**

Weak
- **Rune shaping of the individual increased by 25%.**

Moderate
- **Ether Pool creation of the individual improved by 1% per point.**

Current rank: Moderate level 1.

Rocky felt much better after finally having some success and chose to return back to Toronto. He wasn't sure whether he would tell Sela about his trip to New York yet, but he would tell the Golem Knights about the sapient golems—and recruit them to his cause.

He mounted Azoth and said, "Let's head back to the ship."

CHAPTER THIRTY-TWO

Somehow, preparing the Territory made him feel calm. He had done everything he could. And in the case of his death, people would be able to survive without him. That preparation somehow relieved him. He was breathing easier and had an energy he hadn't before.

The 'borrowed' starship took a total of five minutes to fly south and drop off Rocky and the Golem Knights. It hadn't taken much in the way of convincing for the five to accompany him. Rocky suggesting that the New York golems were sapient was enough for the Knights to sign on. They insisted Adam be left in the Grotto. Rocky hadn't even considered bringing the young man on this possible suicide mission. He hadn't even told Sela.

If this went sideways, the Grotto needed one of its leaders alive and uncompromised. At least, that was what he told himself. If he told Sela, she would try to stop him. He would have loved her help, but what he truly needed were people who believed in this mission as much as he did.

Maybe, if he failed, she would be able to amass enough power to one day save his family. It was a long shot, but he had to believe it.

***

Rocky and Azoth landed beside the area where the Golem Knights had HALO jumped, minus the parachutes. The Knights were pulling themselves out of small landing craters.

Rocky dismounted and turned to his friend, scratching Azoth's chest. "This is as far as we go for now. Go back to help Sela. The Golem Knights will be in touch. Okay?"

Azoth shook his head violently, barely avoiding goring Rocky with his horns in the process. "Azoth. This is an order. You can't help me in New York."

His horns have really grown.

Azoth stomped his front paws and continued shaking his head. "Azoth, please. I can't bring you with me. If I have any chance of finding my family, I need to go without you."

Azoth hung his head and pawed at the soft soil. Then pointed at it with that same paw.

Rocky nodded. "Exactly like the underground Dungeons you couldn't fit in."

Azoth growled but seemed to accept Rocky's order.

Once he had offered a sufficient parting gift to the Chimera—vigorous pets and treats—Azoth loped away, glancing at Rocky over his shoulder. Rocky shook his head and smiled at the creature's antics.

Once he was airborne, Rocky jogged over to Epsilon. "You all understand the plans?"

Gamma answered for Epsilon. "Plan A, if the golems aren't intelligent, sneak you in on our shoulders to find the humans. Plan B, if the golems are sapient, act like you are our slave and join them while attempting to find humans. Plan C, escape if they are hostile and sapient. They aren't very creative plans, idiot, and of course, we know them."

"We will leave you with the humans if we discover them. Then you can find your family. Once accomplished, we will make a trip to inform Sela or Azoth that you are ready for pick up. Are you not worried that you did not tell your Knight about this?" said Epsilon.

Epsilon assumed Sela was his Knight, which might have been amusing if the situation was different. Her lack of immediate support still stung. However, it was better than both of them dying.

"Let's get moving. Daylight is fading, and we need to get to the area where the city used to be."

On the ship, Rocky had shown the Golem Knights the satellite images and the surrounding area. The plans had taken what he had seen of moving golems into account.

The figure that sat on the mountainous throne at the city center intrigued the Golem Knights the most. Rocky never wanted to see it in person, but he feared he might very soon. With the Parliament Buildings beside him, Rocky concluded that the one on-screen was a golem converted from the Empire State Building. The patterned windows and concrete composed its medieval plate armor, and the weapon it wielded looked like the lightning rod that King Kong himself had hung from in Hollywood movies.

Rocky struggled to keep up with the Knights on foot. His stats had increased his speed drastically, and he estimated his speed to be faster than a car on the freeway. However, there was only so much stats could do when your legs were significantly shorter than your companions. Not to mention, they were all Master Classes. For all he knew, their stats doubled his. Eventually, Tao took pity on him, and Rocky clung to the hilt of the Knight's sword.

The trip took far less time when, to Rocky's shame, the golems sprinted at full speed. The fact that these five 'small' golems were this strong meant that the creature thirty times their size was terrifying.

The rubble-strewn city came into view, and the golems revved the speed down, coasting to a stop. Rocky focused on the horrendous honeycomb of perversion below him. Strangely, the city still had a shape, like a sandcastle left out to weather the tide. Piles of rubble, destroyed cars, and outlines of streets were visible. In some areas, the curb highlighted the edges of what used to be a sidewalk and road. The asphalt was gone, though, and only the grey stone remained underneath. The stones were slowly becoming a fine sand. Golems walked in pairs, indicating areas and digging through rubble or breaking large chunks apart. Humans came by and picked up the smaller pieces of debris, loading it into the flatbeds of trucks or trailers.

Over fifty humans hauled on ropes, dragging a destroyed bus over the gravel.

Rocky gasped. "What is this place? Does that thing really need a larger throne?"

"Another question is why all of these buildings aren't golems. There shouldn't be rubble like this. It didn't happen like this in Ottawa—" Omega stopped speaking as one of the scavenger golems pulled a golem's head out of the nearby rubble.

Tao jerked under him, his shoulders rising up toward his ears.

Rocky was going to say something, but a few nearby golems stopped work and began to pay attention to their approach.

Ten golems easily the size of the Ottawa Knights stopped working and studied them. As Rocky and the Knights approached, they arrayed themselves in a defensive position.

Epsilon held up a hand in the universal sign of stopping. His brothers came to an abrupt halt, and he called, "What is going on here?"

The ten golems relaxed at his words, and one of them stepped forward. At first, Rocky couldn't make out what formed the golem. He was far smaller than the converted buildings around him and seemed to contain no joints in the material.

He used Analyze.

William Shakespeare
Master-Bard
Level 51
Health Points 2900 / 2900

Rocky felt his mouth drop open. That was the statue of William Shakespeare? He hadn't seen any statues in Ottawa that came to life.

William Shakespeare spoke, confirming Rocky's suspicions of intelligence. "Welcome to New York, fellow Elders. May I escort you to our Lord Empire?"

"Like, do we have an option?" Omega asked. The other nine golems grew aggressive again, and Omega held up his hands defensively. "It was just a question. Chill, bros."

Rocky Analyzed a white golem with black rings wrapping its body. He could be the Michelin Man's twin. It stepped forward aggressively, pointing at Rocky.

Guggenheim
Master-Artist
Level 77
Health Points 2750 / 2750

"You have one of those flesh sacks on your sword. You can leave it here to join our teams."

Rocky's sphincter clenched, and Tao just nodded. "This one is ours. If we choose to stay, we will place him with the vermin. Thank you for the offer."

"How many of us are there?" Gamma meant sapient golems, and his usual tone of anger was missing, replaced with excitement.

"Golems like us. You mean that are intelligent? Right now, there are probably a couple hundred," said Shakespeare.

Tao whispered, "Rocky, hide your Bag and that weapon. You are lucky they didn't notice it already."

Rocky did as suggested and tucked the Bag of Holding into the inside of his belt, then mentally turned his Soul Sword to its liquid form. He had grown so accustomed to the weight of both the items mentioned that he barely noticed them anymore.

Shakespeare led the way through gravel-strewn streets, giving the Knights a tour of sorts.

"Where are the non-sapient golems?" asked Epsilon when the group hadn't passed any in a good long while.

Shakespeare scoffed and pointed at the pieces of rubble engaging nearby humans with dragging duty. "They are nothing more than hollow shells. Empire ordered their destruction. We are to stack the pieces to create more of our brethren."

"Are you sure that's even possible, bro?" Shakespeare glared, and Omega raised both hands innocently. "Just asking, guy..."

The group walked down a broad gravel path teeming with activity. A mountain of rubble stood a few miles away, Empire seated atop the makeshift throne. It was like a Titan from Greek mythology. Its size and presence so impressive, Rocky thought his soul fled his body. Even Tao had a small hitch in his step.

It took nearly five minutes to walk to the mountain of debris, and the Empire State Building golem continued to grow. By the time they arrived at the creature's sabatons, Rocky couldn't see over the creature's knees even when craning his neck. The sound of a rockslide filled the air as Empire stood to full height. Rocky could swear a cloud must have blocked the view of Empire's head, because he still couldn't see it.

A voice echoed from the heavens. "What have you brought me, tiny one?"

Shakespeare prostrated himself and motioned for the Knights to do the same. "I have brought you a few of our brethren who stumbled upon our birthplace. They do not fit the description of the hollow ones, Lord Empire."

"Do you, lesser ones, have the intelligence to answer questions?" asked Empire.

Rocky tried his best to stay discreet on Tao's back, even as the Knight bowed. Tao shifted beneath him slightly, seeming uncomfortable or nervous while kneeling at the behemoth's boot.

"We can understand your words, interpret them, and respond according to our desire. Why do you call us lesser ones?" Epsilon asked from his respectful bow.

Rocky Analyzed the boot of the Empire State golem, while the conversation lulled.

Empire State Golem
Leader
Epic-Skyscraper
Level 95
Health Points 78,000 / 78,000

It was even stronger than Bathilda and dwarfed the large Dragon by several times. The idea of even attempting to destroy a creature this imposing was incomprehensible.

"Perhaps you have not seen many of our kind? You are but a single step above the hollow ones. Even I am minuscule when compared to the Interstate golems." Empire knelt, and finally, his head came into view. Rocky couldn't see anything in the deep shadows of the plate visor. Empire placed his fingers pinched together near the ground. The fingers stretched apart until they were as tall as Epsilon. Then the gap continued to grow larger than the Knights. "You are small compared to me, like I am small compared to them. Unfortunately, Liberty has failed to bring them around to our cause. One day, we may have to deal with them like Chrysler and I dealt with Park." He pointed to a massive golem head that sat in the rubble pile.

The blood drained from Rocky's face. The head was as big or bigger than one of Empire's Sabatons. It wore a helm of some sort, adorned by a circle plume. He whispered into Tao's ear, "That is one of the tallest buildings in New York. It was probably one of the largest in the world."

Rocky was nothing more than an ant to a creature of that size. He was torn. He sensed it was difficult for his Knights to stare at the decapitated head. But he was relieved that the creature wasn't out there with a magnifying glass. Probably a bad analogy, but how many children stepped on ants, feeling superior due to their size advantage.

"Hasn't Gaia ordered us to protect her Champions? You have enslaved them," said Epsilon.

A booming laugh echoed from Empire, and it lasted far too long. Many of the humans towing along rubble fell to their hands and knees at the sound. A few whips cracked from the slave masters and scored the flesh of the fallen humans.

He growled, but Tao shushed him with a hiss.

"We are not killing her 'champions.' In fact, we are protecting them from the wildlife of the planet. Who is to say that we are not a superior form of life? Gaia may come to one day realize it herself." Empire grew agitated the longer he spoke.

Rocky whispered to Tao, "Go with plan B."

Tao stood and said, "We would like to join you, Great One. Will you have us?"

Empire turned to Shakespeare. "Find them some cattle to herd." He turned back to Tao and Epsilon. "Prove your loyalty, and in time, I may find a use for you. Betray the three at your peril." Empire sat on his throne of golem corpses.

Shakespeare motioned for the Knights to follow him. Once they were a block away, he ordered, "You will leave your slave with one of the other groups. I will split you up and have you work near experienced hands for the time being. You can leave the flesh sack with Flatiron." Shakespeare walked over to a particularly vicious looking Taskmaster golem.

Flatiron was an imposing enough name, but his rank of a high-level Master class proved it. Flatiron cracked his knuckles.

"I will take good care of your pet, don't worry." He sounded anything but sincere.

Rocky climbed down from Tao and joined the line of other humans, pulling a boulder toward the rubble pile.

He didn't see anyone he knew. Working like this would probably have him passing other groups. Maybe he would see his mother and sister. He didn't know how to feel about that. Either his family was being worked to the bone, maybe even whipped, or they were somewhere else, possibly lost to him forever.

But he could sense that they were here. Somewhere. Once he found them, it would be a simple matter of escaping. He swallowed the lump in his throat. Okay, he would need to work on that last part.

CHAPTER THIRTY-THREE

The group under Flatiron joined two other groups of slaves at sunset. The humans formed a line, and each person received a bowl of soup. The soup smelled mostly of grass, with the faint aroma of red meat. Rocky poked at a few chunks of meat and wild vegetables floating in his soup. As soon as each individual received their dish, they sat down to greedily ingest its contents. No one spoke. No one even met Rocky's eyes.

He made a quick search of the other groups that sat with his. His family wasn't amongst them. He glanced over to the three golems off to the side, chatting animatedly. It seemed like this was the common practice, as everyone around him ate and then claimed an area on the well-packed earth.

He turned to his neighbor. "Are we supposed to go to bed?" Rocky whispered and the nervous-looking man shushed him.

Flatiron barked out, "No conversations, blood bags." A barbed whip snapped out, lashing a human over thirty feet from Rocky. His neighbor gave him an accusatory stare. He looked over at the writhing woman. She was in agony, maybe even dying. No one moved to help. He made a motion to stand and his neighbor threw himself onto Rocky's seated legs.

One of the other golems shouted, "Everyone only gets one serving. No fighting for sleeping spots." The golem threw a small pebble, at least it would be considered small for an eight-story building. The head-sized rock impacted Rocky's raised arm, and his radius followed by his ulna collapsed under the projectile.

He fell to the ground and bit his lip to not cry out from pain and anger. His neighbor straightened his broken arm and shook his head at Rocky as he whimpered. His distress went unheard by the three golems. Once straightened, Rocky used Dark Mend discreetly, numbing the area. His neighbor shifted away from Rocky as he saw the Skill manifest. Rocky added a Dark Mend to the woman, writhing on the ground.

These people were utterly cowed. They didn't even attempt to speak at night out of fear. Witnessing the brutality first-hand was a wake-up call. How many times had his family received similar treatment? How many more times would they receive it before he found them?

He entered his Meditative state as the bone fragments shifted back into place under the direction of his Dark Mend skill. Even with Meditation disconnecting from his emotions, a pulse of anger surrounded him. His family was out there, and they may not have the ability to heal themselves from this sort of callous treatment.

He could attempt to sneak around at night under the cover of Stealth and Dark Cloak. With both skills active, he wasn't likely to be caught or run out of Ether during the attempt. But if he attempted it, and Flatiron noticed, he wouldn't be able to come back.

The daily work was difficult, but with his high stats, it wasn't terrible. He had analyzed those around him and discovered many mid-level Apprentice classes. To him, that meant they all had increased strength when compared to the *average* human pre-apocalypse. Their subservience wasn't because of the hard labor. The constant threat of casual violence, like the instances he had just witnessed, ensured the group's complete adherence to the rules.

He looked over, and the woman was still suffering on the ground. No one had dared approach her to help. The skin on her back was shredded by the spiked head of the whip. He cast a second Dark Mend on her. How could these people be so broken? He decided against sneaking around. If Flatiron discovered his absence, he probably wouldn't even be the one who paid the price. A quick Analyze told him that the woman would have been near death from that one casual blow, if not for his Dark Mend.

He lay down where he was, waiting for an opportunity to present itself, waiting for most of the slaves to fall asleep so he could act. He couldn't just sit here doing nothing, but he also couldn't cause harm to those around him. He lay still for a few hours in deep Meditation before summoning his Shadow Clone. As he started using the skill, he thought hard about his second self entering Stealth instantly.

His creation obliged, and he watched through its eyes as it snuck around the sleeping slaves on the ground. He intentionally had it pass by the injured woman, sound asleep and blessedly alive. His clone navigated from rubble to rubble, attempting to find other patches of humans.

The search didn't take long. Rocky found group after group. Each camp of sleeping humans numbered in the hundreds to thousands. He crept through the lines and hunted for his family as he went. Memorizing the location of each group, he searched. He hoped the Taskmasters used the same areas each night.

He picked through the debris and kicked a piece of gravel. A pebble never sounded so loud as it did in the silence of night. His clone froze as the stone pinged from metal sheets to piles of bricks.

A building— no, a hand that used to be a building,—fell onto his clone. His connection to it cut off and a boom thundered in the distance. Through the chill night air, screams echoed from the direction his clone had fallen. His heart shattered as he recognized the screams as those of pain. He swallowed the lump in his throat, hoping that he hadn't killed anyone just now.

A whip cracked out near him, and he started into a sitting position as someone in his group shrieked.

Flatiron barked, "No commotions," and flicked his whip.

Rocky stared at an older gentleman in his sixties, blood pooling under him, and met his eyes.

Flatiron pulled back the whip, and the man's dying body went with it. Rocky reached out a hand, but the man vanished so quickly that he wasn't sure if it even happened. A shadow flew through the air and crashed into rubble nearby. There was a quick scream that instantly cut off. Everything had happened so fast—Rocky could barely register it.

He wasn't sure how many deaths he was responsible for. There were so many camps nearby. He stared at the gentleman's blood sinking into the soil. He had killed at least one person. He clenched his fists as he stayed seated, fixating on the bloody mud until the sun rose.

As soon as a light crested the horizon, golems shouted, rousing the slaves under their control.

Rocky was nearly dead on his feet after the third trip to the rubble heap. He forced himself to move and continued to look at each group he passed, scanning each face in the hopes of finding his sister or mother.

Around mid-morning, he passed Gamma and a group of fifty humans pulling a large tire from a front-end loader. Gamma held up a hand to halt Flatiron. Once Flatiron snapped his whip, the group of slaves dropped the ropes they held and sat down on the ground. Rocky followed suit and listened to the conversation.

"What do you make of this army that is marching north?" Gamma asked Flatiron.

"No army can touch us. No army can hope to win against The Three. Perhaps we should slaughter some flesh bags to punish the attempt?"

Gamma looked unconcerned but clenched his fist. With a steady voice, he said, "Supposedly these humans attacking are more robot than human. The scouts are saying that they are far stronger than other humans they have met. A few of our brothers died trying to learn more."

Flatiron's whip handle creaked under the pressure of his straining fist and arm. He shouted, "Has anyone been told how long until they arrive? I would very much like to meet one of these mechanical fleshies!"

Rocky could tell by the nutjob's voice that it was hoping for revenge. At least the pea brain didn't exact his revenge on targets close at hand.

"No one has told me an exact time, no. They aren't rushing here, but they are destroying any groups of golems and cities they find along the way. They seem to hold a grudge against our kind. We used to consult our slave in these matters— would you mind if I spoke to him?"

Flatiron waved a hand dismissively. "Ask one of your flesh suits. These are mine to control." With that, he cracked his whip, and everyone stood to resume the work of hauling a piece of debris that Flatiron could have lifted on his own.

The Floridians were moving north. Why they were coming north and liberating towns on the way, he couldn't say. Yet, he would guess it had something to do with his flight to New York on the starship. Ernest had warned him not to come south... or he had to consider the much scarier option. Dahrix was beginning to take more control.

Rocky assumed that the Floridians were making their way to New York to find his army or his settlements. Either they were going to attack this place when they discovered humans as slaves. Or they were going to negotiate with Empire.

The Golem Knights were trying to spread misinformation about the Floridians. If they swayed the opinions of the New York golems by the time they arrived, then the conditions would be ripe for a fight.

While it was a good plan, it also meant that this place was going to turn into a war zone. That wouldn't bode well for his family. Or for him. His time was running out. He shuddered as the consequences of last night's search entered his thoughts.

He needed a timeline for the Floridians' arrival. He couldn't just blunder around with his clone every night. Last night proved it wouldn't be easy. It all depended on whether the Mechano-Lords from Florida were the only things moving north, or if they were bringing the vehicle fleet.

For the rest of his labor-filled day, he came to terms with his failure, accepted it, and resolved to do better.

No apologies. No excuses. Just action.

Shortly after Gamma's stop, around mid-afternoon, they ate another bowl of the grass stew. Where the golems were getting the meat was unclear, but there was plenty of wildlife in the surrounding area. For the strong, intelligent golems, he doubted much posed a threat.

At night, he mixed an Elixir of Shortened Sleep into his grass stew. The new concoction nearly made him vomit. He chugged it down and was the first human to fall asleep that night. He woke up an hour later. He needed the sleep to ensure he was wide awake for what he was going to do next. He couldn't afford another mistake, so he summoned his courage and entered Meditation.

Once within it, he summoned his Shadow Clone into Stealth and crept around the sleeping slaves. He knew a few of their names now, but that was only because of Analyze. He had yet to hear a single one of them speak, and if anything, it increased his worry about the situation here. If the humans hadn't been allowed to socialize for two months, their spirits might have broken beyond repair.

Rocky paid close attention to his movements and made his way from camp to camp. He would not make a mistake this evening—this night, he explored until the sun rose. As the sun peeked over the horizon, Rocky sent his clone to join another group of survivors. He ordered it to lay down and follow the commands of the golem Taskmaster.

He may be able to examine its memories later, and perhaps he would recognize his family. He hoped this would double the number of people he examined. Flatiron roused them the same way he had the morning before, with a vicious whip crack and a shout, "Rise and work, useless vermin."

Rocky, much more rested today, looked over everyone who passed him. He didn't recognize a single face, and by his lunchtime meal of grass stew, despair had sunk in. Epsilon sat nearby during his brief mid-afternoon reprieve. He spoke loudly to another golem Rocky couldn't see. "That rumoured ship from the north is supposedly scouting out the city each day. The scouts estimate the robots will be here in three days. Do you think they will both attack to save their fellow humans?"

Epsilon had just given Rocky the timeline he needed.

The other golem said, "They will likely try. Empire has recalled the chosen, which worries me. If these humans weren't a threat, Empire would handle them himself. Right?"

Epsilon shrugged. "Empire is mighty, but he cannot be everywhere at once. These humans seem to be surrounding us. The ones in the north aren't destroying all golems as they approach, at least. The ones in the south can only be coming for our destruction."

The conversation continued, but Flatiron forced his group back to work. The tension radiated off of the golem Taskmaster and Rocky hoped no one would set off Flatiron's anger. He doubted the outcome would be good.

Later in the day, a group of humans 'cut off' their group at an intersection. Flatiron berated their Taskmaster and threatened it with his whip. Flatiron screamed, "Control your cattle, you useless Hollow."

The other golem, Shed, was formed from a silvery material that bulged in odd places as if it had been stung by giant wasps. His voice was like that of a petulant child. "The rules of hauling are clear, you ugly lamppost."

The golems attacked each other. Fists flew, and a few chips of each golem rained down as they fought for dominance. Flatiron quickly gained the upper hand and pinned down the smaller, pudgy golem. "Surpass the other group and continue. This lesser creature shall wait."

The superiority in Flatiron's voice made Rocky sigh with relief. It sounded like a proud older brother, and Rocky kept his fingers crossed that it had worked out most of its aggression. Walking around with a creature on a hair-trigger was stressful. Rocky noted the evident rise in nerves among the golems.

The news of an invasion put everyone on edge, including the humans who still refused to speak but worked with an enthusiasm he hadn't seen the first few days.

CHAPTER THIRTY-FOUR

The worst part of each day was adding the debris to Empire's growing throne. The strength it radiated terrified Rocky. Every time he neared its sabatons, he wondered if he stood next to a god. A soul-crushing god.

If Dahrix was as strong or stronger than this golem, they were in a lot of trouble. He assumed he hadn't felt that power because they had only met Dahrix in the shop. That, or it was his imagination because of Empire's sheer size.

On his third day sweating in the slave camp, Rocky tossed a large piece of metal onto a mound of rubbish near the excavation site. The hulk of metal topped the growing heap, which threatened to teeter if stacked any further. Empire ordered them to tow the pieces to the side of the pile. The irritable golem would stop at nothing to ensure their day was filled with misery.

He dragged a piece of metal that was once a garage door and heaved it to the side. As he turned away from Empire's sabaton, he glimpsed a swish of long hair. His sister.

What used to be vibrant red hair was now nearly a dull brown. Her body looked frail, and her clothes were unrecognizable as the designer brands they once were. Her feet were bare and she didn't look up from the ground. There was no mistaking her. He wanted to run to her and hug her fiercely. It was everything he could do not to scream her name or race over to find his mother—that would cost someone their life. Maybe even hers.

He summoned his clone into Stealth and ordered it to follow her group. The clone made it to the group before it ran out of Ether to supply the Stealth spell. Rocky glanced up at Empire. Any Stealth skill used near it would drastically consume Ether. He held his breath as his clone walked to the rope his sister pulled on. It joined the line and worked alongside her. Her eyes never left the ground.

Please don't let her be broken. Please.

Flatiron's whip cracked and Rocky jumped. Flatiron signalled for the slaves to detach the ropes from the haul and fall into line. He quickly joined his group as they hastened to the task. His spirits, for the first time in days, were buoyed—even while walking beneath the strongest creature he had ever seen.

The remainder of the day, Rocky tried to stay focused, but his mind kept entering Meditation to look through his clone's eyes. He sensed from his clone that his sister's group was harvesting an entirely different part of the city.

He studied his sister's body language and desperately looked for his mother without success. The clone was unable to talk to or get his sister's attention. Lacy continued to stare at the ground. He wanted to scream, wanted to run to her, but timing was everything. During lunch, his group ate near Omega's team.

"Flat bro! Good to see you, man. Heard any newski on the impending invasion?" asked Omega.

The glare Flatiron turned on the surfer golem would have melted stone.

"I heard the scouts are, like, circling the city. If you look over there, you can see the tiny dot hanging in the sky, like a surfer on a colossal wave." Omega pointed at the sky, and every head in the clearing followed his gesture. "You see him, brah?"

Flatiron ground his teeth together and grumbled. "Of course, I can see the dot in the sky. Who cares what it is." Flatiron made a slicing gesture with his hand and then pointed to another silhouette on the ground. "Can you see our forces returning from their recruiting? These mosquitoes don't stand a chance against the combined might of the Three."

Flatiron ordered his group of slaves back to work with a crack of his whip. Rocky sensed that the cruel Taskmaster was worried—its reaction being one of bravado, rather than confidence. He doubted that the Mechanoid devices attached to the Floridians could do any damage to a creature of Empire's size and levels, but golems like the Ottawa Knights and Flatiron were fodder in a war like this. Rocky flashed Omega a tubular sign with his hand as he walked away, hoping Omega understood he had found his family. He received no acknowledgement from the fun-loving golem, so he got back to work.

He checked his clone and found his mother staring into his face. His sister was looking at his clone eyes narrowed, and lips pressed into a firm line. Rocky had missed the events leading to this. His mother appeared injured in some way and looked very weak as she lay on the ground. His sister held a soup bowl to his mother's lips and fed her from it. Two other bowls sat nearby. Evidently, his clone had given over his food to the women. His clone didn't need to eat, but it had gotten a bowl of food and found his mother.

Neither his mother nor sister spoke, which was eerie, and the moment didn't last long, as the group went back to work. His clone and his sister stood as their Taskmaster ordered a start to the afternoon hauling. They left his mother in the resting area with the bowls of food. His sister looked at his clone and made a gesture. She raised both fists and showed him the backs of them. Then banged the palms of the pinky side together in an unmistakable gesture. This was something from a TV show they both loved.

He nearly laughed out loud as his true self pulled the rope tugging a small truck with his group. He made the appropriate response by lacing his fingers behind his neck and banging his elbows together. His sister smiled for the first time, and his gut clenched. He had found them and they were both alive. Now it was time to get them out of here.

That night, all five of the Ottawa Knights camped their 'slaves' at the same place Flatiron did. The Knights' slaves looked healthier than Flatiron's and the other Taskmaster's groups who chose this open expanse of dirt to rest.

His family's group was a few miles away, camping out on the other side of the city. He was desperately working on a plan to get to them when a loud voice spoke over the entirety of the city.

"We have been observing you for a few days now, and it seems you hold no love for humans. Release the one known as Rockland Barkclay to us, and we will leave you be."

The Floridians had arrived. A group of fifty human shapes flew high in the air. One robot form was at the forefront and appeared to be the speaker. From this distance, Rocky couldn't make out the form but he knew the familiar voice belonged to Ernest.

Some of the Mechano-Lords argued amongst each other. A few of the subordinates approached Ernest and then slinked away. Rocky wished he could have heard their discussions. He looked over to the Golem Knights and held up a hand. It was too early to make a move. They needed more of a distraction.

Empire's gravelly voice broke the stillness of the night. "Do you think you have the power to make demands, tiny insects? Liberty, give them a glimpse of what power truly is."

A beam of light lit up the dark sky. The robots swerved out of the way, and tension stirred the air across New York. The voice from the sky laughed, then shouted, "A shot across the bow? I will take it as a sign of greater intelligence and give you another chance. Give us the one human we desire—you can keep the rest."

The group behind Ernest visibly backed away from him. They were upset by the words their leader had chosen.

From the words spoken, Rocky knew that Dahrix had taken full control of his little toy. He felt a pang of regret for everyone up there, as their souls already belonged to another. Even if they disagreed with the actions now, it was too late.

Boosters flared, and a group broke off to fly away. They made it a few hundred meters before they circled back. Their return signaled other groups to attempt an escape—only to suffer the same *change of heart.*

Rocky grimaced and nodded to the Ottawa Knights. This was about to get very heated, very quickly. Rocky triggered Shadow Cloak and Stealth simultaneously and crept toward Flatiron. Epsilon touched his ear and said, "Stand ready."

A few of the Taskmasters gave Epsilon side-eye. But the Knights got into hurried battle stances facing the flying robots. The rest of the golems followed the lead of the Knights a moment later.

Empire finally responded, his gravelly voice booming, "If you want our property, you can come get it."

Lightning streaked through the sky and shot down toward the center of the city, as if Zeus himself had thrown a bolt of blue light from Olympus. Smaller arcs blasted into the night, connecting with robots who jerked and twitched. They didn't fall from the air. Instead, each one spread out, releasing missiles, ballistics, laser beams, and skills onto an unseen target.

That was a signal if Rocky had ever seen one. Skills flew upwards from different quadrants of the city, and one of the Taskmasters in his area threw a green swirling ball into the sky. The ability was slow-moving, and the Mechano-Lords easily dodged it.

Rocky charged his Dark Blade skill five times and struck at Flatiron from cover. He channeled all of his anger and pain into the blow, using a piercing attack and releasing the ability as his blade punctured Flatiron's groin.

The skill tore upward through Flatiron, narrowly missing its core. Flatiron lashed out with his whip and Rocky dove backward as the whip snapped in the area he had stood.

Flatiron cawed, "You think you saw an opportunity. Now I will kill all of the humans here, worm."

Every human on Rocky's team froze the intensity and hatred in the golem's voice. They were conditioned for what followed an angry outburst from Flatiron. Rocky went berserk as he heard the whistle of the whip winding up. He pumped two stacks into Dark Blade and shot it out.

He pulled an Ether Draught Elixir from his Bag of Holding and downed it before charging his Dark Blade again. He heard the whip crack behind him and someone screamed. Rocky slashed vertically, releasing his skill, and the recharged Blade cut horizontally in a split second. The skills chased each other in a grid pattern toward the tormentor.

"Your weak skills mean nothing to me, cattle."

Another whip crack sounded, and Rocky added a triple charge horizontal strike. He felt lightheaded as this skill merged with the others. He pulled another Ether Draught Elixir and glanced at his Ether Bar as he downed it—it was recovering from a quarter full. He had just used upwards of three hundred Ether in seconds, and yet the creature laughed.

He downed a third Ether Draught potion as the retracting whip whistled. He had two options for attack—close in with the charge on his blade, or pierce the golem from a distance. Closing in meant navigating a latticework of danger. His Dark Blades screeched and ground against Flatiron's stone hide.

He added a triple-charged pierce attack and prayed it would be enough. It was times like this where he sharply felt the need for new, powerful skills, but his altered class mostly offered him survival and Etherience boosts.

He punched the point of his sword forward and released the skill. Flatiron grunted as his final attack joined the others with some effect. The golem's whip fell to the ground as it brought its hands together. Flatiron's feet dug into the soft earth as he fought for purchase against Rocky's latticework of skills.

With a mighty heave, Flatiron threw the entire mass of energy away from himself, changing its course on a near right angle. The skill ripped through the ground and took Rocky's fight with it. How was he going to beat a creature that had just thrown a total of ten stacks of his Dark Blade away like a beach ball?

Rocky fell to a knee. His skill collided with a group of Taskmasters grouped together to defend themselves against the Knights. The crisscrossing skill tore through the three other golems from behind like they were paper and screeched into the distance for a few meters before dissipating.

Flatiron's eyes were wild, but his mouth smirked. "The ant has fangs. Time—" Gamma's red glowing ax cleaved halfway into Flatiron's head. The evil creature fell to a knee and its recently smirking mouth fell open before its body crumpled.

Rocky fell onto his butt and looked around, breathing heavily. Five human corpses were on the ground, but the vast majority of the survivors lived. Omega leaped to his side and held out a large green gauntlet. In it was a tiny radio, likely the one from his ear. "Rockman. Sela is asking about you. Get on the airwaves, bro."

Rocky shook his head and pulled his earpiece from his bag, "Rockland Barkclay here. Report. Over."

"Rocky, we have brought the ship and are currently grounded north of the city. Evacuate survivors here—glad you are alright. Over." The last bit was added with a softness in her voice that made Rocky glow.

He turned to the golems Knights, "You heard her. Begin evacuating them—" he pointed to the survivors "—to the north."

Epsilon looked at him and asked, "What do you plan to be doing, Rockland?"

Rocky's clone was currently huddled in a pile of debris with his mother and sister. Other survivors clung to nearby wreckage. The golems in the vicinity hurled skills and rocks into the air, hoping to hit the tiny flying humanoids. Flashes of lightning, beams of light, and balls of green energy exploded in the sky. Red laser beams, missiles, and fireballs lanced toward the ground in retaliation.

His area was unaffected by the barrage. None of the golems there had been able to attack the Floridians yet. He clicked his radio and said, "Sela, I think the Floridians are being controlled by the beacon now. A few tried to leave the battle when their leader suggested abandoning the humans here. However, they all came back after the attempt. Over."

"Selaphelia Ardensai here. Understood, I will fly south with Azoth. Perhaps we can destroy the beacon. Over."

"Epsilon, I am going to save my family, and as many survivors as I can on the way. Can you guys clear a corridor?"

Tao nodded. "This sounds like a knightly endeavor."

"Alright. Omega and Delta, you take this group back— save others as you find them. Stay on this thoroughfare. Tao and Gamma, you are with Rocky and I. We will drop and hold sectors along this route," Epsilon said, taking command.

Rocky downed another Ether Draught, and the Elixir debuff gained a third stack in his UI, along with a drunk debuff. It was a risky move. Time to go.

The group split, and Rocky sprinted to keep up with the Knights. Fifty meters further, Gamma split off as he spotted a group of golem Taskmasters to the right. Half a mile later, Tao did the same to their left. Rocky checked in with his clone. At least another mile to go.

Epsilon called, "This is my stop, Rocky. Don't forge too far ahead, or you will have no avenue of escape."

Rocky gave him a thumbs up. He only had half a mile left. That wasn't too far—at least he hoped not. The path they travelled was empty. Abandoned ropes tied to cars, trucks, golem scraps, and more all littered the thoroughfare. He slowed down for a moment and scanned the rubble for the teams that had been pulling it. Many of them huddled amongst the stones and rocks on the roadside.

He stopped and pointed back down the path. "There is a ship that will take you to safety in that direction. Green golems on or near the path are friendly. Head straight north."

A few brave souls ran, but the majority of the people continued to cower. He didn't have time for this. "Grab your neighbors. Help each other. Go north and stick to this road. Save yourselves."

A few of the people who had run turned back and coaxed others to follow. That was the best Rocky could hope for, and he continued sprinting, stopping every few hundred meters and yelling out the same instructions. At the half-mile mark from when Epsilon left, he checked his clone.

It was off to his right. Mere feet away, ten Taskmasters exchanged fire with the airborne Floridians. Rocky glanced up. Not a single robot destroyed. A few looked injured, splashed by the acid green balls, but unaffected by the strikes of lightning. It appeared Dahrix might have improved on his conversion devices!

The lightning seemed to recharge their skills. He didn't doubt that on the ground, Empire would annihilate them. But up there, in the sky, the skyscraper was limited in its attack options.

CHAPTER THIRTY-FIVE

Getting into the middle of the fighting wouldn't go well for Rocky. He chose to attempt sneaking through the firefight,and use the distraction to evacuate his family and the survivors with them.

He moved within two hundred meters of the golems, and a familiar double-toned voice called, "I know this feeling. Remember—just because I can't see you, doesn't mean I can't kill you."

Drumbeats echoed from his left. The Yin-Yang golem pumped its three fists up and down, striking the earth and stirring up an undulating wave. The earth rolled in a circular pattern, tossing debris, golems, and humans skyward. A hailstorm of stone, metal, and dirt rained down on him. Rocky jumped over the wave of rubble as rocks pelted his scalp and shoulders. He reached up and felt warm blood under his hair.

Damnit, this was the worst time to run into this nutjob.

Yin-Yang golem
Master-Paradox
Level 62

The second wave of Ether had strengthened Yin-Yang further. It had gained nearly thirty levels! This wasn't a fight he wanted. As Rocky jumped over the next undulating wave, he glanced around. Humans attempted to hide in nearby debris. The debris teetered, and a huge slab of stone shifted and collapsed on top of a group of four humans. If Rocky engaged Yin-Yang here, it would cause more carnage and death.

He ran and left off Dark Cloak so as not to highlight his position. The golem called out, "You cannot escape from me; you are a favored enemy of mine now and can never fully hide from my skill."

Yin-Yang stopped its skill and followed after Rocky. If he couldn't escape the thing to stop its rampage, then he had to disable or destroy it before it started again.

He planted his front foot sideways and slid to a stop. He pushed back hard, turning his retreat into a sprint aimed at Yin-Yang. His change of direction surprised the dual golem, and Rocky mentally fistpumped as the golem couldn't *see* him. It could only know when he was near. The surprise didn't last long, and Yin-Yang clapped its two lower hands together. A sound wave buffeted Rocky's ears, and he fell on his face, sliding over the hard-packed earth. His body spasmed.

A stun debuff counted down one second, and as the effect faded, he rolled over. He pushed off with his arms and legs on his first turn, propelling himself out of the impact zone.

Yin-Yang landed where he had fallen, three fists and two feet aerating the ground. The shockwave of the skill strike flung Rocky further away. He was no longer able to control his roll, and he careened to a stop as his back smacked against a scrapheap. He climbed to his feet, spitting out blood, and dodged left as Yin-Yang's fist punched through the air where he had stood. A truck bed lurched away into the distance from the blow.

Its next fist hammered the ground, and Rocky rolled beneath the arm, twisting back up to his feet near one of the golem's legs. It raised its foot as if to stomp, and Rocky charged his Dark Blade, finally given a moment to breathe. He activated Dark Cloak, knowing he couldn't hide in Stealth from his nemesis.

Its foot lashed out, and Rocky stepped behind Yin-Yang's other foot. He slashed out, holding his skill in his sword, as the golem's foot stomped the ground. The blade cut into the onyx and marble like butter, nearly severing the creature's ankle. Yin-Yang shouted and flailed wildly, pushing off and jumping away. The golem successfully disengaged, and spiderwork fractures crackled along his ankle. Rocky charged his opponent. He needed to end this—and fast.

Rocky minimized a notification.

Congratulations! You have learned a new skill.
Hamstring
- **You are particularly good at striking at opponents' vulnerable ankles and achilles tendons. Each strike to a load-bearing limb in the future will impart a movement slowing debuff. The debuff will reduce movement by an additional 1% per point in this skill.**

Current rank: Weak level 1.

Yin-Yang's landing shook the ground, and humans screamed as rubble shifted near him.

Yin-Yang took a first step with its injured foot and cried out. Its leg crumpled, bringing the monster to its knees. In Dark Cloaked form, Rocky charged at Yin-Yang and it struck out at him, punching forward with one hand and simultaneously clapping its other two hands together.

Rocky's body tensed as a half-second stun debuff climbed through his vision and onto the top corner of his interface. The golem's fist connected with Rocky's left arm, spinning him away with a sickening crunch.

He crashed onto the ground, and fire tore across his left side as he rolled over. His adrenaline shot him back to his feet as his hand hung limply at his side. Swallowing back vomit at the sight of his swelling shoulder and bicep, he changed his sword to liquid and grabbed a healing potion while stacking two Dark Mends.

Yin-Yang wobbled as it stood up. The golem's retreat had cost its foot. "I will grind all of your bones to powder. You will die in the worst way imaginable. I will make injuries seem like blessings when I am through with you."

Rocky clenched his teeth as his bones began rearranging themselves in his arm. He downed the Health Potion before walking away. "Next time I see you, I will remove another extremity. 'Til then." He raised his fist with one finger extended over his shoulder, knowing the Dark Cloak covered the gesture but feeling it was necessary.

Yin-Yang howled a string of hatred behind him, and tried to jump toward his retreating form. The unstable leap left the golem nearly defenseless. Rocky turned and added two more Dark Blades into his forming sword, for a combined total of four.

Just as the golem reached its peak and began falling back to the earth, Rocky punched his blade out in a one-handed thrust and released. Yin-Yang had a moment to look surprised before the blow skewered its chest. Thankfully, its body put up enough resistance to change the course of its flight. Instead of falling atop Rocky, its corpse crashed into the ground.

The golem's landing shifted more rubble, and Rocky was too much of a coward to find out if that meant more deaths. He wasn't sure he could handle any more loss. He fixed his gaze on Yin-Yang. This moment should mean so much more, but it rang hollow. So many innocent lives lost.

He was surprised to find that there were no other golems around him—the fight with Yin-Yang would normally have drawn them. Yin-Yang was reckless, tossing other golems skyward with his skills as much as enemies. Perhaps the nut job had alienated his fellow intelligent golems.

If it hadn't wanted to kill me so badly, I would not have won that fight.

He held back a cry as his arm popped painfully, his shoulder joint reforming, then snapping back into proper alignment.

His Health bar was barely half full. Even after a potion. Yin-Yang's blow had been dangerously close to killing him. His Ether bar was worse, sitting at twenty-five points.

The hour timer ticked over, and his Shadow Clone flashed out of existence. An intense headache flared into existence as his Ether Pool attempted to supply the demand, then rebounded into him. It was the first time he had experienced the excruciating sensation, and he fell to the ground. Fighting through the searing pain, he crawled in the direction where his clone had been. His family was so close.

A calm feminine voice reverberated through the city, "Brothers, group up and coordinate your attacks. These mosquitoes only live because of our inadequacy."

Rocky continued to crawl as the city shook around him, evidence of golems moving around. He hoped that would mean that the escape would grow easier.

A golem shouted, "Slaves are escaping to the north. Traitors—" the voice cut off, but the information echoed through other golems.

Empire's voice boomed out. "Golems in the north, engage the escaping slaves. All other golems form on me. It's time to destroy these tiny flying insects." A bright light glowed from the approximate location of the massive mound of rubble.

Rocky continued dragging himself toward his family, gravel digging into his forearms. His Health and Ether continued to increase and the pain in his head lessened. He rose to his feet and limped in the direction. Then walked, and finally sprinted. "Nadine! Lacy! Where are you?"

The dirty red of his sister's hair poked out from behind concrete, and he grinned ear to ear. He rushed over to find her hovering over their mother. Unable to control himself, he pulled both women into a tight hug. When his sister pushed him away, he remembered where they were. He pulled rations out of his bag, followed by two Health potions. "Here, eat all of this and then drink the potion."

His sister didn't take a bite right away, but his mother did. "Who or what was that thing that puffed into black smoke a few minutes ago? It looked like you, but it wouldn't talk to us," Lacy asked.

"It was my Shadow Clone. Now eat."

Nadine Sheals
Apprentice-Gourmet
Level 11
Health Points 55 / 110
Starving

--

Lacy Obs
Apprentice-Witch
Level 12
Health Points 68 / 80
Starving

He quickly moved through his tabs and invited his sister and mother to his guild. then shared all the quests with them. It might mean nothing if he couldn't get them out of this death trap, but it could also mean they would gain a great deal of levels if they survived.

Other survivors inched toward him, and he motioned them over. He handed out rations to those who came close, and that tempted others to join. He withheld the potions, knowing it was unfair, but he only had five left. He added any who accepted to the guild and shared the quests with them. Some tried to ask questions, but he shushed them. There would be time for answers later.

He jogged through the streets back toward Epsilon's last known position. The journey back was much slower with all the survivors in tow, but he was grateful that the food and Health Potion had made a drastic difference for his mother and sister. He clicked his radio and identified himself before asking, "How are we doing?"

Epsilon responded first. "We grouped back up and are perhaps a mile north of my previous position. There are too many enemies to hold individually, but we still have the corridor."

Smith was next. "We have too many survivors already to load onto the ship. We have sent one load back to the Territory and are evacuating north under military escort. Rocky, I estimate there are more than one hundred thousand humans who have escaped."

That was good news. Well, mostly good news. Rocky doubted that there would be a seamless transition into the Territory, but most of these people had spent the last few months as slaves. An explosion a few hundred meters to the left snapped him out of his thoughts. It was far too early to celebrate.

His Ether pool crossed over the halfway mark and he summoned his Shadow Clone. A Mechano-Lord swooped down from above and scanned the area before absorbing some metal and returning to the safety of the sky. Had it seen him?

"Halt, slaves!" A golem stepped into view in front of his group. The concrete construct was composed of grey stone with red accents, its body covered with protruding stone-carved faces. Rocky's skin crawled.

Rocky used Analyze on it.

Metropolitan
Master-Historian
Level 44
Health Points: 4230 / 4450

"I have no desire to destroy you humans, but I cannot let you leave." Metropolitan entered an awkward fighting stance.

Rocky looked his mom and sister in the eyes. "Follow my clone. Get everyone out of here, and I will hold this thing back."

Before his mother could protest, his sister grabbed her arm, tugging her away. The survivors followed them and they broke into a jog.

Metropolitan tilted its head curiously at the side-skirting group. It stepped forward to give chase and Rocky shouted, "Your fight is with me, Museum!"

The golem stopped and looked down, surprised by the confrontation. It towered over him, its eyes flashing away, and its mouth moving silently.

Rocky let it struggle with its indecision and clicked his radio. "Epsilon, I sent my family forward with my clone, I need you—"

An explosion cut him off, narrowly missing the fleeing group of survivors. Four Mechano-Lords coasted down, landing in front of his family and the hundred-plus survivors led by his clone. Rocky cursed at himself in all manner of replacement language.

Ernest descended slowly above Metropolitan and shouted, "It was Rockland, wasn't it? I believe it's time I destroy you and the rebellion you represent." His pattern of speech was off, and Rocky knew it was Dahrix behind the wheel.

"Rockland, what happened? You cut off." Epsilon's voice came through the earpiece.

He couldn't answer, and his brain whirred, searching for an exit strategy for his family. He drew a complete blank, especially with the four Mechano-Lords training their weapons on the group.

Metropolitan picked up a golem arm and slung it like a boomerang at Ernest. The crux of the elbow connected full-on with Ernest's back. Rocky expected the heavy concrete would knock the Floridian from the sky, but instead, his boosters kicked in and untangled his body by blasting him upward and disengaging him with a shriek of abused metal.

Rocky activated his Stealth skill and took off toward the other four Mechano-Lords. If he was going to use his Ether, it would be to save his family. He glanced up and saw his points stagnating at seventy. He pulled out an Ether Draught and chugged it on the run. A fourth stack joined his diminishing returns debuff. He only had three of the Ether potions remaining.

He clicked his radio. "I need help to your south, Epsilon. Ernest is here. Protect my family."

"En route."

He ordered his clone to lead his mother and sister away once he distracted the Mechanos. He climbed a debris pile, clearing his line of sight, and released a double stack of Dark Blade at the four hovering robots. The blades struck and screeched against metal, pushing the boosters for an instant before they compensated.

The boosters flared and pushed Rocky's skill back toward him. "Run, now!"

Just as the four pushed his Dark Blade skill aside, Azoth crashed into two of them, dragging them to the ground. Stunned, Rocky wondered how Azoth was here. He was supposed to be with Sela, flying south. Rocky leaped with all of his strength and skewered a third robot. His added weight behind the thrust disabled the robot, and it fell to the ground.

Rocky's eyes tracked the fourth Mechano as if it moved in slow motion. It turned its back, and for a split second, he was confused, until he spotted its target. The fleeing survivors, maybe one hundred meters away, sprinted for everything they were worth—his clone, sister, and mother in the lead. Pieces of metal broke off from the Mechano-Lord and ignited, creating bursts of intense light. Rocky screamed and threw every drop of Ether he had into his sword. His thrusting Dark Blade ripped from Dark Tidings as a monstrous headache punched him in the cranium.

Everything moved slowly. One second, the six small missiles were beside the robot, and then they inched away. His lancing Dark Blade was on his sword, and then it was closing in. Everything clicked forward again as the explosions rocked the survivors. Rocky didn't even see what his Dark Blade did to the cursed metal. He was too busy watching the humans being flung into the air like bowling pins.

The Mechano-Lord underneath Rocky grabbed his long hair and slammed him into the ground. He looked at the sky and found an impassive face of metal.

"It doesn't matter which of my creations kill you, as long as you're dead," Dahrix's voice spoke through the construct.

CHAPTER THIRTY-SIX

Rocky felt dizzy, his head ringing, as a metal hand attempted to turn his brain to paste. He reacted instinctually, using a disengaging slash from his Seraphim Sword. His spinning wrist and blade scored deep into the mechanical wrist and forced the Mechano-Lord to release him.

He clenched his core and reversed his slash, connecting with the other arm as it came in. The robotic creature took a step back, and Rocky hopped to his feet. He turned his body sideways and returned to a half kneel, narrowly avoiding a laser bolt fired from the tracking eyes of his enemy.

Rocky used his grounded knee and lunged forward, thrusting at the Mechano-Lord's metallic throat. The point of his blade slid across the surface before gaining purchase. With a screech, the point tore out a side of the metal neck.

Black liquid spurted, and the creature clamped a hand onto the wound. Rocky slashed forward, again and again, taking advantage of the close range. This was his domain, and he wasn't going to let this abomination get away.

His opponent finally crumbled into an oily black mess, and Rocky finally had time to catch his breath. Something had happened a moment before—what was it?

All of his strength fled and his knees collapsed. His family! Ernest landed in front of him, waving a hand at Rocky.

He swung sloppily from his knees. Ernest swayed backwards to avoid the strike and started talking.

He wants to taunt me. I will turn him into a grease stain like his friend!

He didn't understand the words. They wouldn't register. He didn't care. He stood and kept attacking. Exhaustion overwhelmed him and Ernest easily parried each blow, toying with him.

Rocky activated Dark Cloak as his anger fueled his frenzied attacks. He didn't use a form, just desperately tried to connect the blade to metallic flesh. Even with Dark Cloak hiding some of his movements, Ernest dodged and batted his sword away.

Ernest fired fists into Rocky's Dark Cloak. The ability maneuvered them away from his body, and Rocky seized any opportunity to hit Ernest. He scored a few strikes on steel before Ernest's attacks overwhelmed his cloak. A fist collided with his head and he spun to the ground.

***

A bell rang and Rocky tried to concentrate on the muffled voices.

"Rockland, snap out of it. Dmitri interrupted the beacon and is in the process of destroying it." The voice was Ernest, and as soon as Rocky registered that the man wasn't hostile, he half stumbled, half crawled to the site of the explosions.

Azoth loped up beside him as he struggled. His pet must have either finished off his two opponents or realized they had reverted to human control. He didn't bother checking. Rocky's mind focused on finding his family.

He found scattered bodies covered in blood and death. He discovered his sister's arm and his mother's leg, but he didn't see them. His Dark Cloak pulsed with each heartbeat. His anger swelled, then left on the tide of the pulses. His brain ached, and he ran from corpse to corpse. None of the bodies were theirs.

He cried then, uncaring if a golem came by and ended his life. His cloak stuttered and pulsed around him, swirling like his tangled emotions. His anger surrounded and extinguished all other feelings.

He wasn't sure how long he sat there, crying. When he stood up, only Azoth was beside him. His radio buzzed a few times with information and he ignored it. He yanked it out of his ear and stomped on it.

His body convulsed and he roared at the sky. Azoth joined his lion's roar, and neither of them stopped until Rocky ran out of breath. Even then, he took another lungful and roared at the ground.

Tears streamed down his face, and Azoth nudged him.

Ernest stepped into his field of vision and said, "I am sorry Rockland, I should have listened—"

Rocky pointed at the hovering robot, and spat. "Don't say it. It is too late now—look around you. Look at the death your 'patron' wants!" His cloak pulsed out and expanded, seeming to attempt to grasp Ernest.

Rocky formed his sword and tried to attack the robotic man, but his head rang and he fell to a knee.

He checked his Ether bar, assuming it had bottomed out, but found it holding near fifty points. His Dark Cloak had somehow disengaged, but the fog still hovered in a wide circle. Engulfing Azoth beside him and nearly claiming Ernest. The spike of pain shook him out of his all-consuming rage long enough to grab a tenuous hold on the reins of his anger.

Before he went on a rampage, Rocky climbed unsteadily to his feet and mounted up. The moment he climbed out of the fog, the Floridian spoke again. "I get it. We will do everything we can to help your people escape. What is left of my men will hold the corridor, for as long as possible. When this is over—please come talk with me."

Rocky's hand shook as he tied himself into Azoth's saddle. Fighting back tears, he choked, "Anywhere but here or the Territory, Azoth!"

EPILOGUE

Sela landed at the evacuation site. She had been heading south with Azoth to destroy the beacon when the satellite team told her of a conflict at the Port. The man Rocky had put his trust in had organized a rebellion to disrupt the signal. Or at least she hoped so. It would have taken her a few hours to fly south, and the evacuation needed her organizational skills here in New York anyway.

She had transformed into her raven form and sent Azoth to find Rocky. She couldn't stop thinking about the stupid man. His decision to come here had seemed so rushed but what she was witnessing made it worthwhile.

What followed wasn't a pretty victory, but they had managed to save thousands upon thousands of humans today. She knew that would cause some issues in the Territory for a time, but she wanted to believe that they could overcome it. Rocky would say something like, "That many bodies working together, will find a solution!"

She thought again about his class change. Sela had never heard of a Chimeran Knight before. She considered it. The class Seraphim was considered extremely powerful because of its reduction in Etherience. What rarity of class was Rocky's if it created *extra* Etherience? This savior quest alone was going to award him a massive bonus!

The flying shape of a mechanoid going airborne caught her attention and broke her musings. The four-legged form that was Azoth flew away from the same location, heading west. She squinted, trying to see if a shape resided on the birdbrain's back. She clicked her radio, "Sela Ardensai here. Rockland, are you ok? Over."

Static hissed, but no response came. She tried her mental connection with Azoth next, <Azoth, where are you going?>

Azoth's presence echoed pure sadness into her mind, <Rocky sad. Azoth and Rocky go hunt. Rocky need space.> She felt her heart catch. The only thing that could have caused this was if his family…

Ernest landed beside her and pointed to the retreating Chimera. "Selaphelia, yes?" At her nod, Ernest continued, "Rockland is leaving on his pet to the south. He won't attack my people, right?"

"What happened out there?"

Ernest looked at the soil beneath his feet. "The person in control of us killed many humans that Rockland escorted. I have only seen grown men cry like that when they lose someone very dear to them." He choked on his words and continued staring at the soil.

Sela watched Azoth shrink into the distance and nodded. He definitely needed some space, but did that include space from her? Every part of her wanted to transform into a raven and follow after the big lout. He needed her, but if she didn't leave soon, Azoth would be out of range.

She prepared to follow Rocky but was interrupted as someone sprinted to her side. She saluted Letoya and commanded, "Report!" She glanced after Rocky's retreating shadow—if Letoya was quick, she could still catch up.

"The Golem Knights are retreating. The enemy is organizing for a response attack. Smith says we have to get out of here now."

Sela froze. Letoya took off to relay her orders to others. Sela looked longingly after Azoth and Rocky. She sighed and let her head fall before looking back up, snapping into commander mode.

Meeting Ernest's eyes, she pointed. "Cover the retreating humans, and help the Knights disengage. You caused most of this—it is time to repent."

Ernest saluted her and flew away. Sela looked over the running, walking, and limping survivors who streamed past her. This was going to be a tough day, and they really could have used Rockland. She shook her head and turned around to see where she could help most, but a figure crossed her line of sight.

She blinked as Rockland limped toward her. She studied him and was horrified to realize he was missing a foot, until she noticed that smoke poured from the wound instead of blood. It was his clone.

The clone carried a body over his shoulders, guiding a second survivor with an arm around their waist. Tears of dark black liquid leaked from its eyes. How had the clone managed to hold itself together? She rushed to it and caught both bodies as the Skill puffed into smoke. She Analyzed them quickly.

Nadine Shealds
Apprentice-Gourmet
Level 18
Health Points 15 / 110

--

Lacy Obs
Apprentice-Witch
Level 18
Health Points 19 / 80

Sela recognized the names and placed the women on the ground. The women's wounds bled freely, and they were each missing a limb. They were dying. Sela had two Health Potions and wasn't sure if they would be enough for the severity of the injuries. She clicked her radio. "Sela here. I need a healer at the retreat point, now! Over."

Nadine's condition was worse than Lacy's. Sela poured a potion down Nadine's throat, praying that it would buy her time.

A response came from the ship. "Scourge. ETA five minutes. Over."

She glanced at the sky and spotted the ship slowing. Five minutes would be too late for one of these women.

She checked her skills page. The ship dropped off nearly twenty thousand survivors and had given her just over forty million Etherience—enough to push her into level twelve. Maybe her skills could help. She had access to a 'heal over time' skill, Rejuvenate, in her third tier, but its effects were not purely healing based. They were more on par with the Elixir of Shortened sleep, but the description said it aided body repair and recuperation.

She sunk two points into it and cast the Skill on both women. Nadine's health bar continued to drop, but Lacy's stabilized. At least she had a chance of saving them. She silently urged the ship to arrive.

She refreshed the Skill whenever her Ether regenerated enough to do so. As the ship descended, she poured her second healing potion down Nadine's throat. It gave her a few more minutes, which was all she needed.

She sighed with relief as a group flooded off the ship with extra Healing Potions and took over for her. She tried to tell Azoth the excellent news, but he was too far away. Her heart panged, and she clutched it. Her other skill option in the third tier was stronger than Rejuvenate. In the long run, she had just placed valuable skill points in a counterproductive way.

What was it about this man? It was far too soon to call this love, wasn't it? Why would Rocky run away from her?

She sniffed and shook off her thoughts. Rockland needed to wait. Sela could find him, but right now, the retreat needed her. She struggled for a few more heartbeats. "Come on Sela, it's just a boy. Get to work," she mumbled to herself.

After setting aside her feelings for Rocky, she walked onto the ship and made her way to the Control Room. She wanted an overview and fumed when she found the Satellite techs studying a shape moving in the ocean. She shouted, "Is that tactically relevant?"

One of the technicians stood and saluted. "The Satellite is not in a location to see our position or the retreat ma'am. We are not the ones in control of the location. That is headquarters."

Sela clicked her mouth shut and nodded. "What are you looking at, then?"

A massive white form frothed the waves as they broke over its rising bulk. The Satellite seemed to be holding position on the object, but by the change in coordinates, Sela realized it was following the shape.

She moved away and got an update on the retreat instead of fixating on the strange white tube. Three golems were forming in the middle of the 'city' for a countercharge. Twenty Mechano-Lords held their attention for now.

The ship loaded up the stragglers and quickly reached capacity. They wouldn't be able to evacuate any more than they already had, and she passed orders. "Tell everyone to stop liberating slaves. We have very little time left, and if we try to save everyone, we will save no one."

A general needed to make the tough decisions—a gasp from the Satellite techs interrupted her pep talk.

She walked over and found herself looking at a body of water surrounded by land. In the center of that water was a black hole, and the white body led directly into it. "Where is this?"

One of the technicians responded. "The Mediterranean Sea, ma'am."

She smiled despite their situation. She had found Atlantis.

AFTERWORD

We hope you enjoyed Earthdom! Since reviews are the lifeblood of indie publishing, we'd love it if you could leave a positive review on Amazon! Please use this link to go to the Ether Collapse: Earthdom Amazon product page to leave your review: geni.us/Earthdom.

As always, thank you for your support! You are the reason we're able to bring these stories to life.

ABOUT RYAN DEBRUYN

Ryan has always been a dream chaser. His first career was as a professional athlete, which taught him the dedication and perseverance needed to chase fantastic goals. A devastating injury removed Ryan from this world before his prime, and taught him the value of an education.

His first book began as a hobby project while he attended Georgian College. Using his hard fought lessons, in motivation, discipline and hard work Ryan published his first book in February 2019.

He is a recent graduate in the field of Electrical Engineering and a full-time author.

Here's hoping you enjoy the worlds he creates as much as he does!

Connect with Ryan:
Facebook.com/RyanDeBruyn
Facebook.com/Groups/RyanDeBruyn
RyanDeBruyn.com
Instagram.com/RyRyDubs
Patreon.com/RyanDeBruyn

ABOUT MOUNTAINDALE PRESS

Dakota and Danielle Krout, a husband and wife team, strive to create as well as publish excellent fantasy and science fiction novels. Self-publishing *The Divine Dungeon: Dungeon Born* in 2016 transformed their careers from Dakota's military and programming background and Danielle's Ph.D. in pharmacology to President and CEO, respectively, of a small press. Their goal is to share their success with other authors and provide captivating fiction to readers with the purpose of solidifying Mountaindale Press as the place 'Where Fantasy Transforms Reality.'

Connect with Mountaindale Press:
MountaindalePress.com
Facebook.com/MountaindalePress
Twitter.com/_Mountaindale
Krout@MountaindalePress.com

Mountaindale Press Titles

GameLit and LitRPG

The Completionist Chronicles Series
The Divine Dungeon Series
Full Murderhobo Series
Year of the Sword Series
By: Dakota Krout

Arcana Unlocked Series
By: Gregory Blackburn

A Touch of Power Series
By: Jay Boyce

Farming Livia Series
Red Mage Series
By: Xander Boyce

Space Seasons Series
By: Dawn Chapman

Ether Collapse Series
Ether Flows Series
By: Ryan DeBruyn

Dr. Druid Series
By: Maxwell Farmer

Bloodgames Series
By: Christian J. Gilliland

Threads of Fate Series
By: MICHAEL HEAD

Lion's Lineage Series
By: ROHAN HUBLIKAR AND DAKOTA KROUT

Wolfman Warlock Series
By: JAMES HUNTER AND DAKOTA KROUT

Axe Druid Series
High Table Hijinks Series
Mephisto's Magic Online Series
By: CHRISTOPHER JOHNS

Skeleton in Space Series
By: ANDRIES LOUWS

Dragon Core Chronicles
By: LARS MACHMÜLLER

Chronicles of Ethan Series
By: JOHN L. MONK

Necrotic Apocalypse Series
Pixel Dust Series
By: DAVID PETRIE

Viceroy's Pride Series
By: CALE PLAMANN

Henchman Series
By: CARL STUBBLEFIELD

Artorian's Archives Series
By: DENNIS VANDERKERKEN AND DAKOTA KROUT

Appendix

Adam Weatherbee – A survivor from Kingston who has a unique class giving him the ability to take control of golems. **Apprentice Stone-Summoner**

Adam's Elites – A group of individuals from Kingston that have now formed a group with Adam and his minion Golems.

Alchemy is the Basis of All – Alchemy guild located on Helion Prime. Is studying gasoline which was traded to him by someone in Florida.

Alex Watt – 11-year-old young man that Rocky met while entering Ottawa. Family was massacred by Corsair's goons. **Died during the Ottawa Exodus Struggle**

Altar of Michabo – A place of power that is linked to the Algonquin Guild. This place of power is billions of years old and was created to link another realm (Spirit Realm) to Gaia. This gives the benefit of Rebirth to our hero but at what cost?

Algonquin Grotto – This is where Selaphelia Ardensai chose to start the settlement of survivors. It was chosen because of its natural defenses in the mountains and cliff faces that surround it on three sides. On the fourth side is a large river that runs through Algonquin Park.

Algonquin Park – Is the full Algonquin Park as seen in our current world.

Algonquin Valley – Is the Territory of Rockland Barkclay, and it sits within Algonquin Park. It is quite large but does not encompass the entirety of the current Algonquin Park from present day Earth.

Amber Dell – A member of the A-Team. A muscular Native American woman who is extremely pretty when she smiles. She also seems to take things a little too literally, often forgetting or not understanding the full meaning of things. **Apprentice-Fencer**

Amelia Nanospark – A Helion, who disguises herself as an Iridescent Kobold. Has a unique class of Nanospark that gives her control over her unique nanobots. With it she has created a resistance on Helion Prime against the tyranny of the Guild Collective.

Analyze – A skill that is common for almost all the individuals of the EtherVerse. When scrutinizing an object or a person, the system will reveal some information based on your level in the skill. Skill can be countered or obfuscated.

Ancestral Guide – A perk of the EtherVerse. Gaia was once predicated on privilege and the power ancestors passed down. Skills, training, gear etc. Ancestral guides were a constant companion that could train the truly fortunate.

Antarctica – A continent on Earth. Google it.

Apep – Essentially a black hole, another form of godly being similar to Gaia but more on par with a Star God. Instead of bringing light to a world, a Void god attempts to subvert worlds away from the light to gain power.

Apep's Void Shoud / Stick – Pieces of gear worn first by the cultists of Apep, but were looted in book 2.

Apothis – One of the countless souls that Apep has at his command. Apep continually spins out his head priest, Apothis, to try to conquer worlds. **Master-Necromonger**

Arbuckle – A very rare metal that can be inscribed with powerful runes, and has the ability to convert hold a large Ether Pool to power them. This metal is required to create a shop, and seed shops. It is somewhat alive and grows more of itself.

Area of Effect (AoE) – A type of skill that creates an effect over a large area. This is usually damage or healing but can be slowing effects or other such effects.

Arena Dungeon – Controlled by the Dungeon core Maximus. This Dungeon becomes the first cardinal Dungeon of the Territory, Algonquin Valley.

Aretrean Bazaar – The Aretrean Bazaar is on Mount Olympus and is the shop our hero has access to currently.

Asgardians – A guild that once resided on Earth but has left when the Ether fled. They are still a powerhouse in the EtherVerse.

Astrid – A member of the Territorial Council. Mid-Forties. Tailoress.

Atlantean Academy – A school Selaphelia attended when growing up. This school was attached to Atlantis and held a neutral faction for the guilds. All attendees were either nobility or very skilled.

Atlantean Guild Tower – This is a greater perk that was earned for the cleansing of the nearby Chalk River nuclear meltdown. This is a tower which links up through a satellite to the EtherNet. Thus providing our hero with more information on the current world.

Atrium – The lower levels of the Guild Tower. The Atrium is a massive cathedral that houses Quest Kiosk's a desk that will house assistants, and an elevator that people on the list can use to access the upper tower.

Azoth – Rockland's pet Chimera. Is able to speak and communicate first with Selaphelia and later with Rockland. Through them both is gaining Sapience. **Dread-Chimera**

Azrael – Rockland's ancestor. Azrael was adopted by the Cathodiem guild and never was considered nobility. A new book is on its way with Azrael's coming of age story. **Ether Flows – Tech Duinn**. Keep your eyes peeled.

Bag of Holding – A bag that has been enchanted to contain a massive Ethereal space inside. Our hero lucked into a very large bag of holding from a dungeon early after the crash.

Bailey – A young girl who first got into trouble for enticing young men to steal weapons from the guards. She has now become an adventurer and was captured and detained by LFD along with 400 other citizens. She continued to break free and farm for Etherience.

Bam-Bam – An Ogre boss that attacks the Territory.

Bancroft – Is a town located on the York River in Hastings County in the Canadian province of Ontario.

Bart – A member of the A-Team. Bart looks like a hell's angel with tattoos, long hair and a biker jacket. There is a deep well of kindness in this man as seen through his deeds, from helping people survive to organizing the Territory.

Barry's Bay – Is a community in the township of Madawaska Valley, Ontario, Canada.

Basalt Golem – A golem that converts from the roads. Tar Golem would also be an appropriate name. But Basalt sounds cooler.

Bathilda the Darkscale – Is the dragon under contract with Gaia. She had a necklace that gives her rights to live on Gaia, but she must obey the commands of Gaia to keep the planet in balance. Essentially an all-powerful bouncer who maintains order on the planet.

Batwing Bird – A type of monster that our group faces during the book.

Bear Tribe – Briefly mentioned by Selaphelia. A tribe within the Beastkin.

Beastkin – A race in the EtherVerse that contains many tribes of difference beast-humanoids.

Blight Skill / Blighted Bog – A skill Sela learned at the Journeyman ranks.

Bloodlust Aura – A skill released by Bam-bam during combat.

Bone Breast Plate – A breastplate dropped by Rattlegore.

Brent – Is a community on Cedar Lake on the Petawawa River in northern Algonquin Provincial Park.

Bullet – Mutated peregrine falcon that had strong, wind-based skills, and that nearly killed Rocky and the group.

Burks Fall – Is an incorporated village in the Almaguin Highlands region of Parry Sound District, Ontario, Canada.

Canadore – A college / university that resides in North Bay.

Cathodiem Guild – Guild that was situated on Gaia over a billion years ago. Guild was very powerful and had great influence with a seat on the Atlantean Council.

Chain Quest – A type of quest that contains multiple parts.

Chalk River – Is a town in Ontario that is near a nuclear research laboratory. A few days after the Ether crash, the converted golem from the plant melts down, prompting a red quest.

Chidi – An emotional representation of a person. A conflicted chidi often means the person is going through emotional turmoil or is an evil person. Good or bad deeds are often reflected on the chidi. Or emotional struggles as seen by our hero.

Choo Sentani – A type of blanket used by Elven merchants. It interacts with the system in the bazaar and can temporarily transfer items across the shops to be viewed or inspected.

Citizen Accessible Shop – An addon for a shop. This allows an assistant to scan through the merchant's wares that reside in a shop and purchase items on the behest of individuals. This limits interactions and messages that can be transmitted through spies. Still, it doesn't stop them...

Class Ranks – Apprentice, Journeyman, Master, Epic, Legenday (Read Ether Flows to learn more)

Construct Command – A skill that Adam Weatherbee uses to control Golems.

Corsair (Jack Jameson) – Sociopathic leader of the Ottawa Militia. Created an inner group of psychopaths who followed his orders to kill survivors instead of allowing monsters to gain more Etherience. **Died during the Ottawa Exodus Struggle**

Crafter – A skill or class a person can have that is for making equipment or consumables that will aid individuals.

Crom – An ancient being from Gelthisar. Whether it is a god or a very powerful combatant is unclear.

Crystals – Crystallized Ether. Crystals is the short form. A type of currency.

Crushed Ether – A component needed for enchanting. Derived from Crystallized Ether.

Cuppa Macht Leaf – A type of leaf from a Cuppa Macht Tree. It is essentially a collapsible cup that contains a biological reaction to cool liquids. The tree is from a dessert region.

Cursed Regalia – Items with counterproductive enchantments that may hinder the user.

Dahrix – Leader of the Mechano-Lords guild. All black metal with Damascus steel filigree. Despite his mechanical body, he is a hot head.

Dario – The current Guild Prime, who runs the guild collective. It is an elected position and he seems to be a bit too wild to be behind a desk.

Dark Cloak – A skill learned by Rockland Barkclay. This cloak hides our hero in a dark fog and also will help to redirect attacks away from him.

Dark Mend – A skill learned by Rockland Barkclay. It uses shadows and darkness to rearrange broken bones and knit back together flesh.

Debuff – An effect that makes a character weaker: a negative status effect.

Delta – A sapient golem who is a member of the Ottawa Knights. He was created from a historical building known as the Parliament Buildings in Ottawa. An intellectual who prefers logic and deductive reasoning to solve problems. **Master-Knight of Gaia**

Delving Dungeon – A type of dungeon that digs down into the ground creating descending levels with increasing difficulty.

Derik – A devious human who was a member of the initial group that is saved from the Onikuma by Rocky. Rocky banishes Derik during the invasion of the Grotto by Apothis and Frank. Derik's banishment is rescinded and he joins the new council, under probation.

Diamond Chip – A type of currency. This is the lowest form of currency. 10 Diamond Chips = 1 Ruby Mark.

Dmitri Gausse – A Russian mobster stationed at the docks in Florida when the first wave struck. He has been crucial in the Floridians survival. He helps our heroes disable the beacon.

Doran Hetch – A brother who makes a horrible decision to kill humans to save himself. Rocky lets them live but tells them to never be seen again.

Dorset – Is a small community located on the boundary between the Lake of Bays Municipality in Muskoka District and the Algonquin Highlands Township in Haliburton County, Ontario, Canada.

Dragonscale – Usually collected from young dragons and prized for their extreme strength. Dragonscale is considered the strongest bio material in the known EtherVerse.

Draksus – Leader of the Ottawa territory. Albino, devastatingly large, and strong.

Dungeon – A creation of Planetary gods to filter Ether to Essence. Each dungeon is rules by a Core that has a personality.

Enchanter's Kit – An item purchased in the shop. Contains a Pen, Mortar and Pestle. This item is a puzzle that Rockland must solve.

Enchanting – A crafting skill that is of immense value. Enchanting uses Glyphs or Runes to circulate Ether and create powerful effects.

Envenom – A skill in the first tier of the Chimera Knight Class.

Epsilon – A sapient golem who appears to be the leader of the Ottawa Knights. He was created from a historical building known as the Parliament Buildings in Ottawa. Extremely devoted to his group of golems and wishes to unite all sapient golems and create a community for them. **Master-Knight of Gaia**

Ernest Ford – Dockmaster. Ernest is in charge of the Floridians and has accepted a Mechanolord conversion seed to help keep them safe. Once he sets up the beacon he is essentially a puppet of Dahrix.

Essence – Essence is the primary resource of a Planetary God. It is filtered from Ether through living beings but can also be recovered from dead organisms. Gaia wakes to find almost all of her vast stores pillaged (oil).

Ether – Cosmic energy of the universe. It is the primary unfiltered raw power that allows life and Planetary Gods to form.

Ether Assisted Protection – A type of protection that helps fledgling Territories. This protection will help turn away powerful monsters.

Ether Converters – A converter that changes Ether into electricity.

Ether Manipulation – A skill that allows individuals to manipulate the Ether internally and externally. Linked with Ether Channels and both have been hidden from Sela during her lifetime.

Ether Pool – A pool of power that skills draw upon to initiate. Synonymous with Mana pool from games.

Ether Tech Helm – A very powerful type of armor. Combines the mechanical advantages of robotic gear with enchantments of Bio Enhanced gear.

Ethernet – A type of global information system used in ancient times. Synonymous with internet.

Exiles – A group of individuals who attacked Rocky during book 2. They were exiled from the Grotto but allowed to hunt in the safety of the Territory.

Fernicular – A type of plant that need Ether to cultivate.

Fire Tornado – A descriptor of the Firestorm skill.

Fireball – A skill Zippo learns in book one.

Firestorm – A skill Zippo learns in book two.

Fennel – A herbalist lady that is mixing ingredients and causes a massive plume of smoke to billow forth outside of the Crafters Hall.

Flatiron – A golem converted from the Flatiron Building in New York.

Florida – A state in the US.

Floridians – The people in the US. As categorized by other humans from earth.

Flow Ridians – The humans of unknown origin as categorized by the Guild Collective.

Flunge – A term used in fencing for a flying lunge.

Frankie Cocozza – Psychologist to the Militiamen on the trip to Algonquin Valley and continues his duties in the Grotto. Turns out he was also the Psychologist for Corsair and his cronies. **Apprentice-Psychologist**

Gaia – Gaia is a Planetary God, specifically the Earth. Each planet is alive and in constant battle with other planets to acquire Essence. What they win if they have the most is still a mystery.

Gaian Plane – The main reality in which our hero resides.

Garnel – A Karacy Salesman in the Aretrean Bazaar. Karacy are often referred to as Dwarfs by other races.

Garry – An older man saved from Kingston. Becomes a member of Adam's Elites off page.

Gamma – A sapient golem who is a member of the Ottawa Knights. He was created from a historical building known as the Parliament Buildings in Ottawa. Hot headed and rash, but also surprisingly good at building. Works hard to help the survivors in the Grotto despite his early complaints to the contrary. **Master-Knight of Gaia**

Gaston – A reluctant healer who wishes to be known as a hero but too scared to actually venture out to fight. He hangs around the military but is not one of them. He also swindles citizens out of Crystals for healing that isn't needed.

Geb – Leader of Bio-Cult and one of the youngest members in a leadership role of a guild on Helion Prime. Likes to call people 'young man' despite her younger age.

Gelthisar – A planetary God.

Gerard – A man from Brent. Some sort of Tank class. Was trapped for most of a week inside LFD.

Glyphs – Another name for Enchanting Runes.

Golden Horseshoe – A term used to describe the Greater Toronto Area. It resembles a horseshoe around Lake Ontario.

Golems – A clever way Gaia has orchestrated to recover a higher percentage of her pillaged Essence. Golems are created from any structure that has no ownership claimed upon it twenty-four hours after the first Ether wave.

Gortuk – A type of monster whose skin was used to create leather that was later turned into a Jerkin of Protection.

Greater Territorial Perk – A benefit that Gaia bestowed for completion of a very difficult Red Quest.

Grotto – Referring to Algonquin Grotto.

Guild Collective – A collection of small guilds that joined together to try to gain a semblance of power that planetary militaries and larger guilds have. They have taken and occupied Helion Prime and are now trying to extend to Gaia.

Guild of Mechano-Lords – Patron of Corsair. Headquarters on Guild Collaborative controlled world of Helion Prime. The leader of the guild is Dahrix.

Guild Prime – Is the leader of the Guild Collective. Currently Dario.

Guild Tent – An item purchased from Garnell. This tent gives a Territory access to guild features at half efficacy without building a true Guild Hall. The guild tower replaces this tent, even skewering it and creating a tent flag for a time.

HALO – High Altitude Low Open

Heartstring – A very powerful item that is created from a Dragon Heart. It can be used to control dungeons, people and is a legendary component.

Hectar – Lieutenant Captain – 'Alchemy is the Basis of All'. Has been running tests on gasoline and his discoveries lead to him being forced to report an emergency finding to the Guild Collaborative prime.

Helion Prime – A planet controlled by the Guild Collective. Originally the home of Amelia Nanospark and her people.

Hollow – A derogatory term used to describe mindless Golems.

Huntsville – Is the largest town in the Muskoka Region of Ontario, Canada.

I-Beam – A metal support beam that looks like an I from the bottom or top.

Initial Increase – A very popular enchantment for tanks. This allows the individual to stand and take a charge from creatures much heavier than themselves.

Initiation Gear – A set of gear that Beastkin use to help them through their trials. All Beastkin must complete the trials to become adults. Due to high death rates this gear was created to increase success rates of participants.

Iridescent Kobold – A race of Kobold's in the Ether Verse. Kobolds are small dragonkin or lizardfolk.

Jack Wareham – A member of the A-Team. A rotund man who is constantly jolly and supportive. He unfortunately dies at the hands of Rockland, when no other options are left to him. **Apprentice-Trapper**

Jason Jackson – 15-year-old young man that Rocky met while entering Ottawa. Family was massacred by Corsair's goons. Has become a member of the party and is fixated on getting stronger. Changes his name to Zippo to distance himself from the tragedy. **Red-Fire Mage**

Jessibihr Windfall – A merchant in the Aretrean Bazaar. Sells skill scrolls primarily. Rockland dislikes him from his actions in book one. Ripped off Rockland in book one.

Joe Flacca – Member of the Ottawa Militia. Becomes its General after the fall of Corsair. Quickly becomes Zippo's best friend but dies sacrificing himself for Rocky. **Special-Trooper. Died during the Place of Power Contestation.**

Joaquim Smith – Joaquim Smith is an initial survivor that was in Algonquin Park during the crash. His group of fifteen is lucky

enough to be saved by Rocky from a giant Onikuma.
Apprentice-Medicine Man

Jorge – A member of the Grotto Council. Hooded and shadowed. Not very talkative.

Karacy – A race native to Gelthisar. Also termed Dwarf.

Karl Keerdint – An engineer who was constructing the crafters hall. Highly attentive to detail and not afraid of authority.

Kata – A Japanese word that refers to patterns of movement. It is often used to teach proper styles for sword and martial arts.

Kingsbraid – A plant that needs Ether to cultivate.

Knight's Action – A skill that Rockland can acquire in the Chimeran Knight class.

Knight's Resolve – A skill that Rockland can acquire in the Chimeran Knight class.

Knowledge Tablet – A tablet that has access to books that are stored in the EtherNet or purchased from other areas of the Ether Verse.

Kodo's Jacket – A piece of Cursed Regalia picked up by our hero during book 3.

Lacy Obs – Rockland's sister.

Letoya Deckman – A friend of Victoria Faris. A member of the Grotto Military and a combat classer.

Lillian Meghan Wright Centre – A educational building inside York Univeristy.

Lingren – An elven merchant inside the Aretrean Bazaar. Somewhat honest but currently disliked by Rockland for his racist slurs and remarks.

Loincloth – An item dropped by Ogres. Ogres use the skin of their strongest foe to craft a loincloth.

Long Forgotten Dungeon (LFD) – Rocky and the gang hide in this Dungeon on the way to Ottawa. Rocky makes a deal with LFD, which he terms Little Friendly Dungeon. LFD will help keep the devastation caused by a nuclear meltdown at bay and, in time, help Rocky's settlement level.

Louisville Slugger – A popular type of wooden bat.

M3 – Is an American .45-caliber submachine gun.

Mages Guild – Guild located on Helion Prime. A guild that is entirely comprised of Mage classes.

Mageleaf – A type of plant that needs Ether to cultivate.

Madawaska – Is an incorporated township in Renfrew County in Eastern Ontario, Canada.

Marcel Grey – A dishwasher in the Mess Hall who has a Geologist class. Gets directed to go to morning trainings and strengthen himself.

Martian Hive – A guild that originated on Mars. Fled when Ether vanished. Still a powerful entity in the Ether Verse.

Maximus – An arena dungeon inside of Algonquin Valley.

McDougall – Is a township in central Ontario, Canada.

Mechanolord – An individual who has been converted into a machine hybrid. They often gain significant power but miss out on a great deal of skill building.

Mechanolords Conversion Seeds – An item that converted biological beings into Mechanolords.

Melee Weapon – A weapon that is used in close quarters.

Meliora Guild – The guild created by Rockland and Sela for the people of the Grotto.

Michabo – A Native American man that resides in the Spirit Realm. He is half rabbit and half man. Extremely old and possibly deceitful.

Minions – A servile dependent, follower or underling.

Minion Golems – Golems controlled by others.

Monsters Bane – An enchantment on an item.

Montessori – The Montessori Method of Education is a individual-centered education approached based on scientific observations of children. Often the teachers learn the materials before sharing it with their pupils. This creates a joint learning environment.

Mortar and Pestle – A bowl and a rod that are used in conjunction to pulp seeds into powders or liquids.

Mr. Pips – A member of the A-Team. Tall wiry man with very blonde hair, and needs food immediately… according to Rocky.

Nadine Shealds – Rockland's mother.

Nanoweave Under Armor – A piece of gear worn by the hero. It is form fitting, self-cleaning, and climate controlled by the nanobots inside.

Nebula – Nebula is a giant cloud of gas in space. This can be caused by explosions of stars or the formation of new stars.

Nipissing – A university / college in the town of North Bay.

North Bay – is a city in Northeastern Ontario, Canada.

NPCs – Non-Power Classes

Odin – The name of the Star God. Otherwise known as the Sun.

Oliver Grees – 13-year-old young man that Rocky met while entering Ottawa. Family was massacred by Corsair's goons. **Died during the Ottawa Exodus Struggle.**

Other Planetary Gods (spoken of) – Mars, Gelth, Krond, Sinfath, Helion Prime (Planet)

Omega – A sapient golem who is a member of the Ottawa Knights. He was created from a historical building known as the Parliament Buildings in Ottawa. A California beach bum

personality that wants to try all the comforts of the old world.
Master-Knight of Gaia

Ottawa Knights – See Tao, Epsilon, Gamma, Delta and Epsilon.

Pan's Cloak – A piece of Cursed Regalia that may billow in unseen winds. It may even pull the user off their feet for no reason. This item was given to Victoria.

Pangaea – Was a supercontinent that existed during the late Paleozoic and early Mesozoic eras.

Parliament Knight Golems – The Parliament golems are five knight brothers that are sapient. They wish to make a place for golems in this new world.

Pebbles – An Ogre boss that controls time magic.

Perception Skill – A skill that highlights things that you might not notice otherwise.

Phalanx – A body of troops standing in close formation. In this book, an inverted triangle formation to break a charge.

Planetary Essence – The secondary tier of energy need by Dungeons and Planetary gods.

Planetary Leaderboards – A feature listing the strongest in multiple categories. Part of the connection to the EtherNet.

Plasma Grenade/Mine – A grenade/mine that uses a Plasma reaction to create a miniature sun.

Poison Pool – A part of the Envenom skill. Our hero can collect poisons and secrete a venom of his own based on the potency of his Poison Pool.

Quests – Can be issued by Gaia directly (Red) or can be issued by Atlantean Net which is the system put in place by ancient Gaians to improve leveling and compatibility with Gaia and Ether.

Questing – Accepting quests and completing them for Etherience. This is a common way to quickly increase levels within the EtherVerse.

Radar Globe – A device on Dahrix's Battleship that he destroys with his laser ports.

Ragnar – Another soul devoured by Apep, and is continually spun out to do his bidding. This individual is far less willing than Apothis and Rattlegore and resists the power of the Void god. His corpse is currently stored in Rocky's Bag of Holding. **Journeyman-Vanir**

Ragnar's Longsword – A sword used by Ragnar and looted after his death. It is later unlocked by Zippo.

Rat Hide Helm – An item that is dropped by the Rat Wolf's and Bat Birds in book 3.

Rattleshirt – Slightly manic soul devoured by Apep. Rattlegore can create a type of skeletal creature that is extremely powerful but territorial. The bones of the creatures he creates are extremely strong and don't burn. **Journeyman–Master of Bones**

Rattleshirt Breastplate – The official name of an item dropped by Rattlegore in Book 2.

Rattlegore – Is a transformation of Rattleshirt using a special Skill and consuming all of Rattleshirt's summoned creatures, however, Rocky and company mostly prevented this.

Journeyman – Obsidian Bone Apostle

Rebirth – A way to return an individual's spirit to a living body. Requires high amounts of Territorial Etherience but can save a person from dying. Often a broken body can be healed to working order after severe damage. The return of the spirit will then revitalize the body and make it useable. Does not need to be the owner's soul to be Reborn.

Red Quest – A quest issued by Gaia herself. These quests are of utmost importance and often return balance to the world.

Research Ships – A ship in the Guild Armada that is meant to research areas they pass through.

Revenant Class – The Apprentice Class of Rockland Barkclay.

Richard Sun – The leader of the Nippissing and Canadore survivors. He was a coach and professor at the schools and lead a great deal of kids to survive the Apocalypse.

Rictus – A nightmarish race that Rockland runs into outside of Garnell's shop, inside the Aretrean Bazaar. Sela mocks Rockland for his fear.

Rockland Barkclay – Distant relative of Azrael, General of the Darkest Night, General of Cathodiem Guild. The main character of the story. If you don't know that, you haven't been paying attention. **Dark-Revenant - Dark-Chimera Knight**

Rune of Protection – An enchanting Rune or Glyph that increases the inherent Ether defence of an item. This helps protect people from damage.

Ryerson – A University in Toronto, Ontario.

Selaphia Ardensai – Granddaughter of Selaphiel. Captain of Cathodiem Guild. Captain of a Century during the War on Mars. Ancestral guide to Rockland Barklcay but not blood related. **Dark-Druid**

Seraphim Seven – A term for a powerful group of individuals in the EtherVerse. Likely a guild and could be the remnants of the Cathodiem Guild.

Shadow Clone – A skill Rockland gained in the Apprentice Ranks. Creates a copy of himself out of smoke that he can utilize in combat or reconnaissance.

Shaman Class – A class that uses totems and often has a bloodlust ability. Assumed base class of Bam-bam the Ogre boss.

Silver Spires – A territory that Sela grew up in. The home town of the Cathodiem Guild and a very beautiful place.

Simon Hetch – A brother who makes a horrible decision to kill humans to save himself. Rocky lets them live but tells them to never be seen again.

Skandranon – Summoned Chimera to serve as Leader of Chimera Roost, which has now become Algonquin Valley. Progenitor of Azoth.

Smith – A nickname for Joaquim Smith.

Snollygoster – Slang. A politician who is guided by personal advantage rather than by a consistent, respectable principle.

Soul Blade – A weapon that is spiritually bound to the user. Gains power and is able to level up. Seems to change as it levels. Currently seems alive in Rockland's hands.

Sphynx – A mythical creature that is immensely powerful and often asks a riddle.

Sphynx Golden Armor – Armor dropped by the Puzzle dungeon. This set is great for tanking and was given to Victoria.

Spirit Realm – A realm that is outside of reality and houses Michabo. Our heroes end up there at the end of Book 2. This Realm was created as part of some long term plan to vanquish an evil.

Stalwart – A class skill learned by Rockland in Book 3.

Stealth Skill – A skill that Rockland learns in Book 1. He purchases it as a scroll in the Aretrean Bazaar.

Steel – Leader of the Steel Wolfpack. Extremely large boss monster who evolved beside an iron mine, which led him to have fur with the tensile strength of steel.

Taskmasters – Sapient Golems that are in charge of teams of slaves inside of New York. Some of the taskmasters are brutal.

Tao – A sapient golem who is a member of the Ottawa Knights. He was created from a historical building known as the Parliament Buildings in Ottawa. Extremely wise and well-versed in some of the mysteries of the EtherVerse. Where he gets his knowledge is a mystery but he is soft spoken and takes over morning training for combat and Meditation. **Master-Knight of Gaia**

Territory – A Territory is a piece of land that will level along with the leader who owns it. The Territory conveys many bonuses to the inhabitants and stabilizes Ether flow, making the immediate area more structured for monster growth.

Territorial Inventory Space (Reserve) – This is a Ethereal Space that is linked to a Territory. It can only be accessed in the Territory and acts like a safe with levels of access.

Territorial Sphere – An item that is created when a Territory is broken down. This sphere can be used to increase an existing Territory size, create a new Territory or sold for a great deal of Crystals.

The Grind – A term used to describe the end of Ranks when the Etherience needed to progress is so high that levels are very hard to come by.

The Scourge – A ship that Amelia traded to the Grotto for allies and information.

Tirahnya – A leader of the Biology Guild in the Guild Collective.

Toronto – A massive city in Southern Ontario, Canada.

Totems – A skill that creates objects with an Area of Effect. The effects vary, but include, shielding, healing, speed and others.

University – The Canadian Equivalent of an American College.

Uplink – A communications link to a satellite.

Victoria Faris – A character introduced in Book 3. A member of the Grotto Military and a tank class. She is powerful and becomes critical to the group's success throughout the book as parties begin to form.

Void God – Opposite of a Sun God. The equivalent to a blackhole that is constantly trying to suck in more Sun Gods and Planetary Gods.

William Shakespeare Statue – A golem that is converted from the Statue in New York.

Did **you** find a word with an X?

Yin-Yang golem – First sapient golem Rocky runs into. This golem is a little bit insane due to its nature.

York University – A University in Toronto.

Yuri – A member of the Grotto Council. A smith who was voted in by the people for all of their hard work in making the Grotto liveable.

Zippo – Nickname for Jason Jackson.